THE RECLAIMED

THE RECLAIMED

ZACH CARPENTER

MONSTER

October 3rd, 2012,

MUTILATED ANIMAL CARCASSES DISCOVERED ALL OVER TOWN, AUTHORITIES SUSPECT NON-HUMAN PERPETRATOR.

Detective Mick Johnson rubbed his bloodshot eyes and then refocused them on the old news headline from last month that he was reading on his tablet. It had been a slow night for the three or so hours he had been here down at the station. He looked at the upper right corner of his screen and checked the time, 10:34 pm.

He reached for his coffee, finished off the remaining half that was in the cup in two big gulps and continued. He scrolled through the news pages till he found the most recent article, the newest one being from a couple days ago.

BODY OF LARGE HUMANOID CREATURE DISCOVERED.

Last night around 10:00pm, New Broken Edge Authorities responded to a disturbance call in regards to sightings of an alleged anthropomorphic creature that stood well over eight feet tall, with the head and features of what appeared to be a giant boar.

A strange glowing liquid was found at the scene. This same substance has also been noted by authorities and witnesses alike as having been present at the sight of multiple crime scenes involving non-human incidents in and around New Broken Edge for the past twelve months. An official statement as to the origin or chemical composition of the substance has yet to be released.

"That's a BLT from Hell," Mick chuckled to himself as he continued reading.

An autopsy showed the stomach contents of the creature contained various animal bones and what DNA tests confirmed to be skull fragments of eight year old Alexa Martinez, who was reported missing in August.

Mick felt his smile drop like a bag of sand at that last part. The Martinez disappearance was one he heard about, but with him being up to his eyeballs in dealing with Federal Agents on the Tick killings, he had only heard the name and nothing more. He scrolled to the little girl's obituary, seeing the smiling face of Alexa in her school photo. Her dark hair was pulled up and wound into a braid atop her head, her prominent dimples and her twinkling dark eyes lit up his screen.

He rested his eyes for a brief second, drumming the fingers of his right hand over the surface of his desk. When he opened them again, he exited out of the website for the *New Broken Edge Oracle,* and brought up his notepad app to tap down some musings.

Mutilated animals found all over town, probably discarded after feeding sessions...Martinez girl being one of the victims... The Porkasaurus-Rex is found with the same glowing substance that has been showing up all over town for a year or so...which is also when those vigilante hunters started showing up...Surveillance on these guys has been next to impossible from what I hear. The task force Scroggins set up can hardly get a beat on them. With the lull in the Tick killings, I've been able to compare notes with some of the guys from the task force. I think there might be a link between this group and what happened back in 95.

"Johnson!" He heard his name and tensed as if he had just had ice water dumped over him. Not because of how the speaker sounded, but because of who the speaker was: Agent Della Pallacios. She was the leading investigator from the FBI that was attached to this case, and she often spoke to everyone else like they were lazy children, or mentally challenged. Often a mixture of both.

Pallacios was a slender, half Hispanic, half Italian woman who wasn't overly attractive but not altogether horrid to look at either. She was someone who expected people to shut up and straighten up when she walked into the room, but didn't command the respect of the other officers to make it happen. Mick had a feeling that due to her level of Nazism, that she was brown nosing someone higher up the chain of command. Either way, having to work under her was painful in more ways than one.

"Look alive! We just got a tip on Terrance Miller's location. He's holding up in the old Broken Edge hospital." She boomed as she moved past his desk in a blur. Mick blinked.

"You're kidding!" He hollered as he nearly flew out of his chair, almost forgetting to grab his jacket.

Mick stood in the one place that had haunted him every night since he was five years old. The ground beneath his feet felt alive with memories, all contained in the blood that had run through it. He kept reminding himself that whenever he felt a gust of wind at his back that it was only just the wind, and not the hand of some specter wailing next to his face. New Broken Edge was called *new* for a reason. It was located nearly twenty miles outside of the *original* city of Broken Edge, Kansas, where Mick was now standing.

Here he was, in the ruins of his hometown. On 25th and Tucker to be exact, watching as paramedics were bringing out an oversized stretcher carrying what looked like a deformed mound of limp flesh. He didn't think they even made stretchers that big! After the initial shock of seeing a stretcher three times bigger than a normal one, the thought crossed his mind, *Wait... That can't be Terrance Miller. He was scrawny!* But as the stretcher got closer, Mick halted the EMT's to have a look.

The face was disfigured, but not so badly that he couldn't tell who it belonged to. The chin was jutting out in an under bite that hurt Mick just to look at it. The rest of his skull looked as if random parts of it were growing at uneven proportions. His forehead was bulging, giving his head the appearance of a wrecking ball. But this was in fact Terrance Miller. The serial killer who the press had begun calling, "Tick," due to his signing each painting of his victims with that name. He would produce a blank canvass and a varied assortment of professional grade paintbrushes, and proceed to sketch the helpless victim while they were tied up, naked and drugged in their own bathtubs. Then he proceeded to bleed them out, painting a portrait of the victims in their own blood.

Helluva a first case to tackle as soon as one makes homicide, Mick thought to himself.

"Looks like your boy contracted Wretch Syndrome while he was away." One of the EMT's said. Mick noticed the shock collar that was fitted around Tick's bulging, veiny neck.

"Couldn't you get in trouble for using that term?" Mick asked smirking.

"Bossman aint around to stop me," The young EMT giggled before continuing, "We revived him long enough to get him walking up the stairs, then we put him under again. He was babbling about white eyes and hot blades slicing him. Take a look," The EMT said as he removed the sheet covering Tick's uneven mass. The word 'MONSTER' had been carved into his flesh. The letters had a dim glow about them, and it was one that he had seen before.

He pulled out his phone, and snapped a few pictures of the creature on the stretcher. The ambulance had been specifically built to transport Wretches, (not the medical name for them, and certainly not the politically correct name for them either.) The ambulance had its own loading platform, which the stretcher was put on and the lift did the rest. Might has well have been an armored cargo vehicle. Just then Mick spotted another familiar face, one that he had grown up with.

"Hey Dick-Head!" George said. They slapped the outstretched hand of the other in a flurry of odd gestures. It was a handshake from their childhood years, and one that was exceedingly, almost unnecessarily complicated. But it had survived the years, and it had survived George's years in the institute he had spent a few years in. George was about ready to sweep the crime scene in that old hospital. When he and Mick were both in college majoring in criminal justice, he had gone the route of Crime Scene Investigator while Mick had pursued Detective. But it worked out as they still got to go to the bar and have a few cold ones after work from time to time.

"You doing okay?" George asked. Mick nodded.

"It's really freaky being back here an all, but I'll be okay," Mick said. He shot a glance back at the hospital. He had been born there, and his and George's family doctor at the time had his practice in that building.

"Well if it means anything man, this is trippy for me too." George said. Mick nodded.

The incident with George's parents that required him to need counseling at such a young age had happened a month before the massacre. He wasn't even in town when it had happened. The experience of finding his parents in their bedroom, both of their wrists cut down the length of their forearms, had caused him to need a few years of therapy.

George was speaking again, "Well we got Tick finally!"

"Right! Now maybe the feds will leave," Mick said as he noted the numerous agents wearing their Kevlar vests, sporting the big bold letters FBI across the chest.

"I heard that!" Mick and George turned, tense irritation coloring their movements. Agent Della Pallacios stood there with her arms crossed, starring down her slightly oversized hook nose at them, almost like they were two kindergarteners who had been caught bullying another kid.

"Well I'm gonna go start the walkthrough. See you in a bit," George said as he strolled off to join the rest of his team.

Jerk, just walk off and leave me then, Mick thought as he made awkward eye contact with Agent Pallacios, fighting back a sudden bad taste in his mouth.

He noticed the coroner's vehicle driving up. According to the tip off there were two stiffs inside. Pallacios was bellowing about something to the other officers present, "Alright we got Miller. Whoever tipped us off knew he was here. The call came in about twenty five minutes ago. I want a perimeter set up and search teams combing the area within a ten block radius in case those vigilantes are still out there!" She ordered. Mick hurried into the building after George.

Mick finally caught up to George, who was taking video footage of the crime scene. He recoiled and pulled out his handkerchief to cover his face as he descended the stairs to the old hospital basement. The stench from down there reached up and grabbed him by the nose hairs, stinging his eyes so bad he had to wipe the water from them twice before he got to the bottom. Stale dog and cat feces, urine, and the smell of blood, mixed with various chemicals almost caused him to vomit. The sound of a barking dog and hissing, yowling cats he could deal with after a few minutes to tune out the noise, but the smell was making him queasy. He hoped this would be a quick walk through. George carefully walked around the two bodies, recording as he went. Mick's eyes scanned the cages that lined the walls. There were several rats in cages, a big pit bull chained up in the corner that was barking at him, plus a few sickly-looking cats. The walls were a nasty brown color, and it was obvious where water had damaged them.

I hope animal control shows up, he thought, and then caught himself wondering just what in the hell was being done with these animals.

Mick looked back up the stairs. Two others were approaching, one of them he recognized as the coroner, Valerie Wellington. She was about five foot eight, strong jaw and defined, yet soft features, a perfect hour glass figure that belonged on the cover of a swimsuit magazine and thick brown hair with natural blonde highlights that she usually wore up in a bun. She was about twenty six years old, only three years older than Mick. The other guy behind her was Matt, some scruffy, hipster looking guy from the crime lab who was going to come in after George and take still shots of the evidence.

"Hey man you about to finish up here? Matt and Valerie are coming down." Mick asked through his handkerchief.

"What?" George asked, raising his voice above the animal ruckus. Mick rolled his eyes and let his face covering down for a bit.

"Val-er-ie, and Matt. Are coming. Down! Are. You. Almost, done yet?" Mick yelled slowly, over annunciating each word and doing hand gestures. He knew George hated when he did that but Mick wasn't in the mood to repeat himself either. George nodded and then sarcastically added, "Yes, mas-ter!" While adding in a middle finger for good measure.

"Good evening Detective." Valerie was right behind him now, and he jumped when he felt her brush up against him.

"…Hi," he said after calming his nerves.

"Didn't mean to scare you there." She said.

"Oh you're fine. Just didn't think you were so close." Mick said nervously, shooting a glance behind Valerie and Matt up the stairs. Matt muttered something indistinguishable as he checked his camera then adjusted his thick rimmed glasses.

Mick nodded in agreement and then returned his gaze to Valerie, "You need a handkerchief?" He said offering her the one he had. Even though Mick was attempting a cheap flirt, he kind of was hoping she would turn him down so he wouldn't have to really give it up. The smell in here seemed to be getting worse.

"Oh no thank you Detective, I'll manage." Valerie said with a straight face.

There was faint glowing rays of light shooting out from the bodies of the two stiffs. They were wearing what look to be medical scrubs. Mick gingerly stepped along the path George had marked. Valerie and Matt followed. Mick knelt down to have a look for himself at one of the bodies. Both appeared to be male. Save for what they were wearing and their gender, the commonalities stopped there. The first man was gangly thin, to the point of looking malnourished. Sparse strands of long greasy black hair fell from beneath his surgeon's cap, and his soiled scrubs were so filthy it was hard to tell what color they had been originally. Empty eye sockets stared up at the ceiling, two fleshy craters devoid of their contents. The second was dressed exactly the same, but looked like a body builder ripped straight from the pages of a protein advertisement. The shafts of light shining out of the bullet holes in his filthy scrubs illuminated the surgical mask covering the lower half of his face, revealing that his eye lids had been stitched shut, a crude job done with wire.

"This one needs a sandwich," Mick said pointing to the emaciated looking one as Valerie handed him a pair of latex gloves as she knelt down.

"He makes a good flashlight," Valerie said as she examined the glowing bullet hole closely.

Mick nodded and continued, "Well looks like those damn vigilantes *were* here. Bullet holes are emitting the same kind of light from all the other crime scenes where these turn up."

Valerie nodded, "Whatever type of ammunition they are using, the bullet fragments dissolve after tearing through the target's body. These look like they possibly belong to a 9mm. Won't know for sure till hotshots over there recover some shell casings." Valerie said.

I wonder if she can cook too, Mick thought as he nodded like he was listening. It would all be in her report anyway.

An abrupt cawing sound from above jolted Mick's nerves. He looked up, shinned his flashlight on the source of the noise. A crow was peeking its head out from an opening in a rotten ceiling tile, perched in a cluster of twigs and other materials that looked like a nest.

"Don't suppose we can question the bird?" Mick asked with a wry chuckle. No one said anything. He was used to that. Most of his attempts at humor either resulted in head shaking and the occasional, "Just stop…" from a co-worker, or were ignored altogether. He was about to ask George something when he noticed something in the crow's beak. A small cylindrical, metallic object that looked like it could be—Mick's eyes widened.

"That bird has evidence!" He said as he stood up quickly.

"What bird?" Matt asked between taking photos.

Valerie suddenly looked up from the cadaver she was inspecting and caught Mick's eye.

"That bird has a shell casing in its mouth," Mick motioned up to the bird in its nest.

"Birds don't have mouths Mick," George said.

"Whatever!" Mick said as he looked for a safe way to climb up to the ceiling tile without disturbing the crime scene. There were some steel bins located against the north wall of this room. For the most part the bins were empty, save for some boxes appearing to contain old medical supplies. He thought briefly about climbing up those, but if there was any evidence in those bins he didn't want to disturb it. So he did a quick once over of the bins, while keeping an eye on that crow. He sorted through the boxes, noting the medical supplies inside them. All from 1995. And that was when he heard the violent flapping of wings. Mick looked up, shielding his eyes and face from the angry bird that dive bombed him.

"Get the bird!" Mick shouted as he felt the thing's sharp beak puncture through his glove and into the soft flesh of his palm. The next second, the thing took off flying up through the stair well in a flurry of loose feathers.

Mick looked at George, Valerie and Matt. Valerie had an amused look on her face as she approached to look at Mick's hand, but George just laughed, as best friends tend to do when such things happen. Matt just stared out through his thick black rimmed glasses before resuming taking photographs.

"Are you okay?" Valerie asked, her tone unapologetically rife with amusement. Mick shook his head, embarrassed and angry that the bird had gotten the better of him.

"Yeah, just hurt my pride is all," Mick said as he removed his punctured glove to reveal the spot where the bird had pecked him. Dark crimson was smeared across his hand as he pulled the glove off.

"Where'd that shell casing go?" Mick asked as Valerie swabbed his hand with an antiseptic wipe.

"We'll find it later Mick. Why don't you go get some air?" Valerie said, her voice sincere.

"Thanks, it's a wonder I haven't already thrown up with the smell of all this crap down here," Mick said as he turned to walk back up the stairs. He cussed under his breath as he got to the top, looked around for Pallacios, and after seeing that the coast was clear of her, hurried through the bustling mass of EMTs, police officers, feds, and animal control to his vehicle to get a bandage for his hand.

MYSTERIOUS WATCHER

After four long hours down at the crime scene, a thirty minute drive from the late Broken Edge, to the station that now resided in New Broken Edge, and filing a report that lasted almost another hour, Mick finally shuffled his way to the elevator in his apartment complex. He pushed the button to the elevator, hoping his rowdy neighbors above him on the fourth floor would be asleep and not making squeaking bed noises. They technically should be asleep, but with those two Mick never knew. He was in that stage of being stupid exhausted, but yet was unable to actually fall asleep due to his mind never being able to shut down. The gruesome sights he had taken in at various crime scenes on the Tick case had stained themselves across the walls of his mind's eye. He looked over his shoulder at the clock that hung in the lobby. It was 5:46 AM. The elevator finally arrived, (He swore that thing dated back to Biblical times) and he stepped inside. Though his claustrophobia protested a little, he told himself that it was a perfectly safe contraption and he was too tired to take the stairs. Plus it would only be a twenty or thirty second ride, he reassured himself. The interior to the elevator had that brown, wood paneling that looked like it belonged back in the 70's, with cream colored flooring, and the light in the ceiling above was dimming.

The doors closed on him, and the elevator lurched as it began its climb up to the third floor. He counted the seconds it took to leave the ground floor and reach his.

One, one thousand, two, one thousand, three, one thousand… His left hand began twitching. He had almost learned how to block out those nervous ticks he got when in an enclosed space. Yet his awareness of them remained, like a blinking light in the background. Like a subtle warning to keep him alert of how compressed his surroundings felt at times.

*Ten, one thousand, eleven, one thousand…*The button to the second floor glowed, letting Mick know he was almost there. And then the elevator lurched to a stop. He hung onto the railing on the walls and cursed under his breath as he tried to slow his frantic heart.

Crap I lost count! He thought as the elevator began its climb upwards again. After seeing the button to the third floor glow, he waited eagerly for those doors to open so he could dash out of this death box.

"Definitely taking the stairs next time." He said to himself as the elevator doors took their sweet time to open. After what seemed like an eternity the elevator finally dinged and the doors slowly rolled open, and true to his thought process, he darted out as fast as he could before those doors could seal him in again and the elevator plummeted him to his certain death.

"Stairs are your friend," Mick said as he started fingering his keys. His apartment was the last one at the end of the hall, and it was straight across from the stairwell. He could have just taken the stairs. He had gotten bored one day and had named the stairs leading up to his apartment—all twenty four of them.

There was Albert, Allen, Aaron, Ben, Benny, Benjamin, Becca, Clarence, Christine…He began the long trudge down the hall to his apartment, vowing he would always take the stairs, no matter how tired he was.

In his apartment, he collapsed onto the futon. There was bunch of documents crammed into a folder on the large cardboard box next to him, the one he used as an end table to set up his reading lamp. He reached for the folder, and let out a long sigh as coroner's reports, crime scene photos, newspaper articles and the like fell out.

He scooped up a few of the documents and thumbed through them. Everything in this folder he hoped could supplement the task force trying to catch the vigilante hunters. Sure since the Tick killings stopped he had still been under the direction of Agent Pallacios, but in his downtime he began gathering information on cases that related to the vigilantes. The glowing light that their ammunition gave off after hitting a target was their calling card. It was definitely nothing like Mick had seen before, and it wasn't like anything in any market out there today, not even the black market. Mick had speculated it might be a new type of military ammo. Given how difficult it had been to track or get a beat on these creeps, it was possible they all had a military background. So if their weapons were experimental military, it was entirely plausible.

Monster hunting was a legitimate, albeit dangerous profession, provided those doing it had the proper credentials to do such a thing. It was a damn lucrative business too. People were willing to pay money they didn't have just to have someone from a hunter division come investigate a strange noise or suspicious looking shadow in their back yard at night. When most of these things could even pass for human beings, all it took was one time of being right to make all the paranoia pay off.

Chemical analysis on the glowing substance had yielded that its properties were unknown. If Mick had to guess, it was a type of acid tailored to have a chemical reaction when exposed to the monster's blood stream, with a bit of prosperous to explain the glowing. But he had seen the chemical analysis reports. All properties were all unknown. It glowed with such an intensity that it was almost hard to look at the stuff. Even with prescription sunglasses. Photos of the stuff had to be enhanced to reduce the glare that the glowing letters gave off on camera lenses. It made the words readable at least.

There was a sketch that had been done by the department's artist of what one of the hunters looked like, according to a witness. It really wasn't much to go on. Given that they only operated at night, and the witness only caught a fleeting glimpse of them, it wasn't very much. The photo was a portrait, like all sketch artists do when trying to render a description, but the face looked like one of those generic, blank faced masks with no expressions. The fact that the mask was black didn't add much detail either. But the eyes were different. The artist put a lot of emphasis on the eyes, while not adding any details like pupils, sclera, or the like. Just two white points of light burning in the two sockets, shining like torch lamps.

Mick pulled the paperclip from the top left corner of the photo, and let a newspaper article about said witness fall to his lap. The article contained two sketches under the headline—One was the same sketch of the masked hunter, and the second was a sketch of what the perpetrator looked like according to the witness. The face of the perp looked mostly human, but with very telling signs to the contrary. An exaggerated hook nose with cartoon like proportions sat above a mouth that housed razors for teeth. Teeth that shot out from the gums in a mess of crisscross, haphazard angles that were suited towards rending flesh. The eyes were far too large, bulbous and bulging. The oddly shaped nose had creases, or folds of skin, on either side of it.

He scooped it up and reread through it:

MASKED MAN STOPS ALLEGED NON-HUMAN INTRUDER.

On the night of August 26th, New Broken Edge Resident Melissa Cline was saved from a home invasion attempt. When authorities investigated her residence for signs of breaking and entering that would specifically be consistent with non-human perpetrators, no such signs were present. A humanoid body was recovered at the scene however. Upon further searching of the residence, discarded clothes, food wrappers and crude but sharp implements stashed within the hollow spaces of her walls were uncovered, which led K-9 units to discover an underground chamber nearly 0.2 kilometers below the structure of the house. This suggests that the perpetrator had been living beneath Miss Cline's residence for some time.

"Until DNA analysis of the evidence can be concluded we can release no official statement as to its origin." Police Chief Theodor Scroggins said.

The rest of the article was quotes from Miss Cline, talking about the masked man who rescued her from the creature. Whoever they were, they were effective at what they did, but the incident with the woman had been too close of a call. He sighed as he felt his eyes starting to get heavy and his mind drifting off into the darkness, that could only be found in that special corner of his mind. Where he dreamed of how the world was before it was mauled by the teeth of monstrous beasts.

The glowing eyes that hid behind the plain black mask watched him intently. Someone peered inside of a window from a fire escape, their eyes glimmering with intensity. The black clad figure produced a small digital camera and brought it up to take a picture, making double sure the flash was off. Luckily for her, Mick Johnson's claustrophobia prompted him to leave a window ajar. The fear of suffocating to death, whether in a tightly enclosed space such as an elevator, or even his own apartment plagued him so. The figure smiled beneath her mask. Johnson had been her assignment since word had reached the Reclaimed of his interest in their activities. She watched him for a moment longer, seeing he was fast asleep there on his couch, holding a few documents in his lap. She waited patiently to ensure he really was asleep before reaching her hand with the camera slowly through the open window, focusing through the LED screen, and took a couple photos of him sleeping there. Then, she was off, quickly and quietly descending down the fire escape on the side of the building.

DOLL FACE

In a room lit only by candlelight, nimble hands were at work, sewing, twisting, and pulling. A teenage girl kneeled at an altar that was draped in a silky black and purple cloth. On the alter were various items, including a small dagger, incense burner, various occult symbols and a clay statue of some grotesque being that was humanoid in shape, but seemed to have multiple faces covering its body. The primary face on its head had a mouth that stretched and gaped. The other faces seemed to be protruding from the thing's torso, like it was growing extra faces out of its flesh. The figure was naked, yet did not feature genitalia of either sex. Resting alongside the statue was the disheveled corpse of a crow.

The young girl kneeling at the alter had lashed sticks together with leather straps, in the literal form of a "stick" figure, before laying the figure onto a large piece of fabric that had been cut out to resemble a rough outline of a person. Then she began to sprinkle various ingredients onto the cloth. A mixture of various herbs and bone fragments from a small animal were then neatly packed around the stick skeleton and the cloth flesh of the doll sown shut. The crow's head, its long beak covered in the dried blood of a human being, was to be sown into the doll's chest. She placed the dead bird on the altar, next to the unfinished doll, and began reciting an incantation. Her voice was fervent, soaking with emotion that suggested she was afraid, on the verge of hysterics. And then, as the girl lifted the dead crow off the altar, she grabbed the head and twisted it off in a sickening crack! The tone and inflection of her voice likewise changed to one of rage and vehement anger.

The bird's head, with blood covered beak facing down toward the doll's crotch, was placed inside the doll's chest, and sealed in. The girl kneeling at the altar breathed heavily, leaning forward on the altar as if to rest their head on their arms. A peculiar hand reached forth from the shadows, clawed and looking as if it was coated in black ink. It rested on the figure's shoulder.

"Rest now, sweet daughter," a strong, fatherly sounding voice said out of the darkness behind her.

"Thank you," The young girl whispered in reply. There was no movement or words from either for what seemed like minutes as the supplicant at the altar labored to catch her breath.

"There is still one last touch to be added." The fatherly voice from the shadows added after a while. With that, the hand slipped off the girl's shoulder, and then extended forth again, holding a pair of scissors and a photograph of someone.

The kneeling girl nodded at those words and took the photograph and scissors from the being's hand. She neatly began to cut out the face of the person in the photo.

The figure in the dark stretched its cold, shadowy hand back into the light of the candle. The girl at the altar produced a safety pin, undid it, and pricked the cold inky black finger of the one standing over her. A dot of thick, black substance oozed out of the pin prick. The substance was dabbed onto the backside of the cut out face, and then pressed firmly to the doll's head, adhering it instantly as steam emitted from the bonding of the two items. Then, she held up the newly constructed doll. The hand from the shadows took hold of the object and there was a soft chuckle of approval that followed.

"Hello, Mick Johnson," the fatherly voice said.

REFLECTION

Mick stood looking into one of the polished glass display cases holding many an abused childhood artifact. Not any from his childhood persay, but many that held certain significance to him nonetheless. Many a child's watch, shoe, and toy sat lonely behind the glass, looking back at him, begging him not to forget. Not to forget what had happened.

He focused his attention on a gnarled *Transformer* action figure of the character *Bumblebee.* He didn't need the sad stares of the preserved toys and charred pieces of clothing to remember what had happened. It was with him in nearly every thought, every dream, and every nightmare. Lurking in the background of each mental photo, like a stalking spirit that refused to let even the unrelated memories go untainted.

"I swear that one is mine," a voice said next to him. Mick turned to see George standing next to him, his finger pointing at the glass at a gnarled action figure. Mick and George had been collectors in their impressionable years. *Transformers* was one of those special things they had in common when they were little, and even now as adults. Mick's home phone was a movie replica model of *Optimus Prime.*

"You wish," Mick said, turning his gaze back to the figure in the glass case.

"Eh…kinda. I would prefer one in mint condition myself. But seriously, I think that one is mine from back in the day." George said.

"It's hard to tell from this angle. Can you see if part of the head is missing?" Mick asked. George smiled. His old family dog, a Grey Hound/Jack Russel Terrier mix, had gotten ahold of it. Mick had been there the day Gracy decided George's beloved action figure was her new chew toy.

"I can tell some of the paint has flacked off, but as far as I can tell the plastic is all intact. But like you said, the angle makes it hard to tell." George said.

Mick sighed, and put his hands in his pockets, "So have you been following me?" he asked, knowing the answer.

"I can always find you here in the morning man. This place is like your *Bat Cave.* "

Mick nodded, "You know me so well."

"I notice you come here a lot after having to deal with Pallacios." George said. Mick nodded.

"This place just calms me down overall. It's almost like my own form of therapy. Only time I have to pay is if I'm in the mood for a tour."

After the two shared in the following silence, Mick continued.

"When I look at all these memories, I find encouragement in how we have risen up from what happened. As a community we banded together to rebuild our lives. The one single event that broke open the floodgates in the media that let the world know monsters exist, and we survived it. Broken Edge is in our blood man. So you wanna get drunk tonight?"

George snorted and dipped his head as his shoulders shook and laughter boiled up out of him. He shook his head.

"Oh wait, you can't tonight huh? Cause tonight isn't your Friday," Mick said, rubbing it in.

"Yeah, I gotta work on the analysis from the crime scene tonight."

"Well I'll drink an extra Jack n' Coke and think of you," Mick said batting his eyelashes in an exaggerated fashion.

"Bite me asshole," George scoffed.

Mick shook his head, "I don't know where you've been,"

"Come on Mick," George said, shoving his hand on Mick's face, squishing his nose and lips like he was playing with clay, "Take a bite. Cannibalism solves world hunger."

Mick grabbed George's hand and shoved it away, "I'll starve thanks," he said. They both laughed their maniacal laughs that they had perfected as children, and turned their gazes back to the toys in the glass case.

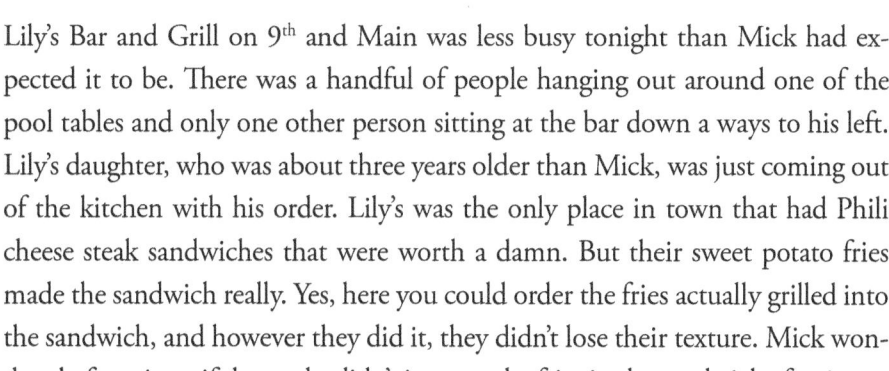

Lily's Bar and Grill on 9th and Main was less busy tonight than Mick had expected it to be. There was a handful of people hanging out around one of the pool tables and only one other person sitting at the bar down a ways to his left. Lily's daughter, who was about three years older than Mick, was just coming out of the kitchen with his order. Lily's was the only place in town that had Phili cheese steak sandwiches that were worth a damn. But their sweet potato fries made the sandwich really. Yes, here you could order the fries actually grilled into the sandwich, and however they did it, they didn't lose their texture. Mick wondered often times if the cooks didn't just put the fries in the sandwich after it was made, but either way, the sandwich was nothing without the sweet potato fries.

"Here ya go sweetie," Mariah said as she set the food down in front of Mick and then topped him off with another bit of Jack. Mick poured a small amount of Coke from the can into the glass and swished it around.

"Thanks Mariah. So all this food and booze is free right?" Mick asked. He asked the random questions on purpose, and he got a kick out of seeing people's faces as his, out of place inquiries gave them a sort of whiplash. Didn't work so much with Mariah though. She had come to expect it from Mick, as he was always trying to playfully get her ire up in some form or another. She was a good inch and a half taller than Mick. She was toned but curvy in all the right places, and highly favored enough by some celestial force to be well endowed but was modest enough to dress in a way that didn't draw *too much* attention to those areas. Mick recalled her wearing a shirt one evening that said, "Eyes up *here.*" Her thick dirty blond hair was often kept in a braid that was wound up behind her head and held in place with clear chopsticks.

"Maybe. Whatcha gonna give me for it?" She asked as she playfully narrowed her eyes at him.

"But then it wouldn't be free. This meal *is* on the house," Mick said, waving his hand out like a wizard, to which Mariah waved him off and replied, "Gimme a million dollars and I'll think about it."

"Damn," Mick chuckled as he began chowing down. It was all in good fun, and she played along marvelously. He looked down at the folder with all his information pertaining to the vigilante hunters that was sticking out from under his butt.

Gotta keep it warm for the Chief, don't want the case to go cold! Mick thought, snickering at his own lame joke. He looked up at the mirror that was behind the various containers of liquor. He saw the shape of someone familiar coming up to him. Mick spun in his bar stool and nodded to Chief of Police, Theodore Scroggins as he approached.

"Johnson, how's it hangin?" Scroggins asked as he squeezed Mick's shoulder and took the stool next to him on his left.

"Like an anaconda!" Mick emphatically exclaimed. Scroggins nodded, chuckling to himself.

"Good to hear son," he said as he turned to place his order.

"So what may I ask is the reason for this secret get together?" Scroggins asked turning in his stool toward Mick.

"Well sir," Mick said reaching for what lay beneath his butt, "I've been putting together a file that pertains to the activity of the vigilante hunters that have been operating in our city for around a year."

Scroggins's eyes narrowed at the folder that Mick set down on the bar in front of him. Mick watched his face in eager anticipation, waiting for him to finally break the silence. Scroggins reached for the folder and flipped it open, thumbing through the statements given by people who had allegedly had some form of interaction with the vigilante hunters.

"Ya know Johnson, most fanboys collect comic books or toys of their favorite heroes," Scroggins said.

"I wouldn't consider myself a fanboy sir, just someone who is seeing a potentially dangerous group on the rise. I have other material in there that may suggest a link between this group and the group of hunters that were in Broken Edge back in 95. I'll admit that is kind of a stretch but it's an angle worth following up on." Mick said.

"And what makes you say that?" Scroggins asked.

Mick pointed to the folder and asked, "May I sir?" Scroggins nodded and handed it over, "We're off duty son, you can call me Ted."

Mick nodded, still flipping through the information, "Sure thing sir." His eyes found the dated photographs from 1995 that were paper clipped together, and then rummaged some more until he found a more recent news article from three months ago.

MUMMIFIED CORPS DISCOVERED IN DUMPSTER.

Mick slid the photos and the news story over to Scroggins and watched his face as he read the story.

"Remember that Jane Doe the city workers found in the dumpster in an alley on Cane Street?" Mick asked pointing to the article. Scroggins nodded, "I do. It was during that lull in the Tick Killings. If I recall, wasn't it you, Valerie and George that got sent out to look over the scene?"

Mick nodded, sliding the photos from 95 over to Scroggins as well.

"I went digging through the evidence archives from back in the day. Thank God these survived the destruction. Corpses in the same exact condition were found in the months preceding the Massacre. Toxicology reports on the victim from three months back matched that of the victims from 95. No illegal substances were found in what was left of the tissues. Hell, there isn't any substance out there that can just wither someone in seconds flat. And who would take it honestly. But that's beside the point," Mick said. He had to stop to inhale again, then he continued, "But the link I'm seeing is that, you will find statements in there from survivors of the Massacre, who saw people wither where they stood, and in every instance, one of those hunters was standing no further away than you or I are in these seats. The fact that we got these new hunters on the scene, and then another corpse turns up in the exact same condition as the ones from back in the day? Come on sir, can you see where I'm going with this?" Mick asked.

Scroggins eyes scanned the information Mick had laid out before him, and then he spoke, "And Pallacios knows nothing about this?"

Mick scoffed, "I don't tell her anything if I can help it. It's not related to Terrance Miller so it doesn't concern her."

"It *doesn't* relate to Terrance Miller, you're right. And that's why I want you to be careful. Until that bitch goes back to Washington, we are still under her authority. *I'm* under her authority. If I say yes to you following through on this, she won't just have your ass but mine too." Scroggins said.

Mick nodded, "I know sir, but…Look can you see where this might lead to? If these guys are back for seconds then I can't have that hanging over my head just because some uppity Fed decides she owns our souls." Mick said.

"Johnson whether those hunters from the nineties perpetuated the attack or not, they died in the Massacre." Scroggins said, like he was explaining to a toddler the meaning of the word 'why.'

"*That* was never fully determined sir." Mick interjected. Scroggins sighed and downed another gulp of his beer.

"But a mummified corpse isn't their calling card," Scroggins offered after his gulp, "was any of the glowing stuff found at the scene of that crime?"

Mick shook his head, "No sir…I was wondering if the odd liquid was a diversion."

"Understood son, but what can you present to prove that?"

Mick sat there for a minute, drummed his fingers on the bar as he thought, "Honestly sir it's just a gut feeling. Just following a hunch."

Scroggins nodded, "I see. You really believe their presence could lead to another incident?" Scroggins asked, putting meaning to Mick's rant.

"Yes exactly. This city has come too far to ever go back to a heap of rubble. I won't let it Chief. I love this city. Can't say much for its people, but the fact that we rebuilt our lives means too much to me to just let them continue operating unchecked."

Scroggins nodded. As far as Mick could tell he seemed to understand, even with bringing up questions Mick hadn't thought of. He wasn't quite buying it but he understood. Mick was going to need more evidence. Personal hunches would only take an investigation so far. They might be the starting ground for a case, and Mick had already collected enough evidence to make his hypothesis coherent. But nothing that screamed, 'We are here to kill you!' If anything, the fact they were operating outside of the law was grounds enough to go after them. The task force that had been set up to monitor their activity had yet to bring them in, always showing up to crime scenes after the fact. There wasn't any clear pattern to determining when they would strike either. But if there were monsters that lurked in New Broken Edge, they found them. Though the existence of non-human creatures was now public knowledge, and had been since the Massacre, creatures of the night didn't just simply go about advertising their presence. They were meticulous planners, only striking when the populace had been lulled back into apathy.

If anything, Mick knew that these hunters were doing the police a favor, going after the non-human monsters so the police could focus on going after the human ones. But as a cop, his loyalties were to the law. That little thing that when followed by people who wanted to live in a functional society, prevented outright chaos and the collapse of the infrastructure that supported their lives. He broke from his thoughts when he realized Scroggins was talking to him.

"Johnson, I can't officially authorize you to continue with this. While the task force has yet to bring them down, they are getting closer. Now that's the state of things as they stand *officially*. But unofficially, I can tell you, that you are a grown man, who knows how to follow procedure. There is nothing stopping you from collaborating with the task force on your findings. On that note, we never had this meeting, and I saw nothing." He said, winking as he sipped his beer.

"Thank you sir!" Mick said, breathing a sigh of relief.

"Damnit Johnson, I said call me Ted. It will make it seem more low-key." Scroggins said. To that, they both raised their beverages and sealed their agreement with the glassy *clink*.

"Keep your involvement with this under the radar," Scroggins warned.

Mick nodded, "Anything you say Teddy Bear," Mick said before he took a drink.

"Don't make me regret this Johnson." Scroggins said.

Mick nodded, "We look out for each other. That's what we do sir."

LIVING MONUMENT

October 3rd, 10:30pm,

The Broken Edge Memorial Museum and its stunning courtyard had closed at eight o clock. Security made their usual rounds within the halls of the museum, but the rounds to be made out in the courtyard weren't for another hour.

An unauthorized visitor sat on one of the benches near the entrance to the courtyard with all its unnervingly lifelike statues. The courtyard, a life size reconstruction of a photograph taken on a decimated Main Street of the original Broken Edge, was adorned with several statues of first responders and military personnel cleaning the street of debris, and assisting survivors that had been pinned beneath fallen walls or beams for several days. The visitor had read the accounts in recent publications of Social Studies textbooks in class. The visitor was a young man of almost seventeen years of age, with an athletic build and of Hispanic descent. Oscar Ramirez sat on the bench, with handfuls of his dark hair clenched in both fists as he rocked back and forth. Blood and raw meat stained the edges of his mouth and down the front of his shirt. The cries of rage and fear of himself that he was trying to suppress came out as *hungry* growls. But that was just it—he *wasn't* actually hungry.

Oscar had always been known as a guy who could put down some food, and he was physically very active in school. Track and football were his sports, and when he wasn't on the field or on the track, he was in the high school's weight room. He could bench 330 lbs. and was working his way up to 345 lbs. He could squat almost as much too. His appetite had earned him the nickname of Garbage Disposal, which he readily accepted, as any food his friends or family didn't eat, he would clean off. But it wasn't until almost two months ago that his appetites gradually took a frightening turn, and tonight it had reached its climax. He had been buying raw hamburger with money stolen from his mother's purse, for the first week, and then began stealing money from his friend's wallets when he was over at their houses. Had already lost one friend over it. The others hadn't caught on to him because he started going through wallets in the locker room.

But tonight, his mother had walked in on him, face buried in a foam tray of raw meat. He had looked up over the tray at her, to see her clutching her mouth to stifle a cry of shock and disgust at the sight of her son eating like an animal. But aside from the sheer embarrassment of being walked in on by his mom, and the shame of stealing money from his friends at school, what had him on the verge of gnawing at his own arm, and scared him more than anything was the fact that he wasn't even hungry. But it seemed like something else inside him was. He couldn't deny that the raw meat had calmed him down. Had satisfied his pallet in ways nothing else ever had. It was like he was eating to feed something else. Whatever it was that was churning through his guts was still hungry.

He winced at the pain as he released a handful of his hair, and sank his teeth into the tissue of his forearm. The teeth finally broke through the skin and ripped into the muscle surrounding the bone. But instead of searing hot pain, his eyes rolled back in sweet ecstasy as the taste of blood filled his mouth. The texture of tendons splitting and veins bursting open as his teeth worked through them like a hacksaw sent him doubling over in an odd mix of satisfaction and unnamable terror as tears finally leapt to his eyes. He sank his teeth even deeper, and by now he could tell he was almost to the bone.

Something moved off in the distance to his right, and he stopped, silently listening to the sounds of the night. The occasional car zoomed by but nothing else...except the sound of light footsteps.

He released his arm, cussing under his breath as he listened. He stood up slowly, eyes looking around, searching the shadows of the courtyard cast from the moonlight. He felt his legs carrying him further into the courtyard.

Another sound, this time behind him. He froze as the bold hunger that had compelled him suddenly vanished, and the fire in his arm flared up, nearly doubling him over. Whatever he did, he couldn't go back to his parents' house now. There was no way they would help him. He didn't even know how to help himself. But whatever he did, he knew now more than ever that he was exposed. If a guard came through here and called the cops, he would just get brought home by the police. After the realization hit him that he had just tried to chew flesh from his own arm, he knew it would only be a matter of time before he tried again with his mother, father or any of his siblings.

He stood stock still and waited for more footsteps to approach, a flash light beam or a shout of, *What are you doing here?!* But he heard nothing. He slowly turned around to look behind him. A statue of a policeman standing watch by a pile of debris starred at him with an unmoving fixed expression.

That wasn't there a second ago, Oscar thought as he slowly back away, keeping his eyes on the policeman. The sounds of scrapping stone could be heard about twenty feet to his left, down the part of the courtyard that was built to look like demolished Calhoun Street. A statue of a small girl stood next to a statue of a fire fighter, facing down the replica of the street toward Oscar.

Oscar had walked this courtyard many times. He came here to hang out during the summer months. He knew this courtyard intimately, and he knew that the fire man was supposed to be pulling the little girl free from the demolished house behind them. Not standing perfectly still where they were now, and facing in his general direction. Immediately he felt icy tendrils snaking out from his stomach and through his entire body, chilling his blood that ran freely down his arm and onto the ground.

He turned to flee, and as soon as he did, stiff, stony fingers encircled his throat. The statue of the policeman had him by the throat, both hands constricting like a vice. He was too shocked to scream, and right now he couldn't even if he wanted to. His vision blurred as he sank to his knees, trying to pry the stone hands off his throat. In the distance he could hear more clamoring, stony foot falls as other statues began to fill in behind the police officer. The fire fighter, the little girl, and many others were shuffling toward him, their stony, unmoving faces closing in around his vision as their hands began to dig their fingers into his flesh.

Another sound filtered in through the sound of the statues. It sounded like scurrying little feet, with the click clack of small claws echoing behind them. Suddenly the policeman statue jerked to the side, releasing its grip on

Oscar's neck, and he coughed and doubled over as the others let him go. Something was distracting them.

In his blurred vision Oscar made out the tiny forms of multiple scurrying creatures. He almost thought they looked like mutant fetuses. At first he thought maybe it was because his eyes were so blurry, but then one of the things bounded over him on all fours like some kind of crazy primate. It was then that he finally saw the things clearly—they *really did* look like mutant fetuses.

A stone head crashed to the ground next to his face. The stony face of the policeman starred back at him, the head broken free from the neck. Black ooze shot from the stump of the neck as the statue's face grimaced and a faint hiss escaped the mouth.

Is that blood?! Oscar screamed in his head as he hurried to his feet. The mutant imp creatures were digging their claws into the statues, flinging bits of stone and chunks of the tarry black ooze along with them. Another statue, this one of a military officer, was being swarmed by four or five of the little ugly things when Oscar heard a loud crack, like part of a cliff face breaking off, accompanied by the sick squirting sounds of what could only be the statues blood.

Statues don't bleed! Oscar screamed in his mind. But then again they didn't try to strangle you either. He turned to see two more standing behind him, one about a foot shorter than the other. Oscar took an aggressive stance, and out of pure survival instinct was about to ram through like he was on the football field. But then he heard the figure speak.

The stranger uttered a phrase in a weird language Oscar hadn't heard before, and immediately he felt himself losing all control of his balance, tumbling arse over teakettle. He landed hard and tumbled toward the two figures he had previously thought to be statues.

"Aren't they adorable?" The shorter one was speaking. Oscar blinked, the sounds of the carnage behind him beginning to die down.

"W-what?!" Oscar responded. The voice belonged to a female, and if he had to guess, one around his age. The two figures stepped closer, their features becoming more defined. Definitely not statues. She was a slender girl of about five feet, seven inches tall. Her green eyes came into focus there in the dark, and Oscar could see she was looking right at him. Then he realized that even though it was dark, he actually could see that her eyes were green. Weird. No more weirder then what was happening behind him, but still weird.

How long have I been able to see in the dark this clearly? He caught himself thinking.

On the girl's head she wore a black skull cap with some artsy design on it. Her long hair fell to her mid back. On her arms she wore stockings with the tops cut off for her fingers to slip through, and holes cut for her thumbs. For the rest of her she was simply clad in form fitting, black jeans and shirt.

"She means the little creatures behind you." The second figure spoke, the taller one, who was clearly a male.

Oscar frantically turned his head back toward the fading sounds behind him. There was now only one of the things left, and one of the statues left as it dragged itself along the ground, the legs apparently smashed to bits, black blood oozing out of the thing's torso and its gaping stony mouth. The one little odd creature that was left pounced on the thing from behind, dug its clawed little bony fingers under the thing's jaw, and with a loud and nauseating *crack*, broke the thing's head free from its shoulders. Chunks of stone mixed with tiny droplets of black ooze flew through the air, and Oscar felt the moisture hit him in the face. Then the small creature faded from visibility, dropping the stone head with the still moving mouth of the statue hard on the ground.

Oscar scrambled to his feet, keeping his arms outstretched in front of him as he began backing away.

"W-what was…Who are you people?! What are those things, and where did the little fetus looking things go?!" He yelled, pointing wildly behind him.

"My name is Craven Grimsbane, and this is my sister Skylah Grimsbane," The male figure said as he extended a hand toward Oscar. He was dressed all in black like she was, and his hair was cut short in the back while the eight inches of dark hair he had in the front was smoothed over his right eye. His wrists were adorned with thick leather bracelets that sported more buckles than were even functional, and clad in a black pullover hoodie. Oscar didn't take his hand.

Craven continued, "Those things that attacked you were gargoyles. And the 'fetus' things, as you called them, belong to me. Our Father calls them Little Outsiders. Not the most original, but it works."

Oscar's wide eyes were still darting to and fro nervously, "W-where did they go?"

"They are back on the astral plane. They drew just enough energy from this place to manifest. Now that we've gotten that out of the way, let's cut to the chase. Your name is Oscar. You started eating raw meat and now you don't have anywhere to go—"

Oscar cut him off, "Whoa, whoa…Just…How the hell do you know my name?! How do you know…anything about me?!"

The girl, Skylah, stepped forward, "We've been watching you for a while Oscar. You weren't that hard to find. Your aura leaves strong impressions wherever you go. It's just like a hunting dog following a scent. We know that the hunger inside of you will drive you mad if you don't come to understand it."

"We know you can't go back home after your dear ol' mother saw what you did. But if you come with us, our Father will teach you to understand what you're becoming, what you were born as." Craven said.

Something about the way he said those last two words caused Oscar's insides to recoil as the tremors of gut wrenching dread tore through his nerves like an electrical current.

"What do you mean, born as? I'm a person. A n-normal, freakin' person!" He protested.

"Do normal people try to eat through their own arm?" Skylah asked, pointing to the gnarled flesh on his arm.

Oscar felt light headed when she said that. A sudden wave of nausea roiled up in his gut and he had to sink down to his haunches as he rocked back and forth, not knowing if he was going to projectile vomit all the gore he had stuffed himself with just hours before coming here.

"I'm…not, hungry…I'm NOT hungry! But I can't stop. It won't let me…I don't know what's going on inside me." Oscar said.

"Our Father can help you. We know you can't return to your family. They won't understand what you're going through. They may or may not have already shunned you. But if you come with us, he will teach you to take that hunger, and derive power from it that you could never comprehend until you ascend." Craven said as he extended out a hand to Oscar again. Oscar eyed his hand for a few awkwardly long seconds before accepting it, and standing to full height.

"You said he could help me understand what I was born as…What am I?"

"Someone he is looking forward to meeting." Skylah said as she moved in closer to him, and slinking one of her arms around his torso, she pulled him tight.

"Welcome to our family," She said.

It had taken them about a half hour to walk from the museum to the house Craven and Skylah had spoken of. The house they were staying in was a two story house about seven blocks from the museum, with an awning over the porch that was supported by pillars, solar lights lining the walkway, and a weeping willow tree on either side of the walkway leading up to the house. As they approached Oscar began to get the impression that this house had been here for decades, which he knew couldn't be true since New Broken Edge had only been established for eighteen years after the incident that he read about in school called the Broken Edge Massacre. The closer they got to the house, the more Oscar felt that the house itself seemed from a different time, even though it looked just as modern as the houses around it. He couldn't quite put his finger on it. Like the house just *felt* older than it really looked.

Oscar's blood froze in his veins as the knob twisted and the door slowly opened to them into darkness, but the more this night went on, the better Oscar's eyes were adjusting. To any ordinary set of eyes it would have looked like the door had opened itself, but Oscar's eyes were different. He could see the clawed, gnarled little hands the color of darkness itself. They held onto the door pulling it open, and a shriveled head with sharp pointed ears peered around the corner, its crimson eyes flaring at the sight of Oscar. Whether it was with hunger or amusement he wasn't sure, which set him on edge even further.

"Do they have names?" Oscar choked out after steeling his nerves enough to walk past the thing. The thing at the door was sniffing the air with gusto, but then Oscar realized it was sniffing in his direction. It muttered something in a language he dared not even try to place.

"I'm sure they used to," was Craven's only response as Oscar heard the door click shut behind him. He followed them from the small receiving area with the coat closet and the mat for wiping one's feet upon entering. He heard the soft sounds of a television playing in the next room over as the two teens motioned him to follow. Into a comfortably large living room they entered.

The glow from the TV lit up the living room, illuminating the gaunt faces of a man and a woman sitting lazily in front of the forty two inch screen as a cooking show kept them transfixed. Their eyes vacantly stared forward into the screen, looking but not seeing.

"They aren't aware of us," Skylah said when she noticed him watching the couple apprehensively. Oscar turned to look at her, puzzled.

"You mean they don't know we're in their house?" Oscar whispered, panic rising in his tone. She nodded and smiled with a wink.

"No need to whisper. They can't hear you." She confirmed.

"How?" He asked as he began following them again, the small creature behind giving him the hungry look.

"We are all cloaked from their perception. Their minds are not able to sense us as long as Father is here with us." She said. Oscar stole one final glance behind him, just in time to see the little creature vault over the couch, and curl up in the woman's lap like a cat. The woman's hand absently moved to stroke the creature behind its ears as she cooed to it, calling it Sprinkles.

The lights overhead glowed softly as they walked toward the stairs that lead up to the second story. He noticed the wallpaper was faded and peeling. He knew that it was of a current style, because he had seen the same kind in stores a couple months back. But it was so faded it looked like it might have been from the seventies.

"Who is your father?" Oscar asked. Craven had stopped at a door at the end of the hall, twisting a knob and stepping aside as the door opened into a gaping maw of darkness.

"He's waiting for you in there." Craven said, his face blank. Oscar nodded, hesitantly putting one foot in front of the other as he felt himself moving toward the open door.

"Come in young man," an echoing voice from inside the room spoke just before Oscar crossed the threshold. The door closed gently behind him, sealing Oscar in the dark room with whoever was in here. He instinctively reached along the sides of the door frame for a light switch, and his heart fluttered with relief as he felt one brush his fingertips.

"Please, leave the lights off. You don't need them, remember?" The voice said. Oscar's mouth went dry as his hand trembled by the light switch. But the voice was right. He didn't need the lights on, because he could clearly see that the room was an eight by ten square foot room, facing the north side of town, with a view of the street from here. He could see the boxes and plastic totes stacked on top of one another. But seated right before him, facing the window that looked out over the street, looked like a man in a recliner…who was covered with a white bedsheet.

Oscar stepped closer cautiously, his hands trembling.

"H-hello?" He asked, his voice only a timid whisper.

"Hello young man." The voice replied. He expected to see the man's face as he rounded the recliner, but he stopped when he saw that the man's head was covered as well.

"What were you doing out past curfew?" The voice asked again. Oscar tried to swallow.

"I…I don't understand what's happening to me. I had to get away. To think. I needed a place I could think." Oscar said.

"To think? About what?" The voice inquired.

Oscar hesitated, trying to find the words. How was he going to tell someone, who was under a sheet of all things, that he had been caught by his mother, eating raw meat and losing himself in rapture at the taste of it? How was he to explain a hunger that wasn't even his own, that compelled him to bite through his own arm?

"The raw meat staining your shirt…is that what you had to think about?" The voice asked. Oscar felt cold beads of sweat racing down his forehead. The sheet looked just as old and frail as everything else in the house.

"I understand you're frightened young man. I do not wish to frighten you further, but I'm not under that sheet," The voice replied.

The shockwave of goosebumps that exploded over his body sent his eyes darting around the room, frantically trying to spot the source of the voice. He swore it had been coming from beneath that sheet. His eyes suddenly landed on a figure standing by the window, only an arm's length away from him. It was taller than him—much taller. The thing's head was grazing the ceiling. It was featureless, and darker than the darkness around it, but three dimensional. It shimmered in a way that made it look like it was liquid, gaseous and solid all at the same time. Its gaze, if it had eyes, or the direction its head was facing, suggested it was looking down at Oscar.

"Oh my God."

"*God?*" It asked, stepping forward. Oscar felt himself being swallowed up by the endless shadows this thing was exuding, as if any shred of light that was coming in from the window was suddenly eaten away by even the slightest movement of this thing.

"It has been ages since any mortal referred to me as a god. I have gone by many titles. Daemon, djinn, dybbuk, a vetala…a god." It said.

"W-what are you?" Oscar managed to squeak out.

"*What* I am is someone who is interested in helping you understand the hunger that lurks within you. As for who I am…I cannot tell you that. Not unless you enter into a certain agreement with me." It said.

Oscar's eyes turned once more toward the man covered with the sheet in the recliner, "W-who…is that?"

The shadow standing before him like a giant didn't have any discernible facial features, even with Oscar's eyesight seeming to improve to superhuman levels in a matter of minutes. But the way that thing cocked its head to the side, Oscar would have sworn he could have seen a glint of a smile, if only for a second. It was so quick he wasn't sure if he had imagined it or not.

"That *was* my body."

Oscar's mind shut down. It was as if every mental structure that had been erected in his brain to house all manner of reason was crumbling at the foundations.

"It's been wearing out over the years. Just like an old pair of shoes. But that brings me to why you are here. You see, I am interested in helping young people like yourself in ascending toward their highest selves. For you to do that, you must understand what you *are.* But this knowledge will come with a price, for anything worth acquiring is never free. If you will aid Skylah and

Craven in helping me make contact with a certain individual, we can begin toward your ascension together." It said.

"W-why do you need their help? Or mine? What are you asking me to do?!" Oscar asked, trembling and on the verge of tears. "I...I can't kill anyone." Oscar choked out, his mind immediately jumping to the worst possible thing he could imagine.

The tall figure reached out an abnormally slender hand and gently drew Oscar's face closer as it bent over to meet his gaze. The figure held his gaze for a time, like he was looking him over or sizing him up in some way. The shadowy hand didn't leave his cheek, but instead remained as the voice slithered out toward him.

"I would never ask you to kill anyone dear boy. All I wish from you, is to be an extra pair of eyes and ears. Nothing more."

"Where the hell would I even start?!" Oscar snapped, tears falling down his cheeks. He immediately regretted it. The fact that this thing didn't have a face or eyes gave him no frame of reference to judge any expression it might have.

"I have someone I wish to make contact with. He merely needs persuaded. That won't be your job however. Just lure him toward Craven or Skylah. They will handle the rest."

"...I...I don't understand. What will happen if..." His voice trailed off, and his eyes wondered again toward the body under the sheet, "A-are you a ghost?"

A chuckle escaped from behind the shifting veil of living shadow that acted as a face, "I suppose you could think of me like that. A spirit separated from its body, seeking out someone of importance to converse with."

Oscar shivered as a pang of hunger zapped through his body once more, his eyes now looking with longing at the body beneath the sheet. If the poor sap was indeed still alive, Oscar could provide a mercy by biting through his throat. Once he realized what he was thinking, his eyes returned to the shadowy mass in front of him.

"Please, it's growing inside of me. I don't know how much longer it will be before I rip someone's throat out!" Oscar sobbed.

"But you couldn't kill." The shadow replied.

"I can't…But *it* could." Oscar said, clutching his stomach and digging his nails into his abs.

The shadow before him was silent for a moment, appearing to study Oscar as it held his face. He suddenly felt a burning, icy chill spread into the pit of his stomach. He tried to pry the shadow's cold touch from his face, but its fingers had turned solid, and had seemed to adhered to his cheek. He could feel something crawling beneath his flesh. Every layer of skin on him seemed to wriggle with icy maggots that eventually spread to his brain. He felt his legs give out from under him, and he dropped to his knees as a name flashed before his mind's eye.

Mick Johnson.

LAST REQUESTS

To: Detective Mick Johnson,

As I'm sure you are well aware, I am scheduled to be executed soon. You are formally invited to be the guest of honor at my grand send off, and it would delight me to no end if you were present. You will note the time and date of my execution on the additional slip of paper I have enclosed within this envelope. Please be a saint and help fulfill a dying man's last request.

With love and expectance, Terrance "Tick" Miller.

P.S. If fate permits, please come visit me as soon as possible before the grand event. I wish to extend my congratulations to you in person, for your exemplary work on putting an end to my 'reign of terror.' I am privileged to have been your first big case.

Mick sat starring at the note that was awaiting him on his desk. Terrance Miller was asking for him personally to be there at his execution! Mick had already asked around the station if anyone else had gotten a note asking them to be present. None had except him. And the way it was written was extremely off putting as well. Who writes an actual invite to their own execution like it's a freakin ballroom dance or retirement dinner?! Mick finally fished out the other piece of paper that was enclosed with the letter. The date of said execution was October sixth, at 11:00 AM. Today was the fourth. He looked at his watch, 11:48 PM.

He knew he didn't *have* to go. With all the atrocities Miller had done, and all for the sake of his 'art', he sure didn't deserve to have any last requests granted to him. But there was one small problem. How did Miller know that he was Mick's first homicide case? It's not like they kept in touch. And why so cordial about the entire matter? Surely being faced with death hadn't given Miller a change of heart *that* fast. Mick shuddered and grabbed his phone out of his pocket, pulled up George's number and placed a call.

The phone rang a couple times before George finally answered.

"What's up?" George's voice came through into Mick's earhole.

"Dude…" Mick felt like he was going to puke as he stood up and started for the men's room.

"There is a letter on my desk from Terrance Miller."

Whatever George was working with on his end clattered against something and he heard George cuss a blue streak before he responded, "Really? Why?"

"I…He says he wants me to be at his execution on the sixth. I'm sorry, I shouldn't have bothered you," Mick apologized as he turned down the hall and caught sight of the men's room at the end.

"Its fine man. You sound like shit though. You feeling okay?" George asked.

"No I feel like I'm gonna puke, thanks for asking!" Mick snapped as he entered the rest room, found and empty stall and knelt over it and waited…nothing.

"Look man we've taken leaks on the phone together but if you need me to get off so you can hurl just say so."

"I'm sorry George, I'm sorry. I don't know what I'm gonna do man. I'm just…Oh God,"

Mick closed his eyes as he felt his stomach do a cartwheel inside and he dry heaved once. He felt the acidic burn in his esophagus as bile shot up from his stomach and out into the toilet.

"…Well I think I'm gonna go now," George said, his voice moving away from the receiver on his end. Mick spit out a glob into the toilet.

"Wait! Dude can you go with me tomorrow please?" Mick asked, and then dry heaved again.

"Tomorrow? But you said the sixth. Today is the forth dude." George came back. Mick nodded his head and wiped his chin with some toilet paper.

"Hello?" George said.

Mick then remembered he was nodding and George couldn't see him, "Yeah. Look I don't think I'll be going to the execution, but…He said some weird things in his letter that I want some clarification on. I'll fill you in tomorrow."

George sighed, "Okay so I guess that means I'm going. Alright man... Well I hope you get to feeling better. When do we need to head out?"

Mick thought for a moment, "Let's do nine thirty."

"So much for catching some sleep after work. Alright man. I'll see ya then." George said.

"Thanks. I'm really sorry for this." Mick said. George sighed into the phone.

"It's what I'm here for man. Quite apologizing, I know you're stressed. It's part of the job."

Mick sighed as he nodded, said bye, and hung up and let his phone clatter to the tile floor. The only image he had in his head was the one of that hulking mass of disproportionate flesh being carried out on a large stretcher, and somehow *that* was supposed to be Terrance Miller. The thing's face looked like him alright. Well, enough like him that if he looked hard enough he could see the similarities, but on the whole, the face that looked blankly up at him from that stretcher looked like a swelling tumor with bleeding pustules. Mick spit out some more of the acid flavor that stained the inside of his mouth and sighed, resting his head against his forearms there on the toilet seat. It wasn't too late to text George and tell him that he had changed his mind. But Mick wanted to know what Tick meant in his letter. Even if it was a bunch of horse crap, Mick would take solace in knowing that Miller would get the needle.

George showed up around nine the next morning, which meant Mick wasn't ready. Still wasn't feeling so great either, but he hadn't told George otherwise on going. He managed to catch an hour of fitful sleep as soon as he got off work, and that long hike up in that cramped stairwell helped to get him ready to doze off as soon as he fell through the door to his apartment.

The queasiness came and went, but gradually grew less intense the further away they got from New Broken Edge. They had just crossed over into Brigsworth County, and soon were driving through checkpoints, showing identification, and also presenting the letter Miller had written to Mick.

Built in the 1920's, Ironswrath Maximum Security Prison had once been a prison for human offenders, until back in the early seventies it was shut down. But ever since the Broken Edge Massacre, it had been reopened and repurposed for holding strictly the non-human types.

The facility was like a maze constructed out of cold dull concrete, barren steel beams, and in some parts, like admissions, brick and mortar from the prison's earlier days stretched as far as one could see around corners or down a dimly lit hallway. It was enough to feed Mick's imagination with images of being swallowed by an anaconda made of brick, concrete and steel, its form writhing as Mick was pushed deeper and deeper into the bowls, to be digested with the other filth it had consumed. There came another bend in the anaconda's infinitely long body, a sharp left turn that was met by two armed guards at a set of double vault like doors. The guards escorting Mick and George filled them in, and they were admitted through.

Mick and George were being escorted by Ironswrath staff that were completely decked out in riot gear. Seeing how heavily armed and armored the guards were made Mick feel almost naked. Two guards leading in front, and two following from the rear. The fully automatic weapons they sported made him feel self-conscious in here about only carrying a Glock. But if anything, his being here would be good experience toward him getting his certification as a Non-Human Response Threat Instructor. He looked up nervously. Some message was playing over a loud speaker somewhere, drowning out the sound of their footfalls on the concrete floor.

"Don't look in their eyes," one of the guards said over their shoulder to him and George.

"Aint gotta tell me twice," Mick said as they approached a long row of cells where discolored arms that ended in claw like talons hung through the bars. Some were excessively hairy, others looked diseased and rotten, but regardless, each was either grossly muscular in some way or sickly thin with unnaturally elongated and bony digits. Mick instinctively drew himself in as far towards the middle of the hallway as he could, trying to make sure none of those unnatural looking fingers touched him. He bumped into George and nearly pushed him away, but managed to restrain the urge.

Immediately, as if sensing his agitation, the hands came up and were grabbing wildly at the guards, trying to get their hands through to touch Mick and George.

"They brought us food!"

"I'm gonna rape every hole in your face!"

"Human filth!"

"I'm gonna make you and your pretty little boyfriend my bitches!"

"Tender flesh!"

Each voice, none of them even vaguely human, continued their proclamation of their intent, most increasingly sexual and cannibalistic. The profanities only overlapped and blurred together as they made another turn, this one to the right, entered through another set of vault like doors, and descended into the basement level of the prison. The west wing of the basement—Block C— housed all the Theriomorph prisoners. The guards had nicknamed the place 'The Zoo.' The east wing, Block D, housed the freaks that weren't so easily categorized. These mostly served as experimental opportunities for those who worked in the labs and morgue down in the subbasement where they were heading. The ones that survived were transported back to their cells until more tests could be thought of to run. Another set of vault doors approached. They were descending deeper into the belly of the anaconda.

"So glad you made it detective, and a whole day early in fact! I was afraid you wouldn't be able to make it!"

Miller's voice cooed in an almost musical fashion. Mick was standing in a large padded room, with about six armed guards present, with a hulking, deformed artist/killer shackled dead center in the middle. An enormous collar was fitted around his bulging, veiny neck, and extending out from it were thick, shiny chains one would expect to see holding anchors for cruise ships. One link of the chains alone looked like it could crush a man's foot if it was dropped, even from a height of three or four feet. They clinked and rattled every time the disheveled mass of muscles and flesh moved.

What remained of his hair were greasy patches. One arm was swollen up about five times the size of the other one, and about four feet longer too. When Miller stood, he almost had to support most of his weight on that giant, muscular sausage he called an arm. He had a terrible hunchback that made

Mick's back ache, and every surface of exposed flesh crawled with snaking veins that seemed to change colors in various areas, blue in some, and black in others. To top it all off, he smelled like rotting meat. Mick, as well as the guards present, were all wearing breathing masks.

Mick swallowed dry as he went to respond, "…Uh…hi," was all that would come out.

Miller laughed a throaty laugh, and eyed Mick down with the one eye that wasn't swollen shut, "Is that all you have to say? I thought you wanted to know why I did it. Oh well, regardless of how much we talk, I plan to have fun at least."

Mick nervously eyed the guards, who were all standing with their weapons trained on Miller, and then looked back at him, "Well, honestly I don't care why you did it. You are a monster and as far as I know, that's just what your kind does." Mick said, trying to sound confident.

Miller's one good eye twinkled, "I'm an artist, Mick Johnson. I can see beauty in death that no mere person is capable of. I'm just the only one talented enough to actually capture it on a canvas."

"You see beauty in the savage killing of innocent people. You are nothing but an animal. Those people you gutted and painted didn't do a damn thing to you." Mick shot back, unsure of where that little bit had come from.

Miller shook his head, not in frustration, but in the way a wise teacher might do before beginning a lecture to a troublesome student. Miller made the *tsk tsk* noises with his tongue before focusing on Mick one more time.

"Has anyone ever told you how rich your eyes are, Mick Johnson?" he said. Mick's eyes instinctively widened, and then when he caught himself doing it he made the effort to quickly avert them.

"What the hell does that mean?" he asked, trying to sound not as unnerved as he really was.

"Have you ever seen the look on someone's face when they are coming to grips with their own mortality? Some people have this look of inner peace, like they can't wait to meet what's on the other side. Others have a look that contorts their whole beings into unearthly terror and madness, because they *know* what's waiting for them past that curtain. But regardless of the expression, it's beautiful. Almost erotic in some ways." He paused.

Mick felt ice cold sweat cascading down into his eyes as his hands trembled at his sides. The churning in his stomach was returning and he suppressed a stale acidic belch, the kind that heralds the coming of a wave of bile.

"I know I'm not the first to try and capture that on canvas, but still the challenge is irresistible to me. And then there is you. Detective…Mick… Johnson." He said, sharpening Mick's name, exaggerating syllables as if he were tasting them.

"You might be wondering why I wanted to see you. After all you weren't even the lead investigator on my case. You were just a supporting role in the grand production of "Tick!" Sure, I could have had that Pallacios bitch come instead of you. I could have gutted her while she slept. I certainly would have gotten off on watching her bleed out, but let's face it. She's no masterpiece waiting to happen. But you…You shouldn't sleep with a window cracked, you know?" he grinned.

Mick felt his knees about go limp and he suddenly felt like his head was detaching from his body. The room was now spinning and he had to hobble a step or two back until he found the cell wall to lean up against.

"Miller, were you in my apartment?" Mick gasped through his breather mask.

Miller smiled nonchalantly, that deformed face cocked to one side like someone who held a secret they would never tell.

"Please, call me Tick. I like it better. It rhymes with *Mick*!" He sneered before he continued, "Your eyes Detective. Your eyes have seen so much. You *have* seen people meet their end before. So much expression in them. I wanted to see them one last time. They are endless wells of inspiration to an artist who is passionate about his craft. And I *crave* inspiration," He said as his voice dropped to a growl on the word 'crave.'

Had Mick not been leaning up against the padded wall of the cell, he would have fallen backwards. His vision went dark for a split second and he pulled the mask up over his face just in time to let loose a barrage of vomit onto the cell floor.

Miller's laughter was so loud he thought he was standing directly above him. Mick jerked back as a guard came over to him and pressed a gloved hand to his shoulder, "Time's up sir," he said. Mick nodded through the haze, spitting out another glob of vomit that had found its way between his cheek and gum. He wasted no time whatsoever as he returned to George out in the hallway.

SECRETS LEARNED

The musty stench of preservatives and faint scent of fur fibers collected in a closet in one of these rooms drew Oscar's attention. As it was now, he was in the room that Skylah had decided was hers while they squatted in this poor couple's home. He starred down into a box full of well-preserved animal hides. The one he was holding now had the almost intact face of a mastiff. The hides were mostly intact one way or another. Some were missing paws or parts of a face here and there. He counted three. Seemed she was a dog person. There was the one of the mastiff he was holding, a Rottweiler, and a German Shephard.

He put the hide back into the box and shoved it back into the closet, and then turned back to the book he had been thumbing through earlier. Skylah's musings didn't really make sense to him, but nevertheless it didn't stop the invisible hand of ice he felt from caressing the nerves around his spine. Craven and Skylah had left at about two thirty this morning to do who knew what, and hadn't returned. Being in a strange house that was, for lack of a better word—haunted—wasn't conducive to getting the best night sleep, so he roamed around, being careful to avoid Sprinkles and the woman who referred to him as such while the husband was away at work. There was once when the woman made direct eye contact with him, yet droned around the room, cleaning, putting things away as if she truly was unaware of his presence. Now that the sun was up though, Sprinkles had made itself scarce. Of course he wasn't too eager to look for the little creep either.

Rituals and incantations, thoughts about creatures from other realms, strange symbols and disturbing doodles covered each page that he flipped through. His eyes roved over to the next entry.

6-27-12

There are those who have sought to distinguish the uses of magic by using such phrasing as, "Black Magic," or "White Magic." Such terms are utterly foolish in that no such colored magic exists. Magic is neither white nor black, nor even gray. It is neither evil nor good, as we humans would define such terms. It is a tool, such as the body is to the spirit, and a tool is completely neutral.

What is good? What is evil? They're just words to distinguish between preferences. For as long as our kind have lived on earth, man has given such invented titles to shelter themselves from what they find uncomfortable. They neither know, nor care what the unknown has to offer their miserable existence. Labelling 'forbidden' that which would make them truly free. They fearfully and violently stamp out what they do not understand. There can be no objective measure for determining what is "good" or what is "evil" when such mechanisms do not exist. Such definitions need not apply to the use of Magic. It is what a practitioner makes of it. It is how I break my mundane chains, and free myself.

7-1-12

Do as ye will, harm no one. That is the law most magic users bind themselves to. The idea that magic is not meant to be used to harm others, because you will be responsible for the karma that you receive as a result.

And it is this law that Father is teaching me to rise above.

We are a part of his coven. Though his coven is no longer a part of this earth. They have ascended beyond the chains of that petty law of Karma. Many who consider themselves Awakened scoff at the idea of manipulating the Hand of Karma. But father has made it possible. He is truly the only one who has ascended, and through ascending, we will become Karma.

"What are you reading?"

The hair on the back of his neck stood up and every muscle in his back tensed. Suddenly he felt naked and exposed, as if he were left to the elements on the side of a mountain for the glaring sun to scorch him to a crisp. Fitting since he suddenly felt his cheeks heating up like burners on a stove.

Skylah was standing in the doorway, her arms crossed and her glaring eyes surgically rending past every excuse he could throw out.

"When—when did you get back?" Oscar stammered.

Skylah stepped into the room, her cold eyes narrowing on the notebook in his hands.

"Look I'm so sorry, I was bored and couldn't sleep and –"

"How far did you read?" She asked, cutting him off. Oscar's mouth snapped shut and he looked back down at the notebook that was now hanging limply in his hand. He held it up to the entry he had just been reading.

"I guess you know me a little bit better than you did last night," She said, swiping the journal out of his hand. Oscar looked down at the ground, shame washing over him.

"It was interesting." He said.

"The blood rituals are my favorite. You can do so much with a single drop of a person's blood. It's one of the truest, most intimate ways of establishing a connection to that person. You can use it to bring wealth and good fortune into their lives, or turn their body into a cesspool for every disease known to mankind." Skylah said, taking her notebook back and sitting on the bed.

"So…your, father. When will he begin helping me understand what's wrong with me?" Oscar asked. Skylah pulled her legs up over the edge of the bed and flipped the notebook open to a blank page to start writing.

"After contact is made with someone special. But you are mistaken if you think something is truly *wrong* with you. It's just what you are, just like this is what I am." She replied.

Oscar sighed, "Well what am I then? And why the hell does he think I can do anything for him?" His tone came out more frustrated than he intended. Her eyes traveled to meet his, without her head turning an inch. It made him feel smaller.

"He knows what you're capable of. He wouldn't have asked if he didn't think you could do it," She said.

"He gave me a name…And it's a name that hasn't stopped echoing in my head ever since he touched me." Oscar said.

"Mick Johnson?" Skylah asked. Oscar nodded, not knowing how to proceed. He felt like he was creeping over a thin sheet of ice to get to the answers he was seeking, and every inch he moved only served to spread the cracks further.

"And that's the person he needs to contact? Like to pass on a message or something?" He asked.

"Something like that," Skylah said as her pen went to work, jotting down what was for her eyes only.

Oscar thought carefully before he opened his mouth to speak again. It was odd she hadn't shooed him out of the room yet. Surely if she had wanted him out bad enough she would have done something to accomplish that, but as of now he felt like she was tolerating him.

"How did he ascend?" He asked.

She looked up at him and drilled him with a dark stare, "Are you one of us?"

Oscar blinked. He had somewhat expected his probing would set off a land-mine. But he figured if he was practically going to be held hostage by forces he didn't understand, it would benefit him to understand as much as he could.

"O-kay I get it. I think I'm gonna go out for some air then." Oscar said. To that, the only reply he received was the continuous sound of her pen gliding over the pages.

INTERROGATION

October 6,

"...Hello?" Mick's phone about slid out of his hand before he tightened his grip on it, forcing his hand muscles to work out of the relaxed limpness that sleep had brought on all his limbs. A voice was talking on the other end, but he barley understood it. He ventured a glance over at his alarm clock, which read 12:36 PM. Recognition was starting to creep in through the back door of his brain, still pickled in serotonin from sleep. It was Chief Scroggins.

"—Got the subbasement and basement levels of the facility back under control at around 9:30 this morning…We took three of them into custody."

Mick rubbed his eyes again, trying to focus on what he was saying through the haze of drowsiness.

"Chief could you start over please?" Mick asked. It came out almost sounding like a mumble.

"Johnson I know how badly you wanted these guys. We got one in an interrogation room waiting for you right now." Scroggins replied.

"Sir I just woke up. Could you please start over from the top?" Mick asked, trying to sound as respectful as his groggy voice would allow.

Scroggins sighed, his exhale creating static in Mick's ear, and then began again, "Ironswrath prison had a riot this morning at about seven o clock. Started in the subbasement level. The power went out and all the electronic locks on every cell in the subbasement were disengaged. Then the power to the basement went out."

Mick felt ice cold sweat oozing from his forehead, and his grip on the phone tightened. The subbasement was where Terrance Miller was. He took the phone away from his ear and looked at the date on the screen. Today was the sixth of October. Miller had been scheduled to be executed today, an hour and a half ago. Scroggins was still talking.

"Prison staff regained control of both levels around nine thirty this morning. About fifty three Ironswrath prison staff are dead, another twenty seriously wounded. Your vigilante hunters were taken into custody shortly afterwards. They were there."

Mick fumbled with the phone as he sat up, now fully awake.

"They were there?! At Ironswrath?! Doing what?!"

"They are all choosing to remain silent. There are three of them here at the station. I need you here ASAP. I know you don't come in till later tonight but we can adjust your schedule when you get here. And Pallacious ended up being called back to Washington. She'll be flying out tomorrow morning, so she doesn't have anything to say about this."

Mick was down at the station in less than fifteen minutes. His heart was racing faster than he could drive. He knew where the speed traps in town were and avoided them on his way there, and then flew out of his car once he found a parking spot. He checked the folder that contained everything he had been collecting on the hunters up to this point. He hurriedly walked and, sometimes jogged down the halls of the police station, pressing and squeezing between any other officers he met on his way to the interrogation room.

Looking through a one way mirror into the soundproof interrogation room was the familiar form of Chief Scroggins. His head turned upon noticing Mick coming down the hall.

Not many words of greeting were exchanged between the two. This was Mick's first real interrogation. The practice ones he did in his Criminal Justice classes felt pretty intense, but honestly he felt his heart hammering in his throat so hard he felt like it was going to burst out and splatter all over the floor.

"Make 'em howl son," Scroggins said, and Mick nodded, held up his folder and proceeded into the small room.

The suspect sat at the small table in the middle of the room. He looked about Mick's age, probably a little older. Twenty five if Mick had to guess. Long thick brown hair was pulled back into a pony tail, and long renegade strands of hair fell lazily on either side of the suspect's face. High cheek bones,

Caucasian, athletic build, dressed all in dark colors—black and gray to be exact. Most notable of all though, was the fact he was looking to his right and was whispering, almost as if he were talking to something that had perched on his shoulder. Mick stood there eyeing him for a couple seconds, until finally the suspect must have felt eyes on him and looked up. He broke off the conversation with whatever he thought was sitting on his shoulder and eyed him with an eagerness that set Mick's nerves even more on edge. He didn't think that was even possible. He seemed too comfortable, and that was another thing that was clawing at the forefront of Mick's mind. These kind of environments were designed to cause suspects to feel uneasy and awkward. It was all a part of the mental manipulation that was necessary to obtaining a confession. But then Mick had to remind himself what kind of person that he was about to speak to.

"Hi there, I'm Detective Mick Johnson," Mick said as he set the folder down on the table between the long haired suspect and himself.

"Hello Mick Johnson," The suspect replied.

"I wasn't made aware if you were read your rights upon arrest, so to cover both our rear-ends, I'm gonna spout those off now," Mick cleared his throat and began, "You have the right to remain silent. Anything you say can and will be used against you in a court of law. You have the right to an attorney. If you cannot afford one, then one will be provided for you by the court…Now that's out of the way, may I know your name?" Mick looked the suspect in the eye.

"My name is Zachary James Stewart. I am twenty six years old, and I have been residing in New Broken Edge for a little over a year." The suspect replied.

He was speaking to a monster hunter, more importantly one that had acted outside of the law. So Mick proceeded with what he thought was a brilliant question to build some type of common ground with the guy.

"You like comic books, Mr. Stewart?" Mick asked.

"Just call me Zach please." Zach replied.

"Okay then, Zach. You like comic books?" Mick repeated.

"Very much," Zach replied.

"*Marvel* or *DC*?" Mick asked.

"I like em both." Zach said.

"Any specific characters you admire?" Mick asked.

"*Nightcrawler, Daredevil, Batman,* the *Green Lantern Kyle Rainer* and *Ror-schach* of the *Watchmen* are all characters that stand out to me." Zach said.

"Why those characters, if you don't mind me asking?" Mick asked.

Zach leaned forward, his hands sporting fingerless gloves as they rested on the table, "*Nitchcrawler* and *Daredevil* because of their faith, *Batman* because of his intellect, *Kyle Rainer* because he is an artist, and *Rorschach* for his conviction."

Mick nodded, "Do you consider yourself a man of faith, like the first two characters you just mentioned?"

"On my better days I like to think so."

Mick nodded, "Does your faith play any kind of role in your nightly, monster slaying activities?"

The look that crossed Zach's face was an unnerving smirk as he answered, "It does."

He's not denying it. Time to move in, Mick thought. Mick opened his folder and started thumbing through the various documents he had been collecting. He laid out various crime scene photos of mutilated bodies that belonged to various creature types. One even looked like it had tentacles or something hanging from its mouth, nostrils and eye sockets. Another was of the body of a strikingly good looking male specimen of about twenty five years old, who had apparently been strangled to death with the white hot links of a chain. The young man would have almost passed completely for a human had it not been for the snake like fangs and the jagged horn like growths sprouting from various areas of the forehead, neck, shoulders and pectorals.

Zach's eyes seemed to light up with a twisted fascination at the scenes splayed before him. Their signature blinding light substance was present in each photograph as well, leaking from the bodies of the deceased creatures.

"You recognize these photos don't you?" Mick asked, more of a statement really than a question.

Zach nodded casually. Mick continued, "I bet your faith must give you some kind of extra boost when you are out there facing these things. I'm sure it helps to believe in something when you are staring down the fanged maw of one of these beauties."

"It does for all of us." Zach said.

"Are all in your group religious?" Mick asked.

Zach nodded, "To a point."

Mick nodded, and then stood up and began to circle around the table, like a vulture getting ready to dine on fine carrion.

"Ya know the people of New Broken Edge should really thank you and your group. You make sure the monsters in the dark stay there, and, you even shed some light on the fact that they are there," Mick said as he pointed to the glowing substance that oozed from the body of a creature with a vaguely insectoid mouth. It appeared to be strung up on meat hooks.

"But we also violate certain laws, such as breaking and entering, hunting monsters without federal or even state licensing, things like that right? Is there an alleged allegation of car theft in there as well?" Zach asked, before Mick could continue. Mick stopped dead in his tracks. He had already made his way back around behind Zach's chair. Damnit this guy was bold...or arrogant. Something about the way he said it though was chilling to Mick. Probably because he had spoken word for word what Mick was going to say next.

"Um...Well, how about you tell me?" Mick asked, trying not to sound like he had just been blindsided.

"About which one in particular?" Zach asked, slightly turning his head to glance behind him at Mick out of his peripherals.

Mick sighed in frustration and balled his hands up into fists, "Let's talk about the car theft," he circled back around the desk, dug through his folder some more and pulled out a security photo taken from an intersection street camera. The photo was zoomed in to capture a figure, half a block away with burning white eyes using their elbow to shatter a driver's side window. The date was from two months ago, and the time read 23:32 pm.

"This 2004 Saturn belonged to a Wilson Shrieder. Did he know that one of you planned to use his vehicle?" Mick asked, trying not to sound overly sarcastic, but it still showed through. More annoyed than anything else...Or shaken up.

"He did not, but if you look back through the reports on that vehicle, I assure you that you will find that on the following morning around ten o clock he reported that same vehicle returned and with a brand new driver's window." Zach replied.

Mick stood with his eyes narrowing on the hunter in disgusted amusement. Who did this prick think he was?

Mick pointed to a couple key areas on the photograph. Another car was driving down the street at the time the hunter was breaking in.

"I don't need to know if this figure here in the photo is you or one of your partners, but I have to ask, why would you be stealing a car on a busy street? Granted it was eleven thirty two at night and there was minimal traffic, but here we got a car driving up on you. Did you just think they wouldn't see you or whichever one of you was breaking into this car and not report it?" Mick asked.

The hunter shrugged, "I can't speak for the one in the photograph, because I know that one isn't me. And as far as we know the owner of the car is the one who reported it, not some passerby."

Ah ha! Gotcha! Mick exclaimed triumphantly in his head, "How do you now it was the owner who reported it?" Mick asked.

The hunter looked at Mick dead square in the eyes and asked, "Are you going to develop a theme now? Isn't that step two of the Reid Interrogation Technique you are using?" His expression sounded bored.

Mick's right hand was trembling. He sucked in a breath to try and begin his rebuttal but then he painfully realized that he didn't have one. His eyes roamed around the small room, noting the location of the table and the suspect's proximity to things like light switches, the thermostat and then the one way mirror. He didn't even want to know what Scroggins was doing on the other side of the glass. Everything about the setting was intended to make the suspect uncomfortable, and emphasis that they have no control over the situation, yet Mick was the one who was suddenly being toyed with.

"You haven't answered my question," Mick pressed, trying not to speak through gritted teeth.

"Oh dear, I've said too much," Zach said, waving his hands around in a mocking gesture, "For your convenience detective, you can skip steps three and four, as I haven't made any denials this far about the evidence or my ties to it, and don't intend on making any." Zach offered.

What's step number four again? Mick floundered in his mind. He rubbed his face and then went for the water cooler, bringing two paper cones full of ice cool water and handed one to the hunter. *I'll try another angle,* he thought.

"Guess I should have asked if you even wanted some right?" Mick asked.

Zach nodded as he sipped on his water and replied, "You're fine. I've clearly rattled you and...Well I *can't* say that I'm sorry, but I can at least advise that if you need a hug, puppies are the way to go."

Mick finished gulping down his water and just looked at Zach. This time he couldn't hide his confusion or irritation, "What is that supposed to mean?"

Zach shrugged, "A hug, ya know, so you can feel better about sucking."

The paper cone in Mick's hand was suddenly a wad of soggy mush as he instinctively crumpled it. He could feel veins in his neck pulsing, and not from being unnerved. This smug bastard had gone way too far.

"Look," Mick said as he drummed his fingers on the table, "I think we've gotten off track here, so how about you tell me how you and the others ended up at Ironswrath this morning? What was your purpose there?"

Zach nodded, "We intercepted a message that originated in the subbasement and was patched through to all guard towers via short wave radio at about seven o'clock this morning. That's how we found out about it." Zach said. Mick nodded, watching Zach's eyes for signs of deception. So far the hunter's eyes hadn't really left Mick's.

"Alright, so you use ham radio, is that it?" Mick asked.

Zach nodded, "among other things."

Would you just give me a straight answer!! Mick cursed in his head, closing his eyes a second to regroup.

"You do know that Ironswrath is equipped with its own response team in the event that a situation such as a riot occurs right? Your team's involvement cost several prison staff their lives." Mick stated. Zach just starred, as if the jab Mick had meant to thrust on the self-righteous crusader hadn't even phased him.

"Of the reports on the incident that are coming in, how many of the known casualties have been identified as non-human inmates?" Zach asked.

"I'm asking the questions, you've done enough talking." Mick said. Zach shrugged and folded his arms.

"What was it, fifty two dead?" Zach continued to press.

Mick could feel his fingernails digging into the surface of the table, "fifty *three* dead...With another twenty injured." He said coldly.

"Of those numbers I can assure you, only five were prison staff, and they were among the injured. I was there, as well as my friends who are all waiting patiently in their cells." Zach said, his tone sharp as steel, and ten times colder than Mick's.

"So the rest are all inmates? Correct?" Mick asked. Zach nodded.

"Is there anything else you would like to know?" Zach asked. Mick shut his eyes and scratched his head.

"Not at the moment. You're obviously aware of the charges, since you quoted them to me earlier in our interview."

"Did I miss any?" Zach asked.

Mick opened his eyes and leveled them at the hunter. If he could shoot lasers from his eyes he would have disintegrated him where he sat and to hell with the consequences. The way he asked, 'did I miss any?' sounded more of a challenge rather than a question. Throughout this whole interrogation, Mick was the one being strung around. Part of him wanted to dive over the table and choke the life out of the hunter. Another part wanted to retreat to his bed, lick his pride and just stew, but only after the former had been accomplished first. Both of those would have to wait.

"No you didn't." Mick replied, cold and flat.

The hunter's body suddenly became rigid as his eyes moved just passed Mick's, like he was looking at something on the wall behind him.

"What?" Mick asked, his patience long gone. The guy's lips started moving sharply and quickly, and a faint sound of what Mick assumed were words could be heard crawling from behind his teeth. Still his eyes remained just passed Mick's.

Mick looked over at the one-way mirror and shook his head. He imagined Scroggins doing the same, as the change in the hunter's demeanor had been startlingly abrupt. But the hunter wasn't looking at the one way mirror. That was to the right. He was looking directly passed Mick, almost like he had locked gazes with something that was peeking out from behind Mick's head.

"Damnit what the hell are you doing?!" Mick yelled. The hunter looked in Mick's eyes again, but it was a fleeting moment that was exchanged for another agitated glance directly passed his head.

"It's behind you." That was all he would say above a whisper.

Mick grimaced and shook his head. He didn't even understand why he was still in here with him. But he instantly became self-conscious about a prickling sensation on the back of his neck as the air conditioner kicked on with a distant *click,* followed by the continuous low hum as cold air began to blow into the room.

"I'm done," Mick said, sliding his chair back and stepping for the door.

SUFFOCATION

Mick stood outside the interrogation room, fuming and irate. He wished he could think of an expletive that accurately encapsulated the torrential wave of face reddening madness that was leaking from every crevice in his face. Then he heard the giggling.

Mick harkened in the direction of the sound. Chief Scroggins was leaning against the one-way mirror, trying to muffle his chortling as Mick made eye contact. He sounded almost like a cheap birthday clown the way he giggled, and had Mick's ego not been beaten to a bloody pulp, he might have found the chief's laughter a wee bit contagious.

"Sir?" Mick asked as he stepped forward, trying not to let on that his pride had just been mauled in the jaws of some arrogant monster hunter.

"Well Johnson what'd you think of your first real interrogation?" Scroggins asked, his face beaming like a lighthouse.

Mick ran his hands through his hair, "Sir please, I know I sucked in there. Can you rub it in next week after I've had time to hang myself?"

Scroggins stepped forward, shaking his head, "Mick how many interrogations have you ever taken part in? And no the ones you did for your classes don't count."

Mick hesitated, not because he had to think, he just wasn't in the mood to talk. But noting the fatherly tone in the chief's voice helped him dislodge the words from his mouth, "Just this one."

Scroggins nodded, his point proven, "Well there ya go. Your first ones gonna have a lot of mistakes. You pick yourself up and you learn from it. And one way you do that is by focusing on what you did *right*. For example you started out laying a strong foundation when you asked him about the comic book thing. Then you went onto validate his faith in his cause."

Mick shrugged and shook his head, "He freakin played me like a fiddle though! It's like he was in my head the whole time and he could have dominated the conversation a lot sooner but he let me get far enough along to get my hooks in him and then he turns around, bends me over and rams it —" Scroggins cut him off.

"Did you not hear a word I just said? You are taking it personally son and you can't do that. You are giving him way too much credit."

Mick shut his mouth long enough for that to sink in. He sighed and put his face in his hands, rubbing his eyes to clear his thoughts enough for him to respond with something that didn't sound like a whiny school brat.

"Okay, okay...I just didn't expect that I would have been the one floundering like that. I saw everything going differently in my head. He confessed to everything and I guess my whole approach was based on him trying to deny everything and I would just sit there and slap him in the face with more and more evidence each time."

Scroggins listened, nodding and adding the sympathetic "MmmHmm," whenever Mick paused. "When you are dealing with smartasses like what's in there," he gestured toward the one-way mirror with his thumb, "you gotta be willing to anticipate those curveballs they throw at you. But you got him to give you details about the Ironswrath riot. You steered him back on track and that's important. There was more you probably could have gotten out of him, but given that you were rattled, you still managed to get some valuable information."

Mick remembered immediately about the ham radio the hunter mentioned. All the police had to do now was find the latitude and longitude of where the broadcast was originating from and follow it to its source. But then he realized that with these guys now caught, who was going to try and reach them? Assuming they had all been apprehended.

Scroggins was talking again, "You've just come off of a big case. I think you should take some time and work on some smaller cases for a while. See what Sergeant Mills has for you."

Before Mick could object, his breath caught in his throat, and his heart felt like a jackhammer in his chest as he almost doubled over. His vision clouded over as he grabbed at his shirt collar.

"Hells Bells Johnson, what's the matter?!" Scroggins asked as he stepped forward. Between gasping for air and trying to stand, Mick looked up and tried to mouth the words, "Need my inhaler." He fumbled around inside his pockets, trying to find the blasted thing, but all he felt was loose change and lint. Mick felt like the ceiling was being lowered on top of him and would crush him like an ant. The precious oxygen being sapped form his lungs was leaving his brain dark. He fought to hold onto consciousness. He dropped down to his knees, trying to make himself smaller to prolong that inevitable feeling of being crushed by the impending ceiling.

"I need an ambulance right away! New Broken Edge Police Headquarters, got a man here who can't breathe!" Scroggins was yelling into his cell phone as he stooped down to put his arm around Mick, but his voice sounded miles away.

Mick's vision blacked out and then came back, but it was darker every time. But with each time, though his vision darkened more and more, something down the hall came into focus just a little more clearly. A masked face, cloaked in pure shadow floated down the hallway through the darkness toward him. It was the glow of the eyes that illuminated the features enough for Mick to know it was even a face. The pupils were so small they looked like tiny black pin pricks, housed inside yellow irises that radiated a glowing intensity deep within them. They were their own source of light deep within whatever scull housed them. A hand reached up and began to lift the mask off with a slick, wet sound following its departure. But before whatever lay beneath was exposed, a voice echoed through his head, *That is enough dear one,* it said. Mick's vision stayed dark after that, and he collapsed onto the tile floor.

The light rain that was being poured out upon the earth made the soil in the backyard so much easier to break through. Skylah threw chunks of soggy earth to the side, her nimble fingers searching for the box she had buried here. She continued reciting an incantation under her breath, the image of Mick Johnson in her mind.

Her fingertips struck the cardboard of the shoebox she had buried. It was beginning to sag under the weight of the soggy earth. She wiggled her fingers deeper, finding the edges of the box with one hand and continuing to throw muddy chunks of soil to the side with the other until finally, the small capsule was unearthed. She opened the lid, her shaking hands clearing away the soggy dirt clods she had packed into the box to cover the object it held. Her muddy fingers clasped around the fragile stick frame of the doll she had made, with Mick Johnson's photograph face starring back at her.

TOWN ASSEMBLY

October 16

New Broken Edge High School, 7:32 p.m.

The auditorium buzzed with the murmuring of parents and students, some discussing the reason for the gathering while others were discussing how Becky had made out with Chad in the boy's locker room. The stage was lit up and the rest of the auditorium fairly dim.

Following Mick's episode at the station, Scroggins ordered him to take three days of paid medical leave, the last day of which Mick found out from George that the hunters now had an attorney, who had managed to cut a deal with the judge.

They would carry out their sentence under the supervision of the New Broken Edge police department, while continuing to hunt—heavily monitored, but unhindered. She was building her case on the fact that they were damn good at what they did, and by having them serve out their sentence by continuing to hunt, they would be aiding the police.

"She believes in them man. And honestly she has a point. The department can barely keep up with all of the human offenders, and God knows just how many of them are making alliances with those things that come out at night. The city could really benefit from this." George had said.

Mick remembered sitting there is his chair, eye twitching as George rattled on, his support for them steadily rising in his voice.

"Dude…These are vigilantes! They are operating outside of the law! Besides, it's not as if we don't already have licensed hunters in the next county over we could call if we ever needed them!" Mick said thrusting both hands out to keep from grabbing his hair.

George just stood there, looking down at the floor for a second, "Mick, is it so wrong to hold out for a little hope that these people can help make our streets even a little bit safer?"

Mick blinked, suppressing the cold rage that ran up through his spine, "I don't know what to say."

George shook his head, "You don't need to say anything."

"So," Mick ventured, "where's Valerie stand on all this?"

George started for the door of Mick's apartment, "You can ask her yourself. There will be a town assembly at New Broken Edge High on the 16th at 7:30pm. She will be going to that."

Mick exhaled and closed his eyes, "What's it for?"

George turned back to Mick, "It will be a Q and A session with the hunters. Maybe you can chew em out then."

Mick spit out a pretty hefty curse and capped it off with, "I'm not going!"

Before George closed the door and winked in Mick's direction, "She's probably gonna ask you if you wanna go." The door clicked shut, leaving Mick standing there in the middle of his living room. He thought the click of the door echoed a little too much, suddenly making him feel self-conscious.

Here he was, standing by one of the entrances to the auditorium, his eyes watching the stage for signs of those insufferable hunters. A row of three chairs were lined up behind a podium, with suspiciously shaped cases underneath them.

"Are there weapons in those cases?" Mick asked Perez, one of the officers who was standing next to him. He nodded.

"They signed a bunch of paperwork. It's okay. They were allowed to bring those in for demonstrative purposes. Just to show off what kind of gear they would be using when out on the streets. Remember, we're here in case anything happens, which I doubt it will," Perez said. Mick gave an unsteady nod and dug out his cell phone. No messages from Valerie. Mick bounced around on the balls of his feet, eyes roving around the heads in the seats to see if he recognized one of them as the hot medical examiner who had actually called and invited him to come tonight, just like George had said. Upon not recognizing any of them, he shot her a quick text.

You on your way? It's about to start.

Sorry, got a late start. Almost there ;)

Cool! She sent a wink!
"I need to get laid," Mick said shaking his head.
"What?" Perez asked, turning his head toward Mick.
"I said when do we get paid?" Mick replied, thinking quickly.

He heard the reverberating thumping on a microphone. Mick's eyes turned toward the stage. The principle was standing at his podium, and three figures were coming out onto the stage on the right. There was Zach, the long haired hunter from his failed interrogation.

Bastard, Mick thought as he saw him take his seat.

Then there were the other two. One with shaggy dishwater blonde hair and a beard. Then there was a very stoutly built black man with muscles as big around as Mick's thigh. They were all muscular in their own right, but he put them all to shame.

Yeah bask in that spotlight, Mick thought as he watched the hunters all take their seats behind the principle.

The principle had a face that reminded Mick of a mouse. He didn't really have buck teeth...per say, but his eyes seemed too big for his face, and his nose turned upward a little bit. His demeanor seemed a tad bit fidgety as well. All those features were wrapped up in a balding head and were sheltered by a rather big pair of thick rimmed glasses that Mick swore belonged back in the seventies.

"May I have your attention, please?" He said into the microphone. The murmuring half-heartedly quieted down as a sea of faces all turned toward him in one way or another before resuming their gossip.

"All right, my name is Wilber Price. I am the principal here at New Broken Edge High School, as most of you all know. Our purpose for gathering here tonight is to give our new friends a chance to speak to us about some things that could really help us and our communities stay safe."

If there was one thing Mick remembered from his days here at New Broken Edge High, it was how Principle Price could ramble. He looked at his phone quickly to start timing the man. Of course why the hunters needed an introduction, Mick couldn't fathom, but it was out of his hands. While Price rattled on, he mentioned a number displayed on an overhead projection on the north east wall of the auditorium for people to text their questions to. The principle had finally given the microphone over to one of the hunters.

"My name is Zach Stewart," said the one with long brown hair drawn in a long pony tail that fell between his shoulder blades.

"Brandon Maxwell," said the one with shaggy blondish hair.

"Name's Parish Larson. Go Twisters!" said the big black dude. At the mention of the high school football team, many in the room began shouting and clapping, to which Parish stood from his seat and motioned with his hands for the crowd to keep up the applause, and they gladly obliged him. God only knew with how badly they were sucking this season, they needed all the encouragement they could get. When it finally died down, Parish sat down next to Brandon.

THE THING IN THE MEN'S ROOM

Oscar looked down at his hands. They were trembling. He gripped the arms of his chair in a frenzy of mixed emotions. He remembered everything from that night. The cold, inky black hands that felt just as real as the wooden armrests he was holding onto. The feeling of mind-rending terror and fascination that compelled him to stay with the witches and learn as much about the one they called Father as he could.

He pulled his jacket sleeve up and looked at his forearms. The bite marks he had placed there from trying to eat the flesh were gone. The bite marks had healed within hours.

Bring me Mick Johnson… You will know him by his scent, the voices instructed. *I don't know who that is!* Oscar protested.

He shut his eyes and tried to calm his breathing. Something was happening inside him. His hunger was mounting as he sat in this big auditorium filled with people. Filled with food. He tried breathing through his mouth to block out the scent of a person, but it did no good. He could taste the scent. *Mick Johnson…*the voice caressed his brain.

The hunters were now taking questions. Principle Price was reading them off and each of the hunters took turns answering them as they passed the microphone around.

"This one is for Mr. Larson…Are you single?" Price read aloud from his cellphone with a chuckle. The question got several chuckles from out in the crowd. Parish was smirking as he took the mic and responded, "If you are over 18 and female, I could be." More laughter ensued.

More serious questions came in regarding topics ranging from home fortification against certain types of monsters, to how long they had all been hunting.

"Does silver really work to kill werewolves? Also, what can kill creatures the government has labeled as Throwbacks? And what are your thoughts as to why that term was chosen to describe them." Price rattled off. Zach took the mic.

"Um, no. Silver does not work on werewolves, or any kind of Theriomorphic creatures. That's a Hollywood myth. The usage of silver in folklore also doesn't really prove anything because in those instances, most alleged werewolves turned out to just be regular wolves. So a silver bullet to the head or heart, who *wouldn't* that kill? Also, silver isn't readily available to be weaponized. As for the Throwbacks, all the ones we have encountered, above ground and below, can be killed through mundane means but it takes a lot of work. Fire is the best weapon we've found. We think they could be a race of subterranean dwelling creatures from a forgotten time in history, hence the name Throwback." He said.

Price interjected with a question of his own, "You said above, and *below*. Are there Throwbacks living beneath the streets of New Broken Edge?"

"Yes there are," Zach said. The crowd's reaction was a mixture of laughter and gasps. To the ones who were chuckling out in the audience, Zach turned his attention to and said, "Yes it's true, and some even like to live in the walls and basements of your houses." Silence washed over the crowd.

The hunter continued, "Next time you think there might be something watching you from inside your closet, give us a call to come and check to see if there is a hallow spot in the wall for something to hide in. That's how they are getting into people's homes."

Mick Johnson.

The voice of Father was intermingling with the voices of those on stage as they answered the crowd's questions. Oscar shook his head to clear them from his brain. It wasn't until then that he felt a cold chill pass through him and he became light headed.

It's strange, all the things one's mind can conjure up while they are standing at a urinal. For Mick it wasn't the usual amalgam of randomness that sometimes clogged his synapses, and that was a novelty. He tuned his ear to listen as best he could to the muffled voices coming from across the commons area and through the closed doors of the auditorium. He did this with only a small amount of success. About the only thing he could deduce was that the principle was probably done with his introduction because he could hear other voices. Mick figured he would still be talking. He looked down at his little friend, and urged him to hurry as he continued relieving himself.

Since tonight's event was a Question and Answer session with the city's "new guardians," (The thought made him twist his face into a sour expression) he thought he would pose a question to them. The format of tonight's event ensured that the questioners remained anonymous. Texting his question to the number displayed from the projector seemed a little too easy. Mick caught himself imagining how events might unfold if he stood up, took control of whatever microphone materialized in his hand in this little fantasy of his, and asked them all point blank, "What are your thoughts on the Broken Edge Massacre of 1995?"

He would stand there on sure footing as the hunters tried to deny knowledge of the incident, or point out the conflicting evidence of how the hunters from that ordeal were not to blame, or that they perished in the event, and in turn he would slam them with the firsthand knowledge of a survivor.

He closed his eyes, rested his head against the wall, and sighed. He knew from his time in the interrogation room with the hunter named Zachary Stewart that nothing of the sort would ever happen. In his time he had spent recovering from his episode, he had vowed to himself not to make such stupid mistakes again. To be teachable by his superiors, to not think of himself as the top dog in the kennel. He still had to grow into his britches, and he knew that all too well. It's amazing the kind of perspective one can gain after a near death experience.

But still, that little day dream of making the hunters look like blithering idiots in front of their now adoring public made him smile.

The sound of footsteps coming up beside him jerked him out of his little world as he noticed someone walking up to the next urinal. When the individual came into view, he could tell they were one of those goth wannabes. He knew a few of those from his high school days. Mick proceeded to wash his hands, looking at his reflection in the mirror in front of him as the person walked up beside him and began doing the same. They made an awkward moment of eye contact in the mirror.

"You here for the Q and A?" The goth asked, breaking the tension. His tone was oddly flat, but still disarming enough to ease the awkward tension of having gone pee next to a stranger.

"Yeah." Mick replied.

"So what do you think about those hunters?" the kid asked.

Mick smirked, "I think they all deserve to be crammed into a solitary confinement cell and forced to share nothing but a single pot to piss in." Mick asked.

"Oh come on now, you want more than that." The goth said, turning the faucet off and flicking water off of his hands.

Mick stopped just before placing his hands under the automatic dryer. He turned back to look at the Goth looking guy, and his reflection in the mirror was looking at Mick.

"Excuse me?" Mick asked, the hairs on his arms beginning to bristle.

The goth turned from the mirror and stared Mick down. The way his eyes landed on him made Mick think of a toddler eyeing a new toy...or a shiny meat cleaver, for the first time.

"There is something of the Massacre about them. No one else can see it but you *know*. You know they have come back to do it again and you want to see their heads on rusty pikes and their headless bodies crucified in the middle of town. You have fantasized about it. If you could get away with it you would be the one to take the saw to their necks yourself."

If Mick could even think straight, he would have been positive he felt all the color drain from his face. He was shaking, and suddenly it was hard to breathe again. For a split second he knew how a prey animal must feel, trying to scurry across a barren field with nowhere to hide as the hawk bore down on him with talons as cold as blades of ice. And then there was the searing hot rage that began to well up in his gut. He felt sweat break out on his face and the only coherent thing that managed to cross his mind was the crippling realization that this guy was *right*. Something about his words ripped something out of the dark reaches of his forgotten sub conscious and into the light before his eyes. The images of the headless bodies hanging on twisted metal crosses, no doubt made from debris of buildings of his childhood city. But realizing it only fueled the churning hot pit of madness within him.

"You don't know anything!" Mick said, stabbing a finger in the air toward the goth's chest, "You don't know me! You…" he growled, shaking as his muscles tensed up.

"I happen to know someone who knows *a lot* about you Detective." The strange goth kid said stepping forward.

Mick frantically stepped back and turned on his heel to storm out of the bathroom, and was stopped as he turned around. There was something blocking the door way. It was a small, deformed mass with legs that bent the wrong way, arms that were longer than a pair ought to be, and some semblance of a face. A fleshy mound housing a gibbering, snapping maw of crooked teeth lashed at the air between it and Mick's foot. It glistened like it had just crawled from a rotten womb, and its sudden overpowering sulfur stench assaulted Mick's nostrils and taste buds. The creature stood to its full height, all of three and a half feet.

It seemed that all faculties in the brain that decided between fight or flight had been compromised as Mick stood there between the goth and the thing that eyed him with a ravenous curiosity.

"My name is Craven," The goth was speaking again, and Mick barely heard it. He wasn't capable of taking his eyes off of the hellish thing in front of him.

"You are not hallucinating, you are not dreaming. The thing you see in front of you is real, and all you have to do to make it go away is agree to come with me. You can meet the one who sent me to find you, and he can give you the power to get the justice you were denied as a child." Craven said.

The thing's unnaturally long fingers dug into the tile, claws scraping out mini trenches in the floor. Judging by the expression in its eyes, it seemed as eager for an answer as this Craven guy was.

"What do you say Detective?" Craven's hand was on his right shoulder.

Mick was aware of the sensation of a hand touching him. But he couldn't yank himself away, couldn't move as the thing in front of him began squealing in a way that reminded Mick of a screaming infant. The squealing came from the fleshy mound on its back that housed those jagged rows of teeth.

"Perhaps you need a little encouragement?" Craven's voice slithered into his ear from behind. His hand gave a tight squeeze on Mick's shoulder. The thing on the ground in front of him let it's toothy maw open wide. With a sick gurgling sound and a bloody, tar like belch, a small hand emerged from the bear trap of fangs. Limbs continued to emerge until the deformed creature that Mick first laid eyes on was a steaming pile of rapidly decaying gore around the feet of a small creature resembling the corpse of a one year old infant, standing up on its own.

With a force that felt like a cannon ball to his chest, Mick felt himself tumbling backwards as his lungs pleaded for the air that had been stolen from them. The tiny creature was slashing at his shirt, sending ribbons of cotton and blood flying all about in every direction. The creature's tiny fingers were like knives as they fileted Mick's chest like a tender cut of meat. With every fleeting ounce of strength he could muster, Mick dug his fingers into the slimy flesh of the horror that ravaged him, and ripped outward. Handfuls of discolored mush oozed between his fingers as he screamed with all his might, but the creature clamped its tiny hands around Mick's Adams apple and squeezed.

The chaos was disrupted with the sound of a sudden electric *pop*, followed by a prolonged muted grunting and the sound of a body hitting the tile floor with an unforgiving impact. Mick opened his eyes. The creature was gone, his shirt and flesh was intact, and there was no steaming pile of muck where an ugly demon baby had just emerged. Craven was on the floor beside him, his body as stiff as a plank with a vein bulging in his neck.

"Get your ass up and come with me!"

Valerie stood there in the doorway of the men's room, holding a Taser. She had worn her hair down this evening. That was a first. Mick almost didn't recognize her, but realization soon came flooding back to him when she barked at him again. Mick scrambled to his feet.

"Y-you fuckin saw that right?!" Mick shrieked, pointing to Craven's stiff form on the ground.

"Sorry I'm late, just come on!" Valerie ordered, taking him by the arm and shoving him out the door.

PANIC

Nearly every head in the audience turned their attention to the muffled sound of a scream somewhere out in the hall. Hushed concerns and the occasional, 'what the hell was that?' zipped through the murmuring auditorium. One of the officers was stepping outside to check on the disturbance.

Oscar's head snapped straight up, his nose sniffing the air and ears twitching. The uniqueness of the muffled scream echoed through his mind over and over again, his pupils dilating. He could smell adrenaline, sweat and an electrical charge from somewhere out there. He guessed it had come from one of the bathrooms. It was then that he noticed the people seated on either side of him were eyeing him curiously.

He felt his entire nasal cavity inside his face shift. Felt the cracks form in his skull around the cartilage as something made his head twitch violently to one side. He gasped and hunched over as blood began to uncontrollably pour out of his nose. The people around him were standing up suddenly, moving away from him.

"Hey, he needs help!" Someone said pointing. Oscar heard a sharp *crack* and threw his head back. Then another sickeningly loud *snap*, and he threw his right arm out. The sharp snapping and cracking of his bones rippled throughout his skeletal structure as bones were dislocated, realigned, and then it happened again, as if whatever force that was doing this to him wasn't happy with the outcome and decided to start over. A fountain of bile erupted from his mouth, showering the floor around him. Screams pierced the air around him now, assaulting his ear drums. He felt his clothes begin to soak through as if he had just been plunged into a warm river. But through the pain he looked down at his clothes—they were soaked through to his skin in deep crimson. His flesh had begun to split open as his skeleton realigned to a new design. It was then that he realized the vibrations he was feeling in his ear drums were coming from his own screams.

"GOOOOD!!! HEEEELLP ME! HELP ME PLEASE!!!!"

His breathe was snuffed out when he felt his jaw unhinge. His vision blacked out momentarily. But there was no mercy to be found there. He was still fully conscious. Every nerve felt as if they were swimming in an acid bath. His vision came back, hellishly blurry at first but soon he could see so much clearer. He looked down momentarily to see two lumps of gooey mush staring back up at him from the floor. The lumps had the same brown irises he had seen all his life when he looked in the mirror.

The faces of each person in the audience was sharper, right down to the individual facial hairs on one guy's chin. He saw the beads of sweat rolling down their tender necks, and each individual bump of gooseflesh that speckled the arms of all the frozen audience members. He noticed the hunters on stage producing items from the cases beneath their seats. He heard all the voices mixing in the crowd.

He could feel the marrow in his bones, as if it had been heated to a thousand degrees. The sound of his bones breaking inside his flesh sounded like splintering wood. His rib cage felt as if it had been snapped open with a pair of bolt cutters, and was now being pried apart by invisible hands. His entire body felt like it was being molded by an indifferent cosmic force that viewed him the same way a child views a fat lump of clay.

The last sensation Oscar's mind could comprehend from his electrified nerves was that of something elongated, bloody and furry thrashing its way out of his unhinged jaw. There was a sound that erupted deep within his gut and escaped the thrashing, lupine muzzle. It sounded like steam escaping a water vessel, followed by a rumbling howl that caused every bit of his remaining self-awareness to diminish. What few precious strands of himself that were left, he could not hold onto. The flesh cocoon that had encased his *true* form all these years continued to split, tear and rend in an eruption of gore as his new body began thrashing violently, sloughing off the membranous fleshy layers that had kept it buried all these years.

The beast that stood on massive triple jointed legs in the high school auditorium sniffed at the air, chasing the new scents that assaulted its snout.

It looked down at its blood matted coat of fur and bloody clawed hands. Charcoal gray fur covered thick, veiny hands that terminated in fingers nearly twice the length of an adult's, the thumb pulled up to a short dew-claw. Its claws were close to six inches long. Its coat, matted and caked with blood and bits of flesh. The creature's massively muscled arms hung down to the floor, and its legs, heavy with bulging muscle, were actually shorter, though still a bit longer than an adult human's legs. The majority of the creature's bulk was supported on its enormously long, tree trunk like arms, which connected to a thickly muscled V shaped torso. Its head and jaws, though lupine in appearance, equaled a Shire horse's head in size.

A symphony of new sounds coursed through every corner of the elongate ears that rose from the top of its head. High pitched screams, but there were a few unique sounds that stood out, partly because they seemed calm—for the most part.

"Hold your fire until all civilians are out of the auditorium!"

And that's when the scent of steaming, hot meat rushed its bloody snout. A pile of flesh and torn clothing lay at its feet. Overcome by ravenous hunger, the beast dove its muzzle into the bloody mess it stood in, scattering more of it around than actually getting in its mouth. The morsels of flesh that it lapped up with its tongue however sent pleasure to every receptor in its brain as it feasted on the pile of flesh at its feet.

Something slammed into the creature from the side, piercing its rough hide in the process. The beast stood to its full height—nine feet and three inches tall, not including the six inches the ears added! It turned its head to the right to see three dark shapes of men with burning white eyes, and veins that burned with white hot power beneath the skin. That's when it noticed the shaft sticking out of its shoulder, and one of the figures reloading a weapon of some sort. The beast focused its eyes on the figure. It had a name tag—Brandon. The others were readying their weapons as well. The sound of every metal slide being drawn back, forearm being pumped, and round being fed into a chamber echoed into the beast's ears.

"What the hell is happening?!" Mick yelled to Valerie as they ran through the lobby toward the doors where an armed police officer was holding the doors open for the stampede of people that was pouring from the auditorium doors.

"You tell me! I only just got here!" Valerie snapped back. Mick decided he didn't like her tone.

"I just stepped out for a second to take a piss! How should I know?!" He yelled back above the crowd. The ear rending howl that was swelling over the crowd from the auditorium like a menacing ethereal voice answered his question. It was so deep it rumbled in his chest and ears, yet it seemed layered with various different pitches. The deep part which rumbled inside of him was accompanied by the high pitched note that set it apart as a howl, but there was something else to it. It almost sounded like a scream of agony was echoing alongside the gut churning howl. It sounded feint at first, but the louder the howl swelled, the more pronounced the scream became, intertwining amidst the howl like a helix.

Oh God. It's happening again! They're using a werewolf! What's happening on the other side of town?! Mick didn't even have time to finish a single line of thought as they began to all jumble together. How many were in the auditorium? Were any of the people in this crowd lycanthropes? At any moment he might feel clawed hands ripping into his back from all directions. Valerie was practically leading him through the swelling crowd of panicked civilians.

Once out of the doors, any semblance of uniform exile the crowd exhibited by fleeing through the confines of the lobby vanished. The stampede spread out into the parking lot like an army of ants after having their dwelling smashed in.

"Who's car we taking?" Mick shouted.

"Mine!" Valerie answered.

Engines were roaring to life and headlights illuminated the terror stricken faces of the city's populace that had gathered tonight.

"Why are you holding my hand?!" Mick demanded, trying to yank himself away. She ignored him and held on tighter as a car pulled out of its parking spot and screeched to a halt in front of them.

"This way!" She shouted, and Mick felt his arm socket pop. There was a sudden sound of metal on metal impact, and a loud horn blaring soon after. Mick looked back to see an SUV had T-boned a pickup.

A chill passed through Mick's chest, freezing his lungs as he fought to breathe. For a moment in time, he was a five year old boy running for his life. It didn't help that he could hear a child screaming nearby. The child, a small boy who looked about five years old, was being clutched tightly to the chest of his father as the man ran. He ran as if the earth would open beneath his feet and swallow him and his son whole. Mick imagined himself falling deep into the suffocating dark void as the ground beneath him cracked and shifted.

And that's when the concrete came up to meet him. For a second Mick was airborne, falling face first into the parking lot. He instinctively threw out his hands to brace himself for the impact, and immediately regretted it. That sudden impact of his poor hands absorbing all the weight of his falling body sent sharp razors of agony ripping through his wrists and up to his elbows.

"Move!" He felt Valerie grabbing the back of his jacket, nearly hauling him to his feet. He only had a split second to marvel at how strong she was, before she yanked him to the side again, causing his left hip to collide into a parked Chevy that hadn't vacated the parking lot.

Wherever Valerie had parked, it was too damn far away. Of course with half the city coming out tonight, and her being late, it was a wonder she even found a parking space at all.

Sirens screamed off in the distance, getting closer. Whatever was happening tonight, he prayed every first responder in New Broken Edge was equipped to handle what awaited in the high school auditorium. Mick nearly feinted with relief when her car was finally visible. He nearly ripped the handle off trying to get the door open. Not soon enough, they were in and hauling it out of the parking lot.

If it wasn't for how badly he was hyperventilating, he would have been impressed that Valerie had handled the car in such a way as to narrowly avoid getting clipped multiple times as they escaped. He lost count of how many fleeing pedestrians alone she had managed to swerve around through the tight spaces of the lanes in the parking lot until she maneuvered out onto the street.

His eyes darted all around out the car windows, searching for signs elsewhere that this city was under siege once again. It made sense, at least to him anyway. Last time something happened in his city and hunters were involved, the creepy crawlies were dragging people beneath the streets through storm drains. But then Mick saw a glimmer of rational thought through the grim slaughterhouse pictures his mind was creating, and he latched onto it with a death grip.

CALL 911 YOU IDIOT!

He dug in his jacket and jerked the phone out. He unlocked it, and the screen washed the inside of the dark cab with light.

"God I hope this is an isolated incident." Mick said putting the phone to his ear.

"911, what's your emergency?" The dispatcher said upon answering.

"My name is Mick Johnson, and I'm with the New Broke Edge Police Department. There has been an incident at New Broken Edge High School—there's been a lycanthrope attack! We need ambulances, fire department, SWAT!"

There was a pause on the other end, some background noise and then, "Alright sir we have received calls about what is going on at the high school, and first responders are already en route. Where are you at?"

"I and a friend are fleeing north on Terminal Blvd. toward city limits." Mick replied.

Mick looked in his side mirror, he could already see the faint red and blue hues of emergency lights off in the distance.

"Sir I need you to stay on the line until you have reached a safe destination away from the school, and then relay your location to me so we can send medical personnel to you. Who else is with you?" The dispatcher asked.

Before Mick could answer, the car was swerving. Mick's eyes barely caught the sight of something small in the road, right before it ducted and vanished from view under the undercarriage. It was fleshy and gray. The same color as that thing that had attacked him in the bathroom. The car bounced and so did Mick's head, right off of the head rest just as the seatbelt tightened and dug into the flesh of his neck. His phone went flying out of his hand, bounced off the dashboard and fell in the floorboard.

Valerie had over corrected. The car was skidding diagonally, straddling both lanes now as Valerie brought it to a stop. But another shape moved out in the darkness. It was far enough away that it was out of the illuminating glow of the headlights, but close enough that Mick could make out some features if he looked closely. A lithe figure with distinctly female features was crouching in the road a few yards away. He couldn't make out any features other than the curves, but even those were obscured by a heavy looking coat the figure was hurriedly wrapping around itself. The girl soon pulled a cowl of some kind over her head. The cowl was honestly far too big for her head and it looked like it had ears and a snout of some kind.

Mick felt his insides freeze as the figure convulsed and bounded toward the car on all fours like a possessed animal. But what he saw next happened so fast, Valerie barely had time to put the car in gear and get it pointed the other direction to escape. As the thing charged at the car, its limbs—once seeming of normal human length—began to elongate. The coat and cowl it was wearing seemed to twist and writhe onto the thing's body, morphing joints and limbs into twisted appendages that were grossly disproportionate to what it had looked like earlier. The details of its face swiftly became visible as the thing leapt onto the hood of the car. From the lower jaw down, it was that of a slender human face. But the "cowl," looked like the decaying face of a large dog. Patches of fur were missing, and the snout was cracked and dried. Yet the eyes looked far too large to belong to a dog. Mick thought for a split second they almost looked human, but the pupils were dilated so much that if there was an iris, it was totally blacked out.

The cowl was stretching to encase the lower jaw of the person inside, stretching as if being pulled by invisible fingers, and bonding itself into the flesh of the person who was wearing the living hide of what used to be a huge dog.

Valerie slammed the car back into drive and floored the gas. The car shot off with the protesting sounds of crunching gravel and spraying dirt as the creature drove one of its appendages through the windshield at Mick's throat.

He didn't have time to move and avoid the thing's grasp. Something that wasn't quite a hand, but wasn't fully a paw either was enclosed around his throat. Mick could faintly hear the sounds of the 911 dispatcher still on the line as his phone slide around in the floor boards.

But his immediate supply of oxygen slipping from his lungs as this thing roared through the windshield was his top priority. The creature's roar had fogged over the windshield on its side. That alone was a mercy just so Mick didn't have to look at the thing's face anymore. His hands were up around the creature's wrist, his fingers desperately trying to lace through the course, furry sausage thick digits that had curled around his throat.

"I'm sorry about this!" Valerie shouted. The deafening squeal of tires exploded into his ears, sending his ear drums screaming in protest as his entire body flew forward and slammed into his seat belt. The dog creature's grip disappeared as the creature's hand shot out through the glass, taking a good portion of the windshield out with it as it rolled on the pavement in a tumbling blur of claws, glass and matted fur.

Mick's head swung forward like a yoyo at the end of a string, and he thought his brains had flown out of his head and landed on the ground somewhere in front of the car. His hands reached up to quell the burn that was now scorching its way through the sides of his neck, and he drew his hand away with traces of blood on them. The thing had took some skin off his neck when Valerie slammed on the breaks.

"Mick look!" Valerie yelled, shaking him with one hand and pointing wildly out of the window with the other. Mick drew his blurry vision toward the direction she was pointing. Dead ahead he could see the creature attempting to stand up. He saw its uneven muscles bunch up beneath the surface of skin and fur that looked like it would tear with the slightest of motion.

But it was what stood in the road beyond the beast that she was pointing to.

Two small lights were approaching steadily toward the beast. In the haze Mick wondered if they were headlights of an oncoming vehicle, but soon realized that wasn't the case. Headlights grow larger and brighter the closer they get. These stayed constant, like two candle flames floating toward the scene. As they approached, Mick quickly realized they were eyes. Housed in a dull expressionless mask. Broad shoulders and thick muscular arms that protruded out of a form fitting tactical vest. A figure was coming into view in the headlight beams, and withdrew a machete. Mick felt his veins frost over at the sight of the figure in front of them. Never before had he seen someone so freakin calm and collected in the presence of a literal monster. The way this guy carried himself felt...alien. Something *non*human. And the way he seemed to casually shift his burning gaze between them and the beast was frustrating, and Mick almost felt himself yell for the guy to make up his mind. But no sooner had the thought crossed his mind than it dawned on him, *It's not that he's indecisive. He is sizing us all up!*

Mick watched as the figure tightened his grip on the weapon, and tiny but clearly visible streaks of light appeared in the blade, spreading up its length until the entire blade glowed with an intensity so bright Mick nearly turned his eyes away from it. Steam emanated from the blade as the creature between them lunged at the figure, and he brought the weapon up to defend. Valerie had the car in reverse and was speeding backwards. She got the car turned back around and they continued on their way out of city limits.

Mick sat there with one arm clutching the seatbelt close to him and the other digging into the arm cradle on the door. He closed his eyes as he took sharp, shallow breathes.

There were more hunters out there. But how many? Three had been taken into custody immediately following the riot at Ironswrath prison. And here he saw another one tonight. He had seen the guy make a machete blade glow in his hand. He looked out of his side mirror to spy another look. No sign of hunter nor beast remained to fill the dark with the sounds of battle.

THE SKINS WE WEAR

Though barely conscious, Oscar could feel with perfect clarity the jack-hammers that were inside his skull, attempting to crush it. He could feel sweat dripping off of him as if he had just slogged out of a sauna. He could vaguely make out through the hammering process inside his skull, that there were voices floating around in the air around him. He thought he recognized them but he couldn't place them at the moment. They were disembodied echoes as far as he was concerned.

You sure?

...Haven't changed in years...

...Wait for Judah...

My beast...

"You awake there puppy dog?"

"Hey, I'm talkin' to you."

Oscar flinched and a low growl burbled up and out of his throat at the deliberate knocking sensation he felt against his head, as if someone was using their finger like a woodpecker's beak. He tried lifting his head up but it weighed a ton. He tried opening his eyelids but the fact he could see pure red through them when they were closed indicated he had a very intense source of light being shone on him from somewhere close by.

"Who's there?" Oscar growled. He realized how his voice sounded and it gave him pause. His muscles tensed but a spasm made them go wild and he felt his shoulders twitching.

"Why do I sound like this?" Oscar asked, his voice coming out gravely, more like a growl that was capable of forming words rather than an actual voice. His teeth felt huge in his gums, and his jaws felt awkward as he moved them to speak.

"You were shifting wildly between your various forms before we were able to subdue you. Thankfully you were more concerned with eating the remains of your flesh body and pissing all over the auditorium, so there were no casualties. We finally apprehended you in your present form. We call it the 'near-man' form. I'm guessing this was your first change." One of the voices said. When Oscar finally got up the nerve to open his eyes and fight through the throbbing in his head to look up, he saw a semi familiar form of a very muscular man sitting in a chair in front of him, just out of the cone of light that was beaming down. The man's eyes were glowing white, and it made the skin around his eyes seem to glow bright red as if a fire was burning inside the man's head. He had shaggy blondish hair and a name sticker that read—Hello, my name is Brandon.

"You…You're one of the hunters from the high school," Oscar said in that voice that sounded more like a belly growl. The hunter named Brandon nodded his head and smiled.

"And you," Brandon said as he leaned forward in his chair, not far enough for his face to come into the light, "are a Lycanthrope. A werewolf. A beast clothed in human flesh. Your true self came out tonight."

"I'm a werewolf?" Oscar asked. Brandon nodded, reached behind him to a table and held out a small mirror for Oscar to look into.

"See for yourself."

Oscar felt heat rise up into his throat and his muscles tensed. The face that stared back at him wasn't the face he had looked at in the mirror every day prior to this. The eyes were bright orange, and even while looking at himself in the mirror, they gazed back with an otherworldly madness and hunger. His nose retained many features of a human nose but was otherwise misshapen and much darker. His lips were blackened and wet, and his face looked like it had been brutalized with a cinder block. But all the discoloration in his face, he noticed when he looked closer, was actually dark course patches of fur.

"When you shifted into this near-man form you are in, you were muttering a name. Mick Johnson. What's he to you and how do you know of him?" Brandon was asking. Oscar looked up wide eyed from the mirror. Oscar hadn't laid eyes on this guy as far as he knew. But he knew that name had significance to the witches and the entity he was staying with. He looked up at Brandon nervously. Something about him made Oscar want to whimper with his ears laid back. The hunter stood up and walked into the light that was showering Oscar, and that's when his eyes changed—went back to normal, human looking eyes. But it was as if something else was looking at Oscar from behind those retinas. Something that was strong enough to dominate him if he dared attacked this man.

"I…honestly don't even know what he looks like." Oscar said, as he felt himself getting smaller and smaller in the presence of this man. He realized he wasn't even bound. But again, he dared not lift a claw to this hunter. He could smell something on him that, in an odd way, almost seemed feral. Something almost of kin. But as soon as he got a whiff, it vanished so quickly Oscar wondered if he had truly smelled anything on Brandon at all or if it was himself he was smelling.

"How do you know the name though?" Brandon pressed.

Oscar hesitated, his achy muscles beginning to shiver, "I…I don't know what it was…it wouldn't even tell me its name, but it wants him. A being. It passed on his name to me. It was dark. Darker than dark. Like a living shadow. It said it would help me to understand what I am if I helped it get to him."

"But on the night of your first change? Seems kind of unfair to me. You would need time to readjust to your true forms. You've been walking in a human suit for so long. What did this thing really expect you to do if you ever found him?" Brandon said.

"It wants him. It said I was supposed to lure him to these other two kids, Craven and Skylah. It said they would do the rest." Oscar said as he fought to remember.

"It wants him for what?" Brandon asked. Oscar shook his head.

"They won't tell me anything. Just that I was supposed to help find him."

Brandon was silent for a moment. Almost too long. The silence was causing Oscar to fidget. But he noticed he could feel the fur receding back into his face. His vision was beginning to dull back to familiar levels, and he could feel the swelling in his gums going down as his teeth seemed to shrink back to their normal size.

"That felt weird," Oscar said as he blinked his eyelids multiple times, and reached up a hand to brush away the water that was accumulating in his eyes.

"You get used to it after a while," Brandon said, as he turned back into the darkness.

"Where are you going?!" Oscar called. The sound of a heavy door was opening somewhere, and Oscar saw Brandon silhouetted in the light from some hallway.

"You can't keep me here! You can't hold me against my will!" He yelled standing up.

Brandon turned around to face him once more, his eyes burning bright in the darkness. Oscar backed up a couple steps, feeling like he was about to be torn apart.

"That law only applies to *humans*." Brandon said, and with that turned and shut the door with a heavy metal clang.

A canine like maw snaps before her face in short mental flashes. She remembered the first time she tried on the skin of a dead animal. Skylah remembered all the components to the spell that she had used in order to call back the spirit of the dead animal to infuse its hide once more. During the ritual the animal's spirit had tried to possess her. But such a desperate attempt was short lived as the creature's spirit suddenly noticed its old remains and dove for the skin that had been neatly laid out like a bearskin rug, its incorporeal muzzle nudging the skin and moving it visibly as it burrowed its way into the hide.

She remembered the first time she bonded with the hide. It twisted and stretched around her bare skin in a ravenous fury. She remembered the pain of her limbs reshaping to accommodate the shape of the dog, her legs breaking and resetting, her shoulder blades becoming like rigid bone slabs that sprang from the meat deep inside her back. Her first form had turned her into an awkward parody of what the creature had looked like in life. A dog that didn't quite stand on all fours just right, and whose paws still had the unsettling appearance of human fingers. But it had bonded to her. She could feel the dog's skin as if it were her own. It felt strange to move at first, but when she got the hang of it, moving as the dog became second nature. With practice she was able to manifest her changes into different forms. The one she had used tonight was that of a hulking human-dog hybrid. But one thing she had never thought to question till tonight as she sat with her wrists shackled to the floor with iron chains, was, had she learned to control the dog in order to achieve those different forms, or had it learned to control her? Had it learned to shape her body to its whims, letting her think that she was really the one doing the choosing?

Such a question was quickly dismissed as she noticed the other men in the room with her. They were all wearing plain black masks, their eyes lit up like flares inside their heads. They appeared to be dressed all in black. Save for the eyes, if she used her imagination, they looked like representations of Father.

But there was one of them whose sheer presence caused her to feel violated. In his gloved hands he held her journal that she had caught Oscar reading. Also the fact that he was the one that ripped the dog's hide from her tonight might have had a little bit to do with that.

The sound of the pages of her journal turning sharply made her flinch with indignation every time. Those burning eyes behind the mask were looking at sacred knowledge! Only those worthy of Father could behold such sacred writings! The words she had penned, the spells, incantations, prayers and lists of various ingredients were a holy text to her! And he was violating it with his burning gaze.

She tore her eyes away from the vulgar sight, and regarded the wards that had been burned into the floor. She assumed they were wards anyway. It wasn't anything she recognized really. She knew the letters were in Hebrew, but that was it. Her eyes darted around to follow the blurs of movement that zipped between each hunter in the shadows. She could see the adorable little forms of the impish creatures she and Craven could call forth from beyond the material plane. But the little darlings could not reach her within this circle, and she could barely muster up enough will to reach beyond it. Anytime she tried, she saw burning flashes in her mind's eye of Hebrew characters like those on the floor. The flashes sent burning spikes into her brain and she had to stop. But the Little Outsiders were incorporeal at the moment. She couldn't pull enough energy to manifest them tangibly. As it was, they were behind the metaphorical glass that separated the material plane from their world. Close enough to look, but not touch. Skylah brought her attention back to the masked hunter that had defeated her and brought her here. He appeared to be done violating her grimoire, and was pointing his fiercely glowing eyes at her.

"Find anything interesting?" She spat.

"As a matter of fact I did," The hunter said, his deep baritone voice muffled slightly from behind his mask.

"The summoning rituals, blood magic, use for various animal pelts were all very interesting. But what I want to know is, who is Father?" The man asked. Her eyes floated around the room. The others that were present stood as silent and as still as statues. She let her eyes fall back on the hunter in front of her.

"He is no concern of yours." She said.

The hunter who was doing the questioning motioned to one of his men, whispered something to him, and then leaned forward in his chair, "I'm going to shoot straight with you little girl. My team found your brother in the boys' room at the high school. He squealed. Police are investigating the property. But they let us pick through it first, which is how we came by your diary."

She smirked. *Father will have known of their coming and will have moved his current vessel.*

"He is the head of our coven." She said.

A chuckle escaped the confines of his mask, "And what about Mick Johnson? I came across his name a couple times. What is he to this coven of yours?"

"He is a friend we wish to initiate," She said.

"Is that *all* you want to do with him?" He asked. His tone was a giveaway that he wasn't buying it.

"It isn't any of your business." She hissed.

"See, he isn't a friend of yours. Here is how I know you are lying. There is this yellow haze around you that gets slightly discolored every time you open your mouth." He said. Skylah's blood ran cold. He could see auras? Her heart sank to the pit of her stomach and settled there like a jagged lump of stone. She could feel a cold sweat beginning to leak out from her pours, being absorbed by her clothes. In the beginning, she had felt like a lioness that had been caged and was waiting to break free and rip them all to shreds. Now she felt like a sheep in the midst of wolves.

"I can see auras too. Only difference between me and you, is I don't have to cheat," He said holding up her notebook. Skylah's eyes shifted toward more movement in the shadows. One of the hunters was bringing something in their arms. The hunter let it flop down with a dry *whump* next to his boss's chair.

It was the hide of the dog she had been wearing that night. Two others were plopped down on top of it. All three of her dog hides she had kept at the house.

Seeing her grimoire in the hands of another person was bad enough, but seeing her dog hides treated with such indifference was more than she could take. The spirits of those dogs were a part of her now!

"Alright, now let's get started shall we?" The one hunter said as he stood up from his chair and began flipping to the front of her notebook. She felt a sharp pain seize her left arm as the sound of a page being torn assaulted her ears.

"For every lie you speak from here on out, I tear out another page to use as kindling on those hides. Are we clear?" The masked man said. It was definitely more of a statement than a question. Maybe she could buy more time? The imps in the shadows were ducking behind the other hunters' legs, digging their claws into the concrete floor with a mad, hungry glare.

"Let's talk about Father for a moment. Who is he?"

"He is wise and cunning." She said, her voice coming out in short bursts. The hunter stood there eyeing her for a moment.

"Well, no discoloration in your aura. But that still didn't answer my question." He said as he began tearing another page, crumpled it up and tossed it onto the pile of dog hides.

Pain stabbed at the back of her right calf, and it was all she could do to not let them see.

"How did you meet him?" The hunter asked.

"He has always known me. His eyes have always –" Pain slammed into her chest, cutting her off midsentence and bending her forward in her chair. She gasped for air as her voice rasped and tried to reform in her throat.

"Now you are *dodging* my questions. Every time you do that, I'm just going to grab a handful of pages and rip." He said.

"Again, how did you meet him!?" He said, raising his voice. Skylah closed her eyes and tried one last time to focus her will through the pain that was wracking her body. She remembered the long nights she had spent at the shadowy apparition's feet, her body twisted and bent at unnatural angles with arcane sigils carved into her flesh. Pain had made her stronger than her brother. There was a reason Father had taken more of a liking to her than he had to Craven. In truth he was more proficient at summoning the Little Outsiders than she was. But pain was one thing she could always outlast him on. That is why it was *she* who performed the blood magic, *she* who wore the skins of animals and had every bone in her body broken and reshaped during the change. She had bled more for Father than Craven ever had.

"He picked me up at a bar one night, said I was cute." She smirked.

The hunter said nothing as he stood there with one hand on a swath of pages, his gloved fingers curled around them. She met his burning gaze only momentarily, but it was enough for her to see that gears were turning behind that mask of his.

The tension shattered at the sound of a heavy metal door screeching open. All glowing eyes in the room, from the hunters to the Little Outsiders that hid in the shadows, turned to see the figure who was attempting to enter.

"What did you get out of him?" The hunter with the notebook asked.

"Nothing we don't already know." Said the other glowing eyed figure entering the room. The hunter with her notebook turned back to her, and slapped the notebook shut and tossed it to one of the hunters with long dark brown hair tied in a ponytail.

"Salt and burn the hides." He said.

Rage erupted within Skylah's chest at those five words. Her vision exploded in various shades of red. There was the power she was looking for. She stood up and strained her wrists against the shackles, letting them dig into her skin and she felt her flesh tear. Just a little more pain. Through the rage, a scream broke free from her chest, or rather, several screams did. She looked around. The Little Outsiders weren't scurrying around in the shadows any longer. They had made it passed the warding circle. If she could not manifest them tangibly, she would offer herself to them. It was their voices that was rising up through her windpipe. She quickly looked down at her skin. It was turning gray.

And then her raging red vision flashed burning hot to white once more.

"SIT DOWN!!!" Ordered the long haired hunter that now held her notebook.

She was thrown backward into her chair again. Her brain felt as if a flaming hand had reached inside of her head and was using her brain as a stress ball. With each throb of her brain, a symbol formed in her mind's eye. A symbol that with each pulse, caused her entire body to convulse as she felt her flesh burning.

The symbol of a Celtic cross, engulfed in radiant white flames, was the last thing she saw before a fiery, enormous figure emerged from the flames in her mind's eye.

PHANTOM RINGTONE

October 17, 4:49 AM,

Sleep was out of the question as far as Mick was concerned. Not after surviving two near death experiences in one night, thank you. He and Valerie had been treated for shock and any other injuries they might have sustained. Mick sported gauze bandages on either side of his neck where the creature's claws had dug into each side. He still was wearing his Glock in the shoulder holster as he paced a trench in the floor of his small living room. He found his muscles clenching as his eyes moved to investigate every noise he heard, or *thought* he heard.

He guessed almost dying twice in one night had something to do with that. Against his better judgment, he had all the windows in his living room open, letting the cold October air fill his apartment like an ice box if it meant he had a way to escape if the walls began to feel closer together.

He never really remembered how he developed the fear of enclosed areas. He couldn't remember much, if anything before he was five years old. Saddest thing he could really say was that his earliest memories were of people getting the skin tore off their backs by nightmare creatures. Things that should have stayed in the movies.

Yet none of this answered his question about his phobia. Whatever had happened to cause that fear must have been tied to the Massacre. Because to his recollection, he didn't have his first memorable episode until a few months after the tragedy. In the years following the Massacre, he couldn't even so much as relax with the covers over his head. Right at the moment he figured that this deliberation was better than allowing himself to be molested by the mental image of that hellish mound of throbbing flesh that spawned the small creature that assaulted him. The sounds of the city outside weren't helping. If a cat yowled down in the streets below his apartment, his mind constructed a quick flash of a quivering heap of flesh hiding under his bed, or climbing in through an open window. A quick blink and it was gone, reassuring him that he was seeing things.

Other mental images formed in his mind's eye. Images of himself as a child in time out, his face in a corner. Putting him in a corner for time out only made him hyperventilate. His parents eventually upgraded to having him stand with his face in the middle of a wall, away from all corners. It worked better than having his face stuffed into a corner. In his teen years, he had to have his room arranged around his bed. Literally, his bed was in the center of his room, away from any of the walls. He had nightmares of being buried alive in debris from his walls caving in on top of him in the night.

He felt his phone vibrating in his pocket. He took it out of his pocket and looked at the screen. George was calling.

"Hey man. Odd time to call don't ya think?" Mick asked, his voice shaking.

The voice that responded on the other end made every inch of Mick's flesh ripple as if he had just been thrown through a wall of ice. His tongue became a useless lump in his mouth as he brought the phone away from his ear and looked at the screen to double check the number.

It *was* George. It was his number, and his voice on the line. But never had Mick heard such raw panic in his friend's voice. The kind of primal, ancient terror that marked mankind's fear of the dark and the doorways to all other alien realms beyond their five senses. That was what George sounded like.

"Y-you got to listen to me Mick! I don't know how much longer I can hold on!" He whispered between sobs.

"George! Dude what in the hell is going on?! Are you alright?! Where are you?!" Mick demanded as he snatched his keys off the coffee table and went for the front door.

"No Mick you can't! Don't come over here! That's exactly what he wants you to do! You gotta stay away from-"

"Whoa whoa man you're not making any sense. Slow down! Where are you!?" Mick asked as he flew down the dimly lit hallway toward the elevator. Each floor had kind of its own vestibule that awaited right outside of the elevator. Each was furnished with an old couch, a small coffee table with a stack of outdated magazines, a book shelf, and a few potted plants. Mick was rounding the corner from the hallway into the vestibule. He wasn't fond of the death box that went up and down, but if George was in trouble, Mick would have thrown himself in front of a bus if it meant saving him.

"Don't go in that elevator!" George screamed into the phone.

A spear of nausea impaled Mick straight through the gut. He felt his knees beginning to give out. Mick's eyes darted all around him now, scrutinizing every corner and crevice of his surroundings for the hundredth time that night.

"George where are you man?" Mick's voice cracked as it came. The sound that emanated from the phone sounded like, wherever he was at, he was shivering and about to pass out from weeping. But the thing that was most disconcerting was the echo.

"I don't know." George's voice came in a horse whisper through the phone. But it was coming from somewhere else as well. That echo, something about it sounded wrong. As if both the echo and its official source sounded electronic. Not the way it would sound if a real person were standing a few feet away and talking on a phone.

"Come on bro. You must have seen me going to the elevator. Just tell me what's going on please," Mick begged as he steadied himself against the wall and chancing another glance behind him. That is when his eyes landed on a naked shape, dragging itself down the hallway toward him. The dim lights in the hall were extinguished in the thing's wake. It was too dark to see its features, but the only thing Mick could truly make out was, it was shaped like a man. It pulled itself along, rather than crawled, as if its legs were broken. Mick felt his phone vibrate in his hand. He pulled it away to see that it was dying. The battery icon flashed, and the screen went pitch black.

"Stay away from it! It's not me!" George's voice said. It was coming from that *thing*, and it hummed with that same electronic resonance as it would if he were hearing it over the phone.

The truck stop on the fringe of New Broken Edge seemed kinda quiet. On a busy day the place would average sixty or eighty patrons, just during breakfast hours alone. Currently it only had one gentleman seated in a booth by the front entrance, three folks ranging from middle aged to elderly at a corner booth under the mounted television set, and Mick and George sitting at a table right out in the middle of the floor. They weren't exactly an island unto themselves. There were other tables that surrounded them, just unoccupied ones. George had found Mick unconscious just outside the elevator on the floor he lived on. George had apparently searched for Mick at his sanctum in the museum, and when that avenue turned up nada, and Mick wasn't answering his phone, then he came to the apartments. Mick told him about everything that happened the previous night. The creepy guy in the bathroom (although he omitted the part about the snarling monstrosity that attacked him), the thing in the road, the other hunter that showed up, and his disturbing phone call and the thing that was dragging itself toward him in the hallway. George listened patiently and non-judgmentally throughout the entire thing...until he got to the phone call part. Then his face twisted into a confused look as he looked at Mick.

"...Okay. That's weird, cause I didn't call you," George said. Mick sighed and shrugged his shoulders.

"For all I know none of it was real. But I swear to God it sounded just like you man. You sounded like you were about to die, like you were being chased by *Michael Myers* or something." Mick said.

He pulled out his cell and brought up the call log for the sixth time this morning, just to make sure he wasn't going crazy. As far as the call log was showing—he just might be. The last phone call from George was from two days ago at 4:23pm. George even showed him his phone, and again, 4:23pm, two days ago. Mick knew that it's easy to delete calls from a call log and feign ignorance, but George had no reason to do a thing like that. He could be a jerk, but he was an honest jerk.

"When's the last time you had a good night's sleep?" George asked, lifting his coffee up to his lips. Mick shook his head. Honestly on his nights off, he barley slept at all. When he got off work early in the morning, he would stay up for a couple hours, but then he would usually sleep most of the day away, and it was hell trying to get to sleep sometimes. He either had a hard time sleeping, or when he did he dreamed about work, the crime scenes he had visited, superiors demanding reports, ect. His body had developed a tolerance to melatonin, so it took about six capsules of the stuff to knock him out as opposed to the normal dosage of one or two.

"What is a good night's sleep?" Mick asked with a heavy grin.

George rolled his eyes and smirked, "Smart ass. Okay well whatever you saw last night was probably a stress induced hallucination brought on by the crazy stuff that happened at the school. Sometimes people can hallucinate if they go too long without sleeping. I mean, we're like bros and so maybe you were worried sick about me and that caused you to lose your shit?"

"You should write sympathy cards for Hallmark, ya know that? Seriously man, you are a master wordsmith! Or maybe you could be a traveling motivational speaker," Mick jested.

They both shared a few more laughs as the waitress brought them their food. The Cajun omelet Mick ordered was a welcome scent, its steamy tendrils soaring up into his nose. The onions, sausage and bell peppers mixed their juices with the melted cheese as he cut into it. The way the stringy ropes of melted cheese stretched as he pulled a chunk of it off on his fork and up to his mouth almost made his knees knock together.

"But one thing that is still bugging me," Mick said between bites, "was I *felt* my phone vibrate in my pocket. I swear the screen was lit up with your contact photo and number. I know I saw that."

George shrugged, "Well, you may very well have felt it vibrate, and even saw the screen all lit up. But I know that I didn't *consciously* call you." He said. They both paused for a second, more to enjoy their food than for the articulation of the conversation. After George washed another bite of biscuits and gravy down with a swig of coffee, he continued.

"My phone does this thing where it will ring on occasion, or will randomly vibrate for no reason. I 'll look at it to see if I got a text or if someone is calling, and there won't be anything there."

"It says, 'George, love me! Worship me!' it's as bad as a clingy girlfriend." Mick said. He looked up and saw the mounted flat screen. The local news station from two counties over was covering the incident from last night at the school. Police line tape had sectioned off the doors to the school that led into the auditorium. School had been suspended for the entire day until forensics was completely finished.

"Aren't you glad you don't have to work that mess?" Mick asked, motioning behind George toward the TV with his fork. George turned around and gawked.

"I'll get to play with everything day crew brings in tonight. So, about Valerie. She sounded like she handled herself pretty well. She sounds like one helluva driver." George said.

Mick nodded in agreement, but before he could say anything to expand more on that point, he saw his phone inching away from his hand as it vibrated. He looked down at it, mouth full, and then back at George.

"You are seeing this right? Like, my phone is actually ringing?" Mick asked as he snatched it up and showed it to George. George nodded his head, "And you better answer it. Looks like Scroggins's number," he said as he took another bite.

Mick answered, "Yes sir."

Mick could hear the background noises of someone closing a door behind them. Probably Scroggins going in his office to talk privately with Mick.

"Are you sitting down Johnson?" He asked. Mick tensed and he felt his breath catch in his throat.

Damnit why did he have to start the conversation like that? Mick thought.

"Yeah I'm sitting down." Mick said, and then took a swig of coffee to try and combat the dry feeling of dread in his throat.

Scroggins sighed and then began, "I'm gonna do this as quick and painless as I can manage. But through some information we obtained last night, we have come to the knowledge that you are a target. Whatever's going on with these hunters, I need you to stay out of the way. You are barred from investigating any further into their activities."

Mick sat there, feeling like he wanted to say something, try to get him to clarify. Eventually, he was able to form a somewhat coherent response.

"Huh?" For Mick, even on a good day, that was pushing it.

"I'm not kidding Johnson! Whatever they are involved in, you seem to be a magnet for all kinds of the crazy that comes with it! You need to –" Finally it was sinking in.

"Whoa Chief, hold on a minute. I'm the one that gathered all the information on them. You gave me the green light on these guys and now you're pulling the rug out from under me!?" Mick protested.

"Watch yourself boy. Might I remind you those britches you are trying to fit into are awfully big." Scroggins voice said, in a tone that could not be argued with. "Now I don't know all the odds and ends, but a couple of them came forward this morning with some information they obtained. Whatever is brewing, you are the focus."

Mick sat there, the mixture of disbelief and disgust that was clogging up his mind making it equally hard to think. George was sitting there looking at him quizzically.

"A couple of them told you this? By a couple of *them*, you mean those vigilantes—" Scroggins started talking again.

"Mick I'm going to have to ask you to turn over all information you have gathered on them to me. I will assign any and all investigations into their activities to another individual who isn't so close to the case. I made a mistake in letting you proceed, and for that I apologize. But I'm not gonna have your blood on my conscience should the worst happen. Now I will expect your files on the hunters on my desk tonight when you come in for work. Have a good day son." And with that he hung up on his end.

Mick sat there staring at his phone, blinking occasionally when his eyes began to sting.

"What's up?" George asked, leaning forward.

Mick looked up, suddenly clutching his phone in his hand, squeezing it so hard he hoped the screen would crack.

"He's taking me off the case. I'm no longer allowed to continue investigating into the vigilantes' activities, past, present or future." Mick said.

"Damn…well, less headaches for you right?" George offered.

THE GRIMOIRE'S SECRET

Mick sat in Scroggins' office that night, his folder full of documentation he had collected over the past year sitting on his lap. He absent mindedly still had both hands laid over it as he nervously bounced his legs on the balls of his feet. He and Scroggins were on good enough terms that he knew he could wait in his office until he got out of the men's room. That was one thing Mick loved about the man. While yes, Mick on occasion still had something to do with his separated parents, it was the Chief that really felt like a true father to him. Those times when the Chief would refer to him as 'son,' wasn't just in passing or flippant.

And it was this fact that Mick kept having to remind himself of while he sat there waiting for Scroggins to hurry up and get back to his office. While Mick felt that he belonged on this case because he had done so much of the ground work in collecting information on the hunters, he knew Scroggins wouldn't have taken him off the case if he didn't think Mick's safety was legitimately at stake. But then again, didn't that come with being in law enforcement? Something had to have scared Scroggins bad enough to want to take him off the case.

The door clicked behind him and he spun in his chair, clutching the folder even tighter.

"Sorry about that," Scroggins said as he side stepped around a stack of boxes. He was still getting moved into his new office. He pulled out his desk chair, hefted a stack of paperwork out of the seat and onto the desk, and sat down in front of Mick. Suddenly a feeling like he was in the principal's office at school washed over him.

Scroggins held out his hand, "Let's have it," he said, that fatherly tone thick in his voice. Mick swallowed, looked down at the folder and sighed while he lifted it up and over the desk.

"Don't suppose you'll reconsider at some point?" Mick asked, trying not to sound too pleading.

Scroggins shook his head, "Not on your life. And I mean that." He clasped the folder in his fingers and began thumbing through everything.

"Everything is in there sir," Mick confirmed. Scroggins nodded, "I'm glad." After a few more moments of the Chief looking through everything, he finally looked up to meet Mick's eyes.

"Since I'm asking you to trust me on this, I owe you the courtesy of sharing the information with you that I received recently." Scroggins said. Mick nodded.

"Shoot," he said, his eyes traveling to rest on the folder.

Scroggins clasped both his hands together under his chin. He looked like he was trying to think how to proceed.

"Sir?" Mick asked.

"Someone is after you Mick. The hunters weren't able to get much information out of the creatures that attacked the high school last night, but they got information on an address where a journal was obtained, belonging to one of them. A girl by the name of Sunny Renee Grisham, along with several dog pelts. Apparently the owners of the house were harboring them, but claimed to have no memory of doing so. They are under investigation right now." Scroggins said.

A spark went off in Mick's mind as he remembered what he saw while Valerie and he were fleeing the high school. He didn't see any facial features, but he remembered very clearly in his mind a female figure, wrapping what appeared to be an animal pelt around her, and then the thing twisting and bending her limbs at weird angels while she—it—bolted for the car.

"Someone this girl referred to in the journal by the title of 'Father' is after you. We think her, the Lycanthrope, and the guy that attacked you in the men's room are all part of some cult, and this Father type is the ring leader. And they got their sights set on you." Scroggins said.

"What the hell for?" Mick asked.

Scroggins swallowed and drummed his fingers on his desk before meeting Mick's gaze, "In the journal the hunters recovered…there are several vague references to you being this Father's new "Right Hand". Without the girl or the lycanthrope giving the hunters anymore to go on, we don't know any more than that."

Something else occurred to Mick, and he pounced on it with both feet.

"What about the guy who attacked me in the men's room?"

Scroggins sighed deeply, looking down at his hands for a moment and then looked up at Mick, his eyes flashing with frustration. For a split second Mick regretted asking. Scroggins already had so much on his plate already. Mick should have known not to push the man.

"He never made it to the station. He was arrested. Had the cuffs slapped on him and had his rights read to him. Soon as the arresting officers arrived at the station and they went to pull him out of the back, officers Thornton and Kinser both said the guy sitting in the back of the car was *not* the guy they had slapped the cuffs on."

They both sat in silence after that.

"So," Mick began, "I wanna make sure I understand this: They arrested the wrong person or…?"

Scroggins shook his head, rubbing his eyes, "I don't fuckin' know Johnson. They both swear they cuffed the guy the hunters had pinned down in the rest room. They both, Thornton and Kinser, walked him outside, one man on each side of him. They are both very insistent that they saw the same kid who they arrested enter the back of the patrol car. He wasn't left unattended. Soon as he was secured in the back of their vehicle, they left. The bastard didn't have time to switch, according to them."

The sensation of feeling his blood freeze overtook Mick, and he twitched. He hadn't really noticed that he was still bouncing his legs on the balls of his feet, until he stopped right then and there. He felt as if he would see his breathe if he breathed out. The cold sensation that overtook him started at the base of his skull and spread from there. He couldn't even think of what to say to that. Every time he tried to open his mouth to ask a question, it fell apart before it could be spoken. Finally, something halfway intelligent came to mind.

"This journal they found, has it been submitted for evidence?" Mick asked.

"It is being analyzed by one of their guys first." Scroggins said.

"Sir forgive me but, two attempts were made at my life last night, which falls into the category of attempted murder, and you're telling me that any evidence that may provide necessary information pertaining to said incidents is being handled by a group of people who aren't even authorized to handle it?!" Mick said, his voice rising steadily with every other word.

Before Scroggins could put Mick in his place, there was a knock at the door. Both of them fell silent for a second before Scroggins hollered "come in!" The door opened, and if Mick could have flown across the room and strangle the person standing there in the doorway, he would have done it. There standing in the doorway of Scroggins' new office, was Zach Stewart.

Mick's blood was boiling as his face flushed. He felt his cheeks burning, the heat spreading down his neck. Stewart nodded in his direction, holding something in one hand. A notebook of some kind.

"I'm sorry to interrupt sir, but here is the journal we got from the girl. Some of the pages were torn out, but we were able to collect them all and put them back into place in what we think is the correct order." He said holding out the notebook for the Chief. Scroggins stood from behind his desk and took the notebook, then gave Mick a look that summed up all he could have said had they not been interrupted.

"Good to see you again Detective!" the hunter said as stuck out his hand.

Mick just sat there, balling his hands into fists. He looked up to meet the hunter's cocky gaze, only to see that he wasn't even looking him in the eyes. He was looking directly passed him. Just like he had done in the interrogation room.

Keep yourself together. He's trying to freak you out. Don't give him the satisfaction.

Mick thought he saw him whispering something, caught the faintest twitch of the hunter's jaw, saw the subtle movements around the lips. He thought he caught the words "you," "have" and "him," but the other words eluded him. The lack of context alone made Mick's mouth go dry as he felt the energy get sapped right out of him.

In the minutes that followed, Mick found himself splashing water on his face in the men's bathroom. He vigorously rubbed the water out of his eyes with his fingers, and blinked out the remaining moisture. He let his eyes rest on those of his reflection in the mirror for some time. He stood there breathing heavily, hands on either side of the sink, and eventually his eyes drifted to the space just passed his head to investigate the small movement he thought he had just seen.

IDLE HAND

Old Broken Edge Ruins, that same evening,

A sharp metallic *clink* jarred Craven awake as he tried to sit up with a start. His body was immediately halted by the thick restraints that was holding him to a bed. He looked around his surroundings. Two figures were present with him in what appeared to have been a child's bedroom at one time. The walls looked like the shredded back of a flogged person, the wallpaper peeling in large ribbons, revealing the rotted walls beneath. What designs he could see on the fragments of wallpaper that still clung to the walls suggested cartoon airplanes, fire trucks and police cars. At least that's what he thought he could make out. It was night time after all, and just by doing a quick look around his surroundings, he guessed he was in a building that hadn't had power for many years.

One figure was standing over a small table, putting away what appeared to be surgical tools of some kind. The thing was about 7 feet tall. It wore a muzzle constructed of scrap metal. Its eyes that bore into him from atop the muzzle were bulbous orbs of black that looked too big for the head. It was shirtless, revealing a muscular physic that seemed to be composed of nothing but scar tissue. Discolored and pulsing, the scare tissue that covered every inch of the creature's upper body was *moving*, like a living blanket of mutilation.

The other one appeared only as a faint outline at first. It was three dimensional in every way, just like the creature who was putting away it's assortment of surgical tools, but even after letting his eyes linger on it, they didn't adjust to make out details in the dark. The darkness around the figure seemed to writhe and twist with a life all its own.

Father, Craven thought.

The figure was silent, yet gave a visible nod, acknowledging his thought. For a long time the amalgamation of writhing shadow matter didn't respond. But then Father gave another nod to the scarred up thing in the muzzle. It grunted and turned to the small table where it had been collecting its instruments. It was rummaging through a sack of some kind. When it turned around, it flung a faintly glowing object at Craven. The thing landed on his chest with a thud. The faint glow that was coming from it illuminated it enough for Craven to see what it was—a severed human hand, cut about three to four inches below the wrist. The glow that was coming from the appendage was from where a hand had enclosed itself around the wrist.

Suddenly, images flashed through Craven's mind. He was back in the men's room at New Broken Edge High School. He now had a glowing scar on his left wrist where one of Father's adversaries had grabbed him. His entire wrist was covered in swollen, raised scar tissue that glowed that same white hot glow of their eyes.

Through the pain of feeling every nerve in his wrist burn with the heat of a dying star, he tried to invoke one of the Outsiders to manifest and come to his aid. But the hunter that had branded him traced a symbol in the air over his face and, the noises that spewed from his tightening throat were only muted gasps for air. Suddenly words came to him, but they were not words his mind had prepared.

"1423 Westhaven Drive!" He screamed. It was the address that he and Skylah had brought the werewolf to. The same place that Father was residing with the current vessel. It was their sanctum. It had been a place for focusing their energies. A gateway of sorts for the Outsiders to enter New Broken Edge. And he had led the hunters and the police right to it.

The vision ended as abruptly as it had started, the darkness rushing back in to rape his vision and render him immobile on this bed. He remembered the night before with such bone jarring clarity, he still felt the phantom burn on his severed hand. He looked back down at the lifeless lump of flesh and bone that lay on his chest.

His breath caught in his throat as he tried to speak. To form a question as to what had happened between now and that moment, why his hand had been removed and what was to become of him. These questions he seemed incapable of asking as the same feeling of his airways being constricted washed over him. It was the same as when he was on his back, at the mercy of the hunter who had branded him and gotten him to talk.

Calm your mind, Father's voice said in his mind. Craven closed his eyes, and tried to slow his breathing. His airways only constricted when he tried to speak.

The hunter has stolen your speech from you…he has saved me the trouble of punishing you, Father's voice said, pressing its way through the sea of tumultuous thoughts that drowned Craven's conscious mind. Father was looming over him suddenly, a canopy of writhing shadow that was humanoid in form.

In time your speech will return. But until then, your new hand is quite capable of channeling all the forces you require to serve me.

M-my new hand? Craven thought.

Father nodded, and pointed a shadowy hand. Craven looked to where the hand was pointing. His left arm was outstretched and bolted down to another crude wooden table with a makeshift metal tourniquet. Where his hand should be, there was a dirty brown sheet covering a twitching thing. He could feel the stare of the large creature in the metal mask boring down into him, as if the creature waited with deranged anticipation for the sheet to be pulled off and the subject to marvel at his work.

You are made whole once again, Father's voice sang with twisted delight into his mind, as the thing beneath the sheet began thrashing, shaking the table it was bolted to. The last thing he heard before passing out, was the guttural laughter from the thing in the metal mask as it moved closer to remove the filthy sheet.

BREAKING AND ENTERING

6:12 AM, the following morning,

Mick trudged up the steps to his apartment yet again, bidding a half-hearted good morning to each individually named stair. The stairwell seemed cramped this morning. He brushed it off as his paranoia from the night before.

He had reported to Sergeant Mills as ordered, and had received his new assignment. He would focus on the particulars of the case tonight when he went in. Leave work at work.

Yeah right. Well in this case, yes, he was more than happy to leave his assignment sitting on his desk until that following evening. Tracking down the driver of a stolen car that had five pounds of cocaine sewn into the lining of all the seats didn't exactly scream "exhilarating," by any means.

He reached the third floor where his apartment was, cringing as he turned the knob and stepped out into the hallway. The sounds of his neighbors in the apartment directly above him were obnoxiously loud to his ear drums.

Though he cringed at the fact that he was now going to have to contend with their rendezvous in his efforts to get some sleep, his cringing soon turned to stark dread as his eyes landed on his apartment door—It was standing wide open.

Mick thought for a second that maintenance had been by to fix the leak in his fridge. They never lock up when they leave—but they never leave the door standing wide open either, and it was after six in the morning. There is no way they would be over this early. It was still dark out.

With his heart hammering in his chest, he looked down the hallway to make sure no one was approaching. Then he slid his hand over his Glock and calmly withdrew it from the holster, along with his small flashlight in the other hand. Holding the gun out with the flashlight crossed under his shooter hand, he approached the doorway. He slid in through the open doorway, keeping his back against the wall as he entered. The entryway opened up first into the kitchen area, which he swept quickly and as silently as possible.

You shouldn't sleep with a window cracked, you know? Miller's words from when he went to visit before his execution came back and sank deep into Mick's stomach.

He went directly into the living room next. The window to the fire escape that he always kept open when he slept out in the living room was closed. If anyone had meant to leave his apartment after breaking in, the fire escape would have been the most ideal route. But it was still locked.

A small shudder escaped him as he spun to address the squeak of a door behind him. The front door was still open like it had been when he slipped in. Looked like it hadn't moved, so his eyes traveled to the bathroom door. It was open a crack, just enough for him to see the beam of his flashlight pass over something reflective.

Was that an eye? Mick thought.

"Come out of there now!" Mick shouted. Only after the last syllable left his mouth did it strike him how truly quiet his apartment was now. He didn't even hear the noises from his upstairs neighbors. The hum of the lights from out in the hallway, the sound of traffic below as people rushed to their jobs—all of it was gone. Muted, as if Mick was standing in a vacuum. The air around him felt thin, and his vision began to blur. Every time he blinked, tears burned his eyes as he tried to suck in a deeper breath. His space felt crowded...violated. Even though the front door was standing wide open, it might as well have been welded shut. He was having another episode. He doubled his efforts to breathe calmly.

Something thudded against the bathroom door on the inside, pushing it shut with a jarring crash, like someone on the other side was wearing boots and had kicked it shut. Mick's body tensed suddenly at the abruptness of the door shutting, and it was enough to jolt him back to action. In his mind, using stealth was now out of the question. He knew someone was here now, and they knew he was aware of their presence.

He flew to the door, took his stance and kicked the door in. Or at least that's how he saw it happening in his mind. Through the needles of pain in his foot he looked down to see he had just rattled the door. It was still latched firmly. He grabbed for the knob, awkwardly twisting it until he had a good grip, and flung the door open.

His flashlight beam tore a path through the inky darkness, revealing his bathroom—much the way he had left it, except for the wet metallic stench that hit him in the face. There wasn't a gradual dispersal of the scent. It was like running face first into a wall. He was smelling blood, so thick and so strong he didn't want to breathe through his nose. He breathed through his mouth, and that didn't help either. He could taste the smell. His eyes watered again.

The shower curtain was pulled back to reveal an empty bath tub. No one was hiding in there. But his shower curtain was the source of the smell. After he checked behind the door for any potential hiding intruders, he wadded up some toilet paper to use as a barrier, and pulled the shower curtain out. Thick crimson letters that oozed little streams of blood down the plastic surface of the shower curtain revealed a message.

WAKE UP

MASTERPIECE

The scent of mold and burning candle wax was filling his nostrils. A splitting pain at the base of his skull, followed by soft throbbing. To make matters worse, he was freezing. A damp cold was soaking through his clothes to embrace his flesh, and to shiver only intensified the brain crushing pressure in his skull.

Mick opened his eyes with great effort, and his surroundings slowly emerged out of the cloak of blurriness. He went to rub the sleep from his eyes, only to feel his arms resisting his movement. That woke him up good. He felt his arms bound behind his back, and he felt something sharp encircling his wrists, but he couldn't feel his hands. He was gradually beginning to be aware of the lively ache in his back and shoulders each time he moved. To make things worse, his throat was a halo of fire every time he tried to swallow. Every time he exhaled, his parched throat would mercilessly throb.

The last memory he had was of going to his Sergeant to receive his new assignment after formally being removed from investigating the vigilante hunters. He couldn't remember any of the details of the rest of that night. He remembered coming home the next morning, finding his apartment door standing open. The rest was dark from there, and to try and remember only made his brain cells scream in pain.

He looked around. He was in a dilapidated room, lit only by a vast array of plain red candles. He could see shelves and counter tops lined with them. The only things he could smell was the burning wax, the scent of the mold in the walls and ceiling above him, the musty smell of mounds of bird droppings, and that overpowering wet stench of copper. He continued surveying his surroundings. Nude mannequins with broken faces and limbs stood in a shattered store front window about twenty feet away from him. He was bound to one of many circular pillars supporting the ceiling, probably with his own pair of handcuffs. That would explain the sharp edges digging into his wrists, and why his hands felt wet and sticky. A few clothes racks with moth eaten garments surrounded him. They looked to be from a couple decades ago, probably mid-nineties. Several art canvasses were mounted on easels, dispersed throughout the clothes wracks.

Mick's blood chilled and the hairs on his arms stood erect. The canvasses he saw weren't blank. Portraits were painted on them in various shades of dark red and rust brown, each depicting a different nude subject in various positions. More unnerving than the fact that he was surrounded by paintings of dead people, was the fact that there was an unfinished portrait a few feet away from him, depicting someone with their hands bound behind a pillar.

A sharp scraping sound behind the pillar startled him and he threw his head to the side, struggling to capture the source of the noise. The scraping was followed by footsteps. A man came around the corner, carrying a small metal tray. All his attire looked like things he probably just picked from within the store—old, and moth eaten. He wore a tattered suit jacket over a tie dye t-shirt, jeans with the knees tore out of them, and brown work boots.

"Ah Detective! You're finally awake!" The man said. As if the voice wasn't enough to give it away, the face sealed the deal. Terrance Miller stood before Mick, holding a tray with something that sloshed out of it and fell on Miller's boot. Images of Miller flashed through Mick's stupefied mind of a bulky, deformed giant that laughed and had to support most of its weight on an arm the size of a tree. He remembered the night he saw the creature being wheeled out on a special gurney by several paramedics, with the word 'MONSTER' crudely carved into its chest.

This was the Terrance Miller he knew from the sketches, but not the one who had contracted wretch syndrome, and who had been executed at Ironswrath Maximum Security Prison.

"I feel the need to thank you again for coming to visit me in prison before my execution. It meant a lot to me," he said as he turned toward the unfinished canvas and set the tray down on a stack of boxes near his feet.

"Where am I?!" Mick demanded. The tight handcuffs around his wrists suddenly reminded him that he wasn't in any position to make demands.

"You don't recognize a place from your home town?" Miller asked over his shoulder as he dipped a brush into the tray he had collected. Mick watched as he began applying various strokes. His heart sped up again.

"You are in the Broken Edge City Mall...or rather, the building it used to be." Miller said, finally answering his question.

How?! Mick thought. The word 'how' was going through his mind a lot now. How was he here, how was Miller alive, how long had he been here.

"Miller...Is that-"

"Tick please...Call me Tick." He corrected. Mick swallowed hard as his burning throat protested.

"Is that...*my* blood?"

Tick nodded, "It wouldn't be right to use another's blood to paint your own portrait. I'll have it completed within the hour. I do hope you plan to stay awake and delight me further with your conversation." He said, and then continued in silence.

Anger was beginning to replace Mick's fear. The shift was gradual though. Anger mixed with horror. Terrance "Tick" Miller, the first serial killer he had helped take down, and was executed, was sitting in front of him painting Mick's portrait in Mick's own blood. Pride wouldn't allow Mick to give Tick the satisfaction of any sort of conversation, but survival was looking like the better option regardless of the means.

"I know your mind must be lively with questions," Tick said, dipping his brush into a cup of water, and switching to another, finer brush.

Mick humored him, "I guess my first question is, how are you not dead?"

Tick chuckled as he continued, "I did die. I was executed on the sixth of this month." He said, very matter of fact and nonchalant.

*He's crazy...*Mick thought, but then he had to remind himself that he was the one who was talking to an executed criminal.

"Dying. It was quite a novel experience I must say. I remember the chemicals being pumped into my neck through the needles built into the collar. I can't say I felt a dire sense of panic, knowing that my final moment had arrived. In fact, I was quite content. It felt like falling asleep. But then I opened my eyes, and I was in my cell. It was dark, save for a single spotlight shining down upon *this*," he said gesturing toward the painting of Mick bound with his hands behind the pillar.

"I saw the finished version of course. It was much how I envisioned my former paintings when I was inspired. While looking at your portrait, I saw each individual brush stroke on the canvass. It was as if I was seeing the big picture, detail by detail, from beginning to end, in real time. A work in progress, yet finished and put on display all at the same time. Then I thought to myself, 'I wonder if this is how God sees the world he created. The whole flow of time, from the big bang, all the way to the day the universe ends from imploding on itself, all while observing the little events that make up human history, one at a time, and all at once.'" He said as he then switched to a que-tip and began dabbing it in Mick's blood.

Mick watched as he used the bloody cue-tip for adding texture to his portrait counter-part's hair. *Keep him talking,* Mick said to himself calmly in his mind.

"So you die…You see the painting of me. What happened next?" Mick asked.

"I was getting to that, let me finish," Tick said as he continued to work on the texture of Mick's hair with a que-tip. When he was done, he sat the que-tip down and stepped back from the painting for a minute to observe. The awkward silence that hung in the air reminded Mick of how cold he was. He finally realized that his clothes weren't actually wet, but had been chilled to such a degree they might as well have felt wet as they were wrapped around his skin. It didn't matter either way, he was cold!

"As soon as those thoughts came to me, I was overcome with a strange mixture of dread and ecstasy that I had never felt before. Certainly not to those levels, and not at the same time. They both fed on and into one another, almost as if the two were making love. As my eyes adjusted, I noticed a figure standing behind the painting. It wasn't like anything I had ever seen before, not because of its shape, but because of the texture of the thing. It was abnormally tall, yet looked like it was composed of a type of living shadow. Like the dark of space, without its stars. I almost hadn't noticed it there in the dark. It touched an oddly tangible hand to the painting, and it spoke to me." Tick said, his eyes finally meeting Mick's again.

"What did it say?"

Tick smiled, "It assured me I was not finished yet. That I had one final masterpiece to create. It told me that it had been the one to prompt me to write to you and request your presence before my execution. Then I awoke. I was no longer in my cell. I was here, in this ghost town, and my body was restored. Though, I'm afraid *this* may never go away," he said pulling up his shirt to reveal the jagged, faintly glowing scars in his flesh where the hunters had carved him up.

The chill had been working its way inside him while he listened to Tick. Now Mick wasn't so sure it was merely because of his cold clothes. The words Tick said were so utterly impossible, yet he articulated them with such clarity and coherence, that he was able to put flesh upon the crazy skeleton of his tale. He didn't sound like a raving lunatic. He sounded like one who had a clear recollection of what they had experienced. There was something in his voice that was, in a way, almost romantic in his retelling of the events. Like revisiting those memories and getting to pass them on was something he had been longing to do almost as much as paint another picture with someone's blood.

"Perhaps I'll finish your portrait another time. Once it's done I won't have any need to keep you. You're such a special subject though. I never had the luxury of taking my time with the others. You're the first one who got to watch me paint them." He said as he took his jacket off, then the t-shirt...then he undid his pants.

"What the hell are you doing?!" Mick shrieked. Here he was, handcuffed to a pillar, bleeding from his wrists, cold, and light headed, and this guy is *stripping!* Mick's eyes began frantically searching around the room. Everything he could possibly use as a weapon was too far away. And even if anything was within reach, he couldn't snap through the cuffs.

"I wasn't *totally* cured of wretch syndrome, but my encounter with the being I described has certainly made the condition more interesting," Tick said with a sneer as he tossed his underwear away from him. He then began going around the room, blowing out the candles.

"What the fuck is that supposed to mean?!" Mick shrieked as his panic rose to a swelling crescendo.

"I'll show you," he said as he began stretching and popping various joints, rolling his neck and shoulders.

"I'm expecting company soon. They may arrive early, and I don't need you present to finish the portrait, but ultimately, I'm just not ready to turn loose of you yet." Tick said as he popped his shoulder. The sound made Mick queasy. The wet sound of bone and cartilage separating was horrendously loud. The flesh on one of Tick's arms looked like it was boiling beneath the skin. He was turning a sickly pale color, almost rotten gray, and his eyes rolled back in his head.

Tick staggered backward as he began coughing up a black, tarry substance. It began oozing from his nostrils and ears, and his eyes too until they looked like sticky black orbs in his head.

"Here comes…the best part!" Tick said, his voice deepening with each word he uttered. He convulsed violently as one arm elongated with a series of cracks that sounded like a wooden board creaking just before it splits apart in a spray of splinters. Tick hunched over, holding his new arm out to steady himself as the vertebras of his spine shot out of his back. The muscles beneath the skin were morphing and growing at such a rate that the skin abruptly split open in various places. The blood that poured from the open wounds was the same black ooze that was coming out of Tick's face. He was growing exponentially, gradually resembling the Tick that Mick had faced in that cell. The legs kicked out like a bucking bull, bending at impossible angles, and elongating with a chorus of snaps that stabbed into Mick's ears. The muscles on one leg expanded quicker than the skin that encapsulated them could compensate for, and the skin was shredded off like old cling wrap.

The grossly muscular, disproportionate parody of a human body hunched forward upon reaching its full height—the head was touching the ceiling. Doing a quick guess, Mick put him at roughly nine feet high. Its posture was that of a deformed gorilla. The face resembled its previous form of looking like a brutalized melon, one eye swollen shut. Thick black veins snaked up and down each deformed limb. Tick grinned down at Mick through blacked teeth that had become a hideous under-bite. Mick instinctually felt himself pulling at the cuffs. He felt the metal edges digging deeper into his wrists, but his hands he couldn't feel at all. With every pull, the muscles in his back and neck rioted in a frenzy of sharp pain.

The beast reached a deformed hand that was the size of a snow shovel around the pillar. Mick almost fainted as he felt both shoulder blades slip out of place. The pain was such that his breath was stolen from him. The gut reaction of screaming almost made him black out. Just when he thought his arms were going to be ripped from their sockets, he heard a small sharp *ping!* His arms fell to his sides, his shoulders sagging unnaturally on either side. He looked through the tears. His arms were free. The skin around his wrists was nearly none existent where the blood stained handcuffs had torn into his flesh. His hands were dark purple from lack of circulation. None of that mattered now though. He scrambled up in a hurry, his dislocated shoulders protesting every movement. Tick was shouting something behind him as he ran toward the shattered glass doors of the department store. All he could make out was the words, "fun," "chase," and "plaything."

RUN!

Mick tore through the shattered department store doors. His arms felt like he was dragging two anchors from his shoulders. His legs shook when he put weight on them, and his thighs trembled from prolonged disuse. His eyes met the devastated landscape of what had once been the Broken Edge Mall. Or at least one floor of it anyway. He saw a couple escalators to his far right, but the way was littered with fallen debris. The fronts of the other stores didn't look much different than this one, all shattered glass and looted merchandise. A gumball machine lay on its side, its enormous glass top obliterated and the dull multicolored gum balls scattered all over hell and back. Mick took off regardless. Survive, escape, and report to the police that Terrance Miller was still alive.

Miller's voice had dropped several octaves. He was shouting something back there as Mick huffed along, attempting to jump over fallen beams. He couldn't understand a word he was saying, partly because he was fleeing, but also because the voice was so deep that it was now distorted. He heard what sounded like some structure collapsing behind him in a twisted chorus of splintering beams and clanging metal. He jerked his head around quickly, causing his shoulders to throb in fiery vengeance. After he blinked the tears from his eyes, he saw the hulking, misshapen mass of Tick lurching out of the department store. His large deformed hands tossed the debris from the entry way to the side and his one good eye landed on Mick. A nauseating grin spread across his face. The inky black eyeball was bulging from its socket. Then the smile vanished and turned to a look that Mick couldn't quite discern with that messed up of a face.

Mick turned on unsteady legs before Tick could launch himself toward him. At this point, his sense of direction was non-existent. Anywhere that the large meaty bulldozer was *not,* could have potentially been his ticket out of here as far as he was concerned. The fact that he was fleeing through near total darkness without a flashlight only occurred to him after the fact. He rounded a corner, his dislocated shoulders screaming for mercy. There was a sky light above him that was letting in a small amount of moonlight. Mick yelped and ducked as a fleshy mass big enough to crush his head slapped at the wall from around the corner. A shower of rotten wall debris crumbled down to the floor as the giant mass of deformed limbs crawled into view right as Mick got his feet under him again and began to run the other way.

"My, aren't you quick!" Tick's voice hammered in his chest.

If Mick's arms didn't eventually pop out of their sockets, his legs would give out any moment. He could feel the shin splints, the muscles around the bone tearing in agony as he pressed onward, trying not to fall and impale himself on anything in the dark. He saw a room to his left side with a roll down cage, lowered almost to the floor. He limped toward it, crawled under the roll down cage and then entered the vest space. Memories came flooding back to him. This was a part of the mall he *had* visited as a child! He saw row after row of classic arcade games, claw machines and shattered glass cabinets that once held coveted prizes, standing tall like silent mechanical sentinels. Glimmers of moonlight seeped in through gaps in the ceiling that reached clear to the roof, but it was still too dark to see what any of the games were. He had no time to process any feelings of nostalgia, as memories of flashing lights and all the chaotic sounds of arcade games clashing in his young ears was suddenly drowned by the incoming cacophony of sharp, ear splitting terror. The sound of the floor and walls of the building being torn apart by the massive growth of disproportionate flesh that was trying to get to him.

"I...hear...blood...through your veins!" Was all Mick could make out as Tick's voice boomed behind him.

Mick bolted as Tick came into view, crashing through the roll down cage. Luckily his eyes were adjusting a little bit. He stopped just long enough to push over one of the claw machines, his adrenaline temporarily numbing the pain in his shoulders. But not for long. Mick chanced a look over his shoulder to see if his obstruction had slowed Tick down in the least, and his heart sank.

He saw his pursuer use one of his large hands to knock it out of the way. The machine and the driving game it smacked into were both obliterated.

Mick began to dodge thick hanging chunks of soggy insulation and rusted metal framing that had been a part of the ceiling, not to mention jumping over the many arcade games that lay on their sides. His eyes eventually landed on a door with the words EXIT ONLY spray painted on it in stenciled letters. He threw himself at the door, knowing before he collided with it that his shoulders were going to pay a price higher than what they wanted to. It hadn't even been worth it. The door only budged a few inches.

"Shit!" Mick yelled, as the sounds of arcade games getting smashed and tossed aside got closer and closer.

"Fi, fy, fo, fum!" Tick's voice boomed, shaking Mick's organs inside his rib cage.

Mick kicked the door that budged ever so slowly on rusted hinges. It finally gave with one last hard shove when he put his shoulder into it, right before a big meaty hand swatted away the chunk of ceiling insulation close to where the door was. Mick practically dove through, tears now blurring his vision from all the abuse his shoulders were going through. He would never take them for granted again if he lived to get them back into their sockets.

He kept moving, his run looking like a pathetic hobble. His current pace gave him some time to take in his surroundings. He noticed in the hallway he was in, other doors, some saying "employee restrooms," or "storage." The vibrations of the ground shaking beneath his feet began to diminish, as if his attacker were withdrawing.

He'll be trying to find another way to get you. Keep moving! Mick thought. This hallway he was in was relatively free from most obstructions. Aside from the mushy ceiling tiles and the occasional hanging cable where maybe a light fixture had hung, this place was practically spotless by comparison. His pace slowed even more, and he rested his hands on his knees, breathing harder than he had remembered doing so in a long time. The ache in his shoulders was swelling like a massive wave about to crush him, and he bit down on his lip through the pain, almost drawing blood. What was that he heard Tick say back there?

I...hear...blood...in your veins...

With his voice being as deep and loud as it was, the words he spoke were so distorted it was hard to hear anything he said. Of coarse while fleeing for his life, Mick couldn't care less what he was saying really. But the part about, hearing blood, if that's what he really said, was bugging him.

Something went *click* behind him, and he spun to adhere to the sound. He had truly come a long way from the door. But standing there down the hall where he had come, still as a statue, stood a black figure. It was so still Mick wasn't sure if in the dark he was actually seeing it…until it moved.

As my eyes adjusted, I noticed a figure standing behind the painting…Like the dark of space, without its stars. I almost hadn't noticed it there. Tick's words came back to him.

Mick drew in a sharp gasp. His eyes widened and his stomach sank. Could that be…? Had it seen him? Mick couldn't move. His feet felt like they had sank into a pit of quick sand. The paralyses spread to his legs. Never before had he been frozen in place with such a sense of unnamable dread and terror. The one time that was even comparable to such a feeling was when he saw the thing that attacked him in the men's room at the high school. If it were merely the sudden shock and fear of being discovered by another here in the dark as he fled for his life, that alone would have been one thing. But there was something *more* about this figure that stood silent and still. Something, alien. Something that didn't belong in this world. As if staring at the thing was opening up a vacuum into a void that Mick's sanity couldn't return from.

He didn't even see the thing move, and Mick was sure he hadn't blinked, but the thing now stood closer. He heard the sound of breathing.

*No…no, no, no, no, no…*Mick thought as he began slowly backing away from the shadow that was becoming more and more three dimensional by the second. He spotted a door to his left. He reached an unsteady hand for the handle, praying to whoever was listening that it would give. It gave with a little resistance, and he heard the click from the latch releasing. The sound of that one little click was far louder than what felt comfortable. Without thinking, he flung the door open and dove through, slamming it behind him. He stood with his back braced against the door for some time, almost like he meant to keep something from coming in. The walls around him shook, jarring him away from the door, eyes zipping around for his attacker. Then he heard it again. When he finally looked up, he noticed where he was. The sky light above shook with the sound of thunder nearby. A set of stairs, leading to the floor below, was straight ahead of him. A huge fountain, fifteen feet high, could be seen from this floor. Mick hobbled over to the stairs, clutching the rails on his way down. The food court was below him. His insides turned to ice at what he saw below.

What he saw occupying the food court, were the still, human forms of what appeared to be male and female store mannequins, positioned at various tables like they were socializing. Some stood facing the dried up fountain in the center. Others stood next to various pillars and were positioned inside the entry ways of the various stores surrounding the food court. Others were posed at the counters of the different food vendors, looking like they were placing an order. Some of the mannequins were missing an arm here, a head there, but most were intact, and all were stark naked.

Lightning flashed, followed by the rumble of thunder about two seconds later. Mick placed a shaking hand on the railing and slowly descended the stairs, his eyes sweeping over each mannequin. The invisible insects crawling beneath his skin caused him to twitch with revulsion at the sight of them. It was like someone was trying to recreate a regular busy weekend at the mall, and then freeze it in time. Mick shimmied through the crowd of still, plaster bodies with blank stares, his eyes meeting every single one of their empty gazes. He was beginning to feel like he couldn't breathe again. Every step he took was labored and every sound his shoes made as they walked across the debris littered floor was like an electric prod to his nerves. He looked up ahead and saw where a sign with arrows hung over an arch way, indicating the general direction of restrooms, other stores, entrances and exits. The arch way split into two different paths, both awash in moonlight from the skylight above.

Mick felt the shock of cold, wet hands around his throat, and his vision became blurry around the edges with tears before he could react. He was being driven to his knees by a pair of hands that were covered in black blood. Though slippery as they were, they held true like a vice.

"Here I was, right under your nose, and you walk right passed me!" Tick's voice sang into his ear. Had he shrunk back down to normal size? Mick blindly flailed his hands around, trying to either get some leverage or to land an awkward punch to Tick's face. Both efforts were a joke compared to the iron grip around his throat that was cutting off the oxygen to his brain.

"Let the Father take you Mick, quickly, before *they* get here!" Tick whispered in Mick's ear.

Mick wasn't sure exactly what he heard echo down one of the paths up ahead. If he were cognizant enough to try and describe the sound he heard right before he was about to black out, he might have described it like a concrete wall being obliterated by a wrecking ball. It sounded like glass shards were in there somewhere. But the sound was evolving. Getting louder. The darkness of the food court, dimly lit by the moonlight pouring in from the skylight, was starting to flee. In his blurring vision, he saw two enormous glowing balls of light, side by side, and then the unmistakable screeching of tires. Then there was a distinct *pop*.

The vice grip loosened tremendously in the seconds that followed however. Mick pried himself free and despite the tremendous throbbing pain in his shoulders, he managed to unsteadily make his way to his feet, hacking and coughing violently. He looked down. Tick was writhing on the ground near Mick's feet, a shaft of light emanating from a hole in his right shoulder. The flesh on his neck looked like it was bubbling, and the sound of cracking bones and tearing skin filled his ears. He was shifting again.

"Mick come on!" a voice called out to him. Mick jumped at the sound of his name being called. He knew that voice!

"Valerie?!" He called out. The features of the vehicle were becoming clearer. It was a large van, and leaning out of the passenger side, holding a pistol aimed at the stirring body of Tick, was Valerie—and her eyes were *glowing*.

The sliding door of the van opened, and out stepped one of the hunters from the assembly—the one named Brandon.

"Get in the van Johnson." Brandon said as he walked passed Mick.

"What the hell's going on?!" Mick demanded, and then wished he hadn't. Brandon turned around so quick Mick almost fell backward. His face had changed. Eyes were still glowing that burning white, but the bones in his face were restructuring themselves. Blood trickled out of Brandon's nose, which quickly flattened itself into a snout. Jagged rows of fangs were pushing themselves out of his gums, causing the human teeth to fall to the floor.

Brandon's meaty, clawed hand shot out toward Mick's shoulder and squeezed. Mick's shoulder erupted like a volcano as magma like agony spread from his socket. Tears shot out from his eyes as he yelped and almost fell to his knees again.

"Get. In. The van!" Brandon snarled, his voice sounding more like a growl than an actual voice. Mick stumbled backward toward the van, his eyes focusing on the body of Tick that was beginning to stand up, its limbs growing larger like overgrown trees. Brandon was on one knee now, his entire body convulsing as his torso, ears, and face elongated, his muscles growing at such a rate as to split the shirt he was wearing.

Mick felt multiple sets of hands grabbing him from behind, jarring him out of his trance. He instinctively began to jerk and flail out of their grips, but the multiple sets of hands overpowered him, and he soon felt something ice cold and metallic around his wrists again. The click of yet another pair of handcuffs was unmistakable.

"Hey!" Mick yelled, but keeping his thrashing to a minimum because his shoulders couldn't handle it. A bag was then shoved over his head. The next thing he knew, he was flung onto the back seat inside of the large van.

"See ya on the other side boss!" One of the hunters yelled before slamming the sliding door shut. With that, the driver slammed the van into reverse, and Mick rolled into the floorboards, trying to keep his cries of anguish to himself.

ONE OF THEM

Here he was, handcuffed (again) with a cloth sack over his head, in the back of some stranger danger type van, speeding off in God knew what direction! How many days had it been since he last went to work? Who was even driving this van? Suddenly, through all the turmoil in his mind, Mick remembered that night he and Valerie were fleeing from the high school. The thing in the road that had looked like a girl wearing an animal pelt but then had morphed into a giant dog/man hybrid. Then the masked man in the road who wielded the glowing machete. His mind flashed back to his last conversation with Chief Scroggins.

How could I have been so stupid?! There were more of them out there and I didn't even think to bring that up! And Valerie is one of them!

Anger was beginning to course through his veins like acid. Blinded by his need for his own personal justice to be brought on them. He was angry for not bringing up the fact to Scroggins that he saw another masked hunter out that night. Come to think of it, he didn't even remember adding that into his report that he filed. It's like his mind had blocked it out. And then there was Valerie. Granted, she and Mick's relationship was strictly professional, not that he hadn't thought about asking her out to dinner though. Regardless, he had kind of always thought of himself, George and her as the Justice Trinity of New Broken Edge PD. She had definitely been one Mick had eyes for but *this* was definitely a deal breaker.

Valerie's voice was reaching him through the cloth sack over his head. He remembered how impressed he had been with her that night she got them both out of the parking lot at the high school. She drove that car like she was in an action movie. Now Mick knew why.

"So you're one of them huh?" Mick asked through the bag covering his face.

"Yep, sure was. The whole time." She said, her conversation resuming with the driver.

Now wait a minute! I'm rolling around in the back of this van, you are working with criminals, and you can't even do me the service of sounding even a little sorry that you lied to me? Mick thought.

"So you employ non-humans too? Just like the hunters from the Broken Edge Massacre." Mick shot off. In his mind, he was probably going to die tonight anyway, so he thought why prolong the inevitable?

The conversation between Valerie and the driver halted. Suddenly the silence that was hanging in the air began to make Mick feel like he was being buried alive by cement. He squirmed, and when his dislocated shoulder blades protested, he whimpered, trying not to sound pathetic.

"I hear you survived that event," said the masculine voice from the driver's seat. Mick's heart skipped a beat and his mouth went dry. He nodded his head but realized how ridiculous he was because his head was covered and he was on his belly in the back floorboards. Mick remained quiet for a long time. As his thoughts raced and crashed through his mind, they continued to turn back to the mental images of the masked hunter in the road.

"So you know who I am?" Mick asked.

"I do indeed." The driver said.

Of course he would know who he is. Valerie was acting as a double agent the whole time. The words that came out of Mick's mouth next felt like trying to expel half-digested spaghetti, but he forced them out anyway. Partially because it was killing him. He had to know, but at the same time everything in him didn't want to know either.

"Are you the one who fought off that creature in the road? The thing in the animal skin?"

"I am."

Eventually the driver's phone rang. Mick listened very carefully through the cloth bag covering his face. He vaguely recognized one of the voices on the other end. It was the hunter who had said, "see you on the other side boss."

"How'd things go Parish?" The driver asked.

"It's done. Terrance Miller is dead. Brandon is dismembering the remains now."

"Good. We are on our way back to you. The whole building goes, so be generous with the gasoline."

"For real," Parish said on the other end.

A few minutes later, after a couple seconds of excruciating pain from both shoulders, Mick found himself standing among the vigilante hunters in the demolished food court. Valerie had been decent enough to pop his shoulders back into place. The ache wouldn't go away for a while, but at least he could move them again, although he was still cuffed.

Before him lay what was left of Terrance Miller. Mick leaned over onto his knees and vomited up bile at the smell. Only then did it hit him, ironically, that he was starving. How long had it been since he had eaten anything? The hulking deformed mass of limbs and a face was now just a glowing, rotting mound of sludge with a rib cage. The skeleton, from what Mick could see, was still intact, but the ammo from the hunter's guns, plus whatever Brandon had done to him, had obliterated any recognizable features. Not that Miller was recognizable when he shifted anyway.

As they all approached, Mick saw in the glow of the remains the eight foot tall, beastly shape of a werewolf; triple jointed and flesh rippling with muscle and veins, all wrapped up in gore and matted fur. The beast's head snapped in their direction, and Mick could see the fiery white glow of its eyes. The claws had steam trailing from them, sizzling the blood they had bathed in. Only when the thing turned to face them fully could Mick see that the teeth, claws and veins of the creature were also burning with the same intense glow beneath the skin.

"Brandon is a natural born lycanthrope," Valerie said.

"But he works for you?" Mick asked, his voice unsteady as he beheld the creature before him.

"He works *with* us. He can make rational choices. He is still a free agent, and has chosen this life and the One we serve. This is how he sates his hunger for flesh." She explained.

Watching the creature transform back into the person Mick recognized was too much. The sounds the beast made as it wailed through the pain of being shrunk down into a body that was too small to contain it was maddening, and Mick tried to block as much of it out as he could by covering his ears. Soon one of the hunters fetched a robe from the van and draped the slowly rising, stiff form of the naked, blood covered man that stood in front of them.

"Hello again," Brandon said, as he approached. Mick only nodded, or he *thought* he nodded.

The hunters Zach and Parish were opening the back double doors of the large van, producing red gasoline jugs and bags of road salt.

"What's all this for?" Mick asked.

The one whose face Mick had not seen yet, the driver, turned towards him finally. The glow in his eyes was fading, making his eyes look human for the time being. His skin was olive and his hair was cut short and looked like it had been confined inside of a ski mask for too long. His face was clad in a full beard, neatly groomed. If his hair had been down to his shoulders Mick thought the guy could almost look like Jesus.

"You believe in life after death?" The driver asked.

Mick hesitated for a second, wondering what that could mean in light of his question.

"I'm not really sure anymore." He replied.

"Brandon," The driver called. Brandon turned toward his superior, carrying a huge bag of road salt over his shoulder, "Yeah Judah?" So that was his name.

"Is Mr. Miller still in the area?" Judah asked.

Brandon's eyes glazed over as he looked out over the demolished landscape that had once been a thriving mall, until his eyes locked on one particularly dark area. Brandon snorted, his grip on the salt bag tightening until Mick thought his fingers would puncture the plastic.

"Yeah. He is over in that corner by the over turned sales booth," Brandon said.

"What the hell kind of bullshit is this?" Mick burst. He noted the hunters pouring the road salt and gasoline all over the remains.

"NO! You're gonna destroy evidence! This is a crime scene! His remains need to be brought back to New Broken Edge to be processed!" Mick erupted, once he finally knew what was going on.

"Well," Valerie piped up, "I'm a coroner. And I can tell you right now that cause of death was gradual trauma of heavy gun fire, mauling of a large animal, and the gradual breakdown of his muscle tissue."

"You won't be coroner for much longer lady!" Mick said jabbing a finger toward her—and then he felt a clawed hand on his shoulder.

Brandon spun him around, his face partially changed. His nose had begun to blacken into a wolf snout, the ridges around his eyes and cheekbones became more pronounced, and his jaw looked like a bear trap. His eyes were glowing white again. But it wasn't really all that which made Mick shut up. It was the direction Brandon's other hand was pointing to.

The overturned sales booth Brandon had mentioned earlier was shielding something pale white, something that shivered and twitched. It stood out in stark contrast to the darkness around it, making the darkness more vibrant than Mick had ever seen it before. The white, twitching thing stumbled out into full view—a wraith, transparent, and with wispy features, stood shaking on wobbly legs. It was skinny and malnourished. Gaunt with hollow black sockets for eyes, but the face was unmistakable. Terrance Miller's spirit, began to stalk forward, groping around blindly.

Blacking out would have been a mercy right now, but it was one that escaped him. Mick's eyes were starting to feel like they were being pushed out from behind his brain. He blinked, but the sensation only grew stronger.

Miller's voice was snaking around through Mick's head. *Your eyes…they've seen so much! They are a fount of endless inspiration. And I CRAVE inspiration!*

A sudden rush of intense heat kissed Mick's face, and he drew back and shielded his eyes from the burst of flame that erupted from within the hollow spirit that stalked forward. He felt Brandon's hand slip off his shoulder, and he crumbled to his knees. Mick's hands shot up toward his eyes, as if to try and keep them pushed inside of his head. He instinctually felt himself ducking behind the robed figure of Brandon, who had opened his eyes to see Miller's spirit depart. If this was their sick way of helping him have closure…he honestly didn't know what to think. When the pain behind his eyes subsided, he looked up. A roaring fire was consuming the heap of disfigured remains in front of him. The hunters were standing around him, watching the fire consume the empty shell of Terrance Miller, but Judah, the driver of the van, was staring down at him.

He wanted to hide. The feeling of being naked when fully clothed made him feel like his very soul had been cast out into an arctic wind, and above him stood an icy titan, ready to scoop him up and devour him. Judah took his eyes off him long enough to nod to whoever was behind him. The next second, his vision turned dark as the bag was placed back over his head again.

PRISONER

The ride to wherever on God's green earth they were taking him was torturous. Thrown into the back of a crowded van, his arms, legs and head all simultaneously being squished against hard immovable surfaces, getting stepped on as one of the hunters adjusted their position, and he couldn't see. Every second, he felt like the van was getting smaller, until the feeling reached its climax and he felt he had been thrown into a casket to be buried. He began thrashing as panic overtook him, causing him to be sat on by several of the hunters until he passed out...again. He was getting tired of that.

Mick awoke to the blinding rays of some fluorescent light hanging above his head. He was unbound. That was one of the first things he noticed. Second was that he was on a very cushiony couch. His heart almost leapt with rapture when it registered that he was on a couch. Until his eyes adjusted and he looked around to see that it wasn't his couch, and he wasn't in his apartment.

The floor was concrete, with bundles or extension cords taped together and secured to the floor in different places. Gun cases lined each wall he laid eyes on, each containing various firearms of many different types. Rifles, shotguns, submachine guns, and pistols. Various other types of cases were positioned in different areas holding crossbows, compound bows. He spotted an area in the distance that appeared to be a work area with dismantled equipment of some kind on different tables. And seated around him in metal folding chairs were his captors. Their eyes appeared normal this time around though. On some of them, like Parish and Judah, a feint white glow could be seen briefly under their skin, like a vein that was aglow, causing the muscle in that area to glow red beneath the skin before it vanished. Was the glowing substance from the crime scene photos literally *inside* them? Flowing through their very veins? Mick felt sick. Whatever they used that could stop a werewolf dead in its tracks was flowing through their bloodstream as he sat with his thoughts racing around like a frenzied hornets' nest. Suddenly the fuzzy chainsaws that bayed at the moon weren't the scariest things he had ever seen.

"W-w-where the hell am I?" He sputtered.

Judah leaned forward, his face stone cold, "You are a guest in our house. It's not an ideal arrangement, but you'll be staying with us for a while."

Mick swallowed, being reminded of the ache in his throat, "Could—could you -?" He stammered, unable to finish a sentence. These people could kill him. They had a freaking werewolf in their trust. Brandon was looking at him right now. They were all looking at him, but *Brandon* was looking at him the same way a dog eyes a steak. He felt like his throat was tightening as he tried to speak, tried to mold a single thought into a sentence, but nothing came out.

"Water!" He finally managed to exclaim.

In response, Valerie came over to him with an ice cold bottle of spring water, which she had apparently undone the lid already. He held it to his lips and his parched tongue instantly absorbed the cold water as it washed down his throat. He finished the bottle in two more huge gulps. Only then did he realize that he should have smelled the water when Valerie handed it to him. The seal on the lid had been broken. He drew the empty bottle away from his lips and snarled, "What was in this water?!"

"Mick, it was just water. Calm down," she said, an exhausted tone in her voice.

"Look I'm gonna be frank with you detective. I don't want you here. But with that *thing* out there looking for you, your safety will be better handled by us than the police." Judah said. Mick looked back at his host.

"Well you guys burned the body of that *thing!* His ghost went up in flames along with his carcass, and the evidence, and the rest of the old Broken Edge Mall for that matter, so what are you worried about?" Mick retorted.

Judah squeezed his eyes shut and sighed deeply. For a brief moment, for all the muscle and imposing build the man had, he looked haggard beyond recognition.

"You…are so exhausting." He said, looking back up at Mick, his eyes flashing white for a second, so brief that Mick thought he imagined it. It was enough to make him rethink his tone.

"Um…Thank you." Mick said, his voice dipping to a whisper.

"The thing I'm talking about wasn't Terrance Miller. I'm talking about the one that calls itself Father," Judah clarified.

For a moment, Mick just sat there. He remembered the conversation with Scroggins the night before he was kidnapped. Now might finally be his chance to get some direct answers. But he was on their terms. Again, he wasn't in control, and that thought alone made his blood boil. Somewhere in the back of his head he kept feeling a small niggle that reminded him, if they had wanted to kill him, they had the chance to do it while he was passed out on this couch. For one reason or another they had saved him from being strangled to death by Tick. Had Valerie had something to do with that? All puppy dog love aside, even if she did have something to do with the fact that Mick was still breathing now, he owed it to her to not screw anything up.

"So who is this Father?" Mick asked.

"Not who...what." Judah said. Silence followed for a brief moment, until Judah leaned forward a little in his chair and regarded Mick like an irritating child who would not stop arguing with a teacher.

"Father is only one title it's gone by. It's something ancient. Not sure at this point where it comes from or what it is, but we know that it wants to make contact with you. Something about bestowing a gift onto you." Judah said.

Mick could feel the nerves in his spine twitching as a chill swept through him.

"And it's in New Broken Edge?" Mick squeaked. He hated the desperation that was beginning to creep up in his voice, but sitting here in the middle of these hunters, made it all far more real than he was ready for.

"It is. And until we can get some protective measures in place, you are staying right here." Judah said.

Mick shuddered, trying to digest everything. Obviously, creatures like Terrance Miller, and other nasties existed. If they could exist, why was he having such a hard time accepting that something ancient could be walking the streets looking for him? At first he thought this guy Father was nothing more than an insane cult leader. But the fact that these hunters were now ascribing *other* attributes to him put this in a new category altogether. And it was going out of its way to find *him* personally.

Mick felt his mouth drawing tight, "The Chief said that it wants me to be its Right Hand. Any of you have a clue what that could mean?" He asked, suddenly feeling like a tentacle of darkness was pulling him down into the ocean.

Judah sighed, but this time it wasn't a sigh of frustration. That sigh scared Mick. Because it was a sigh of a man who was at a complete loss.

"We don't know. But we're guessing that whatever it wants you for, it knows you are in law enforcement. Maybe it wants to use your position and influence to shift suspicion away from its activities." Judah clarified.

Zach was beginning to speak now. Mick thought about tuning him out, but since the information they could provide potentially could make the difference between his survival and a disturbing fate, he listened.

"This thing has marked you. Those times when I was looking right behind you and it looked like I was muttering nonsense? It's got something following you." Zach said. Mick felt like he was sinking in an ever expanding sea of crushing, icy waters.

The recollection of the dark phantom that he saw after interrogating Zach for the first time flashed through his mind. He remembered when he had that insane episode of claustrophobia after the interrogation. A dark figure had materialized down the hallway from him and the Chief. And he had seen the thing again when he lost Miller in the hallway leading out of the arcade at the old mall.

"The first night when you interrogated me, it was standing behind you with its hand on the back of your neck. It looked like a tall shadowy, bald man wearing a long coat." Zach said. Mick twitched at the memory. He had felt *something* touching him that night.

George. Mick's mind suddenly erupted with panic at the recollection of his best friend. He still had no idea how long he had been missing, and George was bound to be looking for him along with the rest of the NBE Police Department. Granted if he hadn't been gone more than forty eight hours he couldn't legally be considered missing.

"Valerie," Mick began, his voice weary and strained, "does George know where I'm at?"

Valerie shook her head, "No, and for his own protection and yours, he isn't going to find out."

"But how long can you keep up the charade?" Mick asked, "I don't know how long I've been missing, but even if it hasn't been two days, I can guarantee you he'll be looking for me. We both know that."

"Well," She began, "I managed to not give anything away in my dealings with you for as long as I knew you were looking into us. And you have been missing since the early morning hours of the 18th. It's the 20th now."

So it's close enough George or someone would have reported me missing, and I know he would be trying to get ahold of me sooner so he would have known something was up, Mick thought.

His mind flew back to what they had said about the entity that was following him. If he had been marked, then he could be found, no matter how safe this place was. His face began to twist into a scowl of rage as he stood up suddenly.

"You said I've been marked! This thing that's following me, can it get in here?!"

"There is a chance that could happen, yes," Judah said as he met Mick's gaze, "But should that happen, it will be on our home turf. It will be causing itself more grief than us."

"You sound awful sure of yourself," Mick said, looking around at each of them.

"We are sure of Yeshua and his power to protect us." Judah said, and with that he stood and began to make his exit.

Who? Mick thought.

"Hey who's that? What's a Yeshua?" Mick called after Judah. The other hunters were filing out after their leader, Valerie included.

Brandon was the last to begin leaving. His eyes were ablaze with predatory fury. The skin on Mick's neck flared with goosebumps when he noticed the hunter that was also a literal monster standing next to him.

"I know you're afraid," Brandon said, "but it would be of great benefit to you, if you could get your fear under control. My beast can smell it, and it's making it hungry."

"Are you threatening me?" Mick asked, his indignation competing for dominance with his unnerved state. Brandon smirked and turned to follow the others.

"Not a threat. A warning." He said, his eyes beginning to glow as he walked away.

FALLEN YARD DECORATIONS

October 21

The thing at the end of Craven's arm wriggled and twitched of its own accord, as if wracked by residual muscle memory from its former owner. It was indeed a hand, to be sure. Anyone who saw it from a distance could see that much. But having stuffed the thing into the pocket in his black hoodie, he would not be giving any passerby's that chance. Because upon a closer look, one could note that the hand didn't look like it belonged to a young man in his late teens. The hand was horridly gaunt and bony, with impossibly long fingers. Its texture felt like sun dried leather to the touch, and it was a diseased purplish color. With his other hand, the one that was still his, he pulled his hood up over his head to shield him from the wind. Dead leaves blew through the cold October air. Gray, overcast skies hovered above the city of New Broken Edge. It had been roughly four days since his operation. The creature who had performed the surgery to attach this thing had removed the staples and wire that had held the flesh in place the next day. The tissue of this alien hand had begun to bond with Craven's flesh within twenty four hours. The energies in the hand had restored his ability to speak, but whenever he opened his mouth to utter words, they came out clumsily, as if he were learning to speak for the first time. The hand was responsible for his successful return to the city. He felt the hand was *speaking* to him. Not in some telepathic voice, but through strong urges to concentrate his energy either this way or that. He remembered focusing on returning to New Broken Edge with such fervor that, in an instant, he remembered his very being evaporating as his molecules flew apart. In another moment, he felt the rush of his particles as they slammed into each other once more, reforming into his solid body, and he fell from a two story window into an alley. The landing was less than pleasant, but the after effects of teleportation were worse. He rolled over just in time to spray a fountain of vomit next to the dumpster he had landed next to.

That was two days ago. He wondered about in the streets, trying out whatever urge the hand impressed upon him. Many things it urged him to do were things he could already do quite well. Things that before his new hand, required him to concentrate heavily just to maintain the energy needed to perform whatever arcane feat he attempted. Now it seemed he could do it innately, without massive amounts of concentration. He had managed to appear in the minds of strangers he met as a longtime friend, which led to him scoring a free meal now and then. Even though his pronunciation of certain words and syllables were disgraceful, those under the charms of his new hand didn't appear to notice. The last time he had performed that illusion, he nearly blacked out as he struggled to maintain it. With the searing pain of the hunter's mark on his old hand, he still had managed to appear in the minds of the two officers that arrested him as another person entirely. Craven thought the looks on their faces would have been priceless had he not been clinging to every ounce of will power he could harness to keep the illusion up. The person that emerged from the back of the squad car that night hadn't broken any laws, hadn't had their rights read to them. Hence, the cops had no reason to legally hold the acne ridden ginger nerd that stepped out of their car, cuffed and looking confused as hell. Craven smirked as he recalled those details. Once they had released him and he had gotten far enough away, *that* had been when he ran into the freak Father had sent to retrieve him. The one who performed the amputation.

He let his eyes travel to take in the view of the street. Trees were stripped bare, and the branches blew about violently in the strong wind. This residential area sat nestled behind the Hispanic owned furniture store on Velvet Avenue. Streetlight poles stood like sentinels, guarding the houses of the common homeowners. This street was known for having the wildest, craziest set up for Halloween in town. One family even sold decorations out of their garage. Craven walked slowly down the street, looking at the different decorations on people's houses and in the yards. He rarely ever left any dwelling he stayed in during daylight hours. The heavy cloud cover was a mercy. Being out in the light of day felt so foreign to him.

Time eluded him, or rather, his sense of time did. He couldn't tell. After using the hand's ability to teleport him anywhere he focused on in the blink of an eye, things like the passing of time seemed irrelevant. His new hand buzzed with a burning sensation. The more he focused on it, he felt the hand twitch as if signals from a different brain altogether were commanding it to do so. But more importantly, he felt like the hand was leading him somewhere, and like a bloodhound on a leash, he could only follow the scent. Without warning, as if whatever source of stimuli the hand was seeking had been found, the burning sensation returned. That creature had done an excellent job at reattaching his nerve endings alright, because Craven *felt* it. It was as if there had been a surge of power that had been building up within the foreign tissue of the thing, only to be ignited in his hand once he reached a certain destination. The hand wiggled its way out of his pocket, causing the rest of him to cooperate in kind. He followed the path it roamed out in front of him with his gaze. He looked like a blind man groping the air in front of him, until it stopped in front of one of the highly decorated houses just a few yards ahead of him.

Halloween decorations stood in the yard—mannequins dressed up as horror movie icons and even a few that were done up after no particular character, but just made to look menacing. *Freddy Krueger* stood on the porch, and *Ghost Face* hovered next to the mailbox, knife raised and ready to strike. A scarecrow sat on the bench in the yard, wearing no hat, an oil stained mechanic's shirt with a name patch embroidered over the left breast pocket, steel-toed work boots, and gardening gloves on each hand. Fake human head replicas made from ballistics gel dangled from the tree limbs above, swaying and knocking against each other in the wind. He could feel the hand pulling him toward this yard. As he approached, he couldn't help but be awed by the scarecrow on the bench. Its frame looked perfectly human. Almost like an actual person dressed up and sitting there, waiting to scare trick or treaters as they passed by. But the thing was completely motionless. Craven watched the chest for any signs of breath. He didn't see any. Normally, yard scarecrows had very rigid frames and were normally constructed out of scrap materials. Whoever had made this one had put some serious time and effort into it. A true labor of love. Craven bent down and with his true hand, picked up a small rock, and chucked it at the thing's head. The rock struck home, knocking the thing on the head with a solid *conk!* It sure didn't sound like the muffled thump of a person's noggin. If he had to guess, Craven would have thought wood. Moments passed without a reaction from the thing. Watching it so intently, Craven thought he saw the thing twitch once or twice, but whatever phantom twitch he thought he saw as refuted by the wind blowing the loose parts of its garments.

The alien hand continued to reach out, feeling the air as if it were feeling some invisible object.

8:34 pm, that evening,

Jack Cramer pushed the broom along in his two car garage, sweeping the wood chips and sawdust into neat piles. He looked back at his work bench briefly, reminiscing on the past year and a half. That was the table his baby had been assembled on. After spending a whole year and a half on that scarecrow, carving the separate pieces that made up the body, all the ball joints and each individual joint of all ten fingers and ten toes, right down to the movable jaw, it was hard to believe he had finished it yesterday.

After the kids had grown up and left for college, he and his wife of thirty eight years, Margarete, had taken up various hobbies. She knitted on occasion, made cute crafts that she hung around the house. He had played golf and gone fishing on the weekends with the guys, but that was during their kids' freshmen year away at college. His carpentry skills had been what he always returned to. After selling off the countless birdhouses, toy fire engines, and rocking chairs, he thought he could feel burnout creeping in through the back door. What he didn't realize was, it was new inspiration. He chuckled to himself, imagining the Blue Fairy from the movie *Pinocchio* appearing to him in his garage to make his scarecrow into a real boy.

The kids had always loved Halloween. And, having raised Carrie and Mark, their two twins, on this street into their teens, they had often taken part in the festivities each year of making their house one of the scariest on the block. One thing Jack had always been fascinated by and terrified of all at once, were scarecrows. When his new wave of inspiration hit him, the theme of the street had been a creepy corn field. And he knew he could make a better scarecrow than any of his neighbors. Granted the creepy corn field had been a couple years ago, so he was late to the party. But it was on display outside right now.

Jack stopped sweeping, almost completely motionless for a whole minute. Something about this garage no longer felt safe. His eyes dared a chance upward to look around. He saw the fishing gear and his red tool cabinet on the wall directly in front of him. His four poles were mounted over his tools where his tackle box sat. He turned slowly, continuing to sweep, but slower this time. The pickup was behind him, parked neatly in its own place. The darkness from the wall on the other side of the pickup shifted vaguely out of the corner of his eye. He turned to face it fully.

"Come out or I call the cops!" He barked, the volume in his voice causing gooseflesh to blossom on his arms. The icy grip of dread encapsulated him. Calling out and acknowledging whatever it was only confirmed that whatever it was, *could* actually be there. And the nanosecond it would have taken for an intruder to give some form of compliance seemed like the split second before diving out of a plane without a parachute. Yet nothing happened, and the longer he stood there, the more exposed he felt. He gripped the broom handle tight, and he quickly and quietly switched out his broom for the shovel that was leaning next to the tool cabinet, then he quietly stalked over to investigate between the pickup and the opposite wall. He only saw the ice coolers and his golf bag shoved in a corner. He lowered the shovel and sighed deeply, his mind still not convinced. He looked up and roamed around the garage some more. If anyone was hiding in here, they would have to be under the truck. He got down on all fours and checked. Sure enough, not a soul.

He didn't have the foggiest idea where that sensation came from just now. He wasn't particularly sensitive to those things, but he guessed there was a first time for everything. Was he going senile?

"I like your scarecrow." A voice whispered behind him.

He felt the nerve's in his fingers tighten as he spun around as is heart felt like it had stopped in his chest for a moment. The act of turning to face the voice so quickly nearly made him feel light headed.

There was a figure sitting on the workbench where the scarecrow had been carved, legs dangling almost to the floor. It had a skinny, lean build, cloaked in the trappings of a filthy black hoody. The figure looked like a homeless young man in his early twenties. He had one hand shoved into the pouch-pocket on his hoodie, and his other hand resting on one knee, each individual finger a different length, and all seeming to bend at the joints with disturbing ease.

"W-who the hell are you?!" Jack yelled, instinctually backing up as he yelled out the question. The figure didn't answer him. Instead, the fluorescent bulbs hanging over the work bench flickered. When they came back on, the figure stood right before him.

"Someone who needs to borrow it." The young man said. His eyes were two bulging black orbs and the skin around them was a diseased looking gray-ish blue. Black veins and arteries could be seen beneath the discolored skin around the black eyes. Jack was frozen in place. Not from fear, but literally, he could not move a muscle.

Anger had replaced any thoughts of fear, and he tried to move his hands to fend off this intruder. But he felt the invisible coiling of some unseen force constricting his limbs. He felt his vision getting dark. He thrashed about in-side of the invisible grasp that had wrapped around him like a boa constrictor, and his heart came up in his throat.

"I also need to burrow *this*," the young man said, as each finger on the one hand suddenly straightened out with a wet cracking noise. The next thing Jack felt was more like a battering ram hitting his chest full force, but with the precision of a knife. His vision blacked out for a second, and when it came back, he could see the young man's arm, buried inside of his own chest! The intruder with the hoodie withdrew his arm, and in his hand, he held the pul-sating heart of Jack Cramer.

"Now he can become a *real boy!*" The intruder gave a knowing sneer and winked, as the force that constricted Jack loosened, and his body fell limp to the concrete.

MY NAME IS

Craven stood over the corpse on the garage floor. There was a lot blood, but not as much as there could have been had the heart stayed inside to pump the rest of it out. As it was, the spongy organ was throbbing in his new hand, its essence spurting out of it with each subsequently weakening pulse.

Suddenly, holding a man's heart in his hand, and standing over that same man's dead body in his garage, Craven began to panic. The legal implications of what he'd just done weren't at the forefront of his mind. He was above that. But it was the karmic implications of what he'd just done.

Do as ye will, harm no one. The creed of witches throughout time echoed through his head as his breathing quickened. He had used his magic to drive people mad, summoning the Little Outsiders to do his Father's bidding, but never had he directly killed someone.

I am ascending, he reminded himself, *I am becoming karma. Father has promised me the gift of ascension. It is I and his coven who will dictate the workings of karma on those we feel are deserving. Because we are karma!*

He kept repeating this in his head like a mantra for some time, trying miserably to convince himself. It was then he felt an invisible, yet familiar pull toward the garage door, and so just like before with the hand's many urgings, he followed the pull. Not to lift up the garage door and duck under it. He kept walking. The garage door came up to meet him, and he kept walking. He felt the touch of the garage door on his face become as cool and as intangible as a wall of fog, and he pressed his body through it, emerging on the other side into the empty driveway. This is how he got into the garage as well, so the urging was familiar. His eyes nervously scanned the yard, his mind questioning whether this was the correct house or not. His eyes suddenly landed on the bench where his prize was sitting. He began making his way to the yard but suddenly stopped. A lot of houses had motion sensors that activated their porch lights. He had no way of knowing if this house did though. It became apparent to Craven right then just how badly he had failed to prepare. He stood there frozen, unsure of what to do. Then he felt another nudge to keep going.

So he walked. He entered the front yard, stepping around the various mannequins that were dressed to kill, until he stood in front of the scarecrow on the bench. Upon closer inspection he could make out more details of the face—or what passed as a face. A burlap sack was stretched over the head, and two uneven holes were cut out for the eyes. A very obvious grin stretched inhumanly from one side of the head to the other, each end stopping where the ears should be. Straw poked out of the stitches in various places, not just on the head, but other places too. Craven reached out his true hand and knocked on the thing's head. Solid, but well insulated with straw. He looked around at the other houses. The street seemed oddly deserted, despite him seeing lights on in the other houses. But even that didn't stop his immediate feeling of being exposed. He was standing in these people's front yard after all.

He fought through the paranoia that he would be seen in a passing vehicle's headlights, or that someone would walk out on their front porch. Then he realized if he stood still, any who did happen to see him would probably mistake him for another mannequin.

He held out the heart of his victim over the scarecrow. The hand squeezed, and the blood gushed out of it. It splattered the scarecrow's face, down the chest, and ran down Craven's arm. The hand kept tightening its grip on the organ, until every drop had run out onto the scarecrow or down Craven's arm and into his sleeve.

Then the hand threw the organ away, over the fence to the right and into the neighbor's yard. Craven felt his eyes return to pitch black. Two orbs of darkness there in his skull were fixed on the motionless thing before him. He knelt down on one knee to the scarecrow's level. He placed his hands on its chest and began reciting an incantation, fervent, like a prayer. He didn't know how he knew this incantation. His only guess in that moment was that the hand itself was speaking through him, using his vocal chords as their instrument. He could feel them moving in ways that weren't humanly possible.

Sweat began pouring from his face. He felt his skin burning. Then suddenly the incantation stopped. Against Craven's will, he leaned forward, and blew on the scarecrow. A shimmer of what looked like heat, like one sees dancing on hot asphalt in the summer, spewed from his mouth and washed over the scarecrow.

It was then that Craven collapsed into oblivion.

Sometime later,

He didn't know how long he had been out of it. All he knew was that his head felt like there was a civil war between two demolition crews raging inside of his skull. Craven fought through the grogginess that clouded his senses, dragging himself back to awareness in the waking world.

He felt a cool breeze blowing over him, which helped to pull him from the grasp of the infinite beyond of sleep. When his eyes opened fully, he saw where he was. He was inside someone's house, laying on the floor. He heard the hardwood floorboards creak under his weight. He looked towards the source of the breeze. What appeared to be the front door to this place was standing wide open. The paneling on the doorpost where the deadbolt would be was obliterated. He focused his eyes on the yard outside. There were mannequins dressed like horror movie icons, and an empty bench. That's when a rush of a thick, wet stench clogged his nose, and he almost dry heaved.

Suddenly everything came rushing back to him. Craven recalled the man in the garage whose heart he had taken, and the scarecrow that had been sitting outside on the bench. The overpowering stench was coppery in nature. He rose to his feet, half looking like a drunkard. He looked at his blood covered, strange hand. It wasn't spazzing like it had been since his recovery from the operation. The sight of it hanging by his side, seemingly resting, but not limp, was a welcome relief. Yet it didn't stop him from feeling like the hand was aware of his glance. Still it remained relaxed. His eyes had adjusted enough to the dark that he could make out the shapes of over turned furniture, and obliterated picture frames that littered the hallway into what

Craven assumed was the kitchen. He listened. Despite the breeze floating in from the open front door, all seemed as still as the congealed blood in a dead man's veins. He treaded lightly through the hall, trying not to crunch broken glass underfoot as he walked toward the kitchen. As he got closer he noticed the faint slivers of moonlight that were washing in the kitchen through the window above the sink. Cabinet doors had been flung open, and their contents spilled onto the linoleum floor. Broken dishes were everywhere. Torn open bags of spices, cereal and rice were strewn about all over the floor and countertops. There was a light coming in from an adjacent doorway. Probably the garage. The light from the garage illuminated a bloody heap on the floor, covered in horrid lacerations so deep the bones were showing. There lay the body of what appeared to have been an elderly woman, her blood matted hair mercifully covering her face.

Craven listened again as his ears picked up the faint sound of something moving out in the garage. It sounded wet, like someone was slapping a hard surface with a wet paintbrush. He eased forward, carefully stepping over the body of the woman, and sliding one eye up to the crack in the door leading out into the garage.

There out in the garage, crawling all over the body of the fallen man who had been its creator, was the scarecrow. It's unmoving, stitched grin almost seemed real. Its gloved hands pawed all over the dead body, sticking its fingers down into the cavity where his heart had been. It slinked off of him like a cat, moving to put its hands to smear the blood into the concrete. It slapped the pavement of the garage floor gleefully, like it had found something it was looking for. It was then Craven knew he had seen the grin move. The scarecrow crawled around on all fours, its joints shaky and bending at impossible angles that only circus performers could achieve, until its back was turned to Craven.

In all his magical practices, Craven had never given a semblance of life to an inanimate object. He had heard of such spells. Ones that could animate the dead were the most common ones he had researched, but never explored first hand.

The scarecrow stopped suddenly, its movement so sharp it made Craven flinch. It knew it was being watched. The thing slowly turned its head back toward the door, and with it, its torso. The two holes cut in the burlap to form its eyes seemed to shift almost like there were actual muscles beneath the burlap controlling their movement.

"Blood memory," it said, its wooden jaw moving beneath the burlap, "Female inside…wrong blood." After it had pawed around on the ground some more, it attempted to stand. Its joints shook unsteadily, not used to movement yet. It looked like it was concentrating its every effort into staying upright. It reached its gloved hand up and ran a bloody finger over the embroidered name patch over the left breast.

"Jaaaaack," It said, dragging out the name, as if it liked the sound of it, "My name…is…Jaaaaack."

CONFESSIONS

It was true what they said, about not knowing how to properly appreciate something until you are deprived of it. While a big chunk of his time in captivity was a blur of darkness behind his eyelids, Mick never felt so grateful for the luxury of hot water washing through his tangled mess of hair as he did right at this minute. And soap! Mana from Heaven! He had begun to shower twice a day just to get the body odor smell out of his flesh. If it had not been for the fact that these people kept clocks in various rooms of this place, he would have lost track of time altogether.

According to Valerie (if she could be trusted, and right now that was debatable) it was the twentieth when he woke up in this place. Since he was obsessive about keeping time by constantly making mental notes each time he glanced at a clock, he guessed that it was going on sixty three hours, so he had been here just a little over two and a half days. So it had to be the twenty third of October.

He surmised that Parish and Zach had regular jobs of some sort, because they always left at a certain time every morning and returned after four, sometimes six in the evening. Valerie he knew about, since he worked with her. She kept to her normal schedule of 10:00 PM to 7:00 AM. In fact, it was because of Valerie he even knew when it was morning and evening. The clocks down in this place were old, 90's office wall clocks that Mick was surprised even worked. The others, Judah and Brandon, came and went at will, with seemingly no predictability to their schedules.

He had met two other prisoners here. Two teenagers, a boy and a girl both around fifteen years old. The girl said her real name was Sunny, but she had gone by Skylah. The boy was Oscar Ramirez, who he later learned had been the lycanthrope that had turned in the high school auditorium the night of the town assembly. They didn't consider themselves prisoners here with the hunters though. In fact they both agreed that they were safest right where they were and that the hunters were looking out for them.

Yep, classic Stockholm syndrome, Mick thought. Probably because they had something done to them, as was evident by the glowing patches of muscle that lit up underneath the girl's skin from time to time just like the hunters. It was because of this, the possibility that something might be done to him in his sleep, that Mick was only surviving on three to four hours of sleep at a time.

His right hand wiped the layer of condensation from the mirror. Whatever this place was, or had been, it was well furnished. It was basically a huge survival bunker big enough to support up to twenty or so people. He wiped his face with the towel before wrapping it around his waist. When he glanced in the mirror he paused for a brief moment. His reflection seemed…off.

He stepped closer to the mirror and studied his face. He touched his chin with his fingertips, and rubbed firmly. Was it a trick of the lighting in this room, compounded by the fog from the shower? He wiped the rest of the mirror and rubbed his cheek.

His skin had a graying hue to it, almost like he had stepped out of an old black and white film reel from the twenties. He grabbed the rag from the shower, looked back into the mirror and scrubbed furiously, trying to get it off. Was there something in the water?

He dropped the rag and began rummaging around through his jeans. The hunters had somehow recovered his wallet, and thankfully, everything in it was intact. He pulled his driver's license from the sleeve. His picture stared back up at him, with that same blank and generic expression that one usually sports for their ID's. His skin had the same grayish pigmentation as it did in the mirror. He set his driver's license on the sink and dug around in his wallet some more for his state ID. His hair was slightly shorter in this picture but it was his face—with the same grayish skin tone.

Had he looked like this the whole time? Memories flashed back to his childhood. He remembered the photos in his parents' photo album. He remembered his memories of looking at the pictures of himself, and as if a curtain had been lifted from his mind, he recalled the gray skin tone that he possessed in every one of them. He remembered the video his mother had taken of his tenth birthday. He, George and everyone in the video had gray skin. Yet his mind was playing that little snippet like it was a long lost detail of the event. If it was a trick of the camera then sure that could be blamed on technology. But when Mick looked down at his arm, still glistening wet from the shower, he couldn't just pass it off as an optical illusion.

Yet when he looked at the color of his flesh, another feeling began to well up inside of him. A feeling that told him he was being a total idiot for wondering whether or not his skin had really always been like this or not. Most people he knew looked like this. He thought back to Chief Scroggins. He was a bit darker gray than Mick but not by much. George too, but he was about as light a gray as Mick had ever seen.

Why was it just now striking Mick in such a way that he was noticing it? He ran his hands through his wet hair, eyes looking back and forth from his ID photos back to the mirror.

"I'm losing it…" He whispered to himself.

"Johnson," A voice from behind him startled him.

"WHAT?!" Mick yelled, whirling around to see young Oscar standing there. Oscar had his own towel slung over his shoulder, a bar of soap in one hand, and was wearing a pair of swimming trunks. His eyes were a shade of bright gold that looked hungrily at Mick. They didn't look like that when he first met him. Sure Mick knew what he was but it didn't stop the unnerving feeling that he was potential prey. And his skin—it wasn't gray like Mick's and everyone else he knew. It was a lighter, tan complexion. Come to think of it…Was Valerie's skin gray? He couldn't remember, and right now, he didn't care. If this thing attacked, Mick would go down swinging. Even if he lost an arm.

"Didn't mean to startle you. Judah says he needs to talk to you when you are done." Oscar said moving into the showers and finding one that was partitioned off from Mick.

"Yeah well Judah can wait till I can get my heart put back in my chest." Mick snapped.

Oscar ignored him. Mick saw the towel and the swimming trunks slap over the edge of the partition like empty flour sacks as the showerhead came on.

About fifteen minutes later Mick found Judah in an odd spot. Parish had to guide him through the various halls of mounted weaponry, passed the surveillance center with a bunch of glowing monitors, passed the research center, where Zach sat pouring over some old leather-bound tomes of some ancient lore, to a small bar. An actual, honest to God bar was down here. There was a beer tap, and various bottles of liquor lined the wall behind the bar. Judah sat at the bar, his back as sturdy as two barn doors, stretching beneath his white t shirt. He wore a shoulder holster, which from the looks of it was holding a Ruger SR40, tactical, fire retarded pants with various pockets of all sizes and a utility belt around his waist.

"Have a seat," Judah said as he glanced back at Mick. Mick nodded reluctantly and did so, his eyes being drawn to all the various liquors.

"You got any Mic Ultra?" Mick asked, apprehensive that this place would actually have anything he would drink. But hell, he had been drinking their water since he got here, and he was still alive, all things considered.

Judah let the liquid in his glass pass down his throat and then pointed toward a small mini fridge in the corner to the left, "Valerie said it was your favorite. She had me pick some up for you last night."

Mick slid off the bar stool and walked around the bar to the small fridge and gave the door a good tug. Cans of Mic Ultra lined the doorway. There was some other kinds there too but nothing he was craving at the moment. He took one in his hand. It was ice cold to the touch. He said a quick silent prayer of gratitude to whoever was listening, popped the tab, and took a swig.

I'll be damned, Mick thought.

Mick made his way back around and sat next to Judah on his stool. While he still didn't trust these people, he wasn't going to turn down his favorite beer.

"Tell Valerie I said thanks next time you see her," Mick said finishing another swig. Judah nodded, keeping his eyes on his own drink.

"She's sorry she had to lie to you," Judah said. Mick closed his eyes and nodded.

When Mick opened his eyes and glanced at Judah again, he noticed his skin tone wasn't gray like his. Had he been like that the whole time? He shot a glance over his shoulder. Zach was white with a little hint of red in his cheeks.

"Do I look gray to you?" Mick asked, suddenly feeling like he was naked in front of his third grade teacher. Judah looked at him curiously, and then regarded Mick for a little while. Was it registering in his head? Did he have to think about this?

"Yeah you do. Why?"

"Why am I the only gray one here?" Mick asked, "I mean…Shit I don't know what I mean. It's not so much the fact that I'm gray. It's…It's that I-"

"You're just noticing it?" Judah finished for him. Mick felt his face sag like a deflated ball.

"Yeah. Like it was never a thing before."

"That means you're aware of your taint," Judah said. Mick slowly turned to look at him. All he could muster was a stupefied, unfitting, "*What?*"

Judah slid his empty glass down the bar away from him and looked at Mick.

"You've always looked like this. You're right about that. Everyone you know, they all look like you too. They just may or may not know it." Judah said.

"So it's normal to look like you? Is that it? And we're all just a bunch of freaks?" Mick growled defensively.

Judah chuckled and slapped the bar, which made Mick jump. His eyes flashed white again and his eyelids lit up red around his eyes as he turned to Mick.

"No Johnson…To look like you is the normal of this world. *We* are the freaks." Judah said.

Mick thought back to Sunny and Oscar. Granted Oscar was a werewolf, so in Mick's mind he didn't totally count, but there was Sunny.

"So Sunny, was she always like you guys? Or did you turn her into a freak like you?" Mick asked.

"She was gray skinned when we found her. Same as Zach over there, Parish, all of us," Judah said. "I don't know how it works, but the taint is part of this reality. No lore has anything on it. As far as we know, people have always looked like this. So in that regard, you look as normal as the next person down the street."

"So then why is it called a taint?" Mick scowled. First he has every ounce of control taken away from him, now he is being called tainted? Inferior?

"This stuff," Judah said, holding up his hand as the veins in his palm began to glow, "is the agent that caused us to look like this. It strengthens our connection to Yeshua. Once you have this stuff flowing through you, the world looks different. It *feels* different. You start to see things you never noticed before. Things that most people just ignore—and you know that those things *don't belong.*"

Mick watched the glowing veins beneath Judah's skin, fascinated, "How does it work?" He asked.

"It helps us see in the dark, see monsters hiding in human form, helps heal injuries. It also increases our reflexes and metabolism, which helps us to stay more fit. This stuff needs a healthy body to reside in. If we don't stay active in some form or another, it'll drive us crazy. Like an itch in that one spot you never knew you had but just can't reach. If we go longer than two days without at least an hour of deliberate, physical exercise, this stuff won't be as potent. That's why you see a lot of us either sparring, working out or anything else that's super physically oriented. It not only helps us stay sharp as hunters, but it helps this stuff not to go dim." Judah said.

"And it also hurts monsters," Mick added. Judah nodded.

"And it's also the conduit for how Yeshua talks to us."

"Okay, I've heard you people mention this Yeshua off and on since I got here. Who the hell is he?" Mick asked. He hadn't noticed until now that his beer was half gone.

"Yeshua is Aramaic. It's the name given to the Son of God in the original language the angel would have spoken to the Virgin Mary. You would know him better as Jesus Christ." Judah said.

Suddenly this all made sense, and confirmed one of Mick's theories. He had been taken in by a cult.

"…I see." Mick said, "And the radioactive juice in your veins, he gives that to you guys?"

"He does." Judah said. This sick bastard actually believed what he was saying.

"And how does he do that?" Mick asked, the tone of a practiced skeptic rising in his voice.

"It's a rather painful process that involves your flesh getting burned off from the inside out. The pain is so intense you swear it can't actually be happening. In fact there isn't any pain at first, but when it sneaks up on you, it feels like being buried inside the core of the sun." Judah said.

Mick just sat there blinking until he took another gulp and finished off his beer. He got up and went to the mini fridge for another one. He was gonna need it.

"Well…Thank you for that hideous, and terrifying, description." Mick said.

"I didn't bring you over here to talk about this," Judah said. Mick popped the tab with a hiss and set the can down. He had seen to a degree what these people were capable of. If he was going to continue to survive, he had to humor them until he could find a way to escape. But then there was the problem of whatever was hunting him outside these walls.

"Okay," Mick said.

"The night we saved your ass from Terrance Miller, you mentioned the Broken Edge Massacre." Judah said. Mick's gaze traveled to meet his. If steel could turn to ice, Judah's gaze would make that happen. Mick felt his insides tense with an expectant dread. The kind of dread you get when you know someone has died and the police car out front only confirms your fear, sending you spiraling towards panic.

"1989. I had spent twelve years in Israeli Special Forces. Was honorably discharged after surviving a combat injury. Four years later I moved to the United States and began the process of getting dual citizenship. The day I got my letter in the mail congratulating me on my test scores, a Kansas Senator shows up on my doorstep, says he had a job for me. I had already had a brush with the supernatural in my time in the Middle East, so I knew this stuff was real. So with that in mind, his job offer didn't seem that strange to me. I and four other recruits attended several 'off the books' meetings with him and a few other senators in pubs and on golf courses. Project Homefront was a state level initiative to put together teams of individuals trained in battling supernatural threats." Judah said, stopping to caress the side of his drinking glass.

Mick's insides coiled with tension. He felt sweat forming on his brow. In his mind's eye he saw the faces of the hunters he idolized as a kid. He could recall vaguely the faces of four of them. There was one that for some reason was blurrier than the rest of them in his memory. And the tension inside only served to give him the deep chilling feeling that this man's face was the correct answer to the blank he was trying to fill.

"It was on the state level because no federal government would risk exposing a large scale supernatural presence to the public. Project Homefront started in Kansas with my team. It was meant to spread to the other forty nine states. After my team was established, two other teams were successfully planted in Oklahoma and Wyoming. My team…" he said, pausing momentarily. Not for effect though. It appeared like he was trying to gather himself.

"My team traveled across the state of Kansas for nine months, until we got to Broken Edge." He said, his eyes finally meeting Mick's. In that moment, the dam broke inside. But instead of a wrathful torrent of rage, all Mick could do was look away, clutch his beer can in his hands, and shut his eyes. He felt like a terrified animal trying to dig its way through the other side of its enclosure as the hand of a cruel owner drew closer and closer. He felt like he was five years old again, teetering on the edge of losing every ounce of control he had over his surroundings as they were invaded by tooth and claw.

"I didn't know what they were." Judah said. Mick chanced a look back at the hunter. His eyes were reddening, and his knuckles had gone white. Mick saw a hairline crack form in the glass Judah had in his hand.

"I swear if I had known what they were from the start, I would have ran the other way and never looked back. If I had known what road it would have taken me down, I would have slammed the door in that senator's face." His voice trembled with rage. Light flashed in a vein on the side of Judah's neck. Mick shot a glance over to where Zach was sitting, only to see he was gone. Mick hadn't realized it, but while Zach was there, he subconsciously felt at ease almost. Now that it was just the two of them, he felt like an animal of prey.

"The day that brought Broken Edge to its knees…And my team was responsible. *I*, was responsible for bringing them there. The day I found out what they were, I tried reporting back to my superiors. But before I could reach them I blacked out. I woke up sometime later. The city was already falling apart." He said.

Neither of them spoke for what seemed like an hour. Mick shot a nervous glance over his shoulder at the clock. It had only been five minutes.

"I don't deserve your forgiveness, so I'll spare you the trouble of having to listen to me ask for it," Judah said, drawing Mick back in.

"But from one survivor to another…I guess I want you to know that you don't have to be alone." He finished, and his grip on the glass eased up. "Also, about my old team…I've noticed some similarities with some references they made back in the day and what's going on with you. Right Hand, Bestowing of Gifts, and so on. I think this thing that calls itself Father might have been influencing them. If its back with its sight set on you, then you should keep that in mind next time you think of sneaking off," Judah said as he slide off of his barstool.

EXAMINATION

There was the pulsing of fire deep within her brain. She remembered the flaming Celtic cross that appeared to her.

"SIT DOWN!!!" Someone had yelled. It had been Zach, she remembered that at least. The words hit her in the chest like a wrecking ball, and she had flown back into her chair. At least that's where her body had stopped. When she opened her eyes, she saw her body laying limp in the chair where the hunters had restrained her earlier. The room they were all in was bathed with the white hot flames of a realm that had invaded her very being. From those flames, the Celtic cross formed, and out of that cross stepped a being that was far too tall to fit in the room, yet he stood unhindered by the ceiling that, in the material realm, would have made one of that size have to crawl on hands and knees. But in this realm, the being stood as a monolithic sentinel, his flaming gaze drilling deep into her core, burning away every layer of darkness that she dared hide beneath.

From the waist up, the figure was naked, and his torso, arms, and face all looked like steel that had been left to burn in the coals of a forge. But the metallic body only looked like a covering for the tempestuous storm that it contained. A storm that would set the cosmos ablaze should it choose to be released. The being's hair, if one could even call it that, looked like a turbulent bonfire. Lightning arcs flashed around the being with nearly every move it made. She couldn't see the entity's lower half. It was obscured by raging flames of every color under the sun. The flames almost appeared sentient in a way as well, and she thought she saw humanoid forms moving about in those flames. Yet there was a nagging suspicion in her brain that told her, this was but one form the being had adopted in order to appear to her.

And then it spoke her name. Her *true* name. The being did not refer to her coven name, Skylah. It called the name that was given to her at birth. The name this being had destined her to have since before the time of her very conception.

Sunny…

All memory of the meeting with the one the hunters called Yeshua faded when she heard her name. Sunny, formally Skylah, turned to see Judah standing in the doorway of her quarters. Upon hers and Oscar's Reclaiming, the hunters had allowed them to stay with them, and each were given their own room.

"Are you ready to go?" Judah asked. Sunny nodded quickly, threw on her new jacket (her entire outfit was new,) and followed Judah out into the dormitory of this underground fortress.

"Are you sure he won't sense me?" She asked. She knew only a taste of Yeshua's might, but here in the material plane where Father and his scions roamed about freely, she still needed the reassurance.

"Your presence is hidden from him for now. He will eventually sense you again, but now that you are Reclaimed, it will be a while before he even recognizes you." Judah said. Sunny took out a small pocket mirror she had bought when Valerie had taken her shopping for the new threads. She clicked it open to take another quick gander at her reflection. She still couldn't get over how pure her skin looked. After her entire lifetime of being one of the grayskins, and not even stopping to question why the people in her life looked the way they did…It was still hard to believe. In a way, her nervous glances into the mirror was her way of making sure it wasn't just a dream, and that the gray hadn't returned.

"So where are we going?" She asked as she followed him up a flight of stairs.

"Valerie's superior is on vacation, so she is holding down the fort at the County morgue, which will make it easier for us to go and check out two bodies that came in recently. An elderly couple was found murdered in their home yesterday." Judah said.

"So why take me?" Sunny asked.

"Two reasons. Number one, we think there could be a connection to the one called Father, and if that is the case, we were hoping you could identify its source for us. Reason number two is, you need to practice using your Higher

Sight. It's when our eyes do this," Judah said, stopping to look at her. His eyes were glowing. He blinked and the light was extinguished from inside his eye balls, like clicking off a lamp.

"You can just turn it off and on?" She asked, more amazed than thrown off guard.

Judah smiled, "It's more a matter of letting it take control of your faculties. We don't control it at all. Similar to how you became a vessel for dark energy when you were tainted. It's a lot like that, but you're playing for a different team."

Twenty minutes later, they were across town. Valerie met them at one of the back entrances, behind the building through an alley, and in less than five minutes, Sunny was staring at the bodies of an elderly couple, mutilated and cold.

"Jack Cramer, sixty-seven years old," Valerie said as she opened one of the cold storage units and pulled out the body on its slab. She undid the plastic covering and gestured to an ugly hole in the man's chest. Sunny winced and covered her mouth at the sight. The edges of the wound were black, and it looked puckered almost like a set of rotting black lips were trying to kiss the open air around them. Like something had forced its way into his chest and then was violently yanked out.

"He was found like this in his garage. His heart was found in the next door neighbor's yard. His wife, Margarete Cramer was found with severe lacerations all over her body, caused by a butcher knife which was discarded at the scene. The killer wore an old brand of gardening gloves that isn't even sold in stores anymore." Valerie said.

"Two different murders in the same house on the same night. Two different M.O.s. Are the police are looking for two different killers then?" Judah asked.

"That's the most likely scenario, although a single killer isn't being ruled out either. Mr. Cramer died about an hour to two hours before Mrs. Cramer was butchered, so there was ample time for a single killer to potentially commit both murders." Valerie said.

"You said the heart was found in the neighbor's yard?" Judah asked. Valerie nodded.

"Yes and had been subjected to intense stress after removal, like someone had squeezed it." Valerie confirmed.

Judah looked over at Sunny, "You ready?"

Sunny took a deep breath and nodded her head, closing her eyes. She took another deep breath and raised her hands up over the cavern in Mr. Cramer's chest.

"Am I supposed to feel something before it happens?" She asked opening her eyes. Judah shook his head.

"Sometimes you feel an intense heat spreading throughout your body. Other times it can feel like a jolt of electricity. It's different for everybody." Judah said. She nodded and shook her palms again.

"Remember, you aren't trying to *become* a vessel. You already are one," Valerie encouraged.

Sunny nodded. That was definitely a switch. Allowing dark forces to take control of her body had been a long process fraught with painful rituals and hours of meditation. This new life she had been given allowed her to just *be*.

She shuddered as a sudden chill swept through her. She looked down at her right hand—she could see a vein glowing just beneath the skin. Suddenly she noticed something trailing from the jagged edges of the puckered flesh around the gaping hole in Mr. Cramer's chest. The black gunk around the edges was shimmering and billowing with black smoke. It had worked!

"Guys are my eyes white?" She asked excitedly.

"They sure are!" Valerie praised.

"Great job!" Judah said.

Sunny tried to keep from squealing. She couldn't remember the last time she felt like such a giddy little girl. These new feelings she was experiencing nearly made her tear up, but she held the tears back as she took a deep breath.

"Anything about the energy coming from the wound?" Judah asked.

Sunny watched a column of black smoke as it curled around in thin wisps, rising upward and upward, but never completely dissipating. Suddenly an image flashed before her eyes, played out within the wisps of the smoke. A hooded figure driving their hand through this poor man's chest, and violently yanking the pulsating heart free. Holding the heart in a long spindly hand that looked like it belonged to a weathered old crone instead of a young man.

Then a face was revealed. She gasped and stepped back. A rush of heat spread through her, starting at her core and permeating every inch of her. She blinked rapidly and wiped her eyes as they readjusted to sight in the mundane world.

The face was that of her brother Craig, or as he had called himself for the past several years, Craven.

"What's wrong sweetie?" Valerie asked as she came close and extended her hand to her shoulder.

Sunny shook her head quickly, closing her eyes for a long time and taking long deep breaths.

"Um," She began, swallowing hard as she tried to keep from tearing up. What had become of her brother? He wasn't capable of ripping an organ from someone's body. And that hand. It wasn't a part of him. It couldn't be.

"My brother did this." She said.

"Your brother. The other member of Father's coven?" Judah asked.

Sunny nodded.

"Did you see anything else?" Judah asked.

"Only him pulling the heart from the man's chest." She said as a tear finally broke free from the well in her eyes and raced down her cheek, "And the hand that he held the heart in. It didn't look like his hand." She said.

"Go on," Judah pressed.

"I-it looked like…The fingers were too long. The fingers each could have made almost two of mine in length. It didn't even look like a real hand. I just saw it in a quick flash in the smoke." She said.

"Okay. You've done good work Sunny," Judah said and then turned to Valerie, "Thanks for working this out babe."

"No problem dearest," She said as she kissed him on the cheek.

INTRUSION

Mick sat at the bar, and by now the empty beer can that was clutched his hands for some time was now an aluminum heap. It had been about forty minutes since Judah's confession to him. The dread that had been coiling around Mick's spine had turned to a hellish icy fist that froze him in place. He could not move as scenes from that day replayed over and over on the big screen of his mind's eye, dull and faded in color like an old reel of film.

He remembered the sky being overcast that day, which added to the oppressive grayness of his memory all the more when his school building lost power. Most of the kids shrieked and were terrified as his homeroom was plunged into the darkness. Although Mick was screaming too, he was just doing it because he thought the other kid's reaction was funny and had been trying to egg it on. He remembered waiting with his class mates for his mom to pick him up. It didn't take terribly long for people to realize that the entire city had lost power. Though they weren't terribly common then, a good handful of people in Broken Edge could afford a cell phone, his parents being among them. It was one of the bulky flip phones with the wiggly antenna. Mom and dad would take turns on who would have the cell phone during the week. It was his mother who had rolled up in the car to pick him up that day. A trivial detail but it was something he remembered.

He remembered how quiet the house was when he and his mother walked through the door. No TV, no underlying hum coming from the refrigerator, no clicking of the second hand on the clock in the kitchen. On cloudy days mom would usually turn the hall light and the kitchen light on to help with lighting up the house. Mick wasn't terribly afraid of the dark but she had a constant fear that if he couldn't see then he would trip over something and get hurt. But now that the power was down, she couldn't do that. And so, while not initially afraid of the dark, Mick recalled how hungry that hallway leading to his room looked. His room, even after he pulled back the curtains to let in some light, still felt like a gray mausoleum.

There was one other detail he remembered. As he sat and pondered it though, he couldn't recall if it had been real at the time or if he was imagining it, but it persisted whenever he let himself get lost in his memories.

It was close to the end of the school year, and for most of his young life the month of May had been pretty dependable as far as weather was concerned. Warm temperatures in the upper seventies and eighties were the norm, and for that year they had been as well. But not on that day. He thought he remembered feeling a chill in his memories as he walked down his dark, family portrait adorned hallway toward his gray, dull room. Even his toys that littered the floor, which his father had been pestering him to put away, seemed…dead. Yes they were toys, but to Mick they were living soldiers that protected his room. The hunters were super heroes that defended his city, like *Batman* and the *Power Rangers*. His toy *Transformers* and *Ninja Turtles* and *G.I. Joes* defended the Homefront of his room. Also he had a few *Star Wars* toys in the mix too. But today everything seemed so two-dimensional.

"Optimus, talk to me please?" Mick heard his younger voice echo through his head as he relived the memory in first person view. His Optimus Prime action figure lay motionless in his hands as he shook it.

"Donatello?" Mick asked, grabbing another action figure. No answer.

Dad came home sometime after that. Said the computers at work were down cause of the power and so everyone in the office got sent home since nobody could do any work.

Suddenly the mental landscape of his room was pitch black and he was in bed, his toys littering the floor around his bed. Little Mick sat up with a sudden jerk, as if he was a flimsy puppet pulled about by a host of strings. A banging on the front door that was so loud, it hammered all the way from the living room, down the hall, and into his chest. *That* had startled him awake.

His dad soon came running down the hall in his underwear, so fast it made Mick scream until it registered in his head that it was his father.

"Mick!"

His father's voice was changing, and his eyes were glowing. Mick blinked. Parish Larson had his hand on Mick's shoulder and was shaking him free of the confines of his memories. The hunter's face was beaded with sweat, the collar of his black undershirt a wet bib of sweat that stretched down his chest. His eyes were glowing and the veins beneath his skin flashed like lightening.

"Something's here." He said, like he was fighting to catch his breath. He was holding his left side, his hand covering up a wound that glowed around the edges as if an atomic light ball were about to spill out. Thick red blood however, ran between his fingers.

Mick wasn't sure how long he looked at Parish's bloody hand before he felt Parish's other hand grab him by the shirt and haul him off the bar stool.

"What happened to you? Where are the others?" Mick gasped, finally once it sank in that he was being drug along.

"It's Zach and me," he panted, "Judah and Sun-shine are out on a little errand, and so are Brandon and Oscar. Just us holding down the fort." He said as his other hand finally released Mick's shoulder. Parish removed his hand and looked down at the swath of flesh that had been sliced away from his side just above his left hip.

"What did this?!" Mick demanded. Parish's other hand clamped itself over Mick's mouth as Parish brought up a bloody finger to his own, his eyes burning white hot like two orbs of fire.

"Whatever's down here can hear just like you an me. You. Be. Quiet." He said. The sound of hurried, yet suppressed foot falls came around the corner. They both turned to see Zach coming around the corner, bandoleers of shotgun shells slung over his chest and a shotgun in each hand. Zach handed one to Parish, and draped one of the bandoleers of shells around his neck, letting him slide into it. Parish winced when the belt brushed up against his bleeding side.

"Did you get a good look at it?" Zach asked. Parish shook his head, "Nah bro. It was too fast."

"Is it the thing that's been following me?" Mick whispered to Zach, since according to Mick's knowledge he was the only one of the hunters who had ever seen it.

"No I don't think so." Zach said as they started off down through the research area.

"You don't *think so?*" Mick asked, nearly losing his composure.

"You really want to get snarly with us now?" Zach asked as he jerked the forearm of the gun and chambered a round.

Well now that you mention it… Mick thought to himself.

"Why don't I get a gun?" Mick asked. Zach stopped and let out a heavy sigh, and then for a couple seconds looked up at the ceiling. Mick saw one of his hands move toward the gun he had tucked into his belt and removed it. He turned to Mick and held out the firearm by the slide, glaring at him. Despite the circumstances, Mick felt a small surge of euphoric triumph over Zach's begrudging compliance. He reached out and took the weapon, looked it over quickly as they started to move again, and turned off the safety.

"You stay close," Zach said, his eyes beginning to light up.

Squeeze the trigger, don't pull. Squeeze, Mick kept reminding himself. He was reminded of the shooting houses he had gone through with pop up cardboard targets, some painted to look like hostiles with weapons, and others who were unarmed civilians. His reaction time to each target as it had popped up was among the top in the class. His discernment of civilians from hostiles however left a lot to be desired. He passed just by a nose hair.

The three men proceeded quickly but lightly, Zach with the stock pressed firmly into his shoulder, sweeping the area before him like a spot light. Mick kept his gun drawn up in both hands by his ear. Parish was staying a couple steps behind, keeping a watchful eye on the dark spaces between the gun cabinets and work benches.

How could either of them not know what had gotten down here? They knew that Mick had been marked, whatever that meant, and was being followed by something, and they still thought bringing him to their hideout was a good idea? How could Parish not have seen what had attacked him? It would have to have gotten pretty close for it to have taken a slab of skin off. How could something get that close and the victim *not* have seen it? But then Mick had to remember, people get attacked all the time and under certain conditions, can't describe their attacker. He kept trying to think like a cop, trying to become cold and detached from the fact that something was down here with him. It could distract him from the gnawing parasite of dread that was telling him he had seen something move in the dark down the hallway they had just passed, even though Zach and Parish both had already inspected it. It would have taken his mind off of the fact that he could hear a faint noise coming from up ahead that sounded like the whimper of something caught in a trap.

Zach halted a few steps ahead of them, and held up his fist. They all listened.

"What the hell is that?" Mick whispered.

Zach stood silent and still for a couple more seconds, "That sounds like a dog," He whispered over his shoulder.

They all listened a bit longer. Mick's blood felt like ice cold mud in his veins. The terrified squeals, whines and howls of whatever it was made Mick feel like every skin cell he had was crawling from a frozen cauldron and clinging to him like an icy wet towel.

They crept forward and followed Zach as he slowly turned the corner. When Mick and Parish came around, Mick froze. Tied up to the handle of a filing cabinet that was over in the surveillance area, was a tiny Boxer puppy that couldn't have been more than six weeks old. A piece of twine had been tied so tight around one of the poor thing's back legs that it's fur was caked with blood. It frantically moved its head back and forth from its little leg, trying to gnaw at the twine with the little nubs that were in its mouth.

The sight of the little pup tore Mick's mind to shreds. Yes, the fact that it was so young and had been cruelly tied up here and left to struggle was horrifying in and of itself, but it only solidified his angst even more that there was something else down here. Or someone. Regardless, whatever had tied up this little pup knew enough about how to tie a knot. Zach rushed forward, withdrew a mean looking karambit from his belt and cut through the twine in one quick jerk.

"Shh shh shhh…calm down little guy, I gotcha," Zach said as he laid the shotgun down and scooped up the dog in both hands. Its cries of panic rose in volume as Zach picked it up and cradled it to his chest before he handed it to Mick.

"Yep, you're a boy," Zach said as he handed the pup over to Mick.

Oh thanks, you're gonna hand me the screaming puppy while we are being hunted, Mick thought.

Parish suddenly brought the barrel of his shotgun up without warning, aiming it off at something beyond the glow of the security monitors.

"Step outta them shadows! I can see ya!" He growled.

Mick and Zach followed his gaze, Zach regaining his shotgun and aiming alongside Parish. Mick held the puppy as close to him as he could while aiming with the pistol with the other hand.

Mick saw just out of the light of the monitors' reach, the shape of what he thought to be an arm move. The puppy looked like it was trying to dig through Mick's chest and that's when Mick figured out that it was trying to get away from whatever was about to move out from behind those monitors.

As the shape slowly staggered out from behind the monitors and into the soft blueish glow they gave off, Mick just about dropped the poor dog. What came walking out from behind them was a tall man about six foot one, wearing a bloody burlap mask that had eye holes cut out and an oversized smile stitched into the cloth. The rest of its raggedy, tattered clothes were stained with some kind of dark substance all over as well. The person gave off a musty but faint scent of copper, and Mick got the feeling the stains in the dark clothing were blood. The man wore a dark long sleeve work shirt with a name patch embroidered over the left breast—Jack.

He wore old, shredded jeans that were stained dark brown. Definitely blood. And on the intruder's feet he wore a pair of steel toed work boots with the leather worn off of the steel toe part. His hands were covered with an old pair of gardening gloves, and…was that, *straw* poking out of the rips and tears in this guy's clothes? He walked with unstable, jerky movements like a life sized marionette. So much so that Mick almost caught himself looking for strings.

The stranger began to speak through his mask. It was a dry, course voice that sounded like tires crunching over loose gravel in a driveway.

"Does…the Mick Joooohnson like…the…gift?" He asked, his head twitching as he drew out Mick's last name?

"Parish, get Mick out of here." Zach whispered sharply.

Mick felt Parish's giant hand close over his shoulder and he was on the move again. He didn't see how it had happened, but a shotgun blast went off behind him. The sound of glass shattering and wood splintering. Zach cussed, and then there was the sound of a body hitting the ground. Something getting overturned. Mick chanced a glance behind him just long enough to see the backside view of the intruder as he advanced toward Zach with a butcher knife—which he had pulled from his own back.

Mick stood mesmerized in complete horror at the sight of this stranger. His back was riddled with various cutting implements. Several long wooden and synthetic knife handles jutted from his back like quills on a porcupine. His movements as he advanced toward Zach were still jerky and sporadic, but they came in rapid succession. Zach's eyes were glowing and so was the curved blade of his karambit as he blocked and parried many of the intruder's thrusts. Not without taking a few lacerations to himself as well.

"What the hell you doin'?! Move it!" Parish yelled as Mick caught the flailing puppy from hitting the floor, and followed Parish.

GET OUT

Mick dashed after Parish, pressing the panicked puppy against his chest. Parish began to slow his pace once they reached a door not far from the couch where Mick had woken up a few nights ago. Mick slid the gun into his belt and tended to the shaking, yelping Boxer puppy with both hands.

"It's okay little guy, it's *gonna* be ok!" Mick said to the puppy, but no sooner had the words left his mouth than he realized he was saying them for his own benefit. His legs felt like jelly, his face was drenched in a cold sweat, and everywhere he looked, every dark corner, it seemed like the cabinets and work benches were getting closer together. It was getting harder to breath.

Parish had quickly sat his shotgun down on one of the work benches and had grabbed a firefighter's ax with a very *intricate* handle. A motorcycle hand break had been attached to the handle. Some type of insulated tubing coiled up the length of the ax handle from the bottom where the break lever was, and stopped at two cartridges that were mounted onto the sides of the ax head. Parish hurriedly hefted the big ax off the bench, clicked a small switch that was somewhere on the weapon's handle, and squeezed the brake lever. The smell of gasoline permeated Mick's nose, invading his nostrils like polluted ethereal tentacles as the ax head became soaked with gas that had shot out of the cartridges. Parish squeezed the lever again and a sudden hiss stung Mick's ears. He jumped back and shielded the dog from the rush of flames that engulfed the head of the ax. Parish scooped his mask up off the workbench and donned it, his eyes two flaming white hot orbs.

"Go through that door," Parish yelled, pointing toward the door they had stopped not too far from, "Take the stairs up to the surface and hide!"

Mick nodded. When a big muscular man in a mask, carrying a flaming ax tells you to do something, you don't ask questions. He dashed forward, wrapped his hands around the door handle, twisted and yanked it open. It led upward, into a dark, narrow stairwell that seemed to go on forever just looking at it. How far down was he really?

Mick turned back to see Parish charging off down the same way they had come. The flames that covered the ax head shimmered and flew off of the ax head as he picked up his pace.

Mick hugged the puppy once more before stepping into the pitch black stairwell and slammed himself in.

The sound of that door slamming shut behind him caused Mick's spine to become taught like a steel cable. He ran up the stairs three at a time, his legs nearly buckling every other hurried step he managed. He flew up the stairs, using the rail to quickly pull himself up rather than for a guide. All the while his lungs screamed for air they couldn't have, burning in his chest as they gradually began to feel smaller with each labored attempt at breathing.

As he flew up the stairs, holding the puppy as close to his chest as humanly possible, he fought the urge to look behind him in the dark. Even though his eyes were beginning to adjust, he dared not look back. He was positive he had shut that door behind him. Somehow he was even sure he had felt the vibration of the latch clicking into place as his hand squeezed the door handle. But still it did nothing to combat the feeling that there were another set of footsteps echoing up the stairwell with him.

His heart felt like it was about to explode in his chest, like a balloon that had exceeded its capacity. But that sound of a second pair of footsteps was persistent, just at the edge of his hearing, causing him to push harder than he felt he was truly capable of.

The stairs came to a landing. Mick reached the top and bent over, holding the puppy close with one hand and using his other to steady himself against the wall to his left for a brief moment. He could push pretty hard when he needed to, but he couldn't get much farther if he collapsed. He sank down to his rump and tried to calm the hysterical pup in his arms.

"It...gonna be...okay." He panted as he kept rubbing his hands up and down the dog's back.

"We're almost out of here, I think," Mick breathed as he held the crying pup close. He felt the rough texture of the twine that was tied around the poor dog's leg rubbing against his arm and he winced for the dog. With all the excitement, the dog seemed to have forgotten about it. Then he felt the quick little wet laps at his face and the calming scent of puppy breath.

A quiet noise slithered up the stairwell and Mick froze, clutching the dog tight against him. He listened, trying to remind himself that he had shut that door behind him. But this stairwell, while narrow, could easily hide someone at the bottom. Probably behind the door he had come in through.

Mick's eyes darted quickly down the stairs. By now he would have been able to make out an odd shape if it moved. But he didn't see anything. But there was that still small noise. It was so subtle he wasn't sure if he had imagined it. He looked to his left, and he could make out the tall rectangular outline of a white door. Had he reached the top, or was this simply another floor? In any case it was a freakin' door and he couldn't stay in this stairwell. He eased himself back onto his feet, assuring the dog in his arms they would both make it out alive. He reached out and felt the cold metal door handle, said a quick prayer to whoever was listening, asking that the damn thing wouldn't be locked, and pulled. The door gave a little, and then he quietly pulled it open and looked around. What he could see was a mop and bucket, shelves with cleaning supplies, a couple brooms, a faucet sticking out of one wall with a hose leading from the faucet, hanging down to the open mouth of a drain in the floor. Just passed all that he spotted another door. He felt hope surging through him as he slipped inside and quietly tried to close the door to the landing.

Mick wasn't sure what he expected to find beyond that door. The thick smell of motor oil and the dry smell of rubber invaded his nose. He clicked the door shut behind him, and stood still, trying to let his eyes adjust to his new surroundings. There were windows, so that was a good sign. The room he was in stretched spaciously out before him, about half the size of the gymnasium at the high school. More concrete floors, and a couple cars up on lifts rested over his head. A tire greasing machine was at the top of a ramp where rows of tires of various sizes were stored on racks.

There were several SnapOn tool boxes on wheels against the wall across from him. A set of stairs led up to a catwalk on the east wall, and to the south, a room that was probably an office of sorts. He could also see a couple water coolers by the tool box wall.

The puppy started to squirm again. Mick held him against his sweat soaked t shirt, and rubbed his head to calm him down. His eyes followed the red glow of the EXIT sign he saw mounted to a wall near the office. Its red glow revealed a glassed in waiting area with chairs and a front desk. It made sense now what at least two of the hunters' jobs were, why they came back smelling like a garage at the end of the day.

Mick felt a strange need to check the door behind him all of a sudden. He looked back at the sturdy door, saw the door handle was one that could be locked with a key. Hopefully it had locked when he closed it behind him. He checked the door handle. It was locked in place firmly.

Then Mick drew back as a shaking sensation from the other side jolted him away from the door. Something *had* been in the stairwell with him! He turned and ran toward the EXIT sign as a deafening *CRASH* threatened to explode his ear drums. Whatever had been on the other side of that door had just smashed its way through like it was a piece of corkboard. Mick turned to look over his shoulder just long enough to glimpse a hooded figure advancing toward him.

"Good to see you again Mr. Johnson! First the men's room and now a garage!" A voice rang out through the dark toward him.

Mick slammed into the exit door, and into the cold October night air. It felt like breaching the surface of the water after being held down to the point of drowning. There was a parking lot with no cars. Just a flat stretch of concrete, which his legs frantically carried him across. The lot was dimly lit up by the flashing letters of a neon kiosk by the side of the road which read 'Tom's Auto.' The 's' and the 'u' however were burned out, making the letters that were glowing spell 'Tomato.' Despite the life and death peril he was fleeing from, Mick felt himself letting out a horse laugh at the simple joke.

He turned back to look again. The door he had just stumbled out of had burst open, revealing the dark hooded form of the person that had followed him up the stairwell.

"Where is my sister?!" his pursuer roared.

The small pup in his arms let out a high pitched series of yips and barks in the direction of the stranger. Mick clapped his other hand over the dog's face, trying to muzzle the echoing barks that filled the empty lot as he took off again toward the highway. He could see the city lights as they lined the horizon. Tom's auto was only a mile or so outside of town. But all Mick had was his legs. Then he remembered the pistol that he had tucked into his pants and stopped.

Mick drew out the gun and aimed it in the general direction of the figure that was now halfway across the parking lot to where he was standing on the curb.

Squeeze, don't pull! Mick reminded himself. The pistol bucked in his hands like a mule kicking against his palm. He let off three rounds in the stranger's direction. Then four. Five. He heard a heavy thump of something hitting the concrete.

Mick didn't know how long he stood there with the gun held out, his lungs on fire. Taking in enough air to breath was difficult. Trying to exhale air that he didn't have was excruciating. He opened his eyes. Apparently he had closed them at some point. He didn't even remember closing them. Probably before the killing shot. He staggered toward the fallen body on the ground, gun extended and finger only a hair twitch away from firing again. The shot that had dropped the pursuer had been to the forehead, just above the left eye. A puddle of blood spread forth from beneath his head across the concrete.

The dog was trying to burrow its way up into his arm pit and Mick had to steady the dog with both hands while holding onto the gun just to keep the poor thing from jumping out of his arms.

Mick saw the face, and instantly dry heaved. He recognized him as the goth kid who had cornered him in the bathroom the night of the town assembly. The one who had violated his soul with the very mention of his childhood. The one who had confronted him about his rage and desire for vengeance against the hunters who had destroyed his world.

Mick felt his finger tighten around the trigger as another round spat forth from the barrel, tearing a hole in the goth kid's sternum. Then out of the corner of his eye he saw a slight twitch, coming from one of the hands.

Mick's gaze went to the elongated, bony hand at the end of one of the kid's arms. A quivering cylinder of diseased looking flesh, adorned with fingers that had too many joints, and bent in all directions. The hammering of his heart was the only sound filling his ears as his eyes remained glued to the twitching, gnarled thing.

What...is it?! Mick stammered, the voice of his own thoughts feeling constricted as the hand snapped and writhed about like a severed tentacle. Mick moved the gun to the hand but couldn't bring himself to fire. His vision began to blur and swirl the longer he looked at it.

Mick turned his gaze away from the thing at the end of the kid's arm, and toward the horizon of city lights off in the distance as he and the terrified pup made their way on foot into New broken Edge.

BROKEN BOND

A sudden impact comparable to a scorching lead rod being shoved through her head stole her breath and made Sunny's eyes roll to the back of her head just as she was climbing into the vehicle. Yet she never lost consciousness. She could see Judah rushing into her peripherals and kneeling down over her. His lips were moving but she couldn't hear any words. A bone chilling sensation swept through her as she became soaked in an icy cold sweat.

"What's going on Sunny?!" Judah's voice came swelling into her hearing, "Talk to me!" His enormous hands had cupped the sides of her face, his rough thumbs brushing her cheeks lightly in a gesture meant to calm.

A quick image flashed through her mind's eye of the same hooded figure she had seen in the black smoke earlier. It was Craig, her brother, lying in a pool of blood that was spreading out from a hole in his forehead.

Sunny sat up and dry heaved, her face and neck awash in ice cold sweat. She scrambled to her feet, stumbling along the way as she clutched onto the side of the vehicle for support.

Though they weren't even twins, Sunny and Craig had always shared a special bond with one another. Their connection was in fact so strong that even as children, if one of them fell at the park and skinned their knee, the other would feel it in the same spot. It made hide and seek an utterly pointless game to play, since either one of them could always *feel* where the other was hiding. That bond was most commonly expressed between identical twins, but her and her brother seemed to be one of the rare exceptions to that rule. Even on occasion when they had not seen each other for a couple days, they always knew if the other one was in danger. This bond only increased to new heights when they got involved with magic. On many occasions she had communicated with her brother telepathically. But it had only ever been with him, and only after they had established themselves in their identities as children of Father.

"Sunny?" Judah asked again. His voice was beginning to come back clearer, and she slowly turned toward him, and when their eyes met, Judah's olive complexion went pale like a cadaver.

"You're bleeding," he said, pointing a finger to her face.

Sunny touched a trembling finger to her face in the place she had felt the scorching impact earlier and drew it away, covered in blood. She felt her ribcage seize up with a chilling gasp, and then she looked in the side mirror. There was a small indentation in her forehead, perfectly circular in its shape. Blood was trickling down her forehead, sloping down her nose. The coppery taste began filling her mouth.

"What's going on?" Judah asked, cautiously stepping forward.

"I—I...My brother..." She said, trying to form the words. The only thoughts she could even form coherently were that they needed to get back to Tom's Auto. But getting them to come out of her mouth was a battle. The same sensation she felt when trying to scream inside of a dream was choking her in this waking world.

"Sweetie, I think you're going into shock. Let's get you home," Judah said as he carefully opened the passenger side door for her, scooped her up in his arms, and hefted her into the passenger seat.

"We'll talk about it when you're ready."

DELUSIONS

Mick had lost track of how long ago it had begun to rain. As the large drops of ice cold dew from the heavens assaulted his body, drenching him to the very marrow of his bones, the small dog wriggled against him, trying in vain to get dry. He felt several sharp icy pricks hitting the back of his head, his neck and all the way down his back. After walking in the rain for as long as he had, he wasn't sure if the raindrops were getting bigger or if it was actually turning to hail. Silvery haloes ringed the street lights in the rain. Building gutters gurgled and gushed, the water racing toward the sewer drains.

The good news was, they were almost to Mick's apartment. Regardless of what he did next, he *had* to get dried off. He had to get some hot food in his belly, and the same went for this little one he held on to for dear life. He ran across the intersection at 4th and Main. His apartment was another two blocks, just straight ahead.

He had to get to a phone too. Everyone at the station, George especially, had to be combing the city for him. Given how long Mick had been missing though, he wouldn't be surprised if by now they were looking for his corpse. If things kept up the way they had been, that might very well be the case.

After about another ten minutes of running, jogging and slogging through the downpour, he was finally bathed in the dim greenish yellow hue of light coming from the foyer of his apartment complex as it shined out through the automatic glass doors. He ducted under the awning and dove into the automatic doors as they slide open to receive him, and then he set the drenched pup down on the ground so it could shake itself off. It cried a high pitched whine that hurt Mick's ears and tore at his heart. This poor thing didn't deserve any of this.

Mick whipped the t-shirt he was wearing off and proceeded to wring it out, holding it out of the doorway. After he had wrung out as much water as he could, he pulled the shirt back on. It still clung to his skin like a wet square of toilet paper clings to the inside of a toilet bowl. He draped the bottom of the shirt down over the handle of the gun Zach had given him.

He held out his hand, whistled for the dog to follow, and then proceeded into the lobby. Stairs be damned, he had been through too much to try and ascend that damned stairwell. After his experience in the stairwell back at the hunters' lair, he wasn't too keen on the idea of being in one for more than a millisecond anyway. He would ride that ancient elevator up to his apartment and do breathing exercises all the way up if he had to. The boxer puppy sniffed the floor, his small nose seeming to pull the rest of him around in all directions as the smells of this new environment flooded his nose.

"We need to get a name for you huh?" Mick said as he pushed the elevator button. He ran through his mental list of generic dogs names he kept stashed under the "Never gonna happen cause no pets allowed in this complex" folder. Fido, Killer, Spike, Fifi, Spot, Steven…Then he remembered a practice of naming pets that one of his friends back in school had talked about. One day for Show and Tell, Jessie, a little red haired girl had brought her pug puppy Skip to school. She said to throw out a bunch of random names, and whatever the dog comes to, no matter how horrible, was their name.

The elevator door dinged, and the old clunky metal doors rolled open. This coffin on cables, awaiting their entry, had arrived. Mick took a very deep breath, and looked at the puppy.

"Come on Spunk, let's go," he said, motioning for him to follow him into the elevator. The dog sat down on its rump and then rolled over, pawing at the air.

"Ya don't like that?" Mick asked, bending down to pick up the wiggly ball of wet fur. He accidentally brushed the puppy's wounded back leg, and the dog yelped so loud Mick flinched.

"I'm sorry! Shhhh! Shhh! Its okay boy. Yeah, you're gonna be just fine." He said as he tried to hold the dog in a way he wasn't going to brush against the sensitive leg.

"How about Floyd? Ya like Floyd?" He asked, not really expecting a response.

The door to Mick's apartment sported a missing poster with his photo on it, which he quickly removed. He tried the handle, and it didn't give.

Sonofabitch, he thought, wishing the hunters could have retrieved his keys as well. There wasn't anyone downstairs in the lobby who could give him a spare, and he wasn't about to go back down again. Not for a while at least. His car was still parked where he had left it down in the complex parking lot. He had locked it when he returned home from work the morning he was taken, and he wasn't about to smash out a window in his own car and hotwire it. Soon as he changed clothes he planned to find a phone and have George come pick him up.

"Hold on buddy," he said as he held the dog close, and brought his foot up and placed it next to the door handle, getting a feel for how he was gonna do this. Kicking down doors was not something he was very good at, but now seemed just as good a time to practice as any. He took a step back, creating just enough distance to get the force of his foot to travel through the door. He took a deep breath and then exhaled, snapping his foot forward. Once his foot connected, he heard the blunt *crack* of the deadbolt separating through the softer wood on the inside of the door frame, and the door swung inward and banged against the inside of the entrance.

Mick sat the puppy down and it reluctantly limped in through the door while Mick entered behind, his trembling hands searching for the light switch. He felt the familiar plastic protrusion in the wall, but when he flicked it, nothing. Mick let out a long, disgruntled sigh as he remembered his electric bill had been due the day he was taken.

The light from outside the hallway was all he had to go by as he cautiously stepped inside. The sound of the rain beating against the side of the building continued to swell with each step he took, until the dark of the apartment was lite up for a brief couple seconds by a flash of lightning. The puppy whined as thunder shook the room following the bright flash.

But then something else began to writhe and chew at the back of his brain like a squirming horde of maggots. Not a feeling of being watched. Mick had experienced so much of that over the last several weeks, he knew it pretty well.

No this was different. While he didn't feel he was being watched, the feeling that someone had been here recently was asserting itself. There wasn't any feint odor. Even though it had been days since he was last home, everything looked as he remembered it. He pulled out the pistol and did a quick look over of his apartment, moving slowly and quietly. His eyes had adjusted enough by that point for him to discern the outlines of some of the cardboard boxes he used as furniture, the futon and the lone TV tray he used for a coffee table.

Still, even with the place being locked up when he got here, he felt like someone had been in here recently. Probably within the last thirty minutes. George did have a set of keys. It was a spare set Mick had made, and given to him, so if he ever lost his main set, George would have the backups with him and he could let Mick in. But this didn't feel like his best friend had been here. He thought maybe he was feeling residual creeps from when Miller had kidnapped him. He could have gotten in, while in his more compact size. But no matter how Mick tried to analyze the feeling, it didn't feel like it was matching with anything he compared it too. The darkness in the room seemed like a gargantuan black hole torn into the fabric of space, pulling his attention this way and that. The pull to investigate each closet, under the bed, was not to find some maniac hiding in his apartment. But to find something out of place. Something that screamed confirmation that the feeling he was experiencing was justified. This was his space, and he knew that there had to be something out of place.

When he got to his room, he noticed a small rectangular object on his nightstand. His heart leapt up inside of him and was overcome with a flood of differing emotions. For one, he had found a phone with which to call George! He scooped up his phone, feeling like *finally*, something was going to go right. He tried turning it on—dead battery.

Mick cussed as he felt the rug get yanked out from beneath his hopes. He looked down at his phone. The other conflicting emotion he felt was that he knew he had this with him the night he disappeared. When he awoke in the mall, he didn't have any personal effects at all. So if his phone was here did that mean Terrance Miller had emptied all his stuff and left them here for him to find? Sounded plausible, although it didn't make sense as to why. This hadn't quite been the clue Mick had been hoping to find as to why he felt his home had been tampered with right before he got home. Of course his home had been violated. Miller had broken into it and kidnapped him. He even, in a roundabout way, admitted to Mick about sneaking in on other occasions through the open window. But still, that wasn't really the source of this uneasiness that kept chiseling away at the lining of his skull. Mick tried to articulate it as he turned toward his dresser and began rummaging around for new clothes. He looked down at the phone again, thoughtful. Miller always wore gloves when he did his deeds. So Mick wasn't too worried about contaminating evidence that might have Miller's prints on it. He felt around on his dresser for the phone charger he kept there. He found that at least. He would have to use one of the outlets out in the lobby on this floor by the elevator. Regardless, he knew he had to contact someone. He quickly changed into dry clothes, grabbed a granola bar out of the cabinet, exited his apartment with the nameless dog, and went and sat down on one of the couches in the lobby. After plugging his device in, and letting the battery get to five percent, he turned on his phone. Apparently he had been a day off on his estimation of how long he had been with the hunters. His phone read that today was October twenty fourth, not the twenty third. Mick brought up the call log, which revealed twelve missed calls on the eighteenth, the day he went missing. Three from Scroggins, one from Valerie, two from an unidentified number, and the rest from George. His voicemail was full as well.

He brought up George's number and hit the green button. The phone rang once, twice, and then a third time.

"Holy Christ Mick! Where the hell are you?!" George's voice rang through the phone so loud Mick felt the concentrated sound through his ear like a fine needlepoint, and pulled the phone away.

"George I'm alright. I'm at my apartment. I need you –"

"Say no more bro, I'm already on my way." George frantically reassured him. Mick heard something clatter to the floor on George's end, and then a thud. George let out a sharp intake of breath and swore. Mick imagined him banging his shin on the sharp edge of his coffee table.

"I'll explain everything when you get here man," Mick said into the phone.

"No dude don't hang up yet! You've been missing for a week! You're staying on this phone with me until I get there!" George informed him. Mick swore he heard his voice crack. There was silence on the other end for a few moments.

"Are you okay George?" Mick asked.

"I'm good man. Just getting a little worked up is all. You're basically my brother and after forty eight hours of you missing, everyone started looking for your body. I knew you'd turn up again in one piece, but..." he stopped for a moment. George was never great with words. Mick looked down at the puppy that had laid down to rest next to his left foot.

"It's been a rough week for all of us," George said, his voice exhaling that last statement as if he had been holding his breath for a very long time. As far as the last few days had gone, he probably had been. Mick felt his eyes watering. His disappearance had obviously shaken George in a way he wasn't accustomed to feeling.

"You promise me you won't ever go missing again." George said, "I mean it too. After my parents died... *You* were the one who helped me face the monsters in my world Mick. I know this might sound weird and girly, but I need you bro." His tone had dissolved into the cracking, uneven terrain one experiences when they are trying their hardest to keep their voice in check, so as not to collapse into a weeping puddle of tears.

Mick's cheeks were now wet and his eyes burned as stinging hot tears pooled in them. He shook his head in earnest, and then again remembered George couldn't see him doing that.

"I promise man. Cross my heart. Now get your ass over here. We have a lot to get caught up on.

The reunion had left Mick with a popped spine, as George wouldn't cease to loosen his bear hug embrace of Mick's person. Honestly though, after what he had been through, having his spine pop all the way from his mid back up to the base of his skull reminded him of how desperately he needed a working over from a chiropractor. The puppy, who was still refusing to come to any name Mick threw out to him, barked profusely when George appeared in the lobby. Poor thing was still shaken up. The little guy had already bonded so well with Mick, it seemed like he was the only one who could even calm him down.

"Remind me to make an appointment tomorrow," Mick said as he opened the passenger side door to George's black 2000 Jeep. It smelled like stale Cheetos in here. Mick brushed off a bunch of fast food wrappers, receipts, and the occasional extra-large cup from Wendy's or Spangles. As trashed as George's vehicle was, his office space down at the forensics lab was immaculate. Not just because of company standards of sterility, but the man definitely took pride in his work. Mick hefted the puppy up into the passenger seat and then sat him on his lap, trying to calm his incessant growling and barking. No matter how cute it had been at first, it was really starting to bother Mick. George didn't seem too put off by it. He loved dogs and said the little fella would warm up to him in time.

"Before we go to the station, there is something I need to show you at the lab." George said, his tone heavy, like a weight was in his stomach. Mick agreed, as if he had a choice.

"But first tell me everything you can remember man, everything!" He insisted as he put the jeep in gear and began toward the lab so fast he neglected to put on his seat belt.

So Mick did. He started with the meeting Scroggins had with him the night before he was kidnapped. Waking up in the old Broken Edge Mall, with a fully restored to life Terrance, "Tick" Miller painting a portrait in his own blood, and how Miller had recounted a meeting with some entity from a darker plane of existence. George listened enraptured by what Mick was telling him. None of his usual smirking or smartass remarks when Mick mentioned something insanely outlandish. In fact, when he told George of how Miller could shift between a normal sized human form to monstrously huge, George only looked toward Mick, puzzled.

"…Can everyone infected with Wretch Syndrome do that?" George asked, his tone suggesting he was still trying to wrap his head around the idea that a person who had their body mutated and mutilated by something in their DNA could be reshaped into the form of a recognizable human figure.

"He made it sound like he was only able to do that because of his meeting with the dark shape." Mick said.

George whistled, "Thank God for that."

Mick continued his account. The more he talked however, he looked over at George, noting the gray tones to his friend's skin that somehow just hadn't been noticeable until his time with the hunters, of whom their colleague Valerie Wellington was one. *That* got George to talking. He wasn't as put off by the notion as Mick thought he would be. Instead George began to gush about how he knew she was really a badass and how the fact she was a monster hunter vigilante only upped her sex-appeal. Although not the reaction Mick expected, he genuinely had to agree with him.

He stopped on occasion to try and calm the puppy, who by now was whining and scratching at Mick's window, and then Mick realized something. It was because of his focus on this little guy that he was even able to recount half of his tale to George without sounding like a jabbering madman. He stroked the dog's ears, ran his hand down its back to reassure it, but it wasn't calming down. At times when Mick spoke he had to speak over the dog. But he held on tighter, holding the dog close to his chest, because he realized this little puppy was the barrier between his sanity and him losing his grasp on reality as he knew it.

It was difficult, but Mick told George of Terrance Miller's final fate at the hands of the hunters who had rescued him. He told him that the one who went by Brandon Maxwell was in fact a werewolf, and they had the werewolf and the skin-walker who had attacked the high school in their trust. They were just kids, not even old enough to legally drink. Information Judah had shared about the taint of gray skin however, Mick kept to himself because he wasn't still really sure what to make of his own experience with seeing the taint in others, let alone his own flesh. He did tell George about Judah and how, much to his dismay, he found out that he was the significant other to Valerie. No wonder neither Mick nor George had a chance in Hell with her.

He told George of how he had escaped, and consequently, where the yappy little mess of wet fur in his lap had come from as a result. George asked questions about the strange attacker who Mick had described as wearing a scarecrow mask and had, in Mick's own words, "A crap ton of knives stuck into his back." To which Mick answered each of his inquiries as best he could. He didn't breathe a word of the kid he had shot dead in the parking lot of Tom's Auto though. Not until he could fully come to terms with the fact that he had shot someone else. Yes it had been self-defense. He knew that. But with no witnesses save for the dog, who was going to believe a word in regards to his innocence?

They pulled up to the forensics lab. The rain had finally stopped, which was a nice change. Mick knew the puppy couldn't come with him into the lab, but George assured him there were people who could help remove the embedded twine in his back leg and bandage it up for him, maybe even get him some food. Letting the little dog go felt like losing one of his arms. If the pup had been crying in George's jeep, it was now doing the puppy equivalent to sobbing and screaming in terror. As Mick reluctantly passed off the puppy to one of the lab staff, the sound it made when Mick turned away was like a screaming child getting burned by a hot fire poker. Mick clinched his eyes shut as the hot tears scalded his eyes.

"So you gonna keep him?" George asked Mick as he led the way to the lab.

"Yeah. I know my place won't allow pets but I'll figure out some way around it. Actually I think after this is all over I'm gonna find a new place. You need a roommate?" Mick asked.

"Hell yeah, someone else to help split the rent and bills. You can move in next week if you want to." George said as he scanned his badge and the sliding glass doors to the lab opened for them.

"So what are we looking at here?" Mick asked as George sat down at his sleek Apple console.

"Well, when Scroggins reported you missing, that's when I started thinking that maybe you had been right about the hunters and I had just gotten caught up in all the hype about them that the rest of the city was starting to fall into. I started keeping an ear open for when they would go out on patrols. Three nights ago myself, Matt, and Jarred get called out along with our lovely Miss Wellington, to go collect evidence at a crime scene where the hunters had dispatched a rather large creature that had apparently been feasting on the local squatters in that unfinished building project over on the north end of town. The hunters were pretty beat up. Well we go through there, do our thing, take the remains of the victims back to the morgue and so on. I notice one of the hunters in the back of an ambulance getting treated. He spits out a huge glob of blood out onto the concrete. So I go over and talk to him a little, try to make small talk, all while guarding his blood sample so no one disturbs it."

"Which one of them was it, do you remember?" Mick asked.

"He had long brown hair." George said, and then continued.

"Took me forever and I felt awkward just standing there trying to talk to this guy, but when he finally had his attention diverted, I was able to collect a sample from his blood. Next morning that Parish Larson shows up at the morgue, talks to Valerie for a bit and then leaves. He had drank some water out of the water cooler and I swiped his paper cup outta the trash can and lifted a sample from it."

"Well look at you being all slick and stealthy." Mick said, looking over his shoulder to see when someone would come get him and tell him the dog's leg was taken care of.

George nodded his head, pleased with himself, "I lifted a sample from Valerie too. That water cooler will be their undoing," George snickered, "But no, when you told me she was one of them that's why I wasn't surprised. What I'm about to show you is something I don't even know what to make of." He said as he moved his cursor arrow to several different icons, typed in a few passwords and then brought up the DNA sequences of the hunters Zach Stewart, Parish Larson, and Valerie.

At first Mick didn't really know what he was looking at. After prodding George to explain further, what followed sent Mick spiraling down toward the murky depths of what precious sanity he had left.

After a brief refresher on the human DNA sequence from George, Mick now understood what he was seeing. These samples from the hunters, had been fundamentally altered in a way that made them so much more, and less than, human. Whatever these hunters were, and whatever had rewritten their genetic code, could explain how they were able to do the things they did. While in their custody, Mick recalled seeing Zach and Judah come back from a nightly patrol, beaten and bloodied. After eight hours of what Mick assumed was them sleeping, they emerged from their chambers without a scratch. They complained of some stiffness in the areas they had taken damage to, but from what Mick could tell, they had fully healed.

It would explain how they could move as fast as they could. The agility Mick had witnessed in their sparring sessions made him dizzy. It would *definitely* explain the glowing white eyes, the glowing veins—the ashen black skin, and the ability to drain the life out of a living organism until nothing but a withered husk of a corpse remained. Mick's mind screamed back to early August of this year, where the withered body of a Jane Doe had been found in a dumpster. She was later identified through dental records as Melany Koehn. It had been during that six month lull in the Tick killings, and he wasn't getting paid to sit around on his hands, so Sargent Mills sent him out on that one. When he got there, George and Valerie were already there. A copy of Melany Koehn's file had been in Mick's case file about the vigilante hunters. He had showed it to Chief Scroggins when they met at Lilly's Bar and Grill.

Mick removed his eyes from the screen, seeing George sitting with his face in his hands.

"You alright?'" Mick asked, putting his hand on George's shoulder. George looked up at him, his eyes watery.

"You remember that Jane Doe we found back in August?" George asked. Mick nodded.

"Yeah I was just thinking about her. Melany Koehn."

George looked at the floor for a moment, looking unsure of what he wanted to say. No, not unsure...*terrified.*

"You remember when we were kids? The school would have us do drills for tornadoes, school shootings and such?" George asked.

Mick nodded, "yeah, they were really fun." He recalled.

"We had done a drill for a school intruder on the day I found my parents dead." George said, his breathing raspy and his voice sounding like a crumbling cliff face about to fully break off.

Mick took a seat next to George, "You want to talk about it?" He asked.

George sat there, wiping his eyes before tears could leap from them.

"There's something I never told you Mick," George began, "I didn't find my parents with their wrists cut. Everything in the papers about their death was a lie."

Mick could feel the tentacles of nausea coiling around him at those words. What had George *actually* seen if he hadn't found his parents with their wrists cut from palm to elbow? Certainly seeing all that blood would have been traumatizing enough to a small child, but if that wasn't the case, what *had* he seen?

"Other than my therapist I had at the children's hospital I stayed at, you'll be the only one I have told. I remember waiting at the school for thirty minutes. Mom had written down all of their contact information and put it in my backpack. Mrs. Goldstone finally called my house to find where Mom and Dad were. She didn't get a hold of them. She called both their cell phones, didn't get 'em that time either. She took me home, and uh..." He stopped to take a deep breath, closing his eyes and shivering as he exhaled.

"She noticed my parents' bedroom window had been left open a little bit. They always left their window open a little, even in the winter time. They both really liked the cold air. She called to them through the window. They didn't answer so she told me to go back to the car as she called the police." He started to break.

"But she didn't see me sneak out of the car and around to the back of the house. She was standing on the front porch and had parked in front of our neighbor's house, so I snuck around, climbed over the fence, and got in through my window. Even before she told me to go back to the car I could feel that something was wrong. The house was a mess. I found my mom and dad in the kitchen. They had been holding each other. Their bodies looked... mummified...dried out."

He sat and began to glare as tears stained his cheeks.

"Those fuckers at the children's hospital told me I had been dreaming! I saw them; they were shriveled up to the bone! I became anorexic. I had to be put on a feeding tube because I almost died once, and I tried to kill myself when we were in 4th grade! Did you know that? And those...idiots have the nerve to tell a five-year-old boy that when someone feels so sad or scared and they don't know what else to do, that sometimes people decide to go to sleep forever. That's what they told me!" he said, trying to stop his voice from shaking.

Here he was sitting with his best friend, looking at the hunters' DNA on a computer screen and hearing the truth of what happened to his parents. Judah had been the link between the two parties he was searching for, and after his stay with them he knew that. But hearing George tell him how he really found his parents seemed to put the finishing touches on the cake in Mick's mind. He knew he couldn't let this affect his objective judgment, but after the things he had seen and managed to survive through by the skin of his teeth, there was no room for debate.

"I thought I had healed, ya know? Buried all that and moved on with my life. And I did. Then we found that woman in the dumpster like that. How can anyone, after having everything sucked out of them, still have such a recognizable expression of maddening terror on their face? She had the same look as my parents had. They didn't deserve to die like that." He said as he buried his head in his hands and broke down. His breathing was reduced to sharp gasping sobs. In truth, Melany Koehn *wasn't* recognizable, but Mick knew what he meant. Despite having no fatty tissue, no bodily fluids, and to just be reduced to skin cells wrapped around a skeleton, the look of paralyzing terror was still recognizable on what was left of the woman's face, if it could still be called a face.

Mick stood from his seat, hands balled up into fists so tight his nails began to dig into his palms. George was attempting to pull himself together, trying hopelessly to wipe his eyes and stop the flow of tears. Mick blinked again, his own eyes watering.

"We need to talk to Scroggins." Mick said, and with that, he knew what he had to do.

FRAGMENTED CRIME SCENE

Though it had stopped raining some time ago, she still stood shivering in her sweat soaked clothes. Sunny held her arms in a futile attempt to shield herself from the penetrating cold within her bones, only exacerbated by the October air.

Upon arriving back at Tom's Auto, where the scene of her brother's death had slammed her mercilessly to the ground a few moments ago, she had expected to find her brother's body. But the figure she had seen in her vision was gone. The parking lot was empty except for the vehicle she and Judah had ridden in. Sunny and Judah were both standing in the spot where she had seen the vision unfold. Craig's body should have been here, but only the freshly rain drenched concrete greeted her gaze. She closed her eyes and felt a surge of hot energy flooding her veins as she balled her hands up into fists. She felt a subtle crackling of that same energy emit from her eyes, jolting them open to her altered surroundings. The darkness of the night sky above her was far deeper than it had been a moment ago. She could *see* the moisture molecules in the air from the previous shower New Broken Edge had just experienced. She could see now, in the spot where she was standing, the atoms that made up the pool of blood where her brother had fallen. She could hear the residual frequency of the gunshot that had put him down, which startled her upon having her eyes opened. She could *smell* the thick, chocking smell of the blood that had seeped into the concrete, mixed with dirt and fresh rainwater. It made her gag, and she pressed a hand to her mouth just in case something solid came out.

She looked down at her feet. Craig's face stared back up at her, eyes wide and pupils dilated. His lips were moving. She stilled her nerves and bent down to get a better look, her eyes trying desperately to read the spectral message that was mouthed from those phantom lips. She recognized a few syllables as the lines to an incantation. She felt ice spreading out from the center of her chest. She felt a spark of primal panic ignited in her gut. She nearly cried out but managed to stifle it back as she back peddled away from what she saw approaching. Another apparition was now standing in her field of vision. She could *feel* the claustrophobic tightness of its features. The thing that lumbered forward appeared in her Sight as a golem of phantasmal tree limbs, now stitched together with blood and shadow. It reached down and picked up the fallen ghostly body that resembled her brother, and hefted it over its shoulder. She remained as still as she could manage, wondering how the thing wasn't aware of her. It didn't react to her presence at all. If it was aware that she could see it, it didn't seem threatened by her prying eyes.

"What you're seeing is just an imprint on reality of something that's already happened. It doesn't see or hear you." Judah's voice said behind her. She blinked and the world around her went back to its muted dull colors and textures. Tom's Auto's marque still had a couple letters shorted out.

Judah was standing behind her, his eyes lit up like torches, searching the ground. When they returned to meet Sunny's gaze, she asked him, "Did you see it too?"

Judah nodded, "Whatever happened to your brother, something picked him up and moved his body. If he was here, then whatever he brought with him tried to attack Mick, Zach and Parish." He said, the urgency in his voice rising.

She followed Judah through the back door to the shop. They made their way through the darkness of the garage where vehicles were parked in various places and or up on their lifts, to a closet deprived of its door. The closet door lay several feet away from the closet itself, hinges sizzling with visible energy that she didn't need her Higher Sight to see. Judah cleared the way of the cleaning supplies and undid the latch to the door on the other side of the room, his movements nearly mechanical.

She followed him down through the dark stairwell. The second she crossed the threshold from the janitor's closet to the stairs, the darkness felt like it was choking her. Each breath of air she fought to take seemed like she was breathing living smoke. Almost without warning, she felt energy crackling through her optical nerves and through her brain. Her thoughts of breathing in smoke were justified once her Higher Sight revealed the congestion of energy that clogged this stairwell. She could only see Judah by a feint outline. She gripped the railing and prayed she wouldn't lose her footing as she descended the stairs. What she saw was exactly what it felt like—she was drowning in thick, vibrantly black clouds of fireless smoke. When she blinked, the stairwell returned to normal.

"Hurry!" Judah's voice called from farther down.

As she descended the stairs, she recalled how Father had her ritually burry Johnson's voodoo doll in that shoebox filled with dirt. Father had told her of Johnson's claustrophobia. How she could make him feel he was being buried alive without ever touching him, and in those moments Father could taste him. He could not inhabit him yet. That would be like indulging in a half cooked meal. But he could sample his delectable vessel at least. As she descended the stairs, fighting for breath, she knew that what she was feeling was Johnson's own panic, his own paralyzing terror that billowed from him in this confined space. Granted she herself had been in far more confined spaces than this. But given whatever her brother had brought upon him this night, how Johnson had to have been fighting for his life, who was she to judge? *Hers* was the hand that heaped handfuls of wet earth on top of him and had buried a piece of him in that shoebox.

By the time she had caught up to Judah, Parish was standing over Zach as he reclined on one of the couches that they had down here. He lay shirt-less, his chest wrapped in gauze that had nearly been turned crimson. Fresh bandages ran up his arms and a few on the side of his face. A bloody parody of someone trying to be a mummy. Strands of his long brown hair, mostly slicked back with sweat, still clung to the sides of his face in places where he wasn't bandaged.

She wasn't sure how much of their report she had missed, but by the time she got to them, Judah was shaking and looking like a caged lion that hadn't eaten in a week.

"What happened? Did you see my brother?!" Sunny asked. Both hunters shook their heads.

"No. Just somethin' else," Parish said. He had his black mask slid up and resting on the top of his head, the strap still clinging faithfully to his sweat soaked scalp.

"What was it? Where is Johnson?" She felt the words escaping from her mouth almost faster than she could think.

"Some kind of magical construct," Zach grunted, shifting his weight on the couch, "It looked like a man dressed like a scarecrow, but as soon as it attacked…I just know it was more solid than a man. Maybe wood. Was too busy trying not to die to really notice anything else."

"Sir I dunno what I was thinking. I should have got Johnson outta here," Parish said, his gaze trying to meet with Judah's, but failing to.

Judah stopped pacing and looked Parish dead in the eye, "You did what you should have. If you hadn't come back, Zach might have been killed. It's what I would have done. Don't you ever forget that!"

"Guys, what about Johnson? Father is hungry! Even after being severed from him I can still feel his energy." Sunny said, trying not to lose herself in the panic that was threatening to choke her.

"We will handle whatever happens next," Judah said, "In the meantime you and Oscar need to get packed. If Johnson escaped and made it back to police headquarters without having a run in with Father, he will have told the authorities about this place. If we go down, you and Oscar can't go down with us." Judah said as he stormed off in another direction.

She turned to see Zach undoing his bloody bandages. Blood residue still lingered on his flesh, had seeped into his skin, but when she looked to see if the damage had healed, she was shocked to see that low and be-hold—scabs that looked at least a week old adorned his muscular torso. She didn't know what she was more impressed by, his rate of healing or his physique. She had never seen Zach shirtless before, so that could have been causing the heat she was suddenly feeling in her face. But now, she could see that horrid, ugly network of gashes that wound their way around his chiseled upper body.

Sunny jumped as a bulky object laded at her feet. She looked down to see a duffle bag resting there, and Judah walking closer to her.

"There is a week's worth of your new clothes in there, some dehydrated food and enough water to last you for a week." He said, and then shifted his eyes to Parish, "Call Brandon, see where him and Oscar are." With that, he disappeared back behind another long row of gun cabinets.

BUSTED

October 28, 9:06pm

The night Mick escaped with his life and made it back and relayed his experience to Chief Ted Scroggins, he put in a call to SWAT. Captain Daniel Mendez of NBE SWAT followed the procedures needed to gain access to blue prints of Tom's Auto. Mick answered as many questions as he possibly could, recalling fuzzy details that were shrouded in the darkness of his memory. Captain Mendez took his personal vehicle down there to have it serviced the next day under a false name, and had his vehicle serviced by Zach and Parish, who were apparently working as employees of the joint. The information Mendez had collected of the building matched Mick's description. While Mendez had been inside, two others of his team had parked vehicles in strategic places to observe the outside from different angles, taking note of the number of windows and doors.

Tonight, Mick was watching Captain Mendez's men ready themselves from the passenger seat of a squad car. One thing Mick could say for certain out of this entire fiasco he had somehow managed to live through, was that his sense of black and white justice felt as violated as his childhood. Not only had these hunters been a link to the ones from his past, with their leader being the one in charge of the ones who helped slaughter his home town, but they had at every turn, *protected* him. The elusive figure they spoke of that they kept calling "Father," had never shown his face. Or *it's* face. They made it sound like this entity wasn't even human. Hell, with what Mick had seen in the past month alone, he didn't have any reason to think it was a far-fetched possibility.

But a question like a rusty nail kept wiggling deeper inside his brain. Was he safe because they truly saved his butt, or was he in even more danger because he had even associated with them? Or was the answer to both of those questions yes? He simply had nothing to go on. Just an achy body, and several days missing out of his memory where he was either knocked out, or deep underground with the people he had been trying to expose. At this point, nothing was really stopping his mind from working up conspiracies. The journal the hunters had gotten from that girl could have easily been written up by one of them. Maybe the girl, the werewolf and the goth kid all worked for the hunters? Was Judah the mysterious 'Father' they all spoke of?

Without any real solid evidence, he was left floating in limbo, and that terrified him more than anything.

Now that things had somewhat calmed down for him over the last few days (as calm as anything ever got for him anyway) it was like every waking moment he lived with a silent dread in his morning routine. When he shaved, was it a draft from the vent by the tub that caused the shower curtain to sway? He eventually ended up just crashing at George's when it got to be too much.

Mick drew in a deep breath and held it for five seconds, and slowly let it out. He was shaking as his hands gripped the door handle to the squad car he had ridden in. He gave the handle a good tug and exited the car, looking up at the marque of Tom's Auto from the parking lot.

Mendez was approaching him, his M4 carbine slung across his back, his helmet tucked under one arm. The man stood all of five foot eight or nine inches tall, had his brown hair cut in a typical buzz cut of someone who had spent time in the military. Though he was rather short in stature, he was as wide as a brick wall, and twice as sturdy as one. The thick mustache that graced his upper lip and his tanned complexion did little to distract one from his rather exaggerated canines that shown proudly when he smiled. Mick thought he looked like a wolf trying to masquerade as a human. His eyes were the eyes of a true predator, but somehow managed to still pull a person in with their warmth. At times Mick would make the joke that he was the wolf from *"Little Red Riding Hood."* Pull the prey in with a flash of those pearly whites, give em a comforting wink, all before they get gobbled up. The thought made the hair on the back of his neck stand up straight as he halted in front of Mick.

"You didn't have to come out here tonight Detective," Mendez said as he extended his hand. Mick took his hand and gave a firm squeeze.

"I needed to. It was more for my peace of mind than anything else." Mick shrugged.

Mendez nodded and turned his eyes back to the armored vans his men were emerging out of.

"Well it's show time. See you when this is all over," he said, giving Mick a slap to the shoulder and running up to direct his men.

10:19pm,

The bust had concluded in less than thirty minutes after Mendez and the rest of SWAT had stormed Tom's Auto. The hunters that were there went without a fight. Valerie had been at the morgue when officers took her into custody. The two teenagers they had with them during Mick's stay were nowhere to be found.

Mick had watched from a one way mirrored window as another detective proceeded to interrogate Valerie. She sat stone faced through the whole interview. Mick looked down at the paper cone in the evidence bag he held. It had a lipstick smear on it. In the other hand he held a printout of Valerie's, Zach's and Parish's genetic code.

The current interrogating detective exited the interrogation room, shaking his head and cussing under his breath. Mick slid passed him on his way out. Valerie looked up only slightly when the door clicked shut behind him. He looked around. It was the same interrogation room he had been humiliated in a couple weeks ago. His movements felt stiff as he proceeded over to the seat at the other side of the table. He wasn't sure if he expected her to even look at him. He wasn't sure why any of this had to include *her*. Regardless of a high school level crush, Valerie had been one that Mick hoped, in time, he could call a friend. They hadn't hung out at all outside of the workplace, and now it was obvious why. As he sat there looking at her, he felt his gut turn, and a tremor of disgust shot through him.

"Guess it's a good thing we never saw each other much outside of work," he said. She didn't even look up.

"I'm not sure what it was about you that made me wish we could have been friends. But I guess I dodged a bullet in that regard," he said as he laid the evidence bag containing her paper cup with her lipstick print on it, along with the printouts of her genetic code.

"George told me how he really found his parents," he continued, his tone steadily getting sharper.

"The papers said they had committed suicide, sliced their wrists in the bathtub. But my best friend found two skeletal figures huddled together, holding each other with looks of complete terror on their faces. *That* was how he found his parents." Mick said. He then tapped his finger on the printout of their DNA sequences.

"I guess whatever you got flowing through your veins must make you awful hungry to be able to suck a person dry of all bodily fluids."

That caused her to look up.

"…What?" She asked, her face wrinkling with disgust. Mick slide the printout and the cup forward to her.

"I'm not gonna say I know what you are. But I know what you're *not*. Certainly no human is capable of the things I've seen you all do." Mick said.

Valerie eyed him intensely, and for a second Mick thought he was going to see her eyes light up.

"I'm as human as you are. I've just been freed from the taint."

A lot can happen in the span of a couple seconds. Mick couldn't even remember those last couple seconds. When the sound of his own voice registered in his brain, he realized he was standing up, bent over the table and he could feel a vein in his neck bulging so far out he began to feel light headed. He didn't even recall the words he had just spoken, but he could feel his face aching with the tension of someone who had just let loose a damn of the hottest hatred a person was capable of producing.

Mick stood there, heaving as he tried to catch his breath. Valerie's eyes were glowing now, and she was standing too, her hands raised in a defensive position. He suddenly heard footsteps and felt hands on him.

"Detective let's get you out of here."

"…You need to rest."

"Have some water…*It's behind you.*"

Mick thrashed and spun around. Three other officers were reaching out to calm him down, and one was standing closer to Valerie with a hand on his side arm and one hand outstretched.

The next second Mick found himself in the men's room, splashing water in his face, trying to remember just what in the hell had transpired in the last two or three minutes.

He looked at his wet face in the mirror. He tried to focus his vision on the water droplets that ran down his face, his bloodshot eyes. Anything other than the fact that the pigmentation of his skin was gray. But the details he tried to focus on in the mirror only emphasized the fact that the face he saw was indeed a hollow, gray face that now looked much, much older than he actually was.

The chills that swept over him felt external at this point. He blinked and what he saw in the mirror behind him was not the urinals of the men's bathroom. He turned around to see he was standing outside, in the ruins of his old home town. Empty building stood on either side of the street he was on, their faces scorched and windows broken out. Some were even heaps of rubble. His shoes crunched over shattered glass, loose chunks of brick and drywall. The sky above, choked with clouds the color of soot as what little of the night sky he saw beyond was a deep, blood red. Lightning chased through the expanse of the dark clouds that threatened to form the hideous face of a dark god. Mick began walking, feeling his limbs pulled in a singular direction.

When he rounded the corner into an alley, he arrived at what had once been a loading bay for freight trucks. In that place, the pulling sensation began to gradually lessen as he came closer to the loading bay.

Five twisted metal crosses stood before him, with five twisted and mangled bodies fastened to the beams with barbed wire. Five pikes, swayed in the gust of wind that kicked up out of nowhere. At their tops, shapes roughly the same size as large melons were perched on top of the pikes.

The rumble of thunder rippled through his body as he staggered closer to get a better look. As he stood under that twisted metal frames of the torture contraptions, a sudden flash of lightning illuminated the forms, revealing them to be headless. Each one had a makeshift sign attached to each body, names painted on small wooden planks that had been attached with a stake through the chest of each.

Zachary J Stewart

Valerie Wellington

Parish Larson

Brandon Maxwell

…Judah…

The words of the goth kid came flooding back through his head, *You know they have come back to do it again and you want to see their heads on rusty pikes and their headless bodies crucified in the middle of town. You have fantasized about it. If you could get away with it you would be the one to take the saw to their necks yourself.*

Mick felt the weight of something in his left hand. A smooth handle that felt like it could have been made out of cold plastic. He looked down. A hacksaw with a jagged blade hung from his grasp. He gripped it tighter as lightning illuminated the swollen and shredded faces of the heads at the ends of the pikes. He barely recognized any of them.

Something twitched out of the corner of his eye, drawing his gaze back toward the collection of twisted metal crosses. He felt his heart drop down to the pit of his stomach as the barbed wire groaned and scraped against the metal beams of the crosses. The headless bodies were struggling, *thrashing* against their barbed restraints.

Mick staggered back, dropping the hacksaw as he saw the body of Judah break free from the restraints and land at the pike where his head began to stir. The beaten and mutilated face twitched as the hands shook, grasping the head on either side and pulling it off with a wet, sluicing noise. The body didn't attempt to reattach the head to its shoulders. It didn't need to.

None of them needed to reattach their heads to speak. Each of them advanced on unsteady legs in jerky movements, holding their own heads in their bloodstained hands. Their mouths each hung open in a wail that encased Mick in a coffin of ice, slamming the lid shut on him and burying him under the crushing weight of eternity.

But it was when the wails turned to a single intelligent phrase that Mick felt himself collapsing, unable to move any further.

"IT'S BEHIND YOU!!!"

CRACKING UP

Mick was on his backside before he felt something slither over his shoulder and apply pressure. Down on his rump in that vulnerable position with something already making physical contact with him from behind made him feel as if gravity had increased on him tenfold, and he struggled to even break the thing's connection to him as it squeezed and shook him by the shoulder.

"MICK! Snap out of it!"

The voice of whatever it was behind him sounded familiar, but it also sounded like it was coming from within a vacuum. He scrambled to his feet across the broken up concrete he had fallen onto, caught a final glimpse of the headless bodies as they limped and jerked forward, and spun to his feet.

The sky above with the menacing dark clouds was now replaced with the grimy white ceiling, lit by fluorescent lights. A row of urinals and stalls stood to his right, a few stall doors cracked ajar. The air felt still, dry and course, like breathing it in was like inhaling sand. Somehow the bathroom seemed dirtier than when he first entered. Or maybe now he was just realizing what had always been there, like his gray skin.

George stood behind him, skin gray as well, his expression plastered with the deepest confusion. His hands were held out slightly, trying to steady Mick as he got his bearings on what was real and what was in his head.

"Dude, what the hell happened in there with her?" He asked, completely bewildered. Mick steadied himself against the sink, breathing heavily, his memory of the last few moments feeling like a chunky whirlpool of muddy water. His time with Valerie felt like it had taken place hours ago. He couldn't remember what had triggered his current mental state, only that he had shouted at her, and his throat was still on fire because of it. The vision he had just seen though; *that* seemed to be the only thing he could recall with clarity. He turned his eyes back to George. He knew it was his friend standing there, and he was solid. He could feel the cold porcelain sink that was holding him up. But somehow everything he saw felt flat. Hollow. Two-dimensional. It wasn't that George didn't look like a real human being to Mick. It wasn't that his reflection in the mirror lacked visual depth and dimension to the shape and texture of his hair, or the contour of his chin, or the slope of his nose. But that everything *felt* like a hollow shell. Only superficially a person, or a sink, and beneath the mask, only stale cold air.

But the vision. The metal crosses. The scraping and groaning of the barbed wire restrains that poorly held the headless bodies in place. The substantial weight of the bloody hacksaw in his left hand. The feeling of the air swirling around his body, biting through his clothes and licking his organs as the air like tongues coiled around them. The wails of the heads gripped firmly in the hands of the hunters'. *That* was the only thing that felt truly real at the moment.

"Mick? Buddy? Hello?" George was talking again, his voice sounding distant.

Mick let go of the sink and looked at his shoes, feeling like they were a hundred feet away and the floor only an illusion.

"Is the floor really holding me up?" Mick asked. His own voice sounded like he was talking into a glass jar.

George's puzzled expression deepened, "What?"

Mick looked up at George and was surprised to feel his belly rumbling, then his chest. The rumble escaped his throat in a distant sounding giggle as he felt the muscles in his face stretch to a grin.

"I don't know what's going on," Mick said, the grin still plastered to his face. George's eyes darted to Mick's side arm, and Mick even through the haze saw the nervous glint in George's eye. With no real rhyme or reason, Mick found himself drawing his Glock from the holster. It felt so light and hollow. Like one of those toy guns with the orange tips. The trigger felt easily flexible as his finger curled around it. The plastic feeling of its curve made it so tempting to squeeze. It would have been so easy. Mick even wondered if he would hear a plastic *click* if he did.

"Am I making you nervous?" Mick asked as he slowly turned to fully face his friend.

"Mick I think you need to come with me, very slowly. But first can you holster that gun?" George said, his voice calm and steady. There was a firmness to it that managed to penetrate through the haze. Mick nodded, giggles still spurting from his parted lips and clenched teeth sporadically.

"I feel like you're not real," Mick blurted out. He was still holding the gun.

George nodded. He seemed to take that rather well, Mick thought. As soon as it registered in some distant shore of his brain that was still fractionally rational, he wondered if he had really been the one that thought it.

"Dude I think we need to get you out of the building. Hell maybe out of this city. Maybe out of this profession, I don't know. But will you come with me out of this bathroom please?" George asked.

Mick gave a noncommittal shrug and holstered the weapon. He could feel the grin on his face spreading wider still. The muscles around his mouth were beginning to feel tight.

"I like you George. You've been a good friend." Mick said. He could feel his jaw flexing and his tongue moving in his head as he said the words. They didn't feel like they had any weight to them. Almost like he was hearing them spoken from *outside* himself, while still managing to manipulate the inner workings of his vocals just to make the words come out.

"Thanks buddy. You've been a great friend too. Looks like right now you really, really need one." George said, inching his way over to Mick and steadily sliding one arm crossed Mick's shoulders, "Let's get you out of here. Maybe get you something to eat. You hungry?" George asked.

Mick just kept giggling.

SAFE HOUSE

October 30, 2:13pm

There is a certain emotional whiplash one experiences when they find out about their supernatural heritage. Even with all the foreshadowing that life and the Universe had been throwing at him, Oscar still struggled to see how he could have been so blind?

You are a dark beast that hunts in the darkness of mankind's nightmares, alien to the fabric of reality…and you had no clue?!

No, despite wondering how he could not have known, Oscar's plate was now filled with bigger things. Floundering eels that threatened to embrace his throat as they mocked and dared him to find a way to cope.

The conversation that was playing through his memory right now was from a couple nights ago. Oscar had picked himself up off the concrete floor, blood pouring from his nose where Brandon's fist had burrowed its way into his face. He could feel his eyes set on fire with white hot rage, burning through the acidic tears that burned their way down his cheeks.

"Since you are so new, literally anything could be a trigger for you to turn," Brandon had said.

"You're *trying* to make me turn?!" Oscar barked, nearly flying back up off of the ground, his fingers turning into claws. Brandon side stepped, caught his arm as it came around, and before Oscar could react, he was on his stomach and his arm was twisted in a way he knew it wasn't meant to bend.

"I'm trying to see what makes you *want* to turn, so that way I can then teach you how to overcome those triggers." He said as he let go of his arm.

Oscar could feel the bones that formed his nasal cavity realigning. He wasn't changing, at least he prayed he wasn't. Soon there was only a dull ache coming from his nasal area, and with each throb, even that began to subside. The watering in his eyes persisted however, much to his annoyance.

"Well I think we can add assault and battery to the list of 'triggers,'" Oscar said.

He was almost starting to think he had been better off with Sunny and that Craven guy. At least they never hauled off and beat the crap outta him.

"I don't want it to take over again." Oscar said, his voice shaking as he balled his hands up into fists.

"You're still thinking of the beast as a separate entity from yourself." Brandon said. Oscar flinched like he had just been touched by a hot iron poker.

"Well...yeah." Oscar admitted. Brandon's face softened, about as much as his face could anyway.

"I've hardly slept since the change." Oscar said as he recalled every fitful night he had been with these hunters.

"Every time I close my eyes I can feel it wanting to burst out. I swear I feel my bones popping without me moving them. I can feel my skin getting tighter and tighter every minute when I'm lying there trying to fall asleep, like I'm going to tear out of it. And I can't stop thinking about it! It felt like someone poured a liter of acid into my brain, and every sense I have was turned up to eleven, and that was just while I was changing! I could feel every nerve ending connected to each bone that broke. I could feel the teeth of that thing pushing their way through my gums. The whole time I'm feeling the vertebrae of my spine ripping through my back, I'm screaming out to God just to make it fucking stop, or to at least let me pass out. But no..." Oscar said, his face rippling with rage as tears burned his eyes. He looked down at his hand he had tried to catch Brandon with earlier. His fingernails had fallen off, and blood was dripping off the ends of new sharp, pointed claws about a good two or three inches long.

"It's deeper than the trauma of your first change though, isn't it?" Brandon asked. Oscar nodded. His entire life growing up, thinking he was a perfectly normal kid. He remembered sitting in front of the TV as a youngster, enraptured by documentaries about wolves. Feeling slightly different from all the other kids at school, until he got to high school and buried himself in athletics. Then it was like he finally had a crowd to fit into, because he was the fastest and strongest on the team. But yet, even because of that, he was still not what he would call, truly, one of the group. Sure it got him all the attention he wanted, but it felt fake. Like none of those other kids ever really wanted to be friends with him because they liked him. They just liked what he did for the team, how he made the rest of them look good. There was always something there, hinting at what he truly had inside of him.

But it wasn't until his first change that all those foreshadowing moments even made sense. And then to find out that he was never really a human being to begin with had brought him to the edge of his sanity. Yet even though he hated admitting it, it was these hunters that had pulled him back from the edge. These hunters, and the one they served. The one Judah kept calling Yeshua.

Oscar's eye blinked away moisture as he returned to the present moment, and with it, a feint glimmer of hope.

Maybe it was the naïve hope of a lost young man, but he hoped he could find the courage to reconnect with his family. But the tearful fantasy of them lovingly embracing him was immediately cut short before he had the chance to enjoy it. He remembered losing himself in the savage hunger of the night he ran away from home. He remembered the hunger that clawed within his guts to be satisfied. He literally recalled the sharp feeling of claws trying to slice through the lining of his stomach as he gulped down the raw hamburger meat he had smuggled into his room. The hamburger meat he had bought with stolen money from his mother's purse. Even then the tribute to the thing inside of him seemed like a piss-off treat. A drop in the ocean of the insurmountable hunger. He recalled the stories he had heard from his many cousins of their times being pregnant. How their eating habits had changed, consuming enough to satisfy the growing thing inside. But in the recent days Oscar had accepted the crippling conclusion that the thing inside of him wasn't a separate entity at all. It was *him*. The boy he had seen in the mirror every morning before school was just a mask. The crushing revelation that there was only a thin layer of skin separating the primal beast from the rest of the world was enough to assault his body with a cold sweat.

All that aside, he thought it was nice of the hunters to at least send him and Sunny to a place that had a TV and an *XBOX 360*. The safe house they had sent them to was a small duplex in a forgotten part of town. Each door leading into the small flats had a CONDEMNED sign plastered over it. These were nothing but forgeries of course. The power that the mini fridge, and television and space heaters ran off of were portable electric generators. No electricity being drawn from the grid of the city. Nothing that could be traced by any power companies. The hunters had gone to great lengths to ensure any safe houses would not be noticed by anyone who could do anything about it. There was also something about wards and blessings over the properties that kept the place obscured from anyone's conscious notice, human or otherwise. Each little flat was stocked to the brim with extra weapons, ammo and other items needed for fighting back the dark. Not to mention mini fridges stocked with bottled water and dry goods to last more than a week. Oscar stayed in one flat, and Sunny was in the one next to him, a wall between them under one sagging roof.

The bullets they used were just regular bullets it seemed. The glowing effect that caused the monsters various harmful effects was produced by the Light being channeled through the Reclaimed Hunter's veins, into the essence of the weapon and more or less, "enchanting" the bullets to be a one stop kill-all for whatever they were facing. Channeling the Light was also a part of experiencing the Higher Sight they talked about. Brandon could do it, even with being a werewolf. Oscar had undergone his own rebirth, or "Reclaiming", but being able to summon the Light to his aid eluded him. He knew deep down that he was being too hard on himself. He still had to find ways to understand the beast that he was, before it would yield and become a conduit for the Light.

Being with the Reclaimed, as they called themselves, made him want the life they were offering even more. He knew any sane person would run the other way and never look back, but he wasn't any sane person. If he was a beast, he wanted to be useful. Not harnessed, or tamed, but he wanted to be able to trust his beast to direct its murderous rampage at the things lurking in the shadows and not at someone who wasn't prepared to defend themselves against it. The Reclaimed were offering him a chance to hunt alongside them. In a sense, they could offer him everything he was lacking right now. Direction, purpose, clarity, and the safety net of reassurance that if he snapped, they would do something about it.

No sooner had he finished his thought than he smelled her approaching. He could always smell her since she was literally just on the other side of the wall, but now he caught her scent rushing toward the back door toward him. His ears heard the air moving under the weight of her feet as she approached, the crunch of the leaves beneath her boots. Her knock was firm, but not jarring. He got up and went to the back door.

Sunny stood there, draped in a purple *Nightmare before Christmas* hoodie, tight hip huggers and black boots.

"Yo," Oscar greeted as he opened the door to her. His eyes saw the feint, round scar tissue over her left eye. She had told him the night they settled here where it had come from. That her brother was gone. While still visible, it was healing nicely. In a couple days she might not even have a scar.

"Hey," She said as her eyes awkwardly lifted to meet his.

"You wanna come in? Join me for some beef jerky and bottled water?" Oscar asked.

She nodded and stepped up into the kitchen while he closed the door behind her.

She sighed and leaned her arms on the counter next to the small sink as he pulled out two bottles of water from the mini fridge and then grabbed a bag of jerky out of the cabinets.

"How you holding up?" He asked.

She answered quicker than he expected, "I'm hurting. A lot. I miss my brother. I miss who he used to be when we were kids." Her eyes turned toward Oscar, full of angst and sorrow, "And I wanted to apologize for dragging you in the middle of this. Honestly, you were meant to be expendable."

He stood there, taken aback slightly as he set the food and water down on the counter next to her, "I *felt* expendable," he said.

She nodded, quickly looking away from him as she grabbed one of the bottles and opened it.

"I know. We treated you like crap. Regardless of my allegiance at the time, I was a pretty crappy person to you. In all the amazing things we've been caught up in over the last couple weeks of being with these hunters, I sort of forgot how shitty I was. Now it takes me losing my brother for me to remember how much of a witch I really was to you. To everyone else who Father didn't want us to approach. I felt like a goddess…And everyone else was an insect. And I'm so sorry for how I treated you." She said as her eyes began to water.

Oscar reluctantly put his hand on her shoulder and gave a light squeeze.

"We're cool," he said. She nodded, wiped her eyes with her sleeve and took a swig of her water. Neither of them said anything for a time, as they both began filling their bellies with Buffalo Jerky Bites.

"Can we be friends?" She asked.

Oscar looked up at her, smiled and let out a small burp.

"I'm down!" Oscar said as he popped another piece of jerky into his mouth. For a while neither of them spoke, and it seemed that neither of them were in any hurry to break the silence as they ate together.

Sunny finished off her bag of jerky quicker than Oscar figured she would, and crossed to the cabinets to have a look.

"Mind if I have another?"

Oscar nodded, trying to chew through the wad of cured meat he was currently working on.

"Thanks," she said as she reached up and began looking through the bags.

"How have you been?" She asked him.

Oscar downed a gulp of water and replied, "Reflective. Like you said, so much has happened over the last few days. Found out I'm a werewolf. Been trying to deal with that. Brandon's been pretty great at helping me."

Sunny nodded, "Yeah he's pretty cool. All the hunters seem so."

"Can you channel the light yet?"

Oscar shook his head, "Nah…Been trying to figure out how to put that gun back together in there. I wanna hunt with these guys so I figure I better get good with the tools ya know?"

"The light is a tool." She said smiling.

"Well yeah…I don't know. I wonder how other hunters do it. The official ones from the government? Cause as far as I know they can't do any fancy light shows in their veins right?" Oscar asked. Sunny shrugged.

"I feel like…" Oscar resumed, trying to think of how to phrase what he wanted to say, "I feel like me, being a werewolf, and learning how to control that might have to come first before I can do any of the cool stuff."

"I can understand that. I would say being a werewolf is pretty cool, but I know better. You saw those dog skins I kept. I used those to change myself like in the old legends. Feeling your body twist and break like that. Only an idiot would think it's a fun time." Sunny said.

Oscar smirked as a thought occurred to him.

"What's so funny?" Sunny asked, a smirk creeping up the side of her face as well.

"Well, at this point, I can literally say that 'I was a Teenaged Werewolf.'"

Sunny closed her eyes like she was about to facepalm. But instead she just shook her head, her smile seeming to stay without fluctuating.

"I've never seen it though," Oscar said.

"No need to when you can live it," She said, her voice taking on a solemn tone. Oscar nodded. He couldn't argue that she had a point.

"But since its one of those older movies it might be all cheesy and goofy. Maybe a light hearted perspective on the matter could help." He said.

"Maybe redbox might have it?" She offered. Oscar shook his head.

"I doubt it. Maybe the library?"

"Road trip?" Sunny offered, and then her face drooped, "can we even watch it here?" She asked looking into the small living room.

"Yeah I have an XBOX we could watch it on." Oscar said.

"Lucky. All I have in mine is a VCR."

"Hey don't knock the classics. VCR's are dope."

"So road trip then?" Sunny asked, handing Oscar another piece of jerky.

"I'm down, let's go!"

A CALL FROM A FRIEND

October 31, 5:45pm,

Mick sat there on George's couch, his eyes cloudy and his eyelids stiff. He moved his fingers, one at a time, feeling each joint flex as the individual digits closed. He drew in a deep breath, held it for five seconds and then let it out slowly.

He remembered what had happened in the men's room at work. He remembered that he had drawn his side arm. He didn't remember if he had pointed it at George or not though. He still remembered the sinister vision that he had experienced that night too, and he struggled to keep the images and sensations of that time and place from invading his mind. His palms began to sweat as something else kept trying to force its way into his thoughts.

The next day Mick had an appointment scheduled with the police psychiatrist. He shaved, had showered twice and even went to the trouble of getting a much needed haircut. Preparing for this appointment felt just like preparing for his first job interview with the NBEPD. He had gone into the evaluation feeling semi-confident. He had spent a good deal of his time trying to psych himself up for it with a lot of positive affirmations, looking at himself in the mirror and telling himself he could pass, and that he wouldn't lose his job and end up out on the streets as a staggering, washed up alcoholic. He felt that it was going extremely well until the psychiatrist began to question his truthfulness about everything he had just been through. Mick hadn't noticed that he was crossing his arms, had put his hands on the psychiatrist's desk, and he expressed some blatant disdain when his claims of what he saw in the men's room were questioned. On some level, after he had regained a measure of his wits, Mick *thought* he knew what he saw was a hallucination. But it was the fact that when they went over it, he honestly had to think about if he was sure in that assessment. The evaluation concluded with Mick exchanging a hand shake and walking out of the office, his face set like stone against the ocean that was threatening to erode him down right then and there.

He opened his eyes and let out his last deep breath. George had been good enough to let him crash at his place, which was more than Mick felt he honestly deserved. He could have shot George when he drew his pistol. It would have been so easy. The gun literally felt like hollow plastic. One would either call George a saint for allowing him to stay there, or incredibly stupid. The apartment was a little bit bigger than Mick's. Two bedroom, second story. Bigger than George needed honestly, but the spare room worked out nicely for Mick, who would have graciously accepted the couch, but George insisted.

"Bro you need to sleep. Real sleep, like you would get on a good ol' fashion memory foam mattress! Not that damn couch that's falling to pieces," George had said, tossing Mick's duffle bag onto the guest bed while Mick protested.

True to form, that night had been the first night in months that Mick had actually slept in such a way he felt he might never wake up. He felt the crushing weight of his own denseness, the tension in his muscles, the ach in his spine, all release as the foam mattress beneath him molded itself to his shape, enveloping him like a living, sentient cloud. Somehow through that night, Mick remembered crying. Lucid dreaming was not something he ex-perienced very often, but for some reason that night, he was perfectly rested, while conscious enough to feel the burning of tears escape his eyes. And he saw shapes dancing in the darkness. Whatever pictures his eyes formed on the screen of his brain crawled toward him there on the bed, rested on his chest, clung to the corners of the walls, but none of them felt malicious. Either that or Mick was so used up he hardly cared anymore. If they were going to take him, he was glad he had gotten to sleep on a memory foam mattress at least. Small blessings could still occur, even in a world full of inhuman parodies of life that crawled on disjointed limbs and clutched at his throat like one of those shadowy forms had tried to do.

He heard buzzing coming from the counter in the kitchen. Mick stood up and made his way over to his phone, each step feeling far heavier than the last. His stomach sank the closer he got to his phone, vibrating there on the counter. If it was Chief Scroggins, it would mean the results of his psychiatric evaluation were in, and Mick wasn't handling the prospect of potentially being deemed unfit for duty very well. But the muscles in his chest relaxed when he saw it was George.

He scooped up his phone, saw it was at 100%, and unplugged it from the charger, then slid the green arrow to the right so he could answer it.

"Hey man, what's up?"

Sharp static shot down his ear canal, and Mick quickly drew the phone away from his ear—but not before making out the sound of his name being shouted through the storm of sharp white noise on the other end.

"Hey, where are you at?" Mick asked, switching ears and jamming a finger down his other ear to stop the throbbing. The static melted away to a light hum that flickered in and out sporadically.

"George?" Mick repeated. He was answered by a sound that was somewhere between sobbing and laughter, and it was George's voice. Mick felt his grip tighten on the phone as the marrow in his bones flushed with frost. He felt like shards of ice were pushing themselves out through his pores, liquefying once upon his brow. George was muttering something in hurried, hushed tones, but what he was saying got drowned out by sudden flares of static. Between the hurried words he spoke, he broke into fits of wailing sobs that sounded distant as if George had been trying to communicate from across the room.

"George where are you man?! Are you hurt? Get ahold of yourself!" The irony of those words stabbed Mick in the back of his brain. Just a few nights ago, it had been George who had talked him down.

There was a *click* on the other end, and the silence from the other end invaded Mick's ears like a roaring phantasm. He looked at his phone, saw that the call had been lost. He pulled up George's number again and hit Call. The phone rang once. Twice. Three times.

GROWING PAINS

October 31, 6:13pm,

W hat...am...I?
It was a question the thing that called itself Father had pondered and asked itself over countless eons. All that time, and still no satisfactory answers had breached the surface of his bubbling consciousness. He faintly recalled ancient civilizations being crushed as the waters of the deep opened their primordial maw to receive them. Now the mortals that sat next to him at this traffic light waiting for it to turn green remember that event as the Flood of Noah.

Did he remember watching the Roman Empire rise? Was he instrumental in its spreading? He couldn't remember. Did he remember fighting in the gladiator pits against foes that had spawned from the nightmares of mankind made flesh? He liked to imagine that he did remember. Emerging as the victor, his body always mutilated beyond recognition, but standing in triumph over the werewolf or griffon or whatever other deformed monstrosity they threw at him.

Did he remember the primordial races that built the Sphynx? Every time he tried all he could recall were vague images of beings of gargantuan stature, with an array of multiple twisting limbs that bent all the wrong ways.

The light turned green, and Father eased the car through the intersection, keeping his speed in check. He knew the speed traps that waited around this area. He could always allow himself to get pulled over. He hadn't fed lately, and surely a cop would make a decent snack. But he wasn't ready to induce a panic just yet. Too many onlookers. He did enjoy dining in peace on occasion. But oh, when the mood struck him, he relished the sweet descent into chaos.

He enjoyed knowing people were running *because* of him. To run from the likes of him meant that the prey's imagination had been captured and molested by terror buried so far deep it only manifested in their nightmares. Terror so pure it harkened back to a time when the creatures of the dark didn't wear human shapes, simply because they weren't necessary and didn't care.

At least, he thought such a time existed. What little fragments he could remember seemed disjointed and conflicted. His day dreams of Rome and other times throughout history, he pondered often as to whether they were true memories of actual events he had experienced, or if they had been formed as waking dreams. Still the question hammered away at him—*What am I?*

Yet for all the uncertainty that swirled about him, at least two things seemed settled in his eyes. Number one, Father was not a recent title. Though a sexless being, offspring had bled into the fabric of this reality through him. The second thing, he was drawn to Mick Johnson.

The offspring though. That was a subject of deepest obsession to him indeed. He had existed long enough to have a few moments of clarity, and he remembered it happening when he had crossed paths with them. Though a rare occurrence, he knew he had met with one of his offspring. Once before recorded history, and again only a blink ago. To be exact it had been about three hundred years ago. Time had been very cruel to one of them, beating it into a form that could no longer be sustained in this physical world. The other one's state of existence and whereabouts though had yet to be determined. Then again there was the issue of remembering exactly how many children he had sired on this physical plane.

Was it two…or three…? He thought. In any case, he amounted that one to old age and memory loss, as some humans would put it.

The line he fed his human worshipers about reuniting with them was probably the only true thing he ever said to them. That indeed was his goal. But his desire to unite with them was not out of a fatherly longing. As he brought the car to a stop in front of a boarded up, condemned one story house at the end of the block, he licked his lips.

Each encounter with his spawn had left a gnawing hunger growing inside of him that no mortal life could fill. It throbbed and screamed for release in the point of its origin—his lacking memory. Whatever his children were, or had turned into, they held the key to his lost memories within their delectable essence. He exited his vehicle and walked up the walkway to the house, whistling a tune he had heard on the radio the other day. He recalled the myth of the Titan Cronos, and how he had devoured his god children. Perhaps the myth was about him? Perhaps his children had escaped the caverns of his belly somehow and that was how they all ended up in this material existence, on this planet called Earth? The thought crossed his mind numerous times. He truly didn't know, and paid it no mind as he unlocked the door and stepped into the darkened house.

He thought one more time about Johnson; obsessively hell bent on his own pursuit of justice. Father was quite obsessive himself. There was a reason Father was drawn to him. There was something about him that drove Father's cravings to a near maddening level. Something he *had* to have. Each person he fed on, touched, kissed, violated, all tasted of the gray taint. As if each human was seasoned by an after taste. With each passing century, he was following a trail, sampling the precious taint from each mortal he interacted with like a buffet. Each one only tasted stronger of the taint his children gave off. The taint which had mutated as *they*, the children, traveled through the DNA of mankind over eons of gestation. They were from him after all, flesh of his flesh. He had a feeling that Johnson would taste very *familial* indeed.

"Are you comfortable?" Father asked off into the darkness where a sheet had been draped over a ratty and tattered recliner that was likely to fall to pieces any moment. Another fine example of his taint. The house had fallen into disrepair the very night he set foot inside of it. His presence had aged the wood so much as to compromise the structural integrity of the house. The fabric of the recliner, though only a couple years old, was now rotten and brittle. A newly married couple had been in the process of moving their belongings into this house when he arrived.

The only reply Father received to his question was a muffled wheezing cough that pitifully escaped from under the sheet on the recliner.

Father stepped closer, through the hallway and into the living room. A couple pictures hung on the wall, a coffee table and an empty entertainment center rested near the south wall. But in the middle of the room was the recliner with the sheet over it. A pathetic, frail form twitched beneath the sheet. He could feel this man's life ebbing away by the minute. This had been the same body that he had kept at the former sanctuary the night Skylah and Craven had brought that werewolf boy. The same body he had said was his, but that was only a half truth. It was one of several he had on standby. A successful hunter has eyes all over the habitat of his prey. This man had been one such pair of eyes. A former hunter himself. Though his body was no longer suitable to hold Father's power, his mind was still potent enough to astral project. Father had made use of this man's spirit in the form of a tall black shape that had appeared often to Mick over the last month. And the entertaining part was that the hunters who called themselves Reclaimed could at times see the black wraith as well.

"It saddens me that our time is almost up old friend," Father said as he circled around the recliner, never bothering to lift the sheet from the man's face.

"I must extend you my deepest gratitude now while I still have the chance. You stayed by my side when the others either fled or burned out altogether. Black Coyote vanished after the Massacre, Swift and Webster couldn't handle my power...But *you* held on. Your mind was so much stronger than theirs. You made a fine host." Father cooed.

The form beneath the sheet attempted to thrash suddenly, but was restrained by an invisible force. A violent hacking fit ensued soon after.

"Shhhh. Preserve your strength. We will yet again recreate a grand and glorious, *New* Broken Edge Massacre," Father said looking from the frail body beneath the sheet, to the tall, shimmering black shadow that now appeared behind the recliner. The bald head reached a height of six foot four, and the wraith appeared to be wearing the black shadowy tatters of a long coat that blustered with the chilling wind of the astral realm. The face of the wraith, though young in features, was haggard and exhausted looking, with yellow eyes and skin the color of ash. Father noted the Hispanic structure of the wraith's face. A much younger astral form of the man beneath the sheet stood there shaking, its lips curling up into a venomous howl of rage. The creature thrashed its face and flung its hands out in all directions, but no voice breached the fabric of reality.

Father smirked, eyeing the wraith with the kind of amusement one would enjoy from watching an idiot try and decode a complex formula.

"I thought that would arouse your excitement."

There was a buzzing sensation coming from one of the vessel's pockets. The small device called a "cell phone," was trying to get his attention. Damn thing had started acting up within the last week. Technology, though a fascinating hobby, was doomed to become a bane to him at this rate. Perhaps it was working right this time?

His lips parted in an impossibly wide grin as he pulled the device out of his pocket and saw who it was. He pressed his thumb over the touch screen's icon of the green telephone and answered the call.

"Hey Mick, what's up?"

The other line was silent for a second.

"George are you okay?" Johnson's voice came through, shaky and unsteady. Father licked his lips again.

"Yeah bro I'm okay, why? Are *you* okay?" Father asked, feigning concern.

Johnson exhaled into the phone and was silent for a second, "Didn't you just call me? I got a call from your number and when I answered it I could hear you on the other end. Sounded like you were crying or…giggling or something."

Father couldn't help the smile spreading across his face as he pulled the phone away from his ear, brought up the call log, and saw that low and behold, only a few minutes before he arrived at the house, a call had been placed through to Mick.

The little worm managed to take control. Oh George you are a determined one aren't you?

"Must have been like that last time you said I called you, remember that? Hey if you aren't busy, you should meet me at Saint Andrews Church." Father said, the mimicry of George's voice, flawless with every word.

"Uh…the Catholic one? Why? Its Halloween dude. And why would you wanna meet at a church?" Johnson asked.

Father rolled his eyes. Defiant child. But again, it was something else that would make bestowing his gift upon him so delightful. He wondered if Johnson would be as successful at taking control at random times like his friend George had. It sounded like a delicious challenge!

"You need to get out of the house man. They are having a special service tonight, and honestly, I think maybe being around some good vibes might help you out." Father said, feeding his will into each word, tasting the honey dripping from is tongue.

Johnson was quiet for a moment but eventually began to rummage in the background.

"Hello?" Father asked.

"Just gotta get my shoes on and find my keys." Mick said.

THE SILENT CONGREGATION

Traffic had been stopped all down the business district for Haunted Main Street, which was New Broken Edge's city wide Halloween event. It was also the main reason Mick had to drive through the south side of town to get anywhere near the church. The strip mall, the plaza and even local fast food places each had booths set up outside of their buildings with an array of games. Trick or treating merged with bouncy houses, face painting, and even free food. Games, squealing children, and even a haunted house in a rented building, littered with torn open candy wrappers and the smell of burgers perfumed every inch of Main Street. The local radio station had set up a booth outside of their building and was blasting Michael Jackson's *Thriller* up and down the street on the outdoor speakers. Police officers, armed to the teeth, and other civil servants stood at each intersection with bags of candy, throwing them out to the children as they passed by. It was often comical to see the young ones scrambling in the streets to claim the bite sized Snickers bar or the tiny bag of Skittles. Curfew was enforced this night more than any other, with the festivities winding down at 10:30pm when parents would be encouraged to get their children home and in bed.

His drive through all the detours had given him some time to mull over why he was even going in the first place, and to *church* of all places. He hadn't been to church since he moved out of his parents' house. If George really wanted him to get out of the house, why invite him there? Maybe George had a newfound appreciation for religion? Still, Lilly's Bar and Grill was their usual hang out spot. In any case, Mick knew George was right. He needed to get outside. He needed to be around ordinary people. Maybe after the service he could convince George to go check out that haunted house. Some cheap jump scares might be kinda fun. The idea of someone waiting around a corner to start chasing him with a fake chainsaw made him laugh on the inside.

He figured by now he had witnessed enough true horror to cause him to go numb. Nothing in a staged haunted house could even begin to compare. The more he thought about it, the more he was made aware of just how badly he needed that. He needed to laugh in someone's face as they ran after him swinging a rubber cleaver. He needed the jump scares to be fake. He needed to laugh at some college girl who screamed and bawled because someone had just touched her butt. He felt his face tightening up into a smile as the thoughts continued to build up momentum. Tonight would be fun, and he was going to enjoy himself. He would grin and bear it through the church service, and then would go to the haunted house with George, and then to make the night really memorable, they would go get drunk.

St. Andrew's Catholic Church was in sight now. The church had its own parking lot located across the street from it, which Mick pulled into. He noted the disturbing absence of other vehicles. Sure he was there, but the only other vehicle he saw was a Sheriff's pickup. He didn't even see George's Jeep. Had Mick beaten him there?

He did *say there was service tonight right? And he said it was at this place,* Mick thought. He got out of his car, the sounds of Halloween festivities trickling into his ears from up the street. He looked up at the church, with its concrete steps leading up toward the metal double doors with the fancy elaborate stained glass shapes set into them. They opened, and a familiar figure emerged.

"Oh there he is," Mick said to himself as he strode across the street. George flung his arms up wide as he saw Mick, and descended from his place on the steps two at a time until they met at the sidewalk.

"Glad to see you made it man!" George said as he pulled Mick into a bro-hug.

"Hey there George," Mick said, his eyes searching again through the parking lot to see if he missed any other vehicles, "are we early?"

George followed Mick's gaze and then chuckled, "Nah man, everyone is inside already. It's getting ready to start." He said as he turned back up the steps.

"So, of all places, a church huh? Lilly's wasn't open?" Mick asked, trying to pretend he didn't actually mean it. George turned to him, his face sporting that trademark smirk of his, "Bro don't worry, there will be plenty of time to get drunk later on. Promise."

Mick followed him up, "Shouldn't we be getting drunk first and *then* come to church? Ya know, to ask for forgiveness?"

Still doesn't explain why there are no other cars here, Mick thought. Mick entered alongside George. He thought he would hear the sounds of an organ playing, people singing, or…*something.* But his ears were greeted with a ceaseless screaming void of silence. The sound his shoes made on the tile flooring in the foyer as he walked were obnoxious, and made him feel all the more self-conscious. He followed George through the modest foyer, onto a ten foot purple and royal blue rug that stretched into the well-lit sanctuary. He saw in the seemingly ceaseless rows of pews gathered many still, somber figures praying where they sat or knelt at the candlelit alter below the pulpit. Almost all of the polished wooden pews were occupied, leaving only minimal seating available. Mick saw George whisper to one prayerful soul at about the middle row of pews in the sanctuary. They nodded and then scooted down so they could be seated as well.

At once, Mick began to notice the queasy, dull gray hue that seemed to be clinging to and exuding from every surface in the sanctuary. He blinked through it, trying to clear the optical illusion from his vision. He focused his eyes on the impressive nine foot tall marble statue of the Archangel Michael pinning Lucifer to the ground under his sandaled feet, holding a drawn sword at the ready to deliver righteous fury upon the old serpent. His eyes traveled around the sanctuary, at times attempting to count the heads of everyone he saw. He tried to see some of their faces, to see if he knew anyone else here tonight, but all those in attendance either had their heads bowed or looked the other direction the moment his eyes landed on them. No one he saw, even from a "back of the head" kind of view looked familiar in the slightest. He eventually gave up counting heads and guessed that there were about two-hundred and fifty to three hundred people here tonight. Everyone was so still, with only the subtle movement of back muscles on occasion just to show they were breathing. Mick was about to play along, bow his head and pretend to pray—or more likely doze off for a short nap—when he looked over at George. His friend also had his eyes closed and his head bowed. His hands were clasped over his lips, subtly twitching. Mick watched, transfixed as his eyes locked onto a spot on top of George's left hand.

A black bruise covered the top of his left hand, like someone had popped an ink bubble beneath his gray skin. Mick immediately began scrambling in his memory for any ounce of recollection. Had he seen that bruise earlier today? How long had it been there? Regardless of what he could or couldn't remember, it didn't explain why the bruise was beginning to flake like ash.

Mick blinked. He blinked hard, trying to comprehend how that was even possible. Tiny flakes of ash floated from the spot on George's hand down to the floor next to his shoe.

Mick began to feel like there were spiders crawling around inside of his chest, wrapping their legs around his lungs and spinning cold wet webs around them. He felt something pinching the base of his brain. Something that felt *very* old, and patient. He could feel the sensation scratching its way into his skull. He wanted to run. Every sense he had was screaming at him to make a break for the doors, but his body remained immobile. Morbid fascination had merged with an ancient dread that came shrieking up through his brainstem as he watched George. His friend with his eyes still closed, began to smile, a knowing grin creeping across his face.

George I swear to God if this is some fucked up prank I'm gonna kill you! Mick kept trying to say in his mind.

"Jack, lock the doors. Me and Mr. Johnson have much to discuss," George said, in a voice that wasn't his.

The shock of someone talking through this reverent silence should have caused a reaction in the crowd. Someone's head should have looked up to see who would dare speak aloud in such a casual tone while everyone else was praying. But no one stirred. Maybe that's how Mick was able to find his strength to bolt out from the pew he was in. He didn't even remember standing up. And if that voice, which was out of place in more ways than one, didn't cause people to stir, the ruckus he was making as he tried to run should have elicited annoyed looks from the prayerful souls gathered around him.

Nothing. Not a single head turned.

Movement ahead caused Mick to slam on the breaks. What he saw next nearly caused him to drop to one knee and clutch at his chest to keep his heart from exploding.

A figure was blocking the doors he and George had walked through. It wore bloodstained, tattered jeans, and muddy steel toed work boots. The figure also wore a bloody burlap mask over its head. As for the rest of it, the being was shirtless, revealing a torso that appeared to be carved out of wood. Its back was facing Mick as it closed the sanctuary doors, sealing Mick in with the rest of the dazed people. With its back turned, Mick could clearly see the assortment of gruesome cutlery that protruded from the figure's back. From one shoulder, swaying by a strap, was a semi-automatic 12 gauge shotgun, and from the other shoulder, an AR-15.

It didn't take him any time at all to register in his mind that this was the one who attacked him at the hunters' lair. Though now he could plainly see that it was no man at all. His mouth went dry as he fought to breath. It felt like just trying to breath was causing his lungs to shrink. He felt like his lungs had been replaced with the lungs of a pre-mature baby.

The thing that was not a man turned its head toward Mick as it withdrew a key from the lock on the sanctuary doors.

"You've met Jack haven't you?" That voice said. Mick struggled not to turn his head. He didn't want to see George's lips moving, only to hear a voice that wasn't his come out.

But against his will, like some other force had taken control of his nervous system, Mick felt himself slowly turning to look behind him. George now stood there, the ashen bruise now beginning to cover his face. He took a step closer and a thin layer of ash fell from one cheek.

"Oh Mr. Johnson, please don't be afraid. Jack had only meant to rescue you from the hunters. And my emissary, Craven's motives were much the same. The one you shot and killed. But, I bear no grudge." The voice went on from George's mouth.

Mick could feel his own lips moving, trying to form words with strained effort. George's hand came up, and Mick felt his struggling cease as a tingling numbness spread over his lips.

"There's no need to talk my dear boy. I understand you are shaken up. To answer your first question: No, I am obviously not George. I cannot give you my name, because I'm afraid I don't remember whether I ever had one or not. But suffice it to say, I have been called Father by many. No doubt you have heard some very, unsavory *lies* about me and my purpose towards you?"

The thing in George's body gave a slight nod as if waiting for Mick to answer, but he couldn't. All he was capable of was standing there shaking as the fiendish presence of the invading voice addressed him from behind the wall of flesh that looked like his friend.

"Let me rephrase; did you ever get the chance to look over the journal of my emissary? The one the hunters claimed to lift from her?"

Mick felt the muscles in his neck release slightly, enough for him to shake his head no. He felt like his neck had turned to plastic, and he was a mannequin fighting for every inch he could move.

"Ah. Then you have no confirmation as to its true contents? And therefore you cannot judge for yourself the authenticity of the hunters' claims or your trusted Chief Ted Scroggins?" Father asked. Mick again felt himself just barely able to shake his head no again.

"A pity your trust in that man was so misplaced. He became a public supporter of the hunters while you were missing. But, he has recanted now that they are behind bars. Hard to put your trust in such a man with such an unsteady backbone. Jack here, along with my other emissaries, were only trying to give you the chance to come with me. I am truly sorry that I have had to hold you in place as I have, but you are exceedingly tenacious when it comes to dealing with my poor emissaries. I'm sorry I had to borrow your friend, but I thought we could talk face to face." The voice said, as George's hand motioned for Mick to sit back down. Without any conscious thought, Mick felt his muscles ease up enough for him to walk back to the pew he and George—Father—were seated at earlier.

"You have such a strong will, Mr. Johnson. It has served you well. Your will has complimented your gut instincts about the hunters. Then their leader arrogantly confessed to you his part in the Broken Edge Massacre, didn't he?" Father asked.

Mick nodded, his insides shaking.

"I don't need to read your mind Mr. Johnson. I can feel the cocoon of energy you are encased in. It saddens me that such a wonderfully created being such as yourself would be bound up with such emotions as fear, rage, and hopelessness, to name a few. Constant fear that your city and the people you care about will suffer next. Fear that next time, you won't be so lucky as to be killed off in the chaos and you'll have to relive the horror every day until you die. Rage, that you were so powerless to stop these new hunters from getting accepted into the public eye. Rage that the brief childhood you had was stripped away from you like the flesh on a live animal as it lay there helpless under the hunter's blade. Fear that the true monsters are the ones who sit in their jail cells plotting your downfall. You were only a small child. They were the ones you looked up to. They were your super heroes. They had violated the trust your impressionable little heart had placed in them. They took your young heart to new heights of terror that none your age can return from whole. I'm truly the one who can give you the power you seek to avenge those poor souls who lost their lives when the Broken Edge Massacre happened. Is that what you want?" The voice out of George's mouth asked.

Mick felt his eyes watering as he sat there, listening to this thing speak to him the words he needed to hear. He needed to have his anguish clearly defined. On the surface he knew it was because his childhood was ripped out from under him at a young age, knew that the hunters he had trusted were to blame. But now, an other worldly being speaking through his best friend of all things, had been able to articulate his grief better than he could. Mick breathed deeply, for the first time since the night had turned on its ear.

"Can I ask you a couple questions?" Mick asked.

"Does that count as one?" Father asked, smirking through George's face.

Mick didn't know whether to smile out of courtesy or proceed to piss himself. The thing inside of his friend was trying to mimic humor.

"You said they lied about you? All those things about me becoming your Right Hand. Giving me some kind of magical gift. Where *those* lies? What does all that mean?" Mick asked, finding just enough confidence to form the words into a question, though just barely above a whisper.

Father's—George's face looked at him thoughtfully, "No they were not. Mr. Johnson, what we have here is a conflict of two differing perspectives.

Both seeking to accomplish and thwart that same goal. These hunters, they're *terrorists*. They know you are capable of bringing them down. You are a thorn in their flesh. They know that if you were to accept my gift, you would be the quarry they could not bag. They seek to "protect" you from me? Laughable at best. They seek to control the key to their downfall. As it stands, you know those cells will not hold them for long. I seek you out for the express purpose of granting you the power truly needed to protect your city, where the power of your blinded justice system and lawmen falls short or is bought by fancy displays of charisma. *You,* Mick Johnson, are the hero that New Broken Edge needs. You survived their first slaughter. You can prevent their next. As for your second question: My presence inside of George's body has caused massive trauma to his vital organs and his brain. I'm not meant to be housed within a third dimensional body for long. I have been trying to reach out to you since you wrapped up the Terrance Miller killings. Perhaps if my emissaries had been successful in drawing you to me sooner, perhaps his condition wouldn't be as dire as it is currently."

Mick's breath caught short. Father had answered his next question before he even had the chance to ask it. He looked at George's body. The bruise had spread up his neck, and with each small movement Father made, more flakes of ash, the uppermost layers of George's skin, fell off, dowsing his red shirt with soot. If his presence inside of him was causing his skin to turn to ash, what was happening to him on the inside? Mick stopped the thought before it could gain enough traction in his mind to become the next conversation piece. He didn't know at what point this thing had started peeking inside of his mind.

Father nodded, "He still has time. But you must choose quickly. He will require swift medical attention. I can get him to the hospital, but George needs your decision quickly."

"Then I've made my choice." Mick said, his eyes blurring over with tears as his voice gained a hot edge to it.

"Then pledge your consent. Save George. Save New Broken Edge."

"I pledge my consent. I accept your gift, whatever it may be. Whatever form it may take, just let me save my friend!" Mick said as images of George from when they were both in kindergarten played through his head. George and him playing with their *Transformer* action figures. Mick reached down deep, deep within him. The fear he felt when he found out George had gone away to that children's hospital greeted him. The bone gnawing terror he felt for his friend as their childhood city was laid siege to by the ones that had come to protect them, wondering if George's hospital had been hit by the monsters too, and having no way of knowing if his best friend was alive. The fear turned to white hot rage that shot through his veins, as he said those words. In that moment, it didn't matter that the other figures gathered were starting to become blurry in his vision as he looked around the room. It didn't matter that the other people gathered here in this sanctuary no longer looked like people to Mick. As their forms became distorted, like a computer glitch, it was as if he was seeing these other people for what they really were. Twisted, hideous, bulky forms of atavistic figures from a time forgotten by the world. Their faces pierced, swollen, stitched together, as if recovering from crude surgeries. Their colors ranged in various shades of gray, blue, green or purple, but all with a glossy, wet coat of sweat or mucus. Many of their limbs were elongated to such a degree as to be jarring to behold, in addition to their hideous faces. One of them had the left side of their ribcage bulging from its chest. Yet they all shared a few commonalities. Their noses were over exaggerated and hooked, the skin on either side of their long noses was creased and sagging, and the eyes were bulging balls of black.

They all matched the descriptions of what witnesses had claimed were Throwbacks. He was in a room full of them, and nothing else mattered. The rage he felt pouring through his veins like a sweet, delicious fire began to feel like thick, freezing mucus that clotted every vessel, every pour, and every crevice inside and outside of his body. His teeth felt like someone had struck a tuning fork and held it against them while it vibrated. He could not shiver, could not breath. But just as panic set in, he realized something—*he* no longer felt like he was the one controlling his lungs. Something else was breathing for him. Something brought him to his feet, jolting the muscles in his legs to tighten as the force inside of him now exerted force upon them to make him stand. His hands lunged toward the pew in front of him, bracing himself as he slowly felt his body being taken over.

His flesh, muscles, right down to the bones felt like he had been dunked into a tank of liquid energy, which had solidified into squishy writhing masses of microscopic slugs that crawled on top of and just beneath his skin. The sensation coated his insides like molasses, the slimy wriggling sensation increasing around his spine, up his brain, and down his throat.

George's body stood to its feet, and the last thing Mick saw before his vision was drowned in the thrashing black fog of crackling energy, was the deformed hand of one of the creatures, placing a jagged, rusty hacksaw in his palm.

Go forth, Mr. Johnson, Father's voice sang through his mind, his chest, down into his stomach.

HAUNTED MAIN STREET

The makeshift floats for the Haunted Main Street Parade, many of which were designed by the community college, had begun their procession down Main Street about five minutes ago. The New Broken Edge high school's orchestra played an arrangement of the *Ghost Busters* theme as they led the parade at a brisk pace. The fire department threw candy to the children as they drove one of the fire engines behind a float with a gigantic, cartoony Frankenstein head. The flat top of the head was the stage on which the college's drama class danced to the tune played by the orchestra. Behind that marched the contestants of the evening's all ages costume contest. Many a slutty pirate, pint size *Power Ranger* and zombie cowboy waved to the throngs of citizens gathered on either side of the street, high fiving the ones close enough.

Father glanced down at the body of the policemen at his feet. The police blockade that marked the end of the parade on Second Street was now a crime scene. Throwbacks hunched over the bodies of fallen officers, were peeling the flesh from off the bodies with their teeth. Many of them looted the fallen officers' belts for their side arms.

Father looked to see Jack emerging from the back seat of a police cruiser, a bandoleer of shotgun shells slung across his chest. One of the creatures stood next to him, holding the AR-15 Jack had with him earlier.

The wraith floated next to Father, "Rufus," Father addressed the spirit by the name it used in its former life as a mortal. The wraith refused to meet his gaze.

"I promise to uphold my promise to you. After the evening's events, you are released. You may go back into your frail old body and die with a measure of dignity, knowing you aided me in accomplishing my dream of finding my children."

The wraith, Rufus, turned its head to look at him, and Father almost felt a subtle amusement as he beheld his servant. The wraith mouthed something and Father felt himself laughing on the inside.

"I know he is. Why else do you think I would want you at my side on this night?"

With that, Father raised his arm, and gave a command in a guttural tongue the creatures around him understood. The orchestra was still very far away up Main Street. Far enough away the carnage that had become this blockade would not be noticeable as a slaughter. With his command, Jack bounded over the blockade, and with him, the throng of grotesque, eviscerated bodies bounded after him.

They cleared two streets ahead in under a minute, and with the first shotgun blast, the first shrieks of panic and terror, Father looked upward into the night sky and breathed deep. Satisfaction filled him as he could feel the vibrations of the bullets puncturing flesh and splintering bone. The sound of other law enforcement trying desperately to herd the crowds of civilians out of harm's way, only to have their throats torn out by one of the flesh warped creatures.

He began to stalk forward, climbed over the police cruisers, and dashed headlong into the chaos of the halted parade.

*Gun...boom...blood...*Jack observed as his wooden index finger squeezed the trigger of the object Father had called a "gun." The gun made a new sound that Jack had never felt before. The humans that ran away from him, Father said they had ears and could hear. Not Jack. No ears.

No ears...no hear...only feel. Feel sounds. Feel words...Vibration of words, Jack thought as he watched the man's head he aimed at explode into a shower of gore, bone and brains. The people that ran away from him, Father called them fleshlings. Jack couldn't understand why they ran from him. It seemed with each step he took in a general direction of them, they ran. Had they not seen a gun? Jack looked beyond the screaming ocean of fleshlings that swirled around him. A large object, larger than anything he had seen, stood in his way.

It looked like a giant head. A man's head with a green face and flat topped head, as big as a building. Perhaps the fat lump of squirming flesh Jack was manhandling by the hair in his other hand might like to go up there? Jack turned his gaze downward to the fat man with sweat running down his flabby face, who was grabbing at his hair with both hands, trying to pry himself free from Jack's wooden grip.

"Do you know who I am?! I'm the mayor of New Broken Edge! I can give you whatever you want! Where are you taking me?!" He screamed.

Jack yanked harder, and the man staggered to his feet, still bent over at an awkward angle from having his hair held fast in Jack's grip. The scarecrow quickened his pace, and hauled the fleshling that called itself 'mayor' up the steps to the wrecked float.

Jack had never been up this high before. He looked down as the fleshlings pounded the road, scattering through the streets as Father's other followers pounced, ripped and tore at their bodies like an army of humanoid meat grinders. Jack turned to look at the fleshling that had called itself mayor, and pointed the shot gun to its head. Mayor flinched, and then Jack noticed the liquid coming out of his face was actually coming from the eye sockets. Jack knelt down closer to the mayor's face and clumsily touched the wet parts of its skin. Mayor flinched back, and Jack drew his gloved hand to his burlap face and touched the moist part to his rough skin. He flinched and drew his hand away, puzzled at the new substance that had soaked into the fabric of his gloved hand.

"Not blood?" Jack asked, looking at Mayor, who only continued to shake uncontrollably as sobs wracked its body. Then, above all the stampede of vibrations that colored the night, a singular one pierced Jack's senses and he turned his head sharply to look at Mayor. The vibration was coming from the Mayor's chest. Jack reached down, his hand slithering into the fleshling's jacket, and found the small, delicate object that was vibrating in his hand now. The small object's surface was bright and glowing! There was a part of the surface that was green, and a part that was red.

Red! Jack liked red. It was like blood. Jack pressed his gloved finger to the red part of the bright surface, expecting to feel the rush of energy that flowed into his being and imparting new knowledge of the world around him through contact with blood…but nothing happened. He set his wooden jaw tightly and tried again. Still, nothing happened. There was no intense surge of knowledge. No smear across the object's surface that indicated he was touching blood. Just a rather bothersome picture of a man with gray hair, a mustache and glasses, and the name, "Ted Scroggins."

"No blood!" Jack growled as he shoved the object into mayor's chest. The fleshling clumsily fumbled with the small object and then suddenly was speaking into it.

"Scroggins…send every officer you can spare…Please, for the love of Christ…Yes," Mayor begged into the little slender object.

Mayor paused for a second as his face scrunched up tightly and another choked sob cracked from his throat. A moment later Jack felt his grip on the handle of the shotgun tighten, and so did his finger as it closed itself around the trigger. The shotgun bucked in his grip.

QUIET STREETS

The six by eight foot cell, with its gray walls, bunk beds with flimsy padded mattresses and toilet weren't much to look at. Much nicer than Judah had expected though. Yet the accommodations merely served to feed the bodiless emanations of heavy dread that threatened to engulf his spirit. He reached deep within his pants pocket and withdrew a small silver band, crowned with a diamond. He closed his eyes as he clenched the ring in his fist, thanking God that upon being processed, the authorities had somehow missed it when they searched him.

As he sat there, he directed the current of his turbulent thoughts toward the place he had fantasized about for months. Him on one knee, holding Valerie's hand, her saying a tearful 'yes!' to his proposal. The smile of an exhausted soul reached across his face as he sat there in the jail cell, letting himself feel the exhilaration, the rush of adrenaline surge through his veins as her eyes lit up. At least, that is what he had planned would happen. He felt the energy of the thoughts shift to snippets from the past. After he awoke to the bloody first night of the Massacre, he found Valerie trying to hotwire a vehicle. She had been packing heat and upon noticing him nearly shot him as he approached. In fact if he recalled right, she *had* shot him. The sight of a man with glowing white eyes approaching her, on a night when man and monster alike were mutilating one another in the streets, her reaction was perfectly justified. He had awoken that night a new man, clothed in the new flesh of his Reclamation, and with the words of Yeshua in his mind.

The girl will help you...

Of course Valerie herself wasn't very fond of the idea, having just met and shot him and all. But it was Judah who soon aided her in fending off a team of ravenous creatures that had descended upon them.

She had been an intern at the Broken Edge Medical Center at that time. He was still just as thankful for that fact now as he had been when she dug her bullet out of his chest. Sure the Light that coursed through their veins did most of the healing work. But she was the one who still reset his bones, stitched up flesh wounds and removed teeth from the nightmarish horrors that had become embedded in his flesh.

He rested with his back against the cold wall and closed his eyes, letting his thoughts drift back to the necklace she had made for him. She had made it for him a year after the Massacre. She told him that the tooth that dangled from the leather thong had actually been from the same type of beast as the ones he had killed the night he saved her. Thankfully he hadn't been wearing it when he was arrested. A sharp object dangling from his neck would be seen as a possible weapon. He wondered how much of his teams' equipment was being confiscated. He hoped that that necklace would remain where it was, tucked safely in a metal tin in one of his dresser drawers in his quarters.

He began honing in on the ringing sound in his ears. That sound had always been one that he found calming. He focused on the ringing, let his breathing fall shallow and listened. He could feel energy prickling against his skin, causing the hairs on his arms to stand erect as the ringing grew louder and louder.

The same entity that had possessed the minds and bodies of his first team was back, and now its intended vessel was out there, unprotected. A tremor shot up his arm as he recalled the vague writings in Sunny's journal. Talk of ascension to higher planes of existence, and how ultimately this being was promising her divinity in exchange for help in acquiring Mick Johnson. Since acquiring her journal, Judah had Zach pouring over every source and bit of lore he could gain access to. But when dealing with a being so ancient, and the extent of their powers was completely unknown, nailing down a source of reliable information was daunting. There was no telling how many faces this thing had worn throughout the centuries. How many cultures had worshiped it? How many names had it gone by? There had been too many variables and not nearly enough time to process them all. But the only thing that was for certain, was it had its eyes set on Johnson, this obsessive, awkward boy with a detective badge and a gun. This boy, who had been a survivor of the carnage his old team had invoked. Valerie, once she had found out about Mick's interest in them, took to being the teams' inside source of information on him. She had gotten him to confide in her about his thoughts surrounding the old hunters. Though Judah's connection with Mick only went as far as the information Valerie had given him, he felt on some level like he had grown to know Mick through her.

Whatever Father was after, it apparently thought Mick was capable of helping achieve its goals. Which again brought Judah back to the very fact that Mick Johnson was out of reach, and now unprotected. Through the ringing, he could feel the vibration of hurried footfalls stampeding down the hallway outside of his cell. The vibrations ran up the wall his back rested against, hammered home into his chest. He could feel the sharp downward swipe of a key card, hear the beeping of electronic locks, all getting closer to his cell where he sat. He opened his eyes and shot his gaze toward the door just as he heard the electronic lock on his cell disengage. He quickly shoved the engagement ring into his pocket just as the heavy metal door flung open and two uniformed officers entered his cell.

Judah gave a nod, "Good evening gentlemen," he said.

"You're being freed, move your ass! All hells breaking loose out there!" One of them said. Judah saw a vein pulsing at the hair line of the officer's crewcut head. Judah allowed himself to be escorted from his cell, out into the cell block where he caught sight of his other hunters.

"The Chief just got a call from Mayor Watkins, who he thinks might be dead now. We got civilians being eaten alive out in the streets, freaks with guns, and a possible dead city official on our hands! You and your team have been ordered released to help deal with what's going on out there." One of the officers said.

"Any idea what's eating people are out there? Lycanthropes? Gargoyles? What do we got?" Judah asked, keeping his tone professional, almost like an exterminator asking for more information on a vermin infestation.

"Dispatch gave us the same info I just gave you," The officer replied as he herded him into the armory, where the rest of his team was waiting. They began suiting up in Kevlar. A moment later, another officer began wheeling boxes out of the evidence room on carts to the armory.

"Damn straight," Parish said as the officer began unloading the boxes onto the floor. Parish began tearing open the flaps to one box and produced his specially modified axe.

Just then a short man with a military haircut, thick mustache and pronounced canines entered the room, dressed in full SWAT gear.

"Well look who it is," Parish said as he cocked the action on the AR-15 he had slung over his shoulder.

"Parish, not now," Judah warned.

"Captain Mendez," Valerie said with a nod as she slid a fresh magazine into her pistol.

"Good evenin' to you Miss Wellington," Daniel Mendez said to her with a nod as he approached Judah.

"You in charge of these goons?" Mendez asked as his eyes swept the room and landed on Judah again.

"These goons are about the only chance your city has, so yes." Judah said reaching into one of the evidence boxes and holstering his Ruger SR-40.

"That's what I wanted to hear," Mendez said, his eyes flashing with eagerness as his radio crackled to life.

"Soon as your team is ready, meet me out front." Mendez said and quickly turned back down the hallway he had emerged from.

Within minutes each hunter was quickly set up with Bluetooth headsets all directly linked up to the command vehicle, an armored titan of a van that was leading the procession of SWAT vehicles down Main Street. Judah and the other hunters went with Mendez in the command vehicle. Judah let his body rock with the momentum of the armored vehicle as he felt Valerie reach over and take his hand.

He felt the ring in his pocket one last time before he looked over at Mendez, who was seated at a control console, looking over data on each building on Main Street that was reported to have civilians hold up inside.

"Captain?" Judah asked over the roar of the vehicle.

"Yeah?" Mendez without turning his eyes away from the monitor.

"Any word on where Detective Mick Johnson is tonight?"

Mendez shook his head, "Haven't seen him since the night we busted you guys, and I'm not at liberty to disclose information on the person who turned you in."

Judah nodded, "Fair enough," he said as he noticed the computer monitor glitch. Mendez noticed and followed Judah's gaze back to the screen. It kept glitching until it went completely black. No ERROR message flashed across the screen, it just went pitch black.

"Ah c'mon!" Mendez said as he stood to check the connection cables behind it, and as he did, the lights in the back of the van began to flicker. Judah felt the energy on his skin flair, and his eyes lit up just in time for the lights to go completely out.

He heard a static ridden, crackly voice come over Mendez's radio, "Vehicles…losing speed…watch out!" In the split second before feeling the impact, Judah reach up, seeing perfectly in the dark, and grabbed the crash safety handle, but his grip was barely enough to keep him stationary as he felt his whole body lurch to the right, slamming into Valerie and Brandon. The sound of metal colliding and grinding with metal exploded in his ear drums, sending jolting shockwaves speeding through him to his core. Zach had grabbed onto Parish and the two had nearly landed in Valerie's lap.

The transport coasted along another ten feet or so before the engine finally died, leaving them encased in an armored coffin on wheels.

Mendez was yelling orders, and trying to get responses from the other vehicles on his Bluetooth, but no such luck. The glowing eyes of the hunters were the only source of light in the darkness of the dead vehicle, dwarfing the LED beam from Mendez's mounted light on his rifle.

"Fancy contacts you got there sir," Mendez remarked.

"Sure. Glad you think so," Judah said, reaching down to help up his other fallen hunters who hadn't been quick enough to grab their crash handles.

Mendez was walking towards the back of the van, "Well," he began, "seeings how it looks like our transports aren't going anywhere and our equipment is completely fried, just wanna stress again, pack in tight, look for any survivors on the streets while me and my boys clear out the buildings!" He said as he undid the latch to the double doors and kicked them open.

Judah sprang up toward the back and landed on the ground next to him. He felt his skin prickling. His glowing eyes began to water. Mendez was holding a gloved hand to his face and coughing as the other officers exited the back of the transport.

The air was thick with columns of smoke, emanating from flaming shells that were once working vehicles. Judah tried to peer through the smoke, his Higher Sight burning a retinal path through. The weight settling in Judah's stomach kept getting heavier with each breath he took. The smell of smoke blended with the smell of death, gore, urine and feces in a vile ensemble of filth and destruction. Main Street had been turned into a maze of wrecked vehicles and blood slicked asphalt. Costumed bodies of various age groups lay face down in pools of blood. Many had been eviscerated by means too vile to speculate. Skulls, torsos and limbs stripped of skin, revealing muscle and bone. Clutched in many of the hands were large bags of spilled candy, each piece now coated in reddish brown, coagulated gunk. At least seven cars that he could count were smashed into each other in odd angles, caddy cornered from one another, creating barriers and or narrow paths.

From what Judah could see, a fire engine sat abandoned four blocks down. Ablaze in the night, and the biggest sources of the smoke, were the remains of what looked like parade floats. Through the crackling of the flames, the scattered sounds of combat boots beating the pavement, and battering rams breaking down doorways, there was a distinct, *stillness* that infested the scene before them. All other noises seemed dampened around them, yet the sound of Judah's breathing sounded crisp and clear. Loud even. Each step he took, though intended to be as soft as feathers, seemed to resonate like an obnoxious click of a pen in an empty office. He took one final look behind him. He could see the outlines of the other armored vans stalled down the street, the Kevlar clad forms of other SWAT officers advancing up the street passed them to spread out and clear buildings.

He turned to look back the other direction. Brandon was sniffing the air, his face becoming more feral and twisting with disgust.

"This was supposed to be a parade right?" Judah asked, stepping forward and raising his M4.

"Haunted Main Street," Valerie replied, "They do it every year."

"They clear streets for parades. These cars," Judah gestured, "something picked them up and positioned them like this." He said, stepping closer and running a gloved hand over a set of claw marks that were on either side of the front end.

"From the looks of this, I gather whatever did this has an arms span of probably eight feet, and probably weighs close to eight hundred pounds." Judah said. Brandon stepped over and sniffed the remains of the car.

"Not one of my kind," He said, "Has a feint sewer smell to it."

Judah pressed forward, motioning them to follow, fan out and stay sharp. With each step, the veins under his skin grew brighter. With each thought, he forced Light through his skin, channeling it into the weapon he held. He concentrated as he stepped cautiously through the bloody maze of twisted metal. His burning white eyes continued to clear a path through the smoke. He blinked, taking shallow breathes as he rounded the back end of an SUV.

Then his eyes began to water. What happened next seemed to Judah like his vision was beginning to *flicker*. He blinked rapidly, trying to focus.

Suddenly the world around him and its colors went dull. Muted and generic. Queasy and sick. He blinked again. His eyes stung with smoke, and he couldn't see. No Higher Sight.

"Guys," Parish was talking somewhere, "I can't see."

What's happening to us? Judah thought.

"I've lost my Higher Sight. I can't see through the smoke. Regroup on me," he ordered.

A TASTE OF YOU

"**B**randon, you got anything?" Judah asked as he took a knee, each of his hunters doing the same once they rallied around him. This was also where the air, though filled with the taste of blood, was also less choked with smoke.

Brandon shook his head, "All I have now is my natural eyesight," He confessed.

"Still that's better than what the rest of us now have," Judah said.

Brandon shook his head, "Because my eyes are more acute than a human's, they are also more sensitive. I'm actually *worse* off in the sight department than you all," Brandon said. Judah grunted, squinting his eyes up over the hood of a nearby car.

"It's taking every effort to keep my stomach in line. I can't abide this smell." Valerie said, her hand cupped over his nose and mouth. Judah rested a loving hand on her shoulder and squeezed.

"We best group up. Brandon, you stick with me, and Valerie, Parish and Zach, take up the back." Judah instructed. As he was talking, he stopped, held up a finger and was silent. The others followed his lead, listening intently. Up through the crackling of the fires rose a distinctively high pitched series of notes that bore a deranged, almost melodic quality to them.

"Whistling," Zach whispered.

It sounded as if it were coming from where the fire engine had parked four blocks down. Not close enough for them to really hear it but yet but it sounded clear as day. They listened, and from what they could make out, it sounded like whoever was whistling was trying to figure out the tune to *Spooky, Scary Skeletons*. But then it changed to another tune Judah couldn't identify.

"Come on," He said, remaining crouched as he and Brandon took the lead, with the others following. Every other wrecked car they passed, they had to stop, take in some new air, and continue. With each new step, Judah could feel his grip tightening on the handle of his rifle. He could feel his chest constricting, as if his ribcage was shrinking with his lungs still inside, fighting against the enclosing bone. He could feel his skin tingling with an energy he could not, *did* not want to identify.

The whistling continued its steady tune, until it switched to something else. *Twinkle, Twinkle, Little Star*, from the sound of it.

Something shifted inside of Judah's chest. He realized it was his heart, attempting to suddenly relocate to his throat. His skin prickled to life as each hair stood at attention, at the sound of a rumbling engine bursting to life. Light washed over them, cutting through the walls of smoke. Judah and the rest of them ducked their heads behind the wreckage of a demolished platform of a parade float. Ever so carefully, Judah looked over the edge of the platform. The fire engine, about half a block away now, had roared to life, its head lights washing over the bodies and debris. The driver's side door flung open, and the body of the driver slumped awkwardly out of the cabin and landed with a wet squelch onto another body. After a pause, another form began to emerge from inside. The glare from the headlights, plus the obnoxious curtains of smoke, still made it difficult to make out any features. All Judah could make out, was that its outline appeared to be that of a human male.

The figure just stood there, appearing to survey the bodies all over the ground, nudging some of them with a foot on occasion.

"What do you see?" Valerie whispered.

Judah's heart was trying to hammer its way free from the confines of his chest. He held up a finger to Valerie—something he knew she hated, but in this instance, he knew he could get away with it.

Judah kept watching. Everything about the figure screamed to be identified in his mind. Though unable to make out much, the outline looked somewhat familiar. The figure turned slightly, just enough for Judah to make out that it had something in its hand. It looked like an old hacksaw.

His blood ran like icy slush through his veins as the man suddenly turned and began walking in their direction, whistling.

Normally, in a situation like this, the fact that *anyone* had been found alive and seemingly whole, would have been a reason for the team to see whoever it was to safety. But in a situation like this, no one is likely to be whistling casually and carrying a hacksaw. Judah ducked back down behind the platform, eyes searching those of his team.

"Stay where you can see each other and him, move up slowly and get the man surrounded," he said, and with that, Zach, Parish and Valerie darted across the street behind another vehicle, and Brandon's neck hairs bristled. Judah signaled, and the two groups began to move up, weaving around debris, and body parts. Stepping lightly so as not to slip in puddles of unnamable bodily fluids, he brought up his hand to signal to everyone to begin closing a circle around the man, whose features continued to be obscured by sudden belches of smoke and flames. Yet the sound of the whistling kept increasing in volume, as did the sound of the man's approaching footsteps.

The sudden sound of metal teeth being drug over the surface of a car hood stopped Judah cold in his tracks, the sound stabbing pain into the roots of his teeth and down his ear canals. The sound made the skin on the back of his neck feel like it would crawl up on top of his head. Judah signaled to his team, and with each signal received, they each stepped out from their concealment, weapons trained on the unidentified figure that was approaching.

As Judah stepped out from behind the truck he had taken cover behind, he knew that there would be no time for the standard, "sir are you injured?" line.

"Get on the ground and identify yourself," he said, his voice sharp as glass and as commanding as a rumble of thunder.

The figure stood there, with its face slumped forward, chin to chest, and the hand that held the hacksaw twitched.

"Oh God," Valerie said when the smoke cleared for just a moment. After blinking the sting out of his eyes from the smoke, Judah could finally see why.

"Mick," Judah breathed. Mick's head came up, and on his face he wore a stupid, drunken grin. However, it wasn't the sight of the unnerving grin that made Judah flinch.

Black ichor was leaking from Mick's eyes, out of his ears, nose and mouth. The substance had stained his clothes, dyeing what remained of his torn up t-shirt into a wet, pitch black mess. His gray skin was at least two shades darker, and black veins stretched down his forearms beneath the surface.

"Looks familiar doesn't it?" Mick asked, spreading his arms out in a sweeping gesture, motioning to all the debris and slaughtered bodies. Further up the street, more forms could be seen. Each of them about the size of a normal man, some much taller, some smaller, yet each one stacked with muscle that could tear through a leather belt. Their bodies stained with blood. Their deformed and misshapen heads slumped forward at uncomfortable angles. Many of the shapes, with a quick jerk and a convulsing roar, sprouted extra limbs out of their backs. Others limbs stretched to inhuman lengths to snatch fleeing human prey, only to pull them back into a bear hug that snapped every rib in their chest. One of the Throwbacks unhinged its jaws, fitting the top of one man's head completely inside its mouth.

Judah looked around at the flaming parade floats, the smashed cars, the carpet of dead bodies, and closed his eyes.

"At least you told him," Mick said—this time with another voice. Judah's eyes snapped toward him.

Judah instantly raised his rifle and squeezing the trigger. He felt the rifle kick slightly as the recoil pad absorbed most of it, and saw the front windshield of the vehicle behind Mick shatter. Judah's hands began shaking. He had him lined up perfectly, and at twenty feet away he hardly ever missed! Judah momentarily took his eyes off of Mick's possessed flesh to meet Brandon's eyes.

"Hurry up the street, those people need you." He ordered. Brandon's expression struggled for a moment. Judah knew he wouldn't willingly leave his side, and for that, he was indebted. But Brandon complied, shedding his Kevlar and began to let his beast out as he circled around, found a path to take, and charged into the fray to dispatch the abominations up the street.

"You should have seen his face when you told him your team were the ones that butchered his old city. But did you? No! You were too busy starring at your glass, recounting your sob story!" The being inside of Mick spat.

"I take it you are Father." Judah stated. Mick's lip curled up one side of his face, and unnaturally so. It was as if his face had become malleable as putty, and the thing inside could form it to whatever it wished.

"Guilty," It said, holding Mick's hands up in mock surrender. Then the hands opened wide, fingers spreading out as if to catch a ball. Valerie was yanked through the air from where she stood, her weapons clattering to the wet asphalt as she literally flew through the air and into Father's outstretched hands. While this happened, Judah felt every muscle in his body tense, and suddenly his feet were whipped out from beneath him. He felt the same force rip the gun free from his hands. He flew backward, and at once felt his back hit the side of the car behind him. All the air he had mustered up to yell left him in a breathless scream as his vision blurred from the impact of his head snapping backward. His ears began ringing again, and his head felt numb for the first six to eight seconds before fiery tendrils began spreading out from the back of his head. When his vision cleared, he could see Zach and Parish, similarly slammed against the side of the building behind them, and Valerie, held fast to Mick's chest, her back pressed firmly against him with one hand clamped around her throat like a vice.

The sight of the woman he loved, held mercilessly in the grip of that monster, set him burning up with rage that throbbed up from the base of his skull. His muscles kicked into overdrive and his heart thudded heavily in his chest as he felt his breath again cut off. Panic filled him to the brim. Panic that soon turned to hysteria, as all the images of him down on one knee, pulling out that ring and asking her to be his wife all came flooding into his brain.

Father pulled her closer to Mick's face, breathing in the scent of her hair. His eyes rolled into the back of his head as he exhaled the sweet aroma that was simply her. The scent of her hair that gave Judah a reason to wake up in the morning.

"This one broke his heart, you know? He thought they could be friends, maybe more than friends, but then he found out she was wrapped up with you in your sheets." Father purred.

"Valerie!" Judah roared, finally getting enough air back in his lungs. Her eyes met his, fierce as she breathed in deep through her nose. He saw her trying to jab elbows into Mick's torso, trying to wriggle free from his iron grip, but the same force that had pinned Judah and the others down also kept her held close to Father's vessel.

Father sighed, looked down at Valerie, and using Mick's tongue, *licked* the side of her face. Her eyes snapped shut as her face scrunched up in disgust and revilement. Black slime trailed up the side of her head and like a string of elastic, stuck to the side of her face by the end of Mick's unnaturally long tongue until it reached its limit and sagged to depart from the vile tongue. Judah saw her skin turn a shade pale, as wrinkles set in around her eyes, and her lips cracked.

"Well now he can say he finally got a taste of her. Before I did this," He said, slipping his hand from her neck, up her face and drawing her head back, exposing her the soft tender flesh of her neck.

"NO!!" Judah yelled as father brought up the hacksaw with his other hand, and in one swift motion, raked the blade across her throat.

MEMORY FEAST

It felt as if a bomb had gone off next to his head. Judah couldn't even hear the sound of the blood rushing through his own ears. The world around him became muted. The only thing he could hear at all, was the ringing. The ringing that drowned out the sound of his own rage filled screams of mortification as he thrashed against the vehicle he was still pinned to.

Father was looking at him now. There was no evil smirk on the face he hid behind. No expression of smug triumph. It looked as if, behind that tar stained face, there was nothing. There was no expression of jubilation at the act of drawing that blade across the throat of the woman he loved. There was nothing but an icy, methodical, *bored* stare.

She was very valiant. Others would have screamed. No wonder she caught your fancy, Father's voice slithered through his head.

"Go to hell!" Judah seethed, though its volume barely touched his own ears. The ringing was still the most prominent sound his brain could process right now.

I've already been there, Father's voice replied, his eyes looking down the street the way the hunters had come. Suddenly the eyes and lips widened into a smile that reminded Judah of the way a child might look when they get a clever idea.

I think I'm going to pay a visit to New Broken Edge's finest. I might even help them clear out those buildings. His voice said inside of Judah's head as he released Valerie from his grip, carelessly letting her fall face first onto the pavement, and began strolling off toward Mendez's SWAT units.

The rush of feeling and mobility back in his limbs left him feeling drained as Judah collapsed there on the blood soaked ground, next to his weapon. Every muscle in his body felt like jelly beneath his skin. Like he had been flexing for an hour nonstop until the muscle fibers just split. He crawled toward the fallen body of his love, each movement taking more of his strength that he didn't have to offer. He willed his muscles to push him closer as his vision blurred. His elbows failed him and he collapsed with one arm underneath him as he let out a cry of agonizing rage. He forced his will into his muscles, making himself get up again, if only to move just an inch closer to her.

The ringing in his ears was beginning to lessen, as he heard the shuffling footsteps of Zach and Parish as they crawled, drug, and helped each other closer to where Valerie lay. When he reached her, he reached a trembling hand out to brush the hair she had scrunched up in the tight bun on the back of her head. Parish and Zach, dragging themselves along, helped him roll her over onto her back, while Judah kept her head steady. Her eyes were wide in a shocked panic. Her mouth gaped wide and was leaking trails of inhaled blood that had been sucked in through the gash. The saw had done more than simply slit her throat. Her larynx had been sliced in to as well. Judah brought a hand up to brush blood from her cheek, and before he knew it, rested his face on hers as the dam broke inside, weeping hot tears onto her face.

He reached a trembling gloved hand up and brushed her eyelids shut, and then lifted her up in his arms to cradle her close to him. He knew that not even five minutes could have passed since he reached her, but every second that ticked by felt like a year. He caught the gazes of Zach and Parish, and they helped him up while he clutched her form close to him.

He pressed his lips to her forehead as a fresh wave of unadulterated wrath began to swell inside of his belly.

"Get her out of here. I don't care where you take her, just take her somewhere safe," he said as he gently hoisted Valerie's body into Parish's arms. Parish nodded, his eyes bloodshot from his own tears as well as the burning smoke. Zach looked at Parish, "I'll keep you covered," he said.

Judah bent down, picked up his rifle, and turned in the direction of the amassing dark aura that surrounded the possessed body of Mick Johnson.

Father drew the blade of the hacksaw along his tongue, tasting the blood of the hunter he had just cut down. Valerie, was it? With the coppery taste came a flood of memories from the fallen hunter. He saw her, going to work, performing her mundane tasks as coroner. He saw her donning her black, expressionless mask, loading weapons, channeling Light from her hands into each bullet that shot forth from her guns.

There was one memory in particular that he lingered on. In this one she had been laying on the muscle hardened chest of the man called Judah, under a blanket down in what appeared to be an emergency bunker, walls lined with guns, tools, and other supplies. They were both laying on an old couch. It was a dark blue, green, checkered upholstered mess that she had felt exceedingly comfortable on, probably because he was underneath her.

"Alright then you big jerk, what are *your* favorite names?" She teased. The tone in her voice was delightful and delicious.

Judah looked thoughtful for a second, scratching his chin before finally answering, "If we were to have a boy, I like the name Isaiah. If we have a little girl, I like Esther."

Father let the memory slip passed once it had run its course, the muscles in his borrowed face twitching on occasion. Something about that memory in particular stirred him in a way he couldn't immediately place. As he let it go in the stream of other memories, he tried briefly to understand why that one was so delicious. He wondered if he had ever experienced anything like that before. The nagging that was tearing at the fibers of his consciousness kept returning to that memory, stirring it back around to the surface of the other memories that played out on the screen of his awareness. He finally gave it up, letting it fizzle out altogether.

He sifted through the memories she had of Mick, all while processing Mick's memories of her at the same time. He smiled at how Mick never had a chance with her, and how much of a true thorn in the side Mick had been to her.

Father found himself chuckling as he approached the dark entry way of one of the buildings. Just before he stepped across the threshold, a wall of flashing blue and red lights caught his eye. Several ambulances were approaching from down the street.

A voice stretched out from the darkness and caught his attention.

"Sir are you injured?"

Father turned his head back to the dark entryway of the building. A flashlight beam was dancing its way toward him, as an armored man with a train of civilians and other armed comrades followed close behind.

"Kill the civilians," Father said, causing the man's head to jerk upward at the sound of his command. The man's eyes clouded over as the pupils expanded to take over the entire eyeball, blacking them out entirely.

Quickly and methodically, like robots programmed for slaughter, each SWAT member turned their weapons on the men, women and children that they had just rescued. The darkness of the building's lobby erupted in a lightshow of gunfire as the barrels of each weapon spat round after round into the bodies of the civilians, dropping them like flies. The ones that tried to flee, quickly found themselves enfolded in Father's embrace, their screams cut short as their life essence evaporated out of their bodies and flowed into his new vessel. Father let their withered, skeletal husks clatter to the floor that was riddled with blood and spent shell casings.

Father stood with his arms outstretched, letting the energy in the room fill his lungs. With a satisfied sigh his eyes roamed about the lobby, seeing each SWAT member standing over the bullet torn bodies of the men and women they had entered this building to save.

"Thank you gentlemen," Father said as he turned to leave the building, "now, each of you draw your side arms, put them in your mouths, and pull the trigger."

The lobby's silence was once again shattered by the sound of pistols being drawn, and fired as the bodies of armed men dropped one by one.

SURVIVOR

Judah could taste the blood particles in the air. It didn't help breathing through his mouth or his nose. Either his nostrils became clogged with the fresh scent of death that clung to every surface, or he was tasting a thick, wet rush of copper that lingered in the air as he stepped around the fresh bodies of the civilians and SWAT team.

"I will say of Hashem, he is my refuge and my fortress, Elohai, in Him I will trust," Judah whispered to himself, feeling slight bursts of the Light energy coursing through him with each word, but nothing more. Nothing that he could sustain. He kept trying.

"He shall cover thee with His evrah, and under his kenafayim shalt thou find defense. His Emes shall be thy shield and buckler."

Whatever that thing inside of Johnson had done to him and his team, it had cut off their ability, at least temporarily, to summon the Light through their bodies. Which meant their weapons were still handy against anything that was in a physical form, but not quite as effective. He kept checking the magazine on his automatic rifle, drawing the slide back just enough to make sure the Light he had channeled into the rounds hadn't faded.

"He shall call upon me, and I will answer him. I will be with him in times of trouble, I will deliver him and honor him. With length of days I will satisfy you and show you my salvation," he continued.

He could hear more gun fire coming from other buildings down the street. He felt like with each step he took, like he was sinking deeper and deeper into gory quicksand, slogging through the bodies that fell because he was too *slow*, too *weakened* by his emotions to have saved them.

More muffled gunfire. More screams, this time coming from within this building! Judah pressed through the lobby at a deliberate pace, taking the curved hallway that was overlaid with black plastic tarps and had the remains of orange and green Halloween lights dangling from nails in the wall. He guessed this building was one of the city's attempts at a haunted house attraction. Fake plastic chains that looked impressive from a distance, hung from the ceiling. A strobe light was flickering by the entrance of one doorway that split off in two directions, left and right. Judah cleared the doorway with the barrel of his rifle quickly, turning to look both directions. The flashing strobe was horribly disorienting, but aside from the stationary shapes of mannequins dowsed in fake gore, all was completely still. He listened again.

The gun fire had halted, and had been replaced with the sounds of heavy breathing. Judah followed the sounds. He could hear a magazine being switched out and an action being worked. Then footsteps were approaching from deeper in the hallway, cloaked in the darkness.

"Hello?" Judah called out.

"Oh thank God!" The voice returned, as the footsteps quickened. A short, armored silhouette with a military buzz cut came tromping into view. Judah recognized it right away.

"Never thought I would be glad to see you," Mendez said, wiping sweat and blood from his forehead, "Where's your team?"

Judah stiffened, "One of our own was killed. Two are getting the body to a safe location and the other is up the street clearing out buildings himself. I assure you, he is capable and can handle himself. What happened to you?"

Mendez pulled out some first aid wrapping and began to apply them to the cut on his head, "We were herding civilians out of here when something waylaid me. I woke up with some guy in a scarecrow mask standing over me and I put him down. I couldn't have been out long because my head still hurts and this gash is still bleeding pretty good. Coms are still down, I can't reach anybody."

Judah felt his arms prickle with gooseflesh at the description of Mendez's assailant, wondering briefly if it was any connection to the creature that had attacked his hunters at Tom's Auto. He shook the notion free of his mind.

"The unit that you had with you in this building is dead, along with the civilians they found." Judah said. No time for tact.

Mendez's face fell, his eyes turned burning hot with rage. He pushed his way passed Judah, his pace quickening. Judah turned back down the way he had come, following behind Mendez. As the scent of the carnage grew stronger, Mendez hurried into a run, bolting into the lobby before Judah could actually catch up with him.

When Judah found him, he was shining the light at the end of his weapon over the dead faces of his men, and the people they were to escort to safety. Mendez stifled a cry of rage with one gloved hand as he sank down to his haunches, clutching his weapon tightly in the other hand. Judah saw the tears streaming down his cheeks, saw the vein threatening to burst under the skin of his forehead. Mendez stood up quickly and surveyed the room one last time.

"I think the same thing that killed…one of mine, also did this to these people." Judah said.

Mendez choked back another torrent of tears through clenched teeth, "These people have bullet holes in them! My men are holding their pistols in their mouths. I-"

Judah cut him off, "I know what it looks like, but whatever it is must have very strong manipulative powers or something, and it's also inside the body of Mick Johnson. Ya know, that guy whose information you weren't at liberty to share with me earlier? It's got him!" Judah said.

"You mean like he's possessed?" Mendez asked, his skeptical tone managing to compete with the grief that was buffeting him.

"I'm going after it, and if you want to avenge your men, you're going to help me." Judah said, stepping passed him. Suddenly he felt Mendez's hand squeezing his shoulder.

"You hear that?" he asked. Judah stayed still, harkening to pick up any stray sounds that didn't belong. At first he didn't hear anything, but he knew that didn't always mean anything special.

"You said you shot a guy in a scarecrow mask?" Judah asked, his voice low. Just then Judah thought he heard something. Something metal and heavy being drug down a hallway.

"Yeah. I emptied an entire magazine into him before he went down." Mendez said.

"We need to go." Judah said, grabbing Mendez by the Kevlar and hauling him out of the entrance of the building.

"Was there any blood when you shot at him?" Judah asked as they hoofed it down the sidewalk, passed formally glassed in storefront windows that were now smashed to bits.

"I don't remember, it was dark. I just saw the mask cause the guy was standing directly over me. I didn't see any other features." Mendez said. Judah turned to look over his shoulder. A figure was emerging from the doorway they had just come out of, and appeared to be holding something in both hands.

Judah ducted into a doorway of another building, and Mendez followed suite. Before them stretched the untouched remains of a furniture store. Only the front entrance had been smashed, leaving the stone titled foyer covered in tiny shards and bits of broken glass. Judah pressed his weight against the double doors leading into the store, but they wouldn't budge. His heart rate increasing, he pressed an eye to the crack of the doors, seeing the lock was set.

"Don't move," Judah said, catching Mendez's eye.

"Whatcha got in mind?" he asked.

Judah poked his head out of the shattered glass door way just enough to see the figure of the thing. A human shape, clothed in the old tattered jeans that appeared to be stained with blood, with a burlap sack for the face. Crude eye holes cut out and an oversized smile stitched into the bottom half of the face. And it was carrying a fireman's axe, the weapon hoisted up onto one shoulder. It looked like it was taking the time to look inside of each of the storefront windows, searching for something to hack apart. Judah listened. Was the creature trying to sing?

"Jack and Jill went up the hill to fetch a pail of water…Jack fell down, broke his crown, and used it to slit Jill's throat. Then Jack through her down a well." Its voice sounded harsh and grainy, like sand being poured down a garbage disposal.

Judah turned back to Mendez, "pray with me."

An amalgam of expressions crossed over the man's face ranging from outright indignation to complete desperation, many of them entangling so far into one another it was difficult to make out where one expression began and the other one ended. Judah chanced another peak out of the door. The scarecrow was two stores down, emerging from the shattered storefront window with the axe in hand.

Judah put a hand on Mendez's shoulder and turned his eyes, and the barrel of his automatic rifle outward toward the door.

"What are you doing?!" Mendez whispered, readying his own weapon.

Judah ignored him, breathing deeply and closing his eyes. When he opened them again, he began.

"Remain absolutely still and stay quiet," Judah said, and then he began, his voice dropping down to a soft whisper.

"Hashem, deliver us in your righteousness, grant us escape. Incline your ear to us and save us..."

He felt Mendez shifting beneath his grasp, and Judah tightened his hold on the man's shoulder.

"O Yahweh, be not far from us: O my God, make haste for our help. Let them be confounded and consumed that are adversaries to my soul; let them be covered with reproach and dishonor that seek my hurt."

The sound of glass and other degrees of rubble being crunched beneath the footfalls of heavy boots drew closer and louder, until the axe wielding form of the wooden scarecrow came into full view there in the doorway. Judah's voice had dropped out of volume, yet his lips continued to move, mouthing lines from the book of Psalms.

The scarecrow stood gawking, axe head resting on the bloody side walk. Its head inclined to one side, and then the other, the crude eyeholes in the mask reflecting the darkness of the store behind Judah and Mendez. Whatever method the creature used for sensing movement, or any sensory input, seemed to just slide passed the two men that stood in the doorway, as if they simply did not exist. Yet none of that eased that tension keeping Judah's finger wrapped around the trigger of his weapon. Every twitch, every subtle fluctuation in the thing's body language continued to tie Judah's stomach into a coil of dread so tight he thought he would pull the trigger at any moment. But the creature just continued to stare *passed* them. Time slowed in that entire moment, each second that ticked by only serving to fuel more adrenaline and the sickening tightness to mount until Judah thought he was going to throw up. But he kept mouthing the words of prayer.

Turning out of the doorway, and starting to sing its modified version of "Jack and Jill," the creature turned and walked out of view further up the demolished street.

Judah eased his finger free from the trigger and he felt Mendez's hand sliding off of his shoulder like a deflated balloon. Judah let out an exhausted breath, and then greedily gulped in a lungful of air, sinking down to his haunches as Mendez rested his back against the wall behind him.

"If I live through tonight," Mendez said turning his gaze toward Judah, "I'm gonna get back in church!"

He gave an exhausted chuckle, and Judah wearily returned it—then he saw the face in the glass behind Mendez's head.

The sound of the glass shattering broke Judah out of his sudden shock as the thing inside drove its hand through the door, curled an arm around the SWAT captain's neck, and pulled him through the glass, into the darkness.

REUNION

Judah felt a dozen claws suddenly ripping at his skin from behind. He spun around. Several mutilated, misshapen, pock-marked faces with slanted foreheads were approaching. Judah shouldered his rifle and squeezed the trigger, shooting their legs out from under them. The creatures staggered and tumbled forward as they lunged for him. He retreated back in through the shattered doorway, his eyes frantically searching around for something he could barricade the door with, if only for a temporary hindrance.

A clawed hand shot through the shattered doorway, nails tearing into his shoulder. Judah quickly spun and withdrew the knife he had stashed on his belt, slicing the exposed flesh of the creature just under the palm. The fingers went limp and slid free from the trenches they had raked into his shoulder.

The scene he saw when he turned briefly to slash again would have almost been comical had the situation not been so intense. Three hulking figures, each with pointed, shredded ears on the side of their heads, had all managed to try and press their collective bulk through the shattered glass doorway at once. The one in the middle had gotten the idea to begin eating its way out. The Throwback clamped its oversized jaws down hard on the side of the throat of one of the obstructing bodies it had jammed with, and ripped. The resulting shriek nearly burst Judah's ear drums as he quickly backed away.

Before Judah could retreat further into the store, another clawed hand, this time much bigger, hairier, and slicked with blood caked fur crashed through the top of the door frame, grabbed onto the head of the thing that had taken a bite out of its friend, and ripped backward!

The creature's lupine face that came into view had eyes that instantly locked onto Judah. The muzzle pressed through the doorway and snatched onto another one of the flailing forms of the flesh warped monstrosities, causing the door itself to be ripped free from the hinges. The werewolf threw the flailing bodies backward in to the horde they had come from. It turned to face them, and got down on all fours. The hands crackled and popped as the fingers shortened into the clawed stubs of paws the size of a grown man's head. The back arched and shortened with a series of wet cracking sounds as the back legs shortened as well. The dire wolf turned its massive head back to Judah, its lips curled into a snarl that heralded a blood rage.

"Thanks Brandon," Judah said, and took off running through the store to find Mendez. He followed the sounds of shattering glass. Sporadic gun fire. Up ahead, the strobe light flashing of a muzzle around that corner. Fists colliding with flesh and bone.

Judah rounded the corner just in time to see Mendez drawing his combat knife, swiping at Mick's body with the skills of a trained fighter. Mick's body had at least five bullet holes in center mass, each leaking streams of the black tar-like substance. Each swipe that connected sliced black spewing gashes into the arms, chest, and once even across the throat! Yet the entity possessing Mick kept walking forward, walking into Mendez's attacks just to show he could!

Mendez brought the heel of his boot up into Father's stomach, and the way his foot collided with Mick's body looked as painful as if the man had just tried to kick a brick wall—barefoot.

"Mendez drop!" Judah yelled as he shouldered his rifle and took aim.

Father's eyes looked up just as Mendez fell, tucking his chin in toward his chest as his back rolled along the ground.

Judah didn't even remember squeezing the trigger. He only saw the muzzle flare in the dark, illuminating Mick's hideous form. Mick's body stiffened with the impact of each fiery round that tore through the flesh, each new bullet hole glowing with the bright radiance of a miniature spot light.

The body of Mick Johnson stood there for a couple seconds that stretched on entirely too long, rocking back and forth on unsteady footing as the Light traveled through the body, illuminating the veins beneath the skin like a glowing spider web. Soon, the body was enveloped in a black aura of swirling shadow as it dropped hard on the floor with an unforgiving *thud*.

"Did we kill it?" Mendez asked as he leaned over on his knees, huffing and wiping sweat from his face with the back of his hand.

The amassing shape that rose from Mick's fallen body was stretching to heights of close to seven feet. Its arms dragged the floor as the grotesquely long fingers searched for something solid to grab onto. The legs twisted and bent in unnatural angles as the thing finally stood up. The head sagged forward on a neck that stretched forth from a hunched back. The face was nonexistent. Not even a mouth was visible. The depth of the darkness grew ever blacker, moving with liquid fluidity. The obsidian shape turned its head in their general direction.

"Well this is unfortunate," said a voice from deep within the humanoid mass of shadow. Its tone suggested a slight bit of annoyance that was unnervingly offset by *amusement.*

"From a non-physical vantage point, you humans all look the same," the figure said as it lurched forward.

Judah fired again, and the shape completely dissipated where the bullets would have impacted it. The form of Father reshaped itself less than five inches away from Judah's face.

"You all look like smeared streaks of bland color," Father said, as Judah felt the icy cold impact of one appendage connect like a whip across his face. He swore he had blacked out for a second. He didn't even remember flying through the air, just hitting the ground with an awkward crash that jarred the vertebrae in his back and might have dislocated his wrist. All Judah knew at present was that his gun was being dismantled in the air in front of him by shadowy tendrils that were slithering out from this thing's mass.

When his vision stopped going out of focus, he could see the Kevlar clad form of Daniel Mendez, slumped over in a corner, out cold.

Suddenly his insides felt like they were being soaked in a bath of liquid nitrogen. His mouth dropped open in a silent scream, and he felt himself lift into the air. The pain stabbed at the nerves in his neck, sending dull razors through his synapses and eyes. He could no longer see, but he could feel the source of the intrusion.

Something wriggled inside of his stomach, and he felt like an eel was thrashing around inside of his intestines, chewing and shredding the contents of his abdomen. He felt himself get slammed against something, and he blacked out momentarily.

"You taste rotten," Father's voice was approaching slowly. He looked up, trying to lift his hand to draw for his pistol. No sooner had his shaking hand touched the handle of the pistol than he remembered he had only channeled the Light into the rounds of his AR-15, which now lay all over the store in pieces. He saw his fingers—smashed, with the skin peeled off the backs of them. The joints crushed, and each little bone bent at a painful slant.

"Your Valerie, was all too delicious." The voice said as the shape of Father's head invaded his vision. The presence of an icy hand the size of a frying pan clamped down onto the back of his neck like a vice, and he felt his heels leave the ground. He felt his neck pop and despite the biting cold from Father's hand, he also felt an opposing rush of heat spreading into his popping ear canals.

The darkness of the store had filled every crevice of his vision, every corner that his eyes could possibly reach was devoid of any light source, ambient or bright. Yet through the darkness, suspended at least a good seven feet in the air, he saw a flickering shape off in the distance. He couldn't make out many features, not from this distance. It looked like it was walking at a calm, yet deliberate pace. About the only other things he could truly make out, with blurring, faulty vision was the billowing train of what looked like an old trench coat. The figure, about six feet tall, looked as if the head were completely bald.

"You're very late," Father hissed. Judah blinked. He still couldn't make out the face.

"As was our agreement" Father said, and Judah felt himself being lowered to the ground in front of the creature. The shape had no distinct feet to stand on, yet it had a stride as it walked. Of the entire shape, the only discernable thing about it was the billowing coat and the bald head. The rest was obscured by swirling shadow, not unlike the essence of the thing that had just waylaid him.

Judah eased over onto his back, every bone in his body screaming as dull, icy torment scrapped through his being. He felt fingers touching him, sliding their way towards his throat. Then, as if materializing out of a cloud of smoke, features started to appear, forming a face that grew closer and closer to his own. The eyes he noticed first. Two dull, yellow orbs that neither glowed, nor were reflective in the darkness. Just two yellow bulbs, housed in a face that once he recognized it, demanded full attention. The skin looked like flaking ash. The teeth, two rows of jagged, yellowed spikes, housed in a mouth as silent and cold as death itself.

"You…" He could barely suck in enough breath to form the word.

The expression on the wraith's face never changed. Without a single word, Judah felt himself being lifted up by his collar, rising to meet the being at eye level. The man's face, preserved as it was in its ashen casing of flesh, looked as young as the day Judah saw it eighteen years ago. Memories flashed, showing the same face laughing as Judah's arm's flailed about, glass shards following his descent as he fell four stories to what was intended to be his death.

A voice began to seep into the crevices of his brain.

Judah, it whispered. He could feel his brain ache at the mention of his name, like the entity of his former colleague had phased his fingers inside of his skull and was mixing his brain like a salad.

I left you to die many years ago…Now it is time that I fix my mistake.

Before Judah could even contemplate what that meant, he felt a rush of wet, cold energy flush through his entire body. He knew he wasn't touching the ground anymore. That was the only thing externally he was aware of at the moment. It felt like he had been caught up in an icy gale of wind so strong it had lifted him up off the ground. He tried desperately to breathe, but even the tiny amount of air he managed to suck into his lungs became spent the harder he tried.

Stop fighting. Let me breathe for you, he heard Rufus say.

Black tar started to eject from Judah's mouth when the icy force finally let him hit the ground. The apparition of Rufus was nowhere to be seen. Instead, when Judah looked down at his hands and noticed they were gray, it was then he heard Rufus's voice inside of his head say, *I betrayed you…accept this act of penance.*

The sounds of hands clapping off in the distance sounded muted to his ears—the ears he was now sharing with Rufus. But the clapping sound grew nearer nonetheless.

"What did you do to me?!" Judah gnashed his teeth as he felt his legs almost buckle. With each word, icy black slime clogged his throat, and he felt himself coughing the substance out of his lungs. The same stuff Mick had dripping out of his face.

"Yes Rufus, tell us. What *are* you doing?" the dark apparition of Father asked as it loomed closer, clapping its hands in amusement.

Judah felt his head turning in the direction of the voice, and then his whole body. He felt his muscles tighten as his arm came up and pointed a finger at the tall shadow. Rufus's doing.

You aren't going to take him. Even if the rest of his team gets killed tonight, I *won't let you take him,* Rufus said, all the while Judah felt his mouth moving in unison with each word the wraith said, using Judah's very own vocal chords.

The shadow of Father stood still for a few long seconds, its head turning this way and that either in confusion or amusement. It was hard to tell. After some time Father spoke.

"You are truly humorous. I don't see how possessing him will give you any edge over me. We are comprised of the same energy Rufus. You are not Light. I could easily rip you from the hunter's body, and devour you."

This isn't about giving me an edge to fight you. I'm doing this for him! *He didn't deserve what I and the others did to him!*

"You made your choice long ago. You accepted my gift just as the others did. The man you now possess is an insect. You were merely doing your job of exterminating such vermin that stood in the way of your ascension."

If this is what it means to be ascended…then you can have it back you hijo de puta! I don't want it anymore!

Father stood there, his featureless head looking around the room. The being sighed and spread its hands out.

"As was our agreement. I have turned over the hunter for you to do with as you see fit, and you are thus unbound from my service. Tonight's outcome, while not what I wanted, will suffice." He then pointed back to the fallen body of Mick Johnson, full of glowing bullet holes where Light coursed through the veins, illuminating the body from the inside out.

"I'm not happy about this. However there are others I can break. His journey into madness was thoroughly rapturous to orchestrate," Father said, his long shadowy arms sweeping the room in a wide arc as he then gave a stylish bow, and then vanished.

UNLESS YOU BECOME LIKE A CHILD

Mick's eyes flew wide open and he screamed. His heart pounded, and his eyes darted from side to side. It was dark in here. It was too dark. He heard footsteps. He heard the creaking of old, wooden planks and then the rusty squeak of old hinges as a door slowly began to open. His eyes continued to search, his mind screaming for a sense of familiarity. Of all the things he could see, there were curtains blowing from an open window. So he was in a room of some kind. He latched onto that fact with both hands, his fragile sanity clawing at the small tidbit of clarity he had stumbled on just by seeing curtains. Everything else was pitch black.

He tried to stand up and walk. It felt like he hadn't used his limbs in ages. His legs wobbled as he put weight on them. He reached out to steady himself when he thought he was going to fall, and his hand bumped something cold. Whatever it was crashed to the ground, which squeaked under his footsteps. The thing he bumped sounded like something breakable.

He let his eyes try to adjust as he bent down slowly to try and feel what it was he had just broke. He felt the jagged ceramic edges of something slightly oval shaped. He could feel more pieces crumbling away at his touch. He continued to work the object over in his hands, the ceramic parts now turning to cold metallic and plastic, until he felt something made of a type of fabric.

Is this a lamp? Mick thought. He could now visually make out a general shape, but that was all. Suddenly a dim light came on close by. Mick instinctively flattened himself on the ground. He waited for a few seconds but nothing happened. When he looked up he could see new shapes. A coffee table. Recliners. A love seat. A large box television with a VCR mounted on top.

Oh God, I'm in somebody's house! He thought. He quickly and quietly scrambled behind the love seat, cursing the squeaking floorboards beneath him as he went. When he felt brave enough to take a peek out from behind the furniture, he looked up and saw where the source of light was coming from.

A hallway to the right now illuminated a pathway through the living room, and now showed a family photo of the people who lived in the house. Mick felt his stomach drop out from him as he looked at the photo.

He had been five when that photo was taken. His curly hair had been combed to the side and he wore a green and purple, crinkle stripped long sleeve shirt. Nineties kid fashion at its finest. He was seated on his mother's lap, and she wore a blue sweater with a double stringed, fake, pearl necklace. His father stood behind them wearing a tweed suite jacket and tie.

Mick remembered the day they went to have this photo taken. They were late to their appointment with the photographer because Mick hadn't wanted to eat his lunch or something like that. When they finally got in the car, it wouldn't start. His dad cursed at the brand new battery they had just put in and made a call to one of his friends from work, named Bill. Bill had been a nice enough guy. Mick remembered his face, but nothing more.

Something moved just out of the light's reach, and Mick ducked. It was something small. He listened, praying to whoever was listening that he hadn't been spotted. Of course why he was back in his old childhood home was also quite bothersome, but that would be the least of his worries if he got caught by something that managed to get here first.

"Hello?"

Mick remained perfectly still at the sound of a child's voice calling out into the living room. His nerves were screaming at him to bolt up, run to the front door and never look back. But he stayed glued to the hardwood floor.

After a couple agonizingly long seconds, the sound of small, shuffling footsteps moved into the lighted hallway. Mick craned his head out from behind the loveseat just in time to see the small form disappear down the hall.

He recognized those pajamas. He recognized that curly mess of brown hair, and that plastic cup the kid was holding in his hands as he trudged back to his room.

This isn't happening…Oh God this can't be happening. This isn't real!

How do you define real? A voice replied from somewhere out in the living room.

Mick sprang up, his nerves set like a hair trigger, and bolted toward the front door. He didn't even bother to search for the source of the voice. All that mattered was escaping. He knew that if he was in his old childhood home, then he must be in the old ruins of the original Broken Edge. While not a pleasant thought at all, at least he could still find his way out of town on foot. From there he wasn't sure how long it would take him to make it back to New Broken Edge, unless he could hail a ride.

His fingers closed around the doorknob of the front door, and it felt like trying to pull a metal door open with one hand. The resistance caused him to grab the door with his other hand and pull. He remembered how heavy this door felt to him as a kid. It was as if the door's weight had increased. He struggled to pull it open, and when it was open enough for him to dart through, he stopped. Because his front yard was not the thing he saw after getting the front door open.

Mick stood there frozen, shaking, and collapsed onto his knees in front of the full length mirror that stared back at him. Only he wasn't a twenty three year old, fresh detective. He was now only about three feet, four inches tall. He was wearing those same pajamas he had just seen his kid self wearing as it went down the hall.

He used both hands and pushed the door shut again with all his might. The door had grown another three and a half feet taller than he was.

Watch your fingers, the voice said again, and Mick instinctively pulled his fingers out of the door before it shut quickly.

Mick spun around, everything towering over him like it did when he was younger.

There was a man standing there behind him. The hall light had gone out, but even though now it was still pretty dark in here, the man seemed to glow without the need of any external light. He wore a pair of oil stained work jeans, steel toed work boots, and a gray t-shirt that might have actually been white at one time.

He was about six foot three. The hair was odd. Mick was blinking rapidly because somehow looking at this guy made it hard for his eyes to focus for long. It was almost like looking into the sun. Even though the guy was glowing, he wasn't shining as radiant as the sun. Surely not enough to cause his eyes to water.

The hair seemed to change each time he blinked. At first it was long, draping his shoulders, and then it was in a ponytail. Then it was medium length and messy. He had a beard though. That never changed. But it was almost like his mind was trying to fit pieces together to try and make a coherent picture of what this guy could look like.

"Who are you?" Mick choked out, as if he were talking through a mouthful of mud. Forming words was now more exhausting, and he felt his body suddenly feeling very sluggish after the effort. The man smiled, knelt down on one knee so he was at Mick's eye level, and said, without opening his mouth, *It's been a long time Mick. You don't remember me, but my name is Yeshua.*

For what seemed like a long time, neither of them spoke. It was as if neither of them had to. The silence between them was enough, and Mick felt himself being drawn to bask in the silence that washed over them. He couldn't help but be drawn to look at the man's eyes. They changed color, but not fiendishly. First they were green, then gray, then brown, then blue, and so on. They were also one of the things that stuck out about him the most. They seemed to be so unaffected by the darkness in the room, that even though they didn't glow really, they were just as visible in the dark as they would have been had the lights been on.

Finally, Yeshua broke the silence. The sound of his voice bounced around inside of Mick's tiny body like a pinball of warm energy that relaxed him, and invigorated him all at once.

You didn't answer my question, Yeshua said, never breaking eye contact. His words resonated inside of Mick's head like a simmering cup of hot tea.

What do you mean? Mick asked, this time responding in his head. Yeshua eased back so he was sitting on the floor. Mick felt himself wanting to do the same, for no apparent reason other than Yeshua was doing it. Something about his presence made Mick feel like he could be the older brother he never had, or the cool uncle or…even the father he never had. He felt himself wanting to imitate everything he did, as kids often do.

You said that this couldn't be real. I asked how you define "real?" Yeshua asked.

Mick looked around at his old living room. Everything was exactly the way he remembered it from the night his father came storming into his bedroom and grabbed him and his mother and ran to the car. He could feel the texture of the carpet beneath his bare feet. The air in the house felt still, yet alive in a way his child's mind just could not grasp, no matter how hard he tried.

Well, Mick began, *I guess how I define real is, anything that is real, I can also feel it and hear and see it, but it also makes sense. The fact that I'm a little kid now, back in my old home, isn't real to me because I remember living as a grown up. I was a cop. I helped catch a very bad man, just like the police from Daddy's TV shows did. So was it all a dream? Did my whole life never really happen and I'm really awake now?*

Yeshua smiled, *Now that would be a plot twist, wouldn't it?*

Mick stared back at him, puzzled, not knowing what that meant apparently.

Mick, Yeshua began, *you are still very much a grown up. Your life that you remember did actually happen. But this place you're in right now, is equally real, if not more real, than the life you've lived.*

A spear of dread shot through Mick, nearly dropping him to his little knees.

Am I dead? He asked.

Yeshua's eyes brightened up, *oh not at all!* He said. *You are out of your body, but you aren't dead. Look down at your tummy,* he said pointing toward Mick's abdomen. Mick looked down, seeing a shimmering, bluish silver cord sticking out from his stomach, through his PJ shirt, and leading into the kitchen. He immediately felt the urge to follow the cord, knowing instantly that it lead back to his body. How he knew that, he didn't know, but he knew it to be true regardless.

Yeshua gently reached out, taking Mick's hand with one of his and the other on his left shoulder, *Trust me little guy, you don't want to follow that cord just yet.*

But I need to get back into my body! Mick replied.

There will be a time for that. You aren't finished living your life yet. But before I let you go back, we have some work to do, Yeshua said, his tone light hearted but also firm. Mick knew as the words hit him that there would be no room for negotiation.

Where am I then? I know this place looks like my old house, but...somehow I don't think it is, Mick asked. Yeshua gave a nod.

The Astral Plane, the Dream World, your Subconscious. All different names to describe the same place really. This is where you go at night when you're physical body is sleeping. This realm is a fully realized reality, existing outside of you. But the gateway to enter it is through your mind, Yeshua said.

Seems like pretty heavy stuff, Mick said. Yeshua smiled, and Mick heard him laugh inside of his head. It was a deep laugh, like the kind you would expect to hear from a lumberjack.

Actually it's pretty lite. See, watch this! Yeshua said as he shot up into the air. He floated over further into the living room and did a cartwheel in the air, floating just below the ceiling fan.

Mick burst out laughing, his voice exploding out of him like a fountain as he crouched down, and then shot off in the air like a rocket. The sight of this man shooting off into the air, in his living room, had ripped a swelling wave of laughter from his chest in a way that nothing ever had. As Mick realized he was now airborne, he felt his stomach do a cartwheel, and immediately the floor to the living room looked so much farther down than he thought it should have. He flailed as panic gripped him. Just as he cried out, until he felt strong, warm arms encircling him and holding him tight. Secured against Yeshua's chest, he stopped struggling, and the two floated there in the air for some time. Relaxation washed through him, and he felt his eyes beginning to close.

A thought suddenly hit him; if he was in the dream world, what would happen if he fell asleep there? Would he just go farther and farther into other dreams? The answers seemed to float right in front of him, yet they evaporated as soon as he reached for them.

So you said I couldn't go back until we do something...what are we going to do? Mick asked.

Yeshua, holding Mick tightly, gently descended until his feet touched the carpet.

Let's take a walk, he said. Mick watched as Yeshua turned his glance toward the front door, and it opened with a loud click, letting in the cool night air.

The cool night air, as Mick found out, wasn't actually coming from outside of the house. The door that had opened, though in his memories and thoughts, was indeed the front door, was now leading instead to another location of the house.

Mick felt the nerves in his fingers tighten as he gripped Yeshua's pant leg. The front door he had tried to open earlier, where instead he saw a mirror, was now yawning deeply into an inky abysmal staircase that Mick recognized at once. The stairs to the basement greeted him with a hungry, breathing sound that softly caressed his face.

But the door to the basement was in the kitchen, Mick thought, his hands trembling as icy shockwaves of dread washed down his spinal column. Yeshua looked down at him and gave a nod.

In here, certain doors lead to different places than what you remember in your world. In your world that was *the front door to your house. In here, that door can lead wherever it needs to at any given time. This is* your *world Mick,* Yeshua said.

Do we have to go in there? Mick asked.

It's what you were brought here for, Yeshua confirmed.

Mick looked down at the ground, feeling the dread begin to spill from his eyes.

You'll come with me right?

Yeshua gently pried Mick's hand free from his pant leg and held it in his own. Mick was surprised at how big and warm Yeshua's hand was compared to his. He could feel warm energy running through it.

Kiddo, I'll always be with you.

The steps, covered with old, yellowish green carpet, creaked under their weight. The stairs leading into the basement seemed to stretch on forever into the darkness when he was little. Now, here in this dimension, the stairs seemed to be mimicking the way he remembered them, not how they actually were. The darkness that swirled around them seemed alive with the presence of other inhabitants. It seemed to stick to him like oil, clinging to the surface of his flesh like cling-wrap.

Suddenly, dim, ambient light lit up the bottom of the stairs and Mick froze. He happened to look down at his hand, still held in Yeshua's. He literally had to look down at his hand to see it, because now as he passed through the darkness, he was now at Yeshua's shoulder. Body swapping between his child self and his adult self was going to be disorienting as hell.

The dim light showed at the bottom of the stairs old laundry baskets full of dirty, moldy clothes, each one wriggling and crawling with roaches. Mick felt his stomach roll in revilement as he tried to step around the roaches that covered the floor, trying not to step too near to them. Old filing cabinets were propped up next to a door on the right that Mick remembered used to be his family's storage room. As storage rooms went though, it hadn't been enough to hold all of his family's belongings. The door was standing open, and Mick suddenly felt the urge to draw his gun.

Placing one hand on his hip, he actually felt its weight there. The butt of his sidearm pressed firmly into his hand and he quickly drew it. The door had always opened outward. It was the same, even here, and it was blocking his line of sight into the storage room from where he stood. He silently crept around the door, peering into the darkness of the storage room.

It looked like another hallway.

Where does this door lead? Mick asked Yeshua, who was scratching at his beard behind Mick's shoulder.

Let's find out, Yeshua said as he pressed passed Mick and into the dark hallway. Mick steadied his nerves as best he could and swallowed. He felt like his feet were glued to the floor. When he looked down he was standing in a congealing puddle of brownish red mush. He flinched when he saw it, eyes darting everywhere to notice that the entire floor was covered in the stuff, and the roaches had all tripled in size.

You coming? Yeshua asked, jerking Mick out of his focus on the sludge and the bugs. Mick flew forward into the doorway, and before he could manage to turn around to shut the door behind him, it slammed shut tightly in his face.

He wasn't sure how long he stood there before he realized how heavy his breathing had become. The sound of a light clicking on somewhere down the hall caused him to finally turn around.

I don't remember this place, Mick said as he began following Yeshua, who didn't respond. The shelves on the sides of either wall gave way to cinderblocks painted a sickly, pale green. It seemed like the walls were becoming narrower, and it was becoming harder to breath by the minute.

The sound of something small falling on the ground up ahead caused Mick's nerves to zing, through his arms, up his throat and into the roots of his teeth. His eyes watered as he clenched them shut at the pain. He looked up to see Yeshua standing still like a statue with one arm held up to signal he stop and listen. Mick noticed the wall to his right turning in a different direction. He looked, and saw what had fallen. Shelves of toys lined the wall of an adjacent hallway. A stuffed animal from Mick's childhood sat there, peering up at him with cracked, glassy eyes. It was a stuffed dog, sewn together from patches of brown and white quilt. The seams had split open in some places, revealing old, moldy stuffing. The dog's name used to be Boy. He remembered it had been a gift from his grandma.

Mick felt the warm touch of Yeshua's hand on his shoulder, and he looked up.

We need to go this way, he said pointing down the direction of the hall lined with toys.

Mick stood up, placed Boy back on the shelf he had fallen off of, and let Yeshua take the lead again.

Another light kicked on in this hallway, many, many yards farther down. It swung like a pendulum, an orb of dull light off in the distance.

Through all this Mick found himself beginning to wonder if all this was really a mass hallucination. Sudden mental flashes of another time came flooding into his head. Him in the men's bathroom at work, waving a gun around at George. Him in the interrogation room with someone who had made him feel like garbage. That one bothered him because he couldn't remember what the person's face looked like. Not here in this reality at least. He let his eyes loom up ahead and linger on the one who had introduced himself as Yeshua. He seemed real enough. Honestly, and Mick felt strange admitting this, but the fact this guy was down here with him was the only thing keeping him halfway sane and calm. Something about the guy put him at ease in a way that was completely alien to him.

Mick halted behind him when Yeshua brought his arm up again. Mick caught a glimpse of something moving just out of the light's reach several yards ahead. He could hear footsteps accompanying a shape that looked fairly human, but was obscured by the deepening shadows.

Don't look, said a tiny voice to his left. Mick's head turned slowly as the goose bumps asserted themselves over his flesh. Another one of his childhood stuffed friends, a hospital gift shop bear, was lying on its side, the head turned at an uncomfortable angle that would have suggested a broken neck if the thing had bones. He had forgotten what he used to call that one, but he had gotten it when he was six and had come down with pneumonia.

If you look…he will see you! The small bear shivered.

Mick stood there, wanting to reach out to the small bear. He felt himself reaching for it, longing to comfort it. Something about the small toy made it look almost malnourished. Years of neglect, locked away down in this eerie, dank hallway with crawling roaches.

His fingers brushed the crusty fabric of the small toy, and a name came into his head at once—*Dr. Muffin.*

Mick felt his eyes swelling with tears as he took the small bear from the shelf in both hands. He remembered how he had cuddled with Doctor Muffin every night he was in the hospital. It was the only thing that helped him sleep while he was in there. Dr. Muffin had been his first stuffy that he had received after leaving all his other toys behind in the chaos of the Massacre.

Who will see me? Mick asked the poor creature. The bear's head just slumped to one side, as if whatever intelligence that had spoken through it had vanished.

Mick cradled the head of the poor bear in his other hand, stroking it gently.

An ear shredding howl crept up on him, roiling up the brink hallway like an unforgiving wave, reaching its crescendo as Mick's nerves screamed in reply. It was so high pitched, if Mick had to guess, it almost sounded like a child's scream. Mick looked up, only to see that Yeshua wasn't standing in front of him anymore. But whatever energy he had been emitting was still present.

Go Mick! He heard Yeshua's voice in his head. Mick took off in the direction of the screams, which now sounded like they were coming from multiple areas. The further and further into this hallway he went, the more he realized one thing. He was in a maze of cinderblock walls, lined with shelves that were sometimes filled with old action figures and stuffies—and other times filled with rusted, sharp instruments.

Mick tripped over something, and he hurdled forward as his momentum carried him through the air. He landed at a four way intersection where the light that had clicked on earlier was still on, still swinging from side to side.

The light illuminated the disfigured faces of toys that lined the shelves in one path, mutilated by fine torture implements. The other path that the light revealed when it swung that way was barren of shelves, but had plenty in the way of messages scrawled on its surface in a dark substance.

DON'T LOOK!!!

HE WILL SEE YOU!!!

IT WASN'T MY FAULT!

WHY ARE YOU DOING THIS TO ME?!

The screams were forming words, but none that Mick could decipher. They were so high pitched that it was difficult to make them out. Just a hurried cadence, and a variation in rhythm were the only signs the screamer was attempting to form words. They were coming from the hallway to the right, the one with the gruesome messages painted into the walls.

Mick shoved himself to his feet and pushed off hard, sprinting through the dark. The further in he ran, the more he could make out that he was coming up to a bend in the wall. Another light was on somewhere off in the distance, somewhere to the left, lighting up the bend in the hall. When Mick rounded the corner, he felt his stomach drop out from beneath him. His grip on the gun felt like a vice, and the heat that rose form his neck threatened to ignite him from the inside out at what he saw.

A figure stood hunched over the tiny form of a child, strapped to a crude chair that looked like it had been fashioned from metal scraps from a junk yard, and held together with barbed wire. The child, if it could even be identified as one, was restrained in the chair by thick leather belts. The child's flesh was eviscerated beyond recognition.

The figure standing over the child, with its back turned toward Mick, withdrew a small scalpel from the back of the child's head, and was now peeling the scalp off with a slick, wet peeling sound. The skull was soon to be visible underneath.

Mick brought up his pistol and fired off three rounds into the back of the monster that held the child's head steady. The bullets punctured the figure in the back, and it stopped its gruesome act. The hands left the child's head as it slumped to one side.

It turned in Mick's direction. But before a face could be revealed, a black blur flew toward Mick, and something that felt like a block of concrete hit him right between the eyes. He fell off balance as another blow slammed into the left side of his head, sending his ear drums ringing like a fire alarm had gone off inside of his head. Hands were grabbing him around the scruff of his shirt and hauling him up.

Mick regained a measure of his bearings in that split second. Enough for him to bring his arms up and slam them down on the fiend's collar bone. Mick heard a loud *crack*, and the attacker let go of him. When his vision cleared, the thing was coming at him again, scalpel in hand, and their face fully revealed.

The attacker was a mirror image of himself. Covered in the blood of a tortured child, face contorted like that of a madman, but still. Mick recognized his own face.

Mick squeezed the trigger again, popping off a round in his doppelganger's face. The thing's head jerked back as the bullet punched a hole in the forehead right above the right eye. But instead of dropping to the floor dead, the thing merely froze there in its tracks, shook itself to get its bearings again, and *laughed*. The damned thing laughed at him, with his own voice!

Rage overtook Mick. His bare hands collided with the thing's throat and before Mick knew it, had slammed the sadistic double down into another crude metal chair. With a thought, sharp blades of scrap metal shot through the double's chest and neck, and barbed wire, as if animated by the sheer power of Mick's thoughts, wrapped around the creature's bloodied form.

But it was still laughing.

Mick grabbed onto the double's left hand, gripped one of the digits tightly, and jerked. He felt the popping of joints and the fracture of finger bones all at the same time. The double gave a mocking howl of fake pain, threw its head back and then said something under its breath.

"What did you say?!" Mick screamed, this time using his mouth. The thing continued to cackle, its teeth stained with the blood from the bullet hole that dripped down its face. *Mick's* face.

"I said," the doppelganger began, "that it's happening again. I live for this shit!" It said and then spat out a tooth at Mick's feet.

Mick! Yeshua's voice shook Mick all the way to his core, rattling his spine. Mick slowly turned to see Yeshua standing behind him, and in his arms he held the bloodied, mutilated form of the child that had begun to have their scalp peeled off. Through all the blood, Mick began to make out certain features. Its hair, though slick with blood, was curly, and the blood stained garments it wore had airplanes, firetrucks and police cars on them. The pajamas were his. The child, which Yeshua held in his arms, was him as well.

"What the hell is happening here?!" Mick screamed as he felt his knees beginning to buckle. His hands were shaking so badly he dropped the gun, and it clattered to the gore soaked floor.

Yeshua's eyes burned with the fiery rage of a volcano, and it made Mick feel smaller than he ever had in his life. The weight of his stare was causing him to *have* to look away as Yeshua held the small mutilated form of Mick's younger self close to his chest, staining it with blood.

Mick felt words caught in his throat. His stomach was like a boiling cauldron of red hot rage, gray despair, and the sickening puss color of yellow disgust.

Ever since the night of the Massacre, you've hated yourself so much. You hated yourself because you saw how easily your power could be taken away from you. You believed the lie that because it happened so easily, that must be proof that you never had any power to begin with. You've done nothing but perpetuate this cycle of torturing yourself ever since, because you thought you were too weak. But Mick, you were only five years old!

The surge of primal, raw emotion that spilled from him caused a rush of lightheadedness, and Mick felt himself collapsing into a puddle of his own burning tears. Every muscle in his body contracted with sobs. When he got the strength to do so, he looked up at the doppelganger in the chair. It was still looking at him, smirking. He turned his gaze to the body of his child self in Yeshua's arms. The tiny chest rose in sharp gasps for air as the eyes looked off blindly into the distance.

What happened wasn't your fault Mick, Yeshua's voice said in his head.

Your sense of justice was birthed from that tragedy. And that is honorable. But it's been misguided. You've turned your rage on those who didn't deserve it, Yeshua said, holding the tiny mangled body in his arms out to illustrate.

You are not a monster Mick Johnson. You are this precious child that I'm holding in my arms right now. You are every ounce of love that you poured into your stuffed animals and action figures. You are the boy who survived the tragedy that showed the world at large the dark things that lurk in the shadows. Every time you and your family almost died while trying to escape, it was me that made a way through the chaos. I've been watching over you from the day you were born Mick, and I cannot watch you do this to yourself anymore!

The room was turning brighter as shadows were chased away into the depths of oblivion. Mick dared to look up. Yeshua was towering over him now, at least eight feet tall now. His skin had fallen away and underneath he looked like burning hot steel, or gold that was so pure it was transparent. The hair was now flowing in fiery waves from the back of his head, the flames dancing as if being licked and tossed about by a wind storm. The eyes were the brightest thing, framed in that scorching hot face of cosmic radiance. In his arms, the tiny form of his child body was fully healed. Not a trace of blood could be seen anywhere on the small body. Every laceration, every fracture, or gash was nowhere to be seen, and not even a trace of a scar could indicate that they were ever present. Mick's first thought as he saw his child body held against the bare, scorching metallic flesh of Yeshua, was *how has he not gone up in flames?*

Cradling the tiny body in one enormously muscular arm, Yeshua reached out his other hand toward Mick—and that was when Mick noticed it.

There in the wrist, just below the palm, was a glowing hole that seemed to radiate a familiar energy. Images shot through his head of the hunters from New Broken Edge. Their eyes, their veins. Somehow, in this plane of existence, it was almost like he could feel the residual energy from the Light they each gave off when he was with them. It was the same, pulsing power that was coming from the hole in Yeshua's wrist.

"You really are him…" Mick breathed out. Yeshua nodded.

I am.

Mick looked and noticed his feet had two of the same holes.

"That's where you were…"

It is. He said.

Mick wasn't sure how long he stayed there, just soaking in the sight before him. It could have been a lifetime for all he knew, and yet neither he nor Yeshua seemed to mind. As terrifying as this being was to behold, the feelings that were washing through Mick were those of utter serenity, complete acceptance, and most of all, love. Love of every breath he had drawn. Love of every picture he had painted in kindergarten, every pet he had ever owned, every other kid he had played with. Everything flashed through his awareness in a series of chronological bursts of thought. Every experience that Mick had ever treasured in his life came rushing back to him, even the little things. Yet he wasn't remembering them from his own perspective. It was as if he was seeing them from Yeshua's. He was seeing just how much every bit of the person, Mick Johnson, truly mattered to Him.

Yeshua extended one hand out to him. Mick reached his hand out and took hold of Yeshua's, ignoring the fact that his flesh may very well be burned off in the process. But he figured if the kid version of him wasn't going up in flames, then he should be just fine.

Suddenly Mick heard a soft buzzing sound that gradually swelled louder and louder. As the sound increased, the child version of him opened his eyes and looked at him. Mick felt himself being pulled towards the small body, felt like he was being squeezed through a hole too small for him to fit through. The buzzing sound became a deafening *whooshing* noise, and his vision exploded into a brilliant prism effect of colors he had never seen before. There were also colors he knew from earth, but these were indefinitely brighter and more *alive* than their mundane counterparts. The sensation felt like he was traveling at light speed. For a second he thought he was going to disintegrate, or vibrate, right out of existence.

It was only when he began to hear himself screaming, did he notice the fact that his flesh was now burning.

THE RECLAIMED

Judah could feel the muscles in his legs flexing, pumping, and straining as he struggled to stay upright. He felt like a marionette in the hands of an unexperienced puppet master. His hand reached out to steady the rest of his body against one of the support pillars he was close to. When he realized that *he* wasn't the one trying to steady his own body, he tensed up, instantly attempting to jerk his arm back, which threw him off balance. He hit the ground awkwardly, feeling the sudden impact of the floor as his body crashed like an unmanned aircraft.

This would be easier if you wouldn't fight me, Rufus sighed.

"Get...out...of me!" Judah growled, feeling the urge to claw open his chest, Kevlar or not.

I understand that you hate me for what I did to you. I don't deserve your forgiveness. But your fingers, as well as three of your ribs are broken, and there are still creatures roaming the streets. If you would let me take control, I can get you out of here.

The sensation of cold, oily snakes roiling through his stomach, his muscles and even the very bones in his body, was working its way up to his brain. Judah immediately focused what little will he had left around the traveling sensation. Amid the other sensations he felt, one emanated from his brain and collected at the base of his skull, cutting off the icy tendrils that threatened to insert themselves into the base of his skull.

"Rufus...I forgave you years ago," he said, "but I don't have to trust you."

I suppose that is fair, Rufus said as Judah felt his own shoulders shrug noncommittally.

"Stop doing that!"

Judah began limping to where Mendez was probably lying unconscious.

"If you're gonna be along for the ride, then you'd better start talking."

Somewhere inside of him he could feel a sigh of resignation passing through his whole body. The voice of Rufus was silent for a few seconds before it stirred within him again.

I couldn't watch him level Broken Edge a second time. While he got a pretty good start on his plans, he's gone now. I've learned a little about him from my time trapped here. If he sees a task that no longer presents a worthwhile payoff, he abandons the pursuit. Sure I used you as a bluff against him. Wasn't sure it would work. But you're not dead, and I'm not bound to him anymore. So we both win.

Judah felt himself, actually *himself* and not Rufus, trying to wrap his broken fingers around the handle of his pistol. The pain felt like dull razors trying to dig through the meat of his fingers and he winced.

With each limping step, Judah remembered the feeling of falling, the sight of the car that would break his fall coming up to meet him a lot faster than he had anticipated. The feeling of his stomach, lungs and everything else trying to escape his body before the impact.

This isn't personal amigo. Just the natural order of things. This is what happens when a god meets an insect! Rufus's voice echoed through his head as the memories flashed before him. He remembered the voices of his other team mates, worshipers of this entity, discussing what to do with him, and urging each other to make a decision before he blacked out, so he could be conscious for whatever they had planned.

Rufus was being quiet now. Too quiet. Judah wondered if he too, had seen his memories playing on the screen behind his eyes. Judah moved his left arm, testing it to see not only how much he could move it, but to see if it actually felt like him moving it. Sure enough, it was his own dwindling strength, his own mental signals that were causing his arm to move.

"You still in there?" Only silence followed his question.

Rufus had saved him—in the most invasive and vile way possible. He would live to fight another day. Yet here he was, nearly beaten to death, and hobbling to try and find Mendez. Johnson was dead for all he knew. He'd seen the damage his body had taken in the knife fight with Mendez, and being shot countless times. He felt a rush of agonizing rage flush through him as he remembered the saw blade being drawn across Valerie's throat. Yet as quick as the overwhelming heat of rage nearly swallowed him up, it was redirected.

Father had been the one holding the saw. Holding them all in place, with no way of doing anything. Their power had been easily stripped from them and the love of his life made an example of.

He heard shuffling footsteps behind him, coupled with disgruntled moans of undoubtedly sharp pain. Judah turned slowly to see SWAT Captain Dan Mendez hobbling into view, holding his semiautomatic rifle at the ready.

"You okay?" He panted when he saw Judah.

"Barely."

"Where did it go?"

"It left when it saw it wasn't going to get what it came for. Not only that, I ruined its vessel," he said pointing toward Johnson's fallen body. Mendez's eyes just about bugged when he saw the beams of Light pulsing through the bullet holes, as if his memory was finally jogged enough to remember.

"Say, who were you talking to just now?" Mendez asked, looking around.

"Let's get Johnson out of here," Judah said, ignoring the question.

"You gonna be okay to walk? You look worse than I feel."

"I'll be fine," Judah grunted.

The sound of a steady *pit pat, pit pat* on the roof of the building was beginning to creep up in Judah's hearing as he wearily limped toward Mick. The sound of distant thunder boomed off in the distance. He prayed that the rain would be enough to wash away all the blood that now coated the streets, even though he knew better.

An inhuman gasp escaped from the throat of the body at their feet as Judah touched it. Mendez drew back, weapon trained at Mick's head. Judah found himself stiffening, yet tightening his grip on Mick's arm with his good hand.

Mick's body thrashed on the floor and Judah rolled him over onto his back, where Mick's hands went straight for the gray skin on his own face. The fingernails scraped and dug deep into the skin, itching like something was crawling beneath it. The eyes flew open to reveal two white glowing orbs from which glowing blood vessels trailed all over his face.

"What the hell's happening to him?!" Mendez yelled.

Judah turned his beaten gaze toward Mendez, and despite aching facial muscles, he smiled.

"He's changing."

"Into what?!"

"One of us," Judah said.

Judah felt a sudden tingle in his eyes—a warmth that originated in the back of his head and was shooting out to the rest of his body. He looked down at his own hand, the one with the broken fingers. His exposed tissue where the skin had been ripped off was glowing pure white. He felt the rush hit his eyes full force, and it was enough to cause him to blink rapidly, as if he had turned his gaze toward the sun. When he blinked away the water in his eyes, his sight revealed the darkness of the furniture store to be like the light of day.

This would have come in handy twenty minutes ago. Judah thought as he shook his head. The thrum of the warm energy as it pulsed through his body sent shockwaves through his stomach and heart, numbing the pain where the ribs had been broken, and spread all the way through every inch of his body that had taken its beating.

Judah turned his gaze back toward Mick. His hoarse screams escaped his throat as his body flailed and writhed on the floor, his hands searching all over his own body for the source of the burning. The fingers dug through the bloody fabric of his shirt, and ripped. The fingernails dug through the skin like they were hot blades swimming through a tub of butter. The wet ripping sounds that followed as slabs of melting skin were torn off and cast aside were accompanied by the sound of thunder outside as rain hammered the building. As the wet sheets of bloodied, gray epidermis were flung aside, they disintegrated as if they had been cast into the sun, leaving only an ashy residue floating down through the air.

The exposed areas of flesh where Mick had ripped through his own skin, were glowing a brilliant white that to a tainted eye, would have obscured the details of the flesh beneath. Yet Judah saw clearly. Fresh, peach colored skin, smooth and moist like a newborn who had just breached the birthing canal, shown through the brilliance.

The canvas of black that blanketed Mick's vision slowly opened, and he registered blurry outlines of two humanoid forms, one shorter than the other. He abruptly snapped his eyes shut, though not out of fear. His eyes physically hurt to open. The tiny view of the outside world they had glimpse only briefly had been enough to nearly overload them. The floor beneath him was crawling with something he could barely identify. His skin felt icy and wet and he swore he could feel every molecule in the air as they coated his body. The forms that hovered above him were breathing, talking to one another—and their voices thundered like two timpani drums pressed against either side of his head.

"Johnson? Can you hear me?" one voice asked. He recognized that voice. Sounded like the SWAT Captain Daniel Mendez.

Mick forced his eyes to open, blinked rapidly against all the new lights and colors that invaded his vision. Mendez was indeed there, and he saw the towering figure of the one the hunters had called Judah. His eyes burned with the same fierce power he had seen the night he and Valerie escaped from the high school. He approached, and his very footsteps sent vibrations so powerful Mick felt them all the way up his spine. Yet for all the swirling memories that began to wash through his mind, Mick could not bring himself to feel anything akin to fear or hatred for the man. Mick remembered what it felt like to be back on that bar stool, listening to the man recount the tale of what started him as a hunter, and what ultimately led to the destruction of Mick's city. But he was seeing those memories with a different set of eyes this time. Through the eyes of the one who had saved him from himself. He carried with him into the waking world, the lingering energy of his encounter with the one called Yeshua. The memories of flying through the air in his old living room. Of the descent into the basement. Strapping his dark double to a chair and breaking his fingers, only to realize that Mick had been his own torturer the entire time. Judah and his current team of hunters had never been the enemy.

Judah stretched out his hand. It felt like the most natural thing to do, and Mick took hold of it. He felt himself being lifted up off the ground by a force he likened to that of a crane arm.

Standing up proved to be too much outright however, and he nearly toppled over. Judah and Mendez caught his limp body between their own bulk, supporting him on either side.

"Welcome to the Reclaimed, Mr. Johnson." Judah said.

MEMORIAL

November 7th,

Mick stood looking at his reflection in the mirror in his quarters beneath Tom's Auto. He still couldn't get over the new skin. Every time he looked in the mirror he stared for what seemed like hours. He would look closely and see the pores, feel the stubble on his face. He was new, having literally shed his old skin. The thought was overwhelming. He still felt electrical tingles shoot through his stomach on occasion. Judah had said it was the Light getting acquainted with its new host. Still moving in, clearing the cobwebs out. Sometimes it felt like the furniture was being rearranged, but they said that wasn't uncommon either.

It had taken about three days for his eyes to adjust. He couldn't believe how well he could see everything. Colors looked so much deeper and richer in comparison to how he used to see the world. It was like he was seeing through a high definition set of eyes compared to the obsolete sight organs he was born with.

He still had not channeled the Light the way the others had though, which he figured would come with practice.

Like he had figured would happen in his previous life, he had failed his psych evaluation with the police department, and as a result, turned in his badge and his gun. It would take some time getting used to no longer seeing the word 'Detective' in front of his name anymore.

When he was cognizant enough to be somewhat rational, the hunters asked him how much he remembered from Halloween. The last thing he remembered was meeting George at St. Andrews, and nothing after that. The hunters and the police department had gained access to security cameras from buildings and traffic light cameras from that night, which did nothing to prove or capture the events. Most electronic equipment had shorted out in the wake of the slaughter. The one known exception seemed to be the Mayor, Jacob Watkins's, cell phone he had used to communicate with Chief Scroggins.

Slowly but surely, the hunters helped him to fill in the gaps, through which he was able to piece together enough information to find out about George. The weight filled up his body like wet cement and settled in his chest as he tied his tie in a knot. In frustration he undid the troublesome thing and threw it down on the floor. Here he was, fumbling with his tie when he should have already been at the church in his seat and ready to speak his eulogy for his best friend's memorial service!

A knock at the door startled him. He turned around.

"Do you want some help with that?" Valerie asked, standing there in women's slacks, and a black button up blouse. Her hair fell freely down her shoulders, stopping just below her shoulder blades. The jagged scar that rimmed its way around her throat looked like an ugly stretch mark.

Mick nodded and sighed, picking his tie up and handing it to her. Her nimble fingers worked the knot free and she straightened it out and put it around his head like she was placing a medal on him.

Mick's eyes remained fixated on the scar that encircled her throat, and he worked hard to suppress the twitch in his left eye when he saw it. As she worked the tie around his neck, lifting up his collar flaps and pulling it tight, Mick closed his eyes. She had never been this close to him before.

"Something on your mind?" She asked as she flattened out his collar flaps over the freshly tied tie.

Mick opened his eyes again to meet hers, but they inevitably returned to her scar.

"Some of the guys say that…I did this," He said pointing to the scar.

"Mick," She began as her hands slid off of him and rested on her hips, "You weren't in control of your own body at that time. It wasn't you that killed me that night."

"But it was my hand that held that saw," He said, turning his eyes away from her as he felt them begin to swell with tears.

"Mick listen to me," She said, taking his face in her hands, "You, Mick Johnson, did not kill me. You were not in control of yourself when it happened, and to be perfectly frank, that was your *old* body that thing was using. You are a completely new man. These hands," she said grasping both of his hands and holding them up in her own, "these are your *new* hands. Not the ones that held the saw that night."

"Try telling that to a judge," Mick said, his voice dropping to a whisper.

Mick caught movement in the doorway behind her as Judah entered with a knock. Mick barely recognized the man outside of the Kevlar and tactical gear he was usually wearing, but for the occasion he was dressed like a Wall Street investor. Who knew Judah owned a Calvin Klein suit?

"You two ready?" Judah asked as he bent down and kissed Valerie on top of the head.

Mick breathed deep, blinking the moisture from his eyes and nodded.

"Ready as I'll ever be I guess." He said.

The drive to the Methodist church took about fifteen minutes longer than it normally would. Even though Main Street had been cleared of the debris from the events of last Halloween, road crews from the State had it blocked off to repaint the lines, and in some places, replace parts of the road that had been damaged. More than enough time for the dam to break and the cascade of emotional turbulence to hit Mick in the center of his chest, like a burning hand reaching in and pinching off the aorta valve to his heart.

First—Something had taken over his body and slaughtered a few hundred people, Valerie being one of them. She had described the events that transpired with her that evening in small tidbits. She recalled floating with Yeshua and had actually watched Mick's Reclaiming from the astral plane with him. Mick had a hard time believing that one since *he* had been with Yeshua, but then again if what they said about him was true, about being omnipotent and all, it was more than possible for him to have been with her and him at the same time. She said she recalled waking up in her body around the time Mick began to claw his old skin off. Zach and Parish had stolen a car and were driving her body back to Tom's Auto when she awoke. The jagged canyon carved into her throat was glowing white hot as the flesh pulled itself back together. Mick had asked her why the scar didn't heal. She shrugged and smiled.

"I'm not worried. Sometimes our scars can be useful."

Second—Regardless of the fact he wasn't in control of his body at the time, it was still *his* body, old or not. The fact that no cameras that they knew of had captured him leading a small army in gleeful slaughter, was altogether a twisted relief, and a weight in his gut. Not matter if the one called Father had actually done it or not, no court would take that into consideration. His body had been the vehicle used in the slaughter of New Broken Edge's people. And no matter how *new* he was as a person, that fact wasn't going to stop haunting him any time soon. This thing had practically bathed in the blood of the townspeople, and as of right now, Mick was technically off scot free. No matter his official standing with the police department, you can't remove the cop from the man, and Mick's inner cop was screaming for him to turn himself in. He knew that from a criminal justice point of view, even though Father was primarily to blame, Mick was an accessory to the mass murder that had taken place. But the controlling entity couldn't be put on trial, so no matter what—it was all on his shoulders. He could never look Scroggins or anybody from the department in the eye ever again as long as he knew what he knew.

All of this brought him back around to the third conundrum he faced. His best friend had been reduced to an urn of ashes. At least that's the state they were in now. A member of church staff at St. Andrew's had found a partially cremated pile of gore, seasoned with ash in the sanctuary. Lab tests had confirmed it to be the remains of George Turner, from the department's forensics lab. The fact he could remember meeting him at the church, but not what transpired afterwards, was chewing on his insides like a persistent mantis. Mick closed his eyes and breathed deep when the thought occurred to him, *for all I know, I could have been the one who killed him too.*

When they had arrived, Mick separated from the hunters, Oscar and Sunny included, who had come to support him. He took his seat up at the front row which had been reserved for family. Only two other people were seated in the front row, and Mick only recognized one of them, a cousin George had from when they were little. A spear of anger shot through his chest, replacing every other raging emotion he had experienced up to that second. Sure, his parents were dead, and he was an only child. But not even George's uncles and aunts could even be bothered to show up to their own nephew's service?! Mick closed his eyes and fought back the urge to scream. Most everyone else here were people from the police department and the forensics lab. Mariah and her mom Lilly were there. Mick and George were two of their favorite regulars. It was good to see them, even if Lilly's makeup had been put on too thick. The curator from the New Broken Edge Memorial Museum was also there. About forty people gathered in the sanctuary, not including Mick and the hunters. The sanctuary that was capable of holding about two hundred and fifty, to three hundred people. Sure, George had other friends outside of work. He was always more of a socialite than Mick was. But Mick didn't recognize anyone else here as a friend from George's other circles.

Guess you find out who your true friends are when you die, Mick thought.

Mick watched the preacher bless those gathered, and then they prayed. George's urn was on the elaborately decorated marble table in front of the red carpeted stairs leading up to the pulpit. His portrait was framed and propped up next to the urn, both of which were surrounded by various flower arrangements.

Mick barley heard his name called when it was his time to go up and speak. One of the cousins nudged Mick's elbow, jostling him back to reality.

Mick nervously clenched his hands into fists, feeling how dry and cold his skin felt. His mouth felt dry as he swallowed. He took the microphone from the preacher, and stood there behind the pulpit awkwardly for some time, not daring to bring his eyes up to meet those who had gathered.

He breathed deeply and bit his lower lip to get control before he found the strength to lift his head.

"I met George back in kindergarten," he began, "I remember the day we met, he was the new kid and it was nap time. He didn't want to lay down on the blankets like the other kids. He wanted to climb on the counters and sleep there but the teacher wouldn't let him." He said, pausing to gather himself.

"I remember he slipped and fell off when the teacher had her back to him, and he landed hard on his arm. I was trying to go to sleep, but his screaming woke me up."

Some quiet chuckles rippled through the small congregation. He fought through the tightness in his chest as he took another deep breath.

"All throughout kindergarten, up until the death of his parents and he got sent away, we were *so* annoying. As we got older, I truly felt sorry for our teachers who had to put up with us. I remember one day the entire class brought their lunch trays back to the classroom and we ate lunch in there with our teacher. Another kid had thrown his cookie in George's face, and it had bounced off of him and went in the trashcan. George, being George, picked it out of the trash, and the kid dared him to eat it. Instead, ya know what he did?" Mick paused, looking out at the crowd.

"The bastard made *me* eat it."

The congregation nearly exploded into a raging torrent of laughter, snickers and deep throaty giggles. Even the preacher standing off to the side had his hand over his mouth, but his face was becoming tight as he shook, trying to contain his own giggles.

"When the Massacre happened, he was already out of town at the children's hospital that was counseling him after the death of his parents. I didn't know where he had been taken off to so when we had to evacuate, my biggest concern was finding out where he was and if he was okay. We met up again in grade school. His aunt and uncle," Mick shot a glance toward the nearly barren front row, where they should have been, "they had taken over as his legal guardians. The new and improved grade school we had when we rebuilt the city was huge, and he eventually learned all the cool places to hide. The district has grown in the years since. A lot of new schools. A lot of places he would have loved to explore. He talked about wanting to be an urban explorer." Mick said, stopping to take a breath as more memories washed through him.

"I remember all throughout high school we both took college courses whenever we could so we could both focus heavily on our majors. He was a forensics nerd and I wanted to be a detective. We would stay up stupid late, both of us having had four or five Redbulls each, cramming for tests that we had to take in a few hours. When his aunt and uncle were having problems and ended up fighting constantly, he would always crash at my house and that's where we would study for our exams."

Mick felt the weight of the object in the pocket of his slacks. He reached inside of his pocket and withdrew the bulk of an old *Transformer* action figure. The yellow paint had been nearly bleached by the sunlight, dirt clinging to the fine crevices and packed into the ball joints of the things' appendages. Part of the head was gone, the jagged plastic gnarled in the place where George's dog Gracy had chewed on it.

He felt the warm sting in his eyes as they blurred over, and he wrapped his fingers around the figure that had become a symbol of their friendship. The action figure that had been housed behind the glass at the New Broken Edge Memorial Museum *had* belonged to George. Mick had obtained it from the curator yesterday.

"All throughout our childhood, and even when we were in high school and college, our joint fandom was *Transformers*," Mick said, holding up the battered action figure that had survived through the impossible.

"I want to thank the Curator of the New Broken Edge Memorial Museum, Denise Hickert, for allowing me to reunite this piece of our childhood with my brother," Mick said as he stepped down from the pulpit, approached the urn and set the toy down next to it.

But just before his fingertips left the small figure, Mick felt a tiny niggle at the forefront of his mind.

I have been trying to reach out to you since you wrapped up the Terrance Miller killings. If perhaps my emissaries had been successful in drawing you to me sooner, perhaps his condition wouldn't be as dire as it is currently.

He stood, frozen with his hand still on the action figure, eyes on the urn as something else slithered into the forefront of his memory. It felt like a searing hot branding iron as those words—that voice—burned their way to the front of his recollection. He was remembering another detail from that night.

It had been enough for him to wonder, if the words of that parasite that called itself Father could be trusted, just how many times in the last several months had George really been *George?*

CRAWLING TOWARDS LIFE

The sting of icy darkness filled his atrophied lungs. It was the only air he could breathe down here. No, not down here. Was it down?

Rufus could feel the crackling energies of a distinctly lower vibration as they hummed through his body, causing him to feel as if his body was composed of lead. He staggered to his feet. Even the simplest of movements felt like it was taking years to accomplish. He knew that the darkness that was swirling around him was no mere darkness of earth. The darkness here was alive. It clung to him like tar, setting his nerves ablaze in the burning cold. The feeling was very much like the way he felt when Father had imparted his essence into him. This time though, none of the endorphins flooded his brain with the ecstasy of power. Through the gusts of wind that threatened to tear his face off, he swore he felt droplets of—something, hitting his head. It couldn't be moisture. Not down here.

After saying his piece to Judah, he departed. Not to the astral plane, but further away from what the natives of other realms called the third dimension. The physical world, or as those still living like to call, the *real* world. But the realm his feet touched was far more real than anything the ignorant living could even imagine. Everything felt denser. The droplets hitting his head actually started hurting like weighted pin pricks. He dared not look up, lest his eyes be impaled by some sharpened hailstone.

He looked at his hands. They were certainly real. The long tattered duster he wore years ago still clung to his frame—or a version of it at least. His body wasn't brittle and frail here as it was in the physical world. It still resembled what he looked like on the day it happened. He had read somewhere that the physical body mimics the soul's appearance, not the other way around.

Though his physical body had withered, his soul was still the ashen wraith it had been all along. So in a way maybe it was only partly true.

As the memories of pandemonium in the streets of Broken Edge came flooding back, he looked up. A lone building stood off in the distance, barely visible against the backdrop of the infinite bubbling blackness on the horizon. On earth it would have been called the night sky. Here, it simply was. No night, no day. Just an endless void of darkness. A dome of such vast proportions that the expanse of it felt oppressive and heavy. Almost like the infinite black dome above could collapse at any moment.

Rufus recognized the building as he trudged his way toward it. With great effort that left him almost at the verge of collapsing, he hefted the weight of his coat over his bald head to provide a meager barrier to shield him from the falling projectiles that rained down.

He was looking at the ruins of the Broken Edge Mall. The remains of the mall stood tall and dark, a massive silhouette against an equally dark backdrop. The tall grass in the parking lot was nearly flattened by the wall of wind that originated with no direction, but simply just was, like everything else here.

He looked around, expecting to see other buildings surrounding it as they had back when he was a hunter, but the mall stood solo, it's only other companions the unnatural growths that were mimicking grass that had sprang up through this place's version of a parking lot.

Time only seemed real when Rufus recalled memories from his life as a hunter, and as he trudged across the blackened wasteland of whatever godless realm that had claimed him as its soul inhabitant, he realized this. Time, even in the form of old memories, seemed to be the one thing keeping his sanity held together. He measured how long to took him to trudge across the distance of the parking lot and the tall grass which stretched on for uncountable lengths. The building never appeared any closer, nor farther away. Like everything else here, it just was.

The more memories filtered through his being, the more he began to question the wisdom of his decision to use the memories as a means of measuring time.

The memories knotted themselves inside his brain, throbbing there in a manner that dropped him to his knees. He remembered his father, that rowdy Irishman that had swept his Latino mother off her feet and was later put to shame when she drank him under the table.

The faces of everyone he interviewed when out gathering information. The faces of every person whose withered carcass he had discarded like packaging on food, only to suckle at their precious life force. The energy fields produced by the bodies of his prey called to his recollections, and he found himself salivating here in this dark world.

He found himself digging his fingers into the substance of the ground beneath him. He didn't think it accurate to call it dirt, or cement or anything found on earth.

He snapped his head up. Something was clawing at him in the back of his mind, demanding his awareness. In spite of the wind threatening to uproot him in spite of his greater density, in spite of the shower of shrapnel that descended on him in unforgiving waves of icy wrath, something called to him in his mind. It rattled his insides, ringing down his spine from the base of his brain. Something ancient called to him. A form of energy he had only experienced once in his lifetime as a small boy in Mexico.

That source of the energy that flowed through his mind, coating the void where his heart used to be, was a single name. A name he was not sure where he had ever heard it spoken, or by whom, but a name that he remembered from somewhere. A name his cracked and dried lips were begging to be able to utter.

"Y…Yeshua…"

Utterance of the name drained him of what precious little strength he had left. His arms had faltered beneath his weight. His face descended onto the substance beneath him. There he lay, his body feeling like it had been flayed by the storm as a gale of subzero wind threatened to rip his coat from off his back.

The faces of every victim he had drained flashed before him again. The screams of a city which had been lured into their trust, only to be decimated by their power, filled every orifice of his shattered body. Resignation settled his form deeper into the ground, as if the substance had turned to a form of quicksand.

"I know…that I don't deserve your forgiveness. But I ask now that whatever judgment awaits me—may it be a fair one. I will go willingly into the abyss for my crimes…Only know that my utterance of your name was sincere." He prayed, not knowing where the strength to utter such words came from.

The screams that were playing through his ears were rising higher and higher with the storm, and with it—the sound of a chain.

The sound of something familiar from earth caused him to instinctually attempt to lift his head. He barely had the strength for that simple motion, but he managed a look upward. Off in the distance, walking out of the ruins of what posed for the Broken Edge mall, a dark creature was towering just outside of the entrance. It looked like it could have been eight feet tall. It stood naked, with no obvious genitalia, but the humanoid build suggested a masculine dominance. Its flesh was nearly as black as the sky around it. The only reason Rufus could visually make it out was because it was moving. The sound of chain links clinking as the long chain dangled from its hand was the only thing that set it apart from the rest of the environment. If it had not been for that, he would have never noticed it. The entity didn't appear to have a face, no matter how hard Rufus tried to make one out.

Yet as Rufus let his eyes adjust to make out the details of the figure, he could hear that the screams that washed over him like a tidal wave were all originating from *it*. The screams of every man, woman and child he had fed from, all their cries of anguish and terror, their panic stricken gasps for air, their pleas all melded together in a chorus so deafening it rivaled and intertwined with the wind that threatened to pick him up and carry him off toward the thing making its way toward him.

And then, silence. Silence so abrupt and jarring, like the sudden impact from a car crash, but without the luxury of blacking out. Without the airbag to catch ones face from flattening across the dashboard. Silence, replaced by the slimy, wet sound of what could have been lips parting, and a great, red eye appeared on the thing's head, right where a mouth would be located on a normal head.

The red eye landed on him and the pupil dilated as the red orb the size of a softball bulged in its unnaturally placed socket. The great chain it held in one hand lifted off the ground, ending in a three foot long double pronged weapon. Held in the other hand, was something that appeared to be an oversized grappling hook big enough to rip a man's head free from their shoulders with its prongs.

It began walking straight toward him, crudely shaped bident gripped in one hand while the other wiped the chain around like a lasso. The sound of the hook as its rotation sliced through the air sounded like a gust of wind, one that battered his broken form mercilessly.

With what little will he still possessed, Rufus dug his fingers into the substance of the ground beneath him, and pushed against the gravity that was bearing down upon him. His lungs screamed for air, his muscles threatening to explode beneath his ash textured skin. His eyes burned as the storm remained constant, showering him with—A coppery taste.

The ground beneath him was soaked a deep crimson. He closed his eyes as the thing continued to stomp toward him, sending explosions of blood red mud gushing up around its legs at the impact of its steps.

Faces bombarded his mind's eye. The life force of everyone he had ever fed from. Names were etched into the walls of his brain.

Kenneth Rose
Barbarra Jeffreys
Benny Turner
Carla Beth Turner.
Juan Rios.
Stacey Adams
Grant Haller
Melanie Mendelsohn

The names went on and on as he struggled to get up, to stand and face the creature bearing down on him, resigned to his fate. He knew his judgment was just, now he planned to face it with what dignity he had left. Each drop resonated with the frequency of each person's last moments, their hysteria and mortification.

With strength he knew not where it came from, he pushed himself to his feet, and rose to meet the thing as it came for him.

He looked up to see the creature less than ten yards away. It was releasing that chain in his direction, the hook soaring through the air, cutting a path toward him. Rufus closed his eyes, clenching his teeth, and waited for the paralyzing impact that would rend his body like tissue paper.

He heard a sound next to his ear on the right side of his head, and he flinched. But nothing happened. He was still standing, his hands balled into fists that were shaking with the agonizing anticipation of final death. Yet he felt nothing, save for a warm energy that was utterly alien to this plane. It was radiating next to his head where the creature's hook should have struck.

The thing that jolted his eyes open was the ear shattering shrieks of the creature. Rufus stared wide eyed at a glowing hand that held the grappling hook, right where it would have connected with his head. The hand was bigger than his own head, and was connected to a figure that stood about the same height as the dark apparition before him.

A man stared down into his eyes, his face glowing as hot as steel pulled straight from a blacksmith's forge, and the hair was like a cosmic firestorm that blazed with the intensity like that of the sun.

The man casually tossed the hook back at the creature, its weight like that of a cheaply made toy. The creature shot up an immense hand and caught it, much the same way the Bright Man had. Lightning and fire sparked to life in the palms of the Bright Man's hands, and he sculpted it into a pair of flaming scimitars. The hilts of each blade looked just like his skin—glowing red hot, with tiny flames escaping between his fingers, crawling up the length of the blades.

"I'm glad you called me Rufus," the Bright Man smiled as he took a stance, stepping between Rufus and the creature, which was rearing back for another swing.

The sounds of clashing metal and the swinging of that chain seemed amplified somehow. He looked up to see the two beings, ducking, slashing, thrusting their blazing metallic instruments of wrath and mercy in a dizzying array of slashes and strokes that hurt his eyes to behold.

Why is he fighting for me?! I deserve to be served up to that thing! Rufus screamed in his mind as mental flashes of his victims' final moments continued to play over his mind.

The darkness that surrounded the creature had fled from its visage, revealing a repulsive frame that looked very much like the human body deprived of the skin, though still its color was completely black. The face of the thing was nonexistent even still, save for only a single red eye that kept trying to land on him. The muscles, tendons and veins were split open by several patches of bone spurs that had ripped through the forearms, at the knees, and had apparently grown out of the thing's skull. The crown of bone it wore on its head glistened as the Bright One's fire glanced off of it, leaving various areas of flesh melting and beginning to run down the sides of its head as it fought to claim its prize.

The Bright One's blades moved as off-synced partners, one quickly behind the other. The dark creature's bident stabbed straight for his abdomen. He drove his own blade through the prongs and twisted, slashing upward, cutting the prongs off of the weapon's shaft. The chain zoomed through the air, and again he dodged, parried with one blade, quickly following up with the other.

Rufus looked down at his hands. The veins beneath his ashen skin were glowing.

The dark, abandoned and lonely house that was to be the happy home of a newly married couple remained still and quiet. The few belongings they had moved into the house, along with the house itself, had begun to fall into disrepair. The crumbling, pathetic recliner that rested in the living room still held the withered, frail body of a deceased male that the obsidian shadow known only as Father, had been using as a backup vessel.

The body beneath the sheet was as cold as if it had been sculpted from a block of ice. Yet just beneath the sheet, two points of reference gave off a warm glow. The glow spread out through the still, frail body beneath the sheet.

A gasp for air pierced the night, as one of the hands shot up from under the sheet and towards its face. The bony fingers grabbed a handful of the dirty covering and ripped it off. Along with the sheet, a wad of papery thin skin came free with a wet ripping sound. Beneath the withered skin of the skeletal figure, a radiantly blinding glow of white hot energy shot forth from the torn face. Where the surrounding areas of skin were stretched thin with wrinkles a mile long, the new skin beneath was firm, smooth, and young looking.

The Bright One, Yeshua, stood over the stick thin body as the man it belonged to clawed his way through the void of darkness, his old body having become a portal back into this world.

Welcome back Rufus. Let's start again.